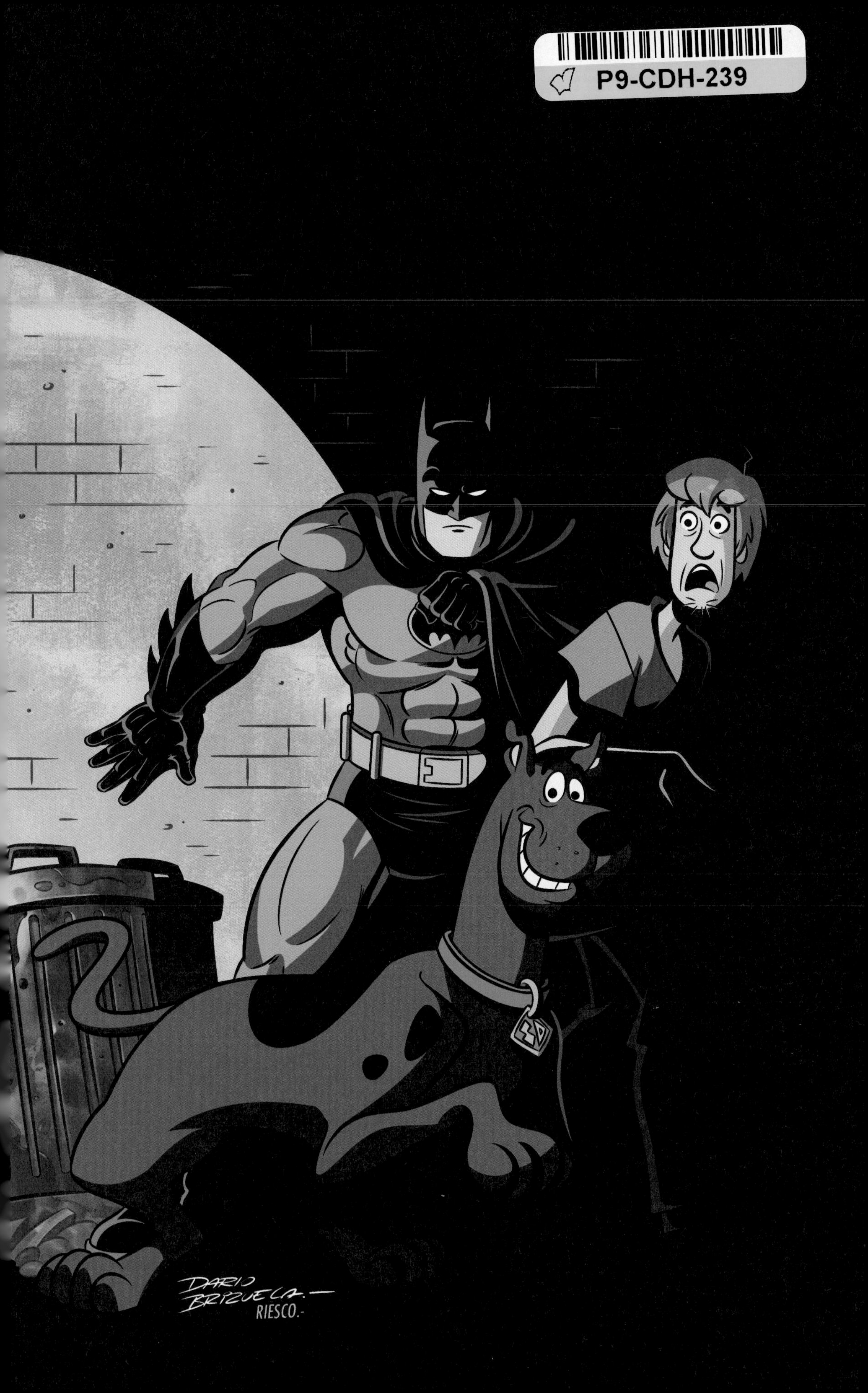
DARIO BRIZUELA.—
RIESCO.-

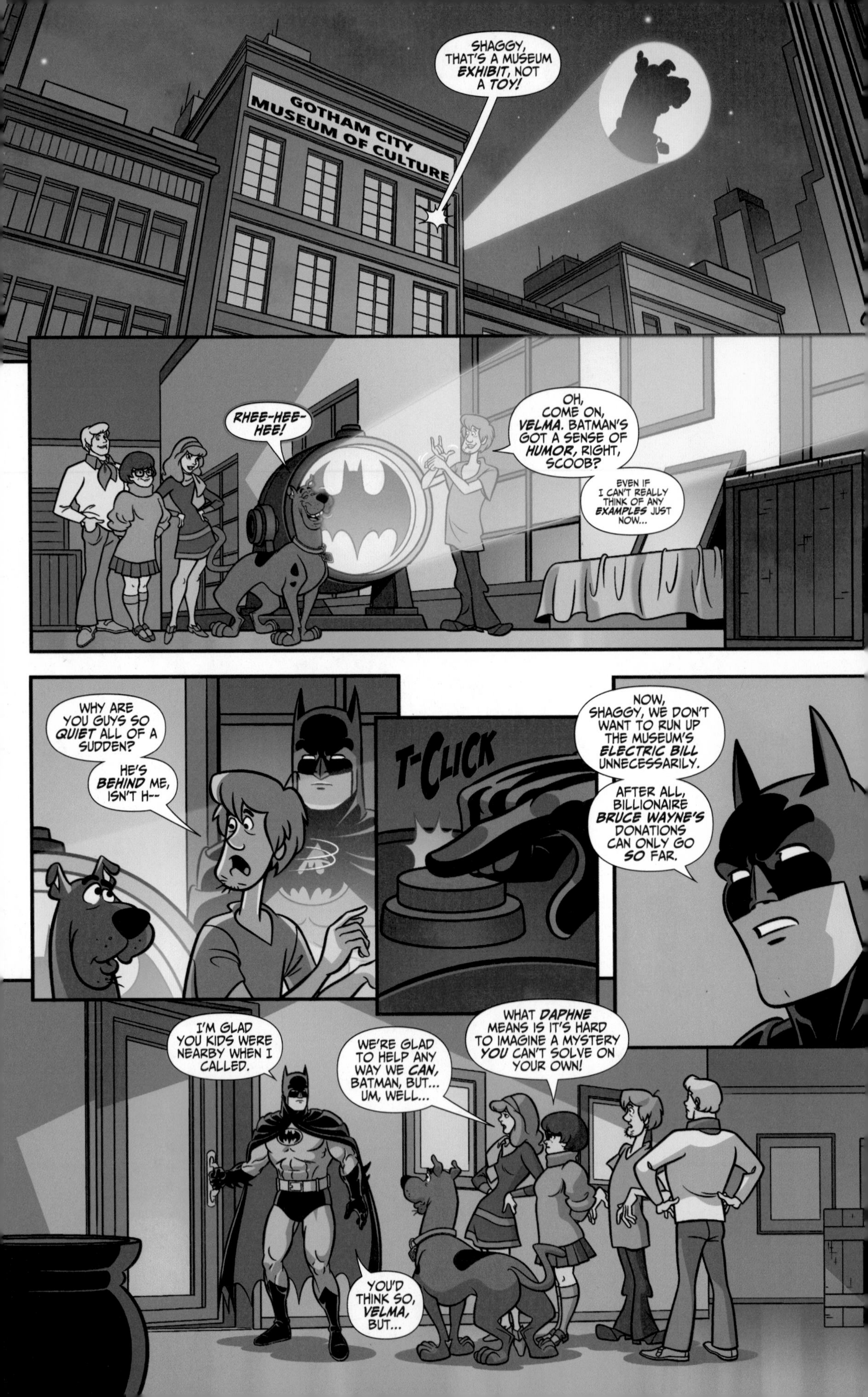
GOTHAM CITY MUSEUM OF CULTURE
SHAGGY, THAT'S A MUSEUM EXHIBIT, NOT A TOY!
RHEE-HEE-HEE!
OH, COME ON, VELMA. BATMAN'S GOT A SENSE OF HUMOR, RIGHT, SCOOB?
EVEN IF I CAN'T REALLY THINK OF ANY EXAMPLES JUST NOW...
WHY ARE YOU GUYS SO QUIET ALL OF A SUDDEN?
HE'S BEHIND ME, ISN'T H--
T-CLICK
NOW, SHAGGY, WE DON'T WANT TO RUN UP THE MUSEUM'S ELECTRIC BILL UNNECESSARILY.
AFTER ALL, BILLIONAIRE BRUCE WAYNE'S DONATIONS CAN ONLY GO SO FAR.
I'M GLAD YOU KIDS WERE NEARBY WHEN I CALLED.
WE'RE GLAD TO HELP ANY WAY WE CAN, BATMAN, BUT... UM, WELL...
WHAT DAPHNE MEANS IS IT'S HARD TO IMAGINE A MYSTERY YOU CAN'T SOLVE ON YOUR OWN!
YOU'D THINK SO, VELMA, BUT...

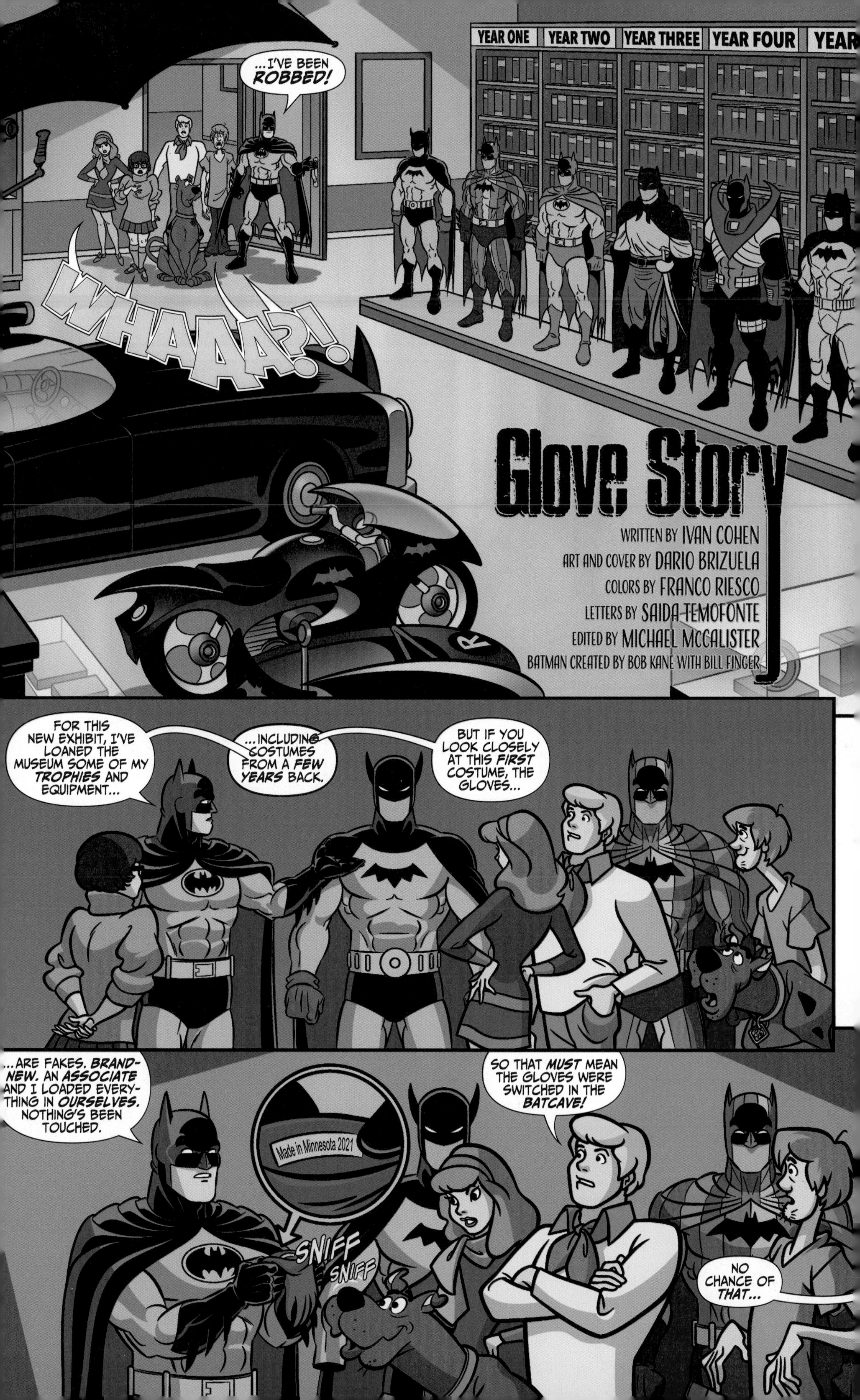
YEAR ONE
YEAR TWO
YEAR THREE
YEAR FOUR
...I'VE BEEN ROBBED!
WHAAA?!
Glove Story
WRITTEN BY IVAN COHEN
ART AND COVER BY DARIO BRIZUELA
COLORS BY FRANCO RIESCO
LETTERS BY SAIDA TEMOFONTE
EDITED BY MICHAEL McCALISTER
BATMAN CREATED BY BOB KANE WITH BILL FINGER
FOR THIS NEW EXHIBIT, I'VE LOANED THE MUSEUM SOME OF MY TROPHIES AND EQUIPMENT...
...INCLUDING COSTUMES FROM A FEW YEARS BACK.
BUT IF YOU LOOK CLOSELY AT THIS FIRST COSTUME, THE GLOVES...
...ARE FAKES. BRAND-NEW. AN ASSOCIATE AND I LOADED EVERY-THING IN OURSELVES. NOTHING'S BEEN TOUCHED.
Made in Minnesota 2021
SO THAT MUST MEAN THE GLOVES WERE SWITCHED IN THE BATCAVE!
SNIFF
SNIFF
NO CHANCE OF THAT...

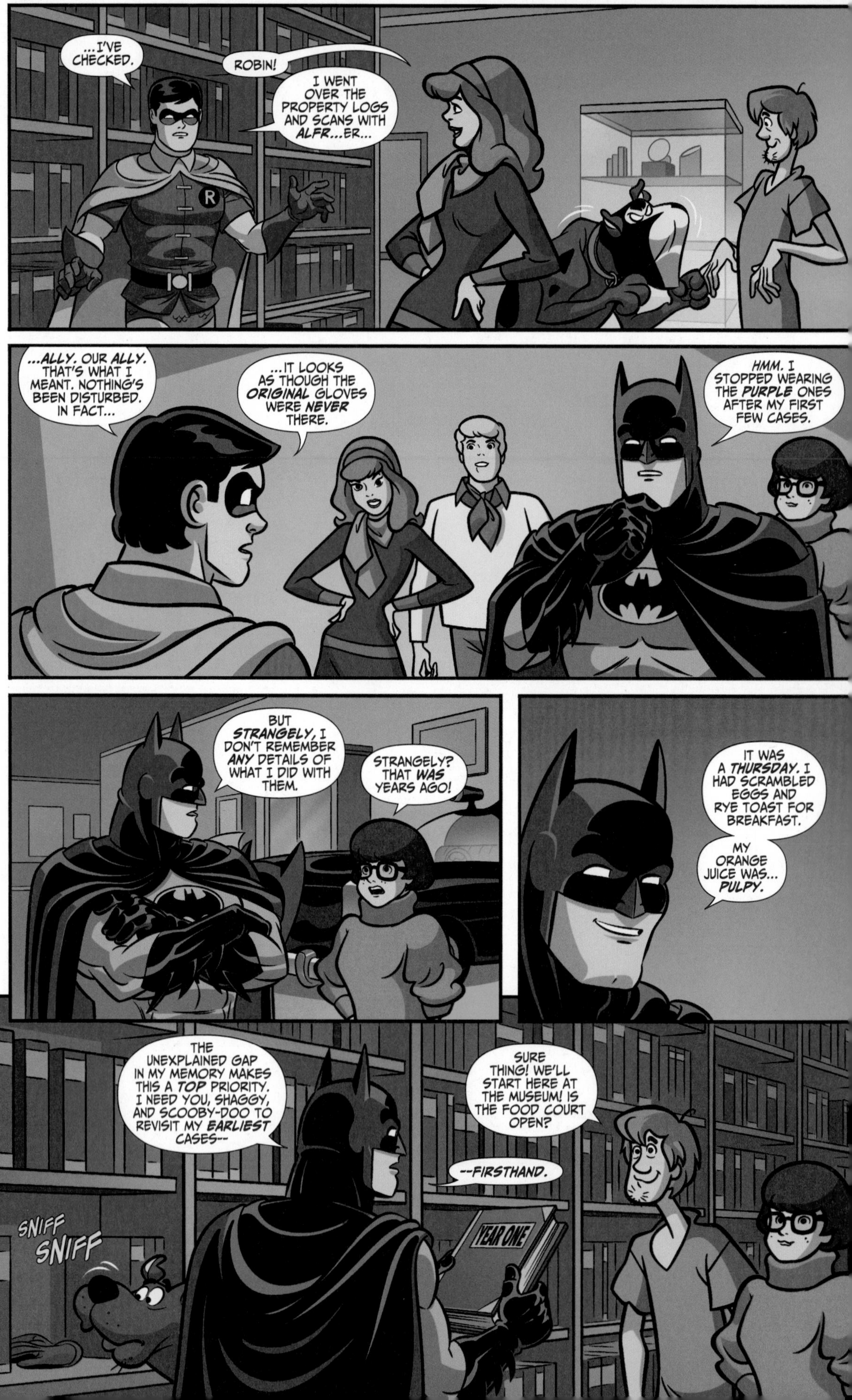
...I'VE CHECKED.
ROBIN!
I WENT OVER THE PROPERTY LOGS AND SCANS WITH ALFR...ER...
...ALLY. OUR ALLY. THAT'S WHAT I MEANT. NOTHING'S BEEN DISTURBED. IN FACT...
...IT LOOKS AS THOUGH THE ORIGINAL GLOVES WERE NEVER THERE.
HMM. I STOPPED WEARING THE PURPLE ONES AFTER MY FIRST FEW CASES.
BUT STRANGELY, I DON'T REMEMBER ANY DETAILS OF WHAT I DID WITH THEM.
STRANGELY? THAT WAS YEARS AGO!
IT WAS A THURSDAY. I HAD SCRAMBLED EGGS AND RYE TOAST FOR BREAKFAST.
MY ORANGE JUICE WAS... PULPY.
THE UNEXPLAINED GAP IN MY MEMORY MAKES THIS A TOP PRIORITY. I NEED YOU, SHAGGY, AND SCOOBY-DOO TO REVISIT MY EARLIEST CASES--
SURE THING! WE'LL START HERE AT THE MUSEUM! IS THE FOOD COURT OPEN?
--FIRSTHAND.
YEAR ONE
SNIFF SNIFF

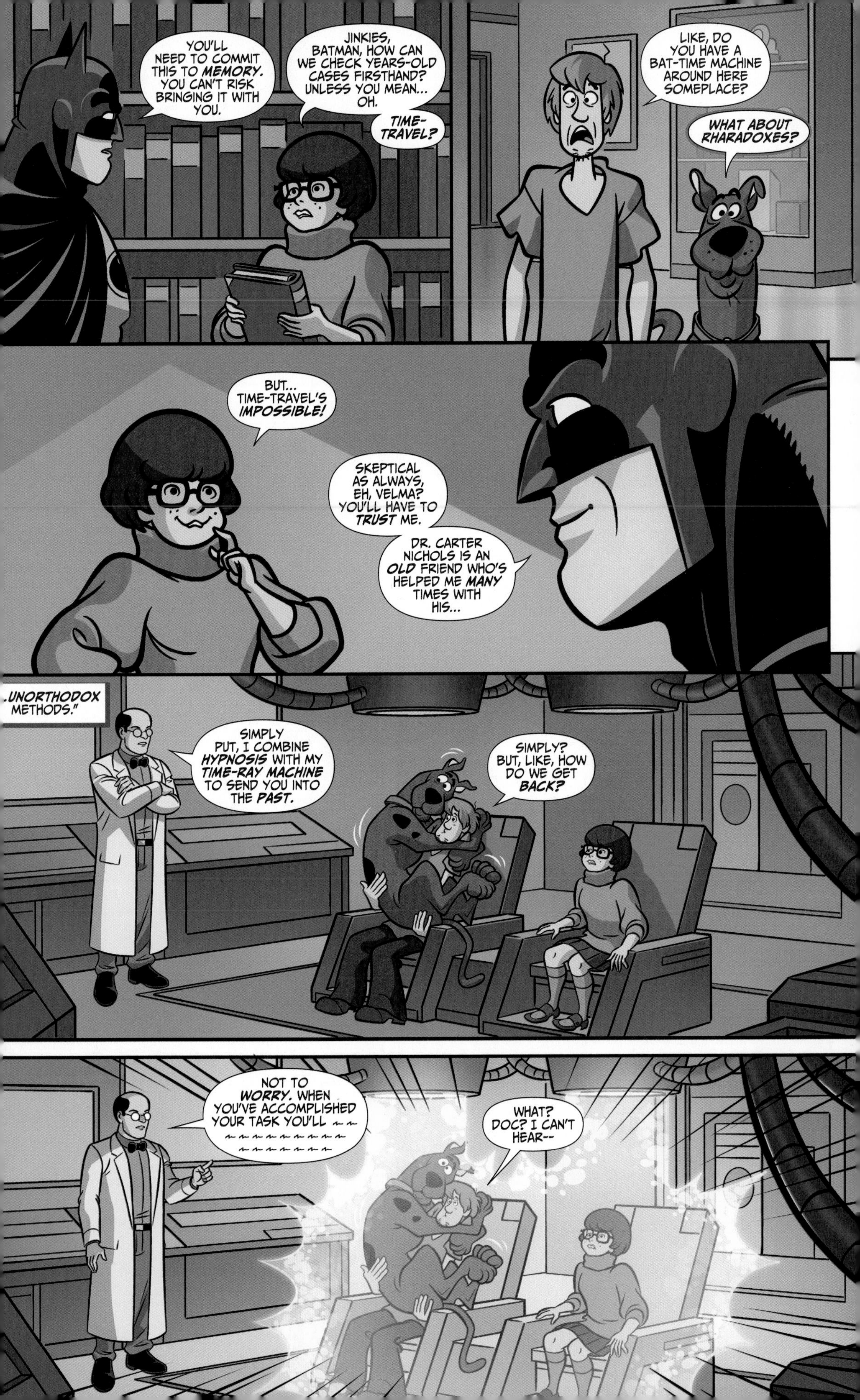
YOU'LL NEED TO COMMIT THIS TO MEMORY. YOU CAN'T RISK BRINGING IT WITH YOU.
JINKIES, BATMAN, HOW CAN WE CHECK YEARS-OLD CASES FIRSTHAND? UNLESS YOU MEAN... OH.
TIME-TRAVEL?
LIKE, DO YOU HAVE A BAT-TIME MACHINE AROUND HERE SOMEPLACE?
WHAT ABOUT RHARADOXES?
BUT... TIME-TRAVEL'S IMPOSSIBLE!
SKEPTICAL AS ALWAYS, EH, VELMA? YOU'LL HAVE TO TRUST ME.
DR. CARTER NICHOLS IS AN OLD FRIEND WHO'S HELPED ME MANY TIMES WITH HIS...
...UNORTHODOX METHODS."
SIMPLY PUT, I COMBINE HYPNOSIS WITH MY TIME-RAY MACHINE TO SEND YOU INTO THE PAST.
SIMPLY? BUT, LIKE, HOW DO WE GET BACK?
NOT TO WORRY. WHEN YOU'VE ACCOMPLISHED YOUR TASK YOU'LL ~~ ~~~~~~~~~ ~~~~~~~~
WHAT? DOC? I CAN'T HEAR--

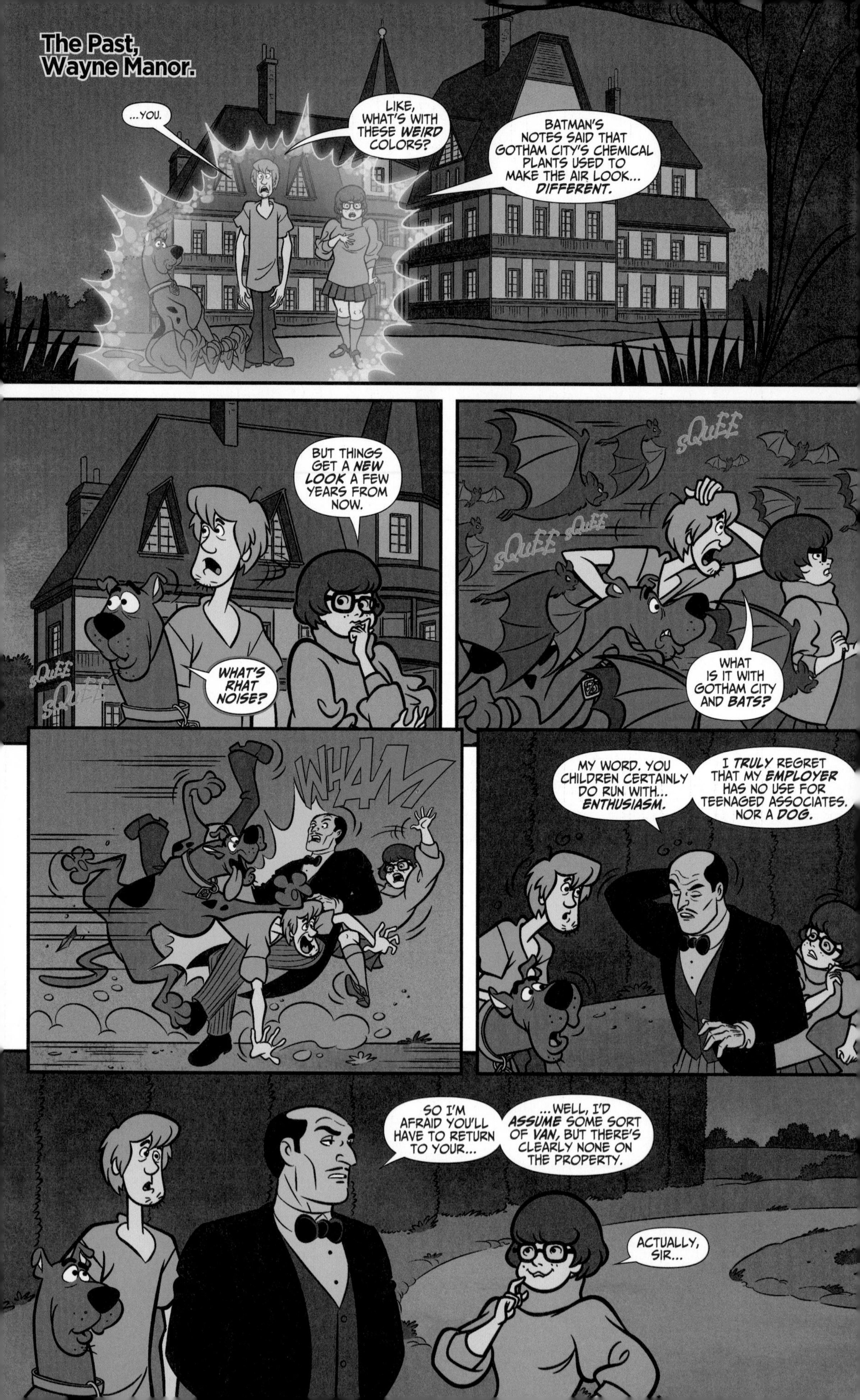
The Past, Wayne Manor.
...YOU.
LIKE, WHAT'S WITH THESE WEIRD COLORS?
BATMAN'S NOTES SAID THAT GOTHAM CITY'S CHEMICAL PLANTS USED TO MAKE THE AIR LOOK... DIFFERENT.
BUT THINGS GET A NEW LOOK A FEW YEARS FROM NOW.
SQUEE
SQUEE
WHAT'S RHAT NOISE?
SQUEE
SQUEE SQUEE
SQUEE
WHAT IS IT WITH GOTHAM CITY AND BATS?
WHAM
MY WORD. YOU CHILDREN CERTAINLY DO RUN WITH... ENTHUSIASM.
I TRULY REGRET THAT MY EMPLOYER HAS NO USE FOR TEENAGED ASSOCIATES. NOR A DOG.
SO I'M AFRAID YOU'LL HAVE TO RETURN TO YOUR...
...WELL, I'D ASSUME SOME SORT OF VAN, BUT THERE'S CLEARLY NONE ON THE PROPERTY.
ACTUALLY, SIR...

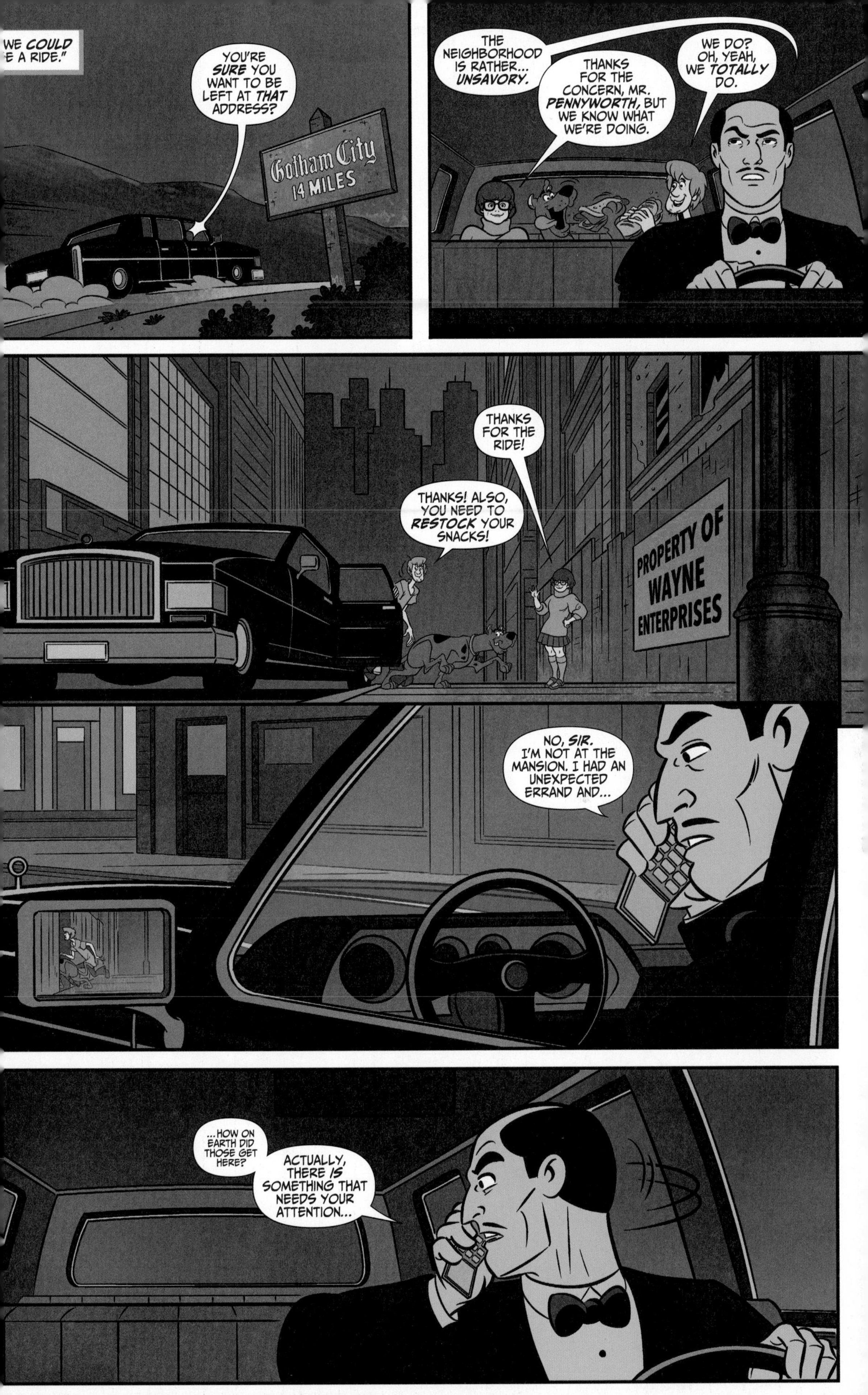
WE COULD
E A RIDE."
YOU'RE SURE YOU WANT TO BE LEFT AT THAT ADDRESS?
Gotham City
14 MILES
THE NEIGHBORHOOD IS RATHER... UNSAVORY.
THANKS FOR THE CONCERN, MR. PENNYWORTH, BUT WE KNOW WHAT WE'RE DOING.
WE DO? OH, YEAH, WE TOTALLY DO.
THANKS FOR THE RIDE!
THANKS! ALSO, YOU NEED TO RESTOCK YOUR SNACKS!
PROPERTY OF WAYNE ENTERPRISES
NO, SIR. I'M NOT AT THE MANSION. I HAD AN UNEXPECTED ERRAND AND...
...HOW ON EARTH DID THOSE GET HERE?
ACTUALLY, THERE IS SOMETHING THAT NEEDS YOUR ATTENTION...

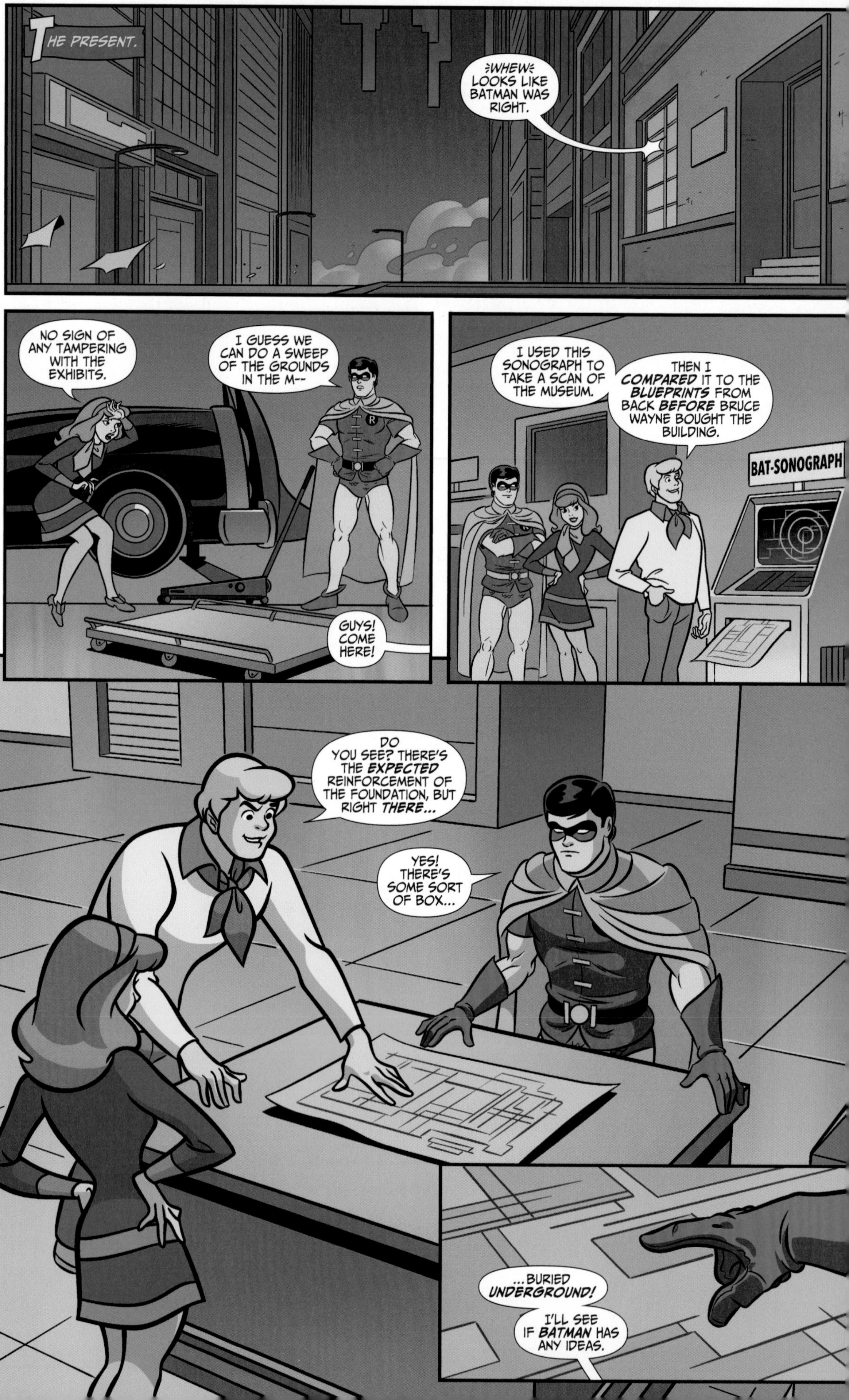
THE PRESENT.
WHEW LOOKS LIKE BATMAN WAS RIGHT.
NO SIGN OF ANY TAMPERING WITH THE EXHIBITS.
I GUESS WE CAN DO A SWEEP OF THE GROUNDS IN THE M--
GUYS! COME HERE!
I USED THIS SONOGRAPH TO TAKE A SCAN OF THE MUSEUM.
THEN I COMPARED IT TO THE BLUEPRINTS FROM BACK BEFORE BRUCE WAYNE BOUGHT THE BUILDING.
BAT-SONOGRAPH
DO YOU SEE? THERE'S THE EXPECTED REINFORCEMENT OF THE FOUNDATION, BUT RIGHT THERE...
YES! THERE'S SOME SORT OF BOX...
...BURIED UNDERGROUND!
I'LL SEE IF BATMAN HAS ANY IDEAS.

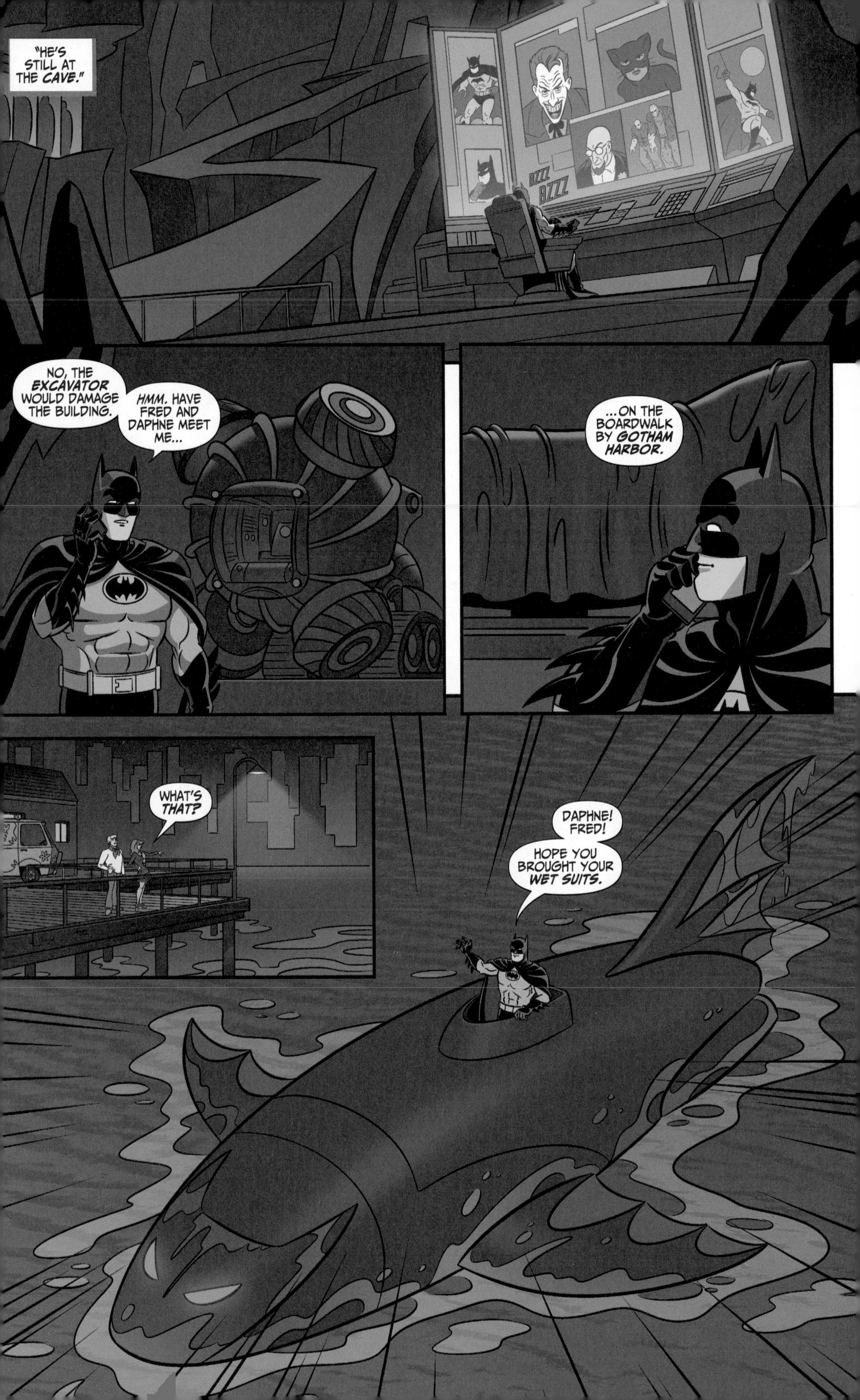
"HE'S STILL AT THE CAVE."
BZZZ BZZZ
NO, THE EXCAVATOR WOULD DAMAGE THE BUILDING.
HMM. HAVE FRED AND DAPHNE MEET ME...
...ON THE BOARDWALK BY GOTHAM HARBOR.
WHAT'S THAT?
DAPHNE! FRED!
HOPE YOU BROUGHT YOUR WET SUITS.

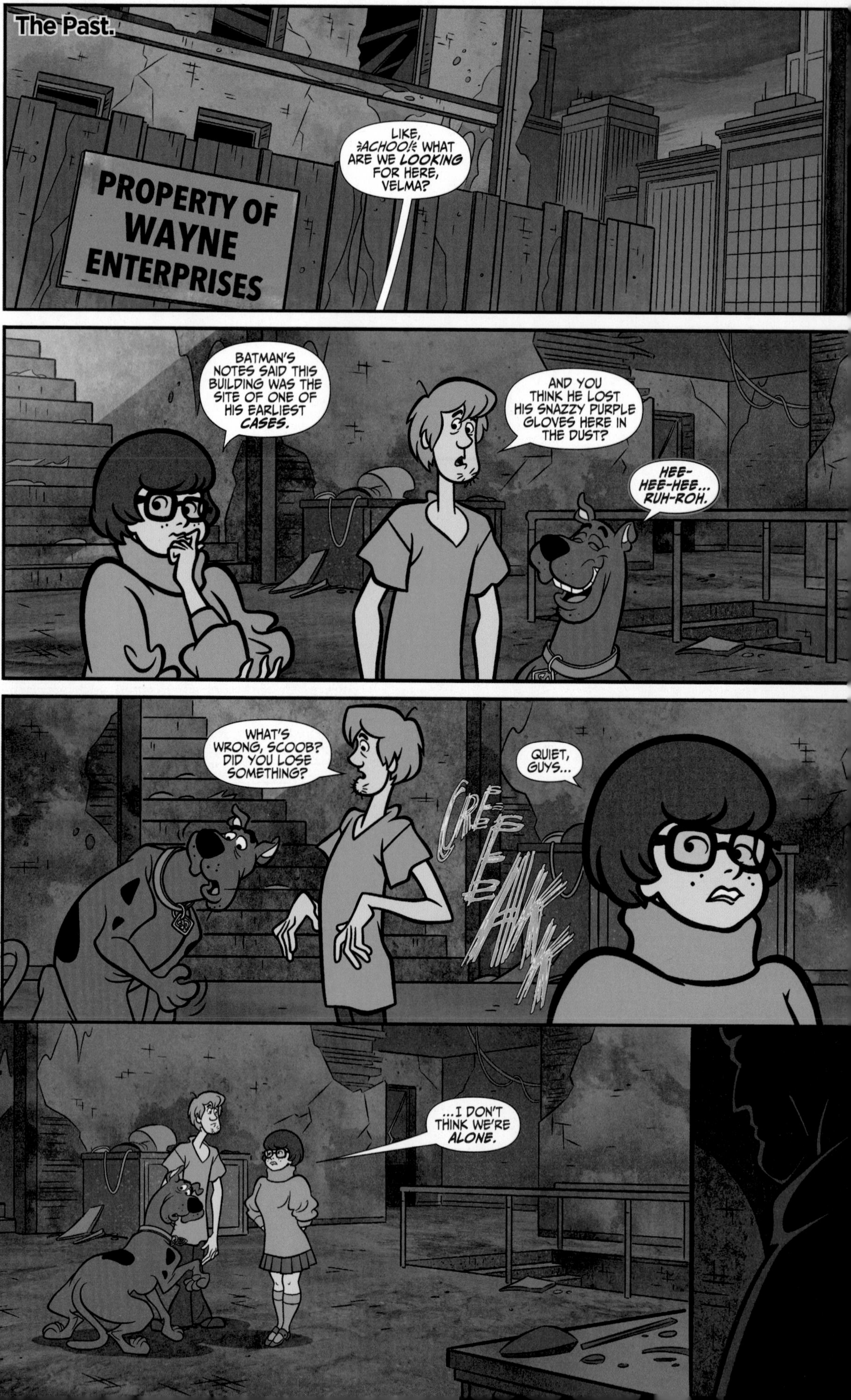
The Past.
PROPERTY OF WAYNE ENTERPRISES
LIKE, *ACHOO!* WHAT ARE WE LOOKING FOR HERE, VELMA?
BATMAN'S NOTES SAID THIS BUILDING WAS THE SITE OF ONE OF HIS EARLIEST CASES.
AND YOU THINK HE LOST HIS SNAZZY PURPLE GLOVES HERE IN THE DUST?
HEE-HEE-HEE... RUH-ROH.
WHAT'S WRONG, SCOOB? DID YOU LOSE SOMETHING?
QUIET, GUYS...
CREEEAKK
...I DON'T THINK WE'RE ALONE.

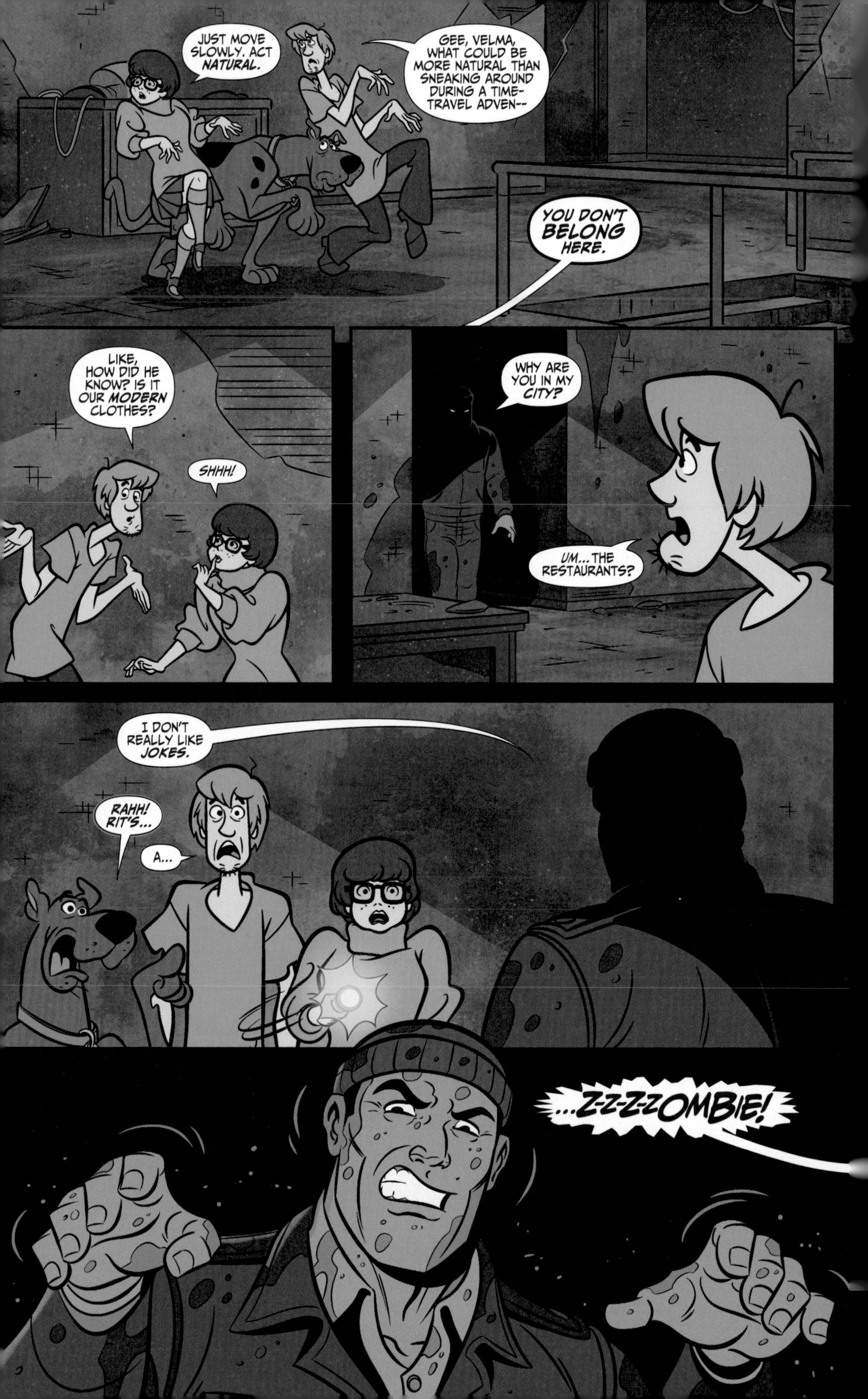
JUST MOVE SLOWLY. ACT NATURAL.
GEE, VELMA, WHAT COULD BE MORE NATURAL THAN SNEAKING AROUND DURING A TIME-TRAVEL ADVEN--
YOU DON'T BELONG HERE.
LIKE, HOW DID HE KNOW? IS IT OUR MODERN CLOTHES?
SHHH!
WHY ARE YOU IN MY CITY?
UM... THE RESTAURANTS?
I DON'T REALLY LIKE JOKES.
RAHH! RIT'S...
A...
...Z-Z-Z-ZOMBIE!

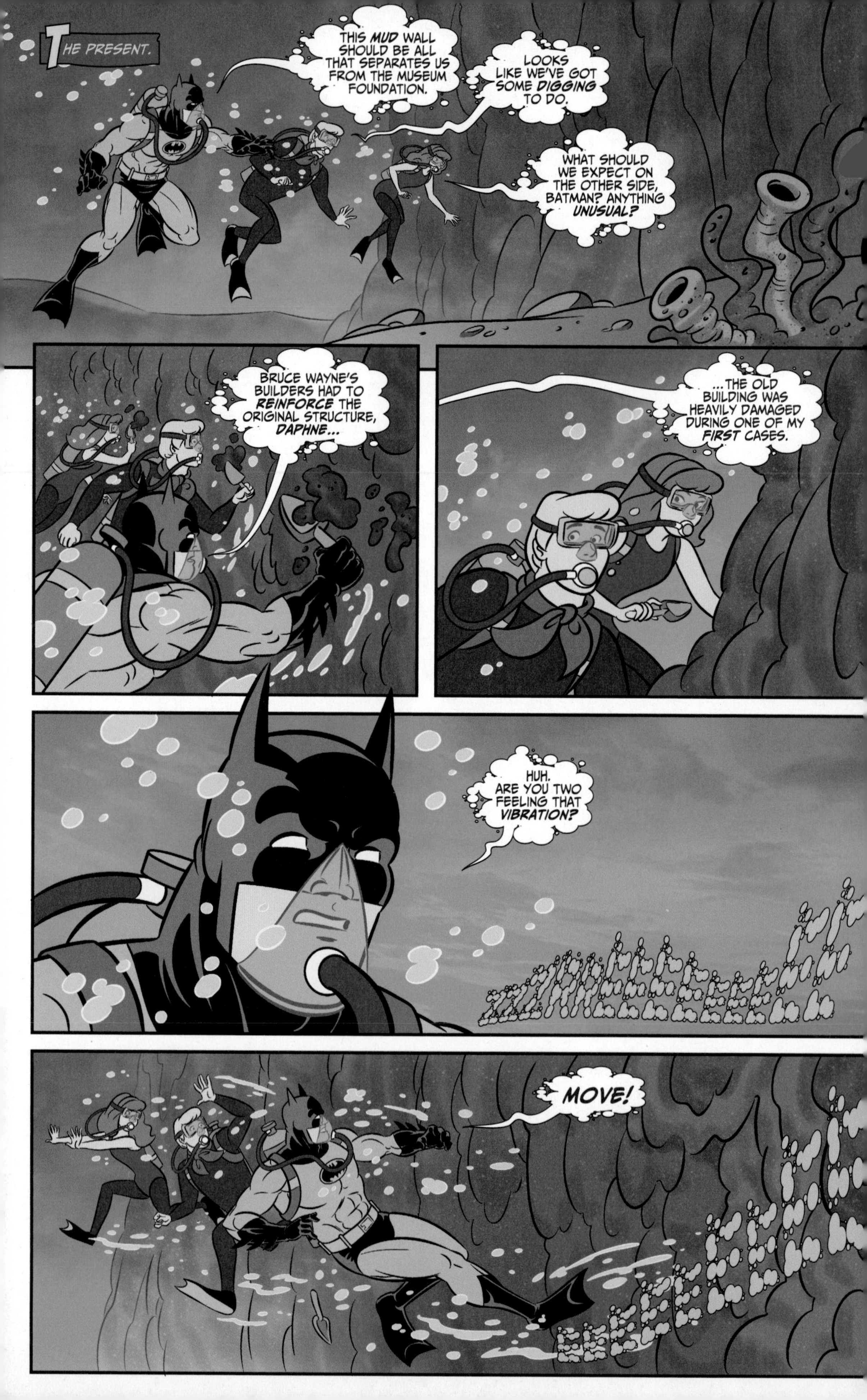
THE PRESENT.
THIS MUD WALL SHOULD BE ALL THAT SEPARATES US FROM THE MUSEUM FOUNDATION.
LOOKS LIKE WE'VE GOT SOME DIGGING TO DO.
WHAT SHOULD WE EXPECT ON THE OTHER SIDE, BATMAN? ANYTHING UNUSUAL?
BRUCE WAYNE'S BUILDERS HAD TO REINFORCE THE ORIGINAL STRUCTURE, DAPHNE...
...THE OLD BUILDING WAS HEAVILY DAMAGED DURING ONE OF MY FIRST CASES.
HUH. ARE YOU TWO FEELING THAT VIBRATION?
MOVE!

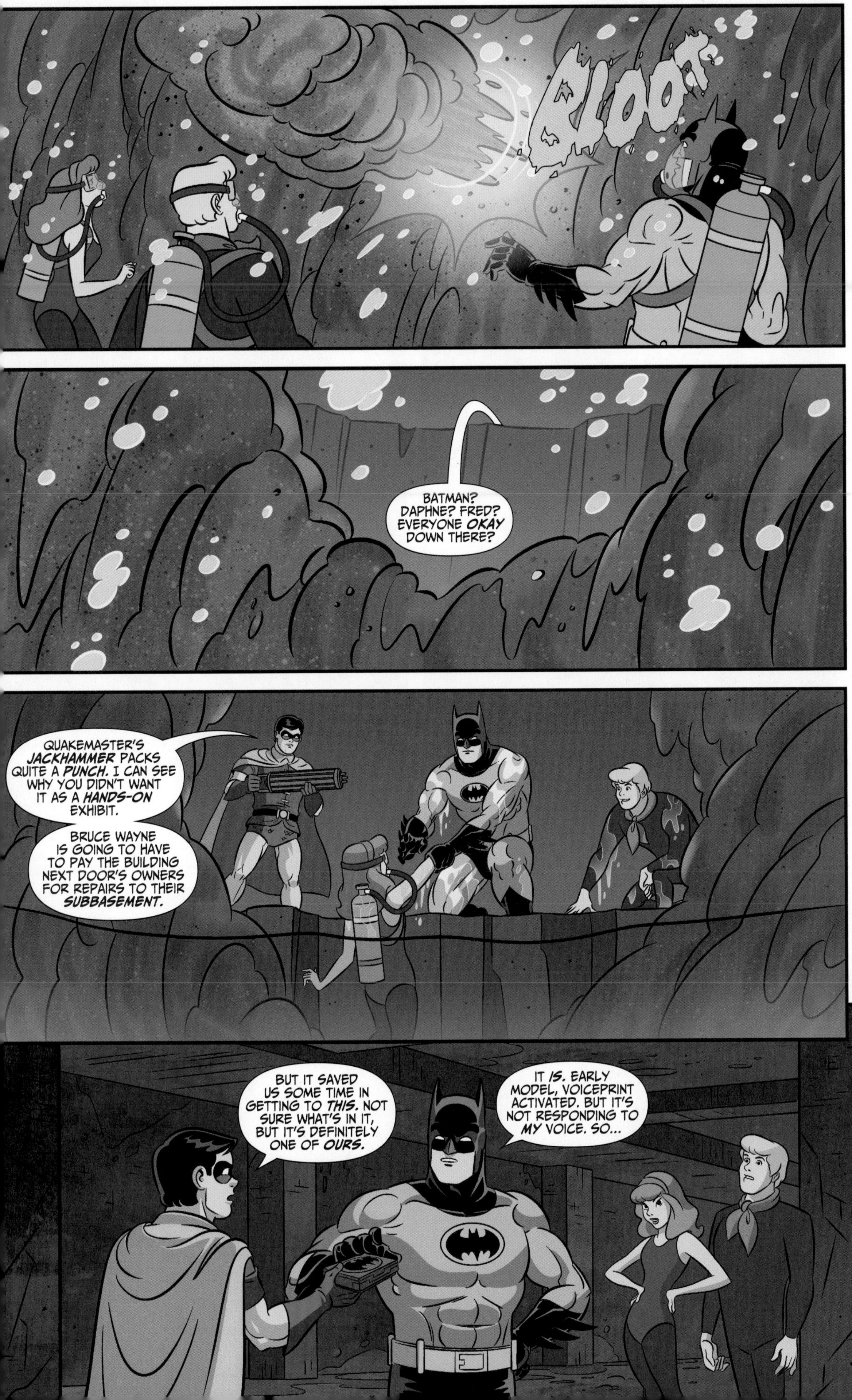
BLOOT
BATMAN? DAPHNE? FRED? EVERYONE OKAY DOWN THERE?
QUAKEMASTER'S JACKHAMMER PACKS QUITE A PUNCH. I CAN SEE WHY YOU DIDN'T WANT IT AS A HANDS-ON EXHIBIT.
BRUCE WAYNE IS GOING TO HAVE TO PAY THE BUILDING NEXT DOOR'S OWNERS FOR REPAIRS TO THEIR SUBBASEMENT.
BUT IT SAVED US SOME TIME IN GETTING TO THIS. NOT SURE WHAT'S IN IT, BUT IT'S DEFINITELY ONE OF OURS.
IT IS. EARLY MODEL, VOICEPRINT ACTIVATED. BUT IT'S NOT RESPONDING TO MY VOICE. SO...

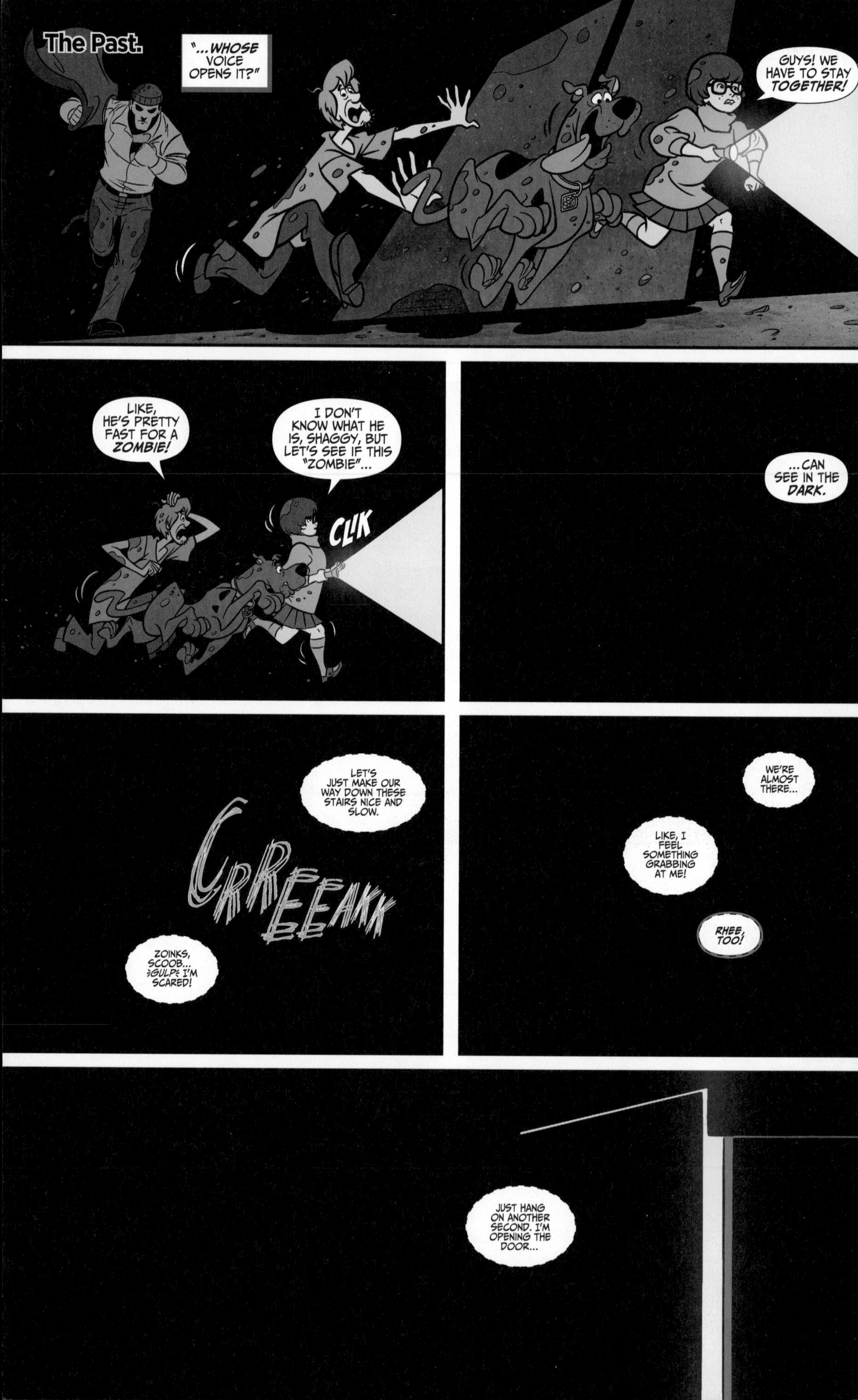
The Past.
"...WHOSE VOICE OPENS IT?"
GUYS! WE HAVE TO STAY TOGETHER!
LIKE, HE'S PRETTY FAST FOR A ZOMBIE!
I DON'T KNOW WHAT HE IS, SHAGGY, BUT LET'S SEE IF THIS "ZOMBIE"...
CLIK
...CAN SEE IN THE DARK.
LET'S JUST MAKE OUR WAY DOWN THESE STAIRS NICE AND SLOW.
CRREEAKK
ZOINKS, SCOOB... ≠GULP≠ I'M SCARED!
WE'RE ALMOST THERE...
LIKE, I FEEL SOMETHING GRABBING AT ME!
RHEE, TOO!
JUST HANG ON ANOTHER SECOND. I'M OPENING THE DOOR...

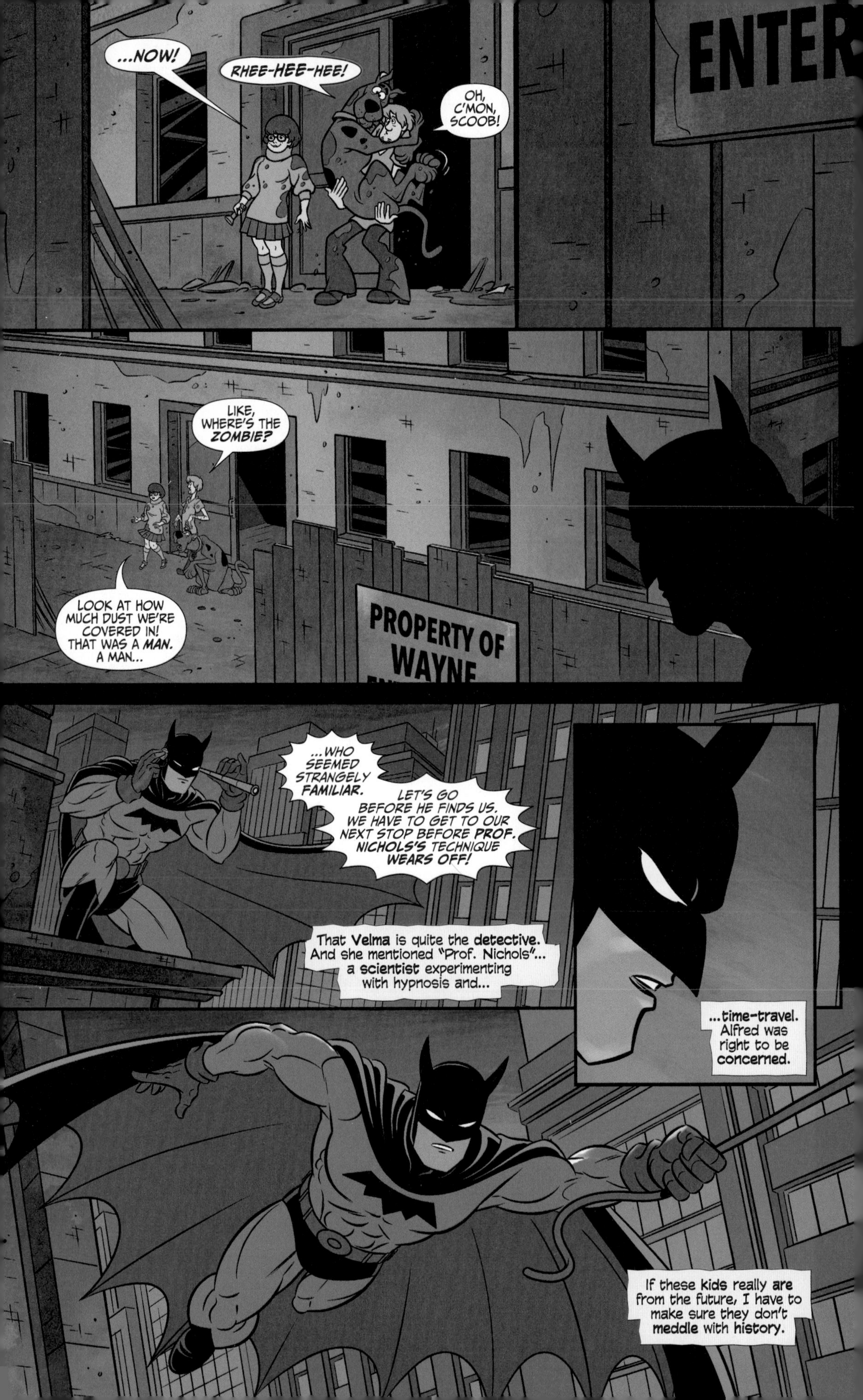
ENTER
...NOW!
RHEE-HEE-HEE!
OH, C'MON, SCOOB!
LIKE, WHERE'S THE ZOMBIE?
LOOK AT HOW MUCH DUST WE'RE COVERED IN! THAT WAS A MAN. A MAN...
PROPERTY OF WAYNE
...WHO SEEMED STRANGELY FAMILIAR.
LET'S GO BEFORE HE FINDS US. WE HAVE TO GET TO OUR NEXT STOP BEFORE PROF. NICHOLS'S TECHNIQUE WEARS OFF!
That Velma is quite the detective. And she mentioned "Prof. Nichols"... a scientist experimenting with hypnosis and...
...time-travel. Alfred was right to be concerned.
If these kids really are from the future, I have to make sure they don't meddle with history.

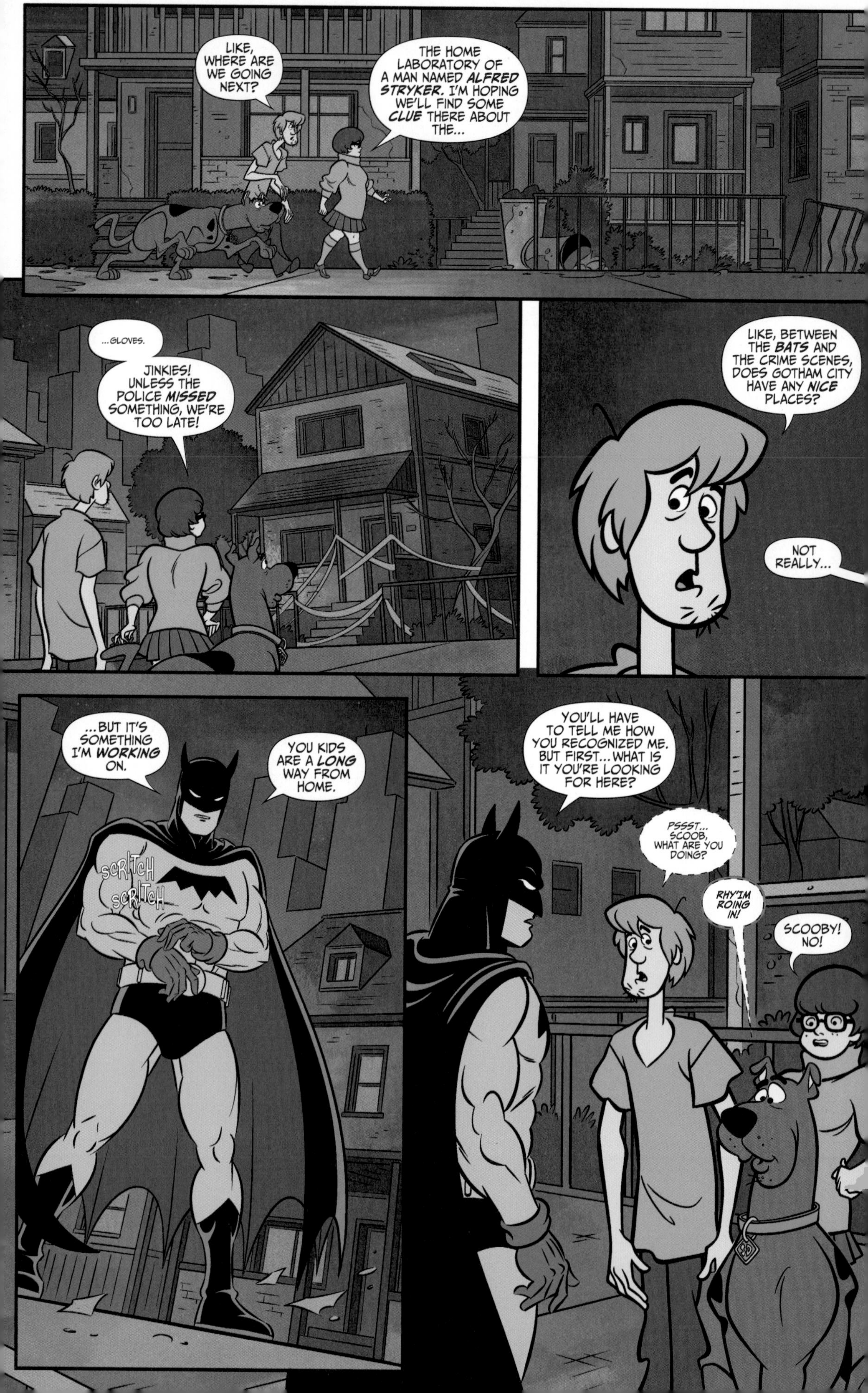
LIKE, WHERE ARE WE GOING NEXT?
THE HOME LABORATORY OF A MAN NAMED ALFRED STRYKER. I'M HOPING WE'LL FIND SOME CLUE THERE ABOUT THE...
...GLOVES.
JINKIES! UNLESS THE POLICE MISSED SOMETHING, WE'RE TOO LATE!
LIKE, BETWEEN THE BATS AND THE CRIME SCENES, DOES GOTHAM CITY HAVE ANY NICE PLACES?
NOT REALLY...
...BUT IT'S SOMETHING I'M WORKING ON.
YOU KIDS ARE A LONG WAY FROM HOME.
SCRITCH SCRITCH
YOU'LL HAVE TO TELL ME HOW YOU RECOGNIZED ME. BUT FIRST...WHAT IS IT YOU'RE LOOKING FOR HERE?
PSSST... SCOOB, WHAT ARE YOU DOING?
RHY'IM ROING IN!
SCOOBY! NO!

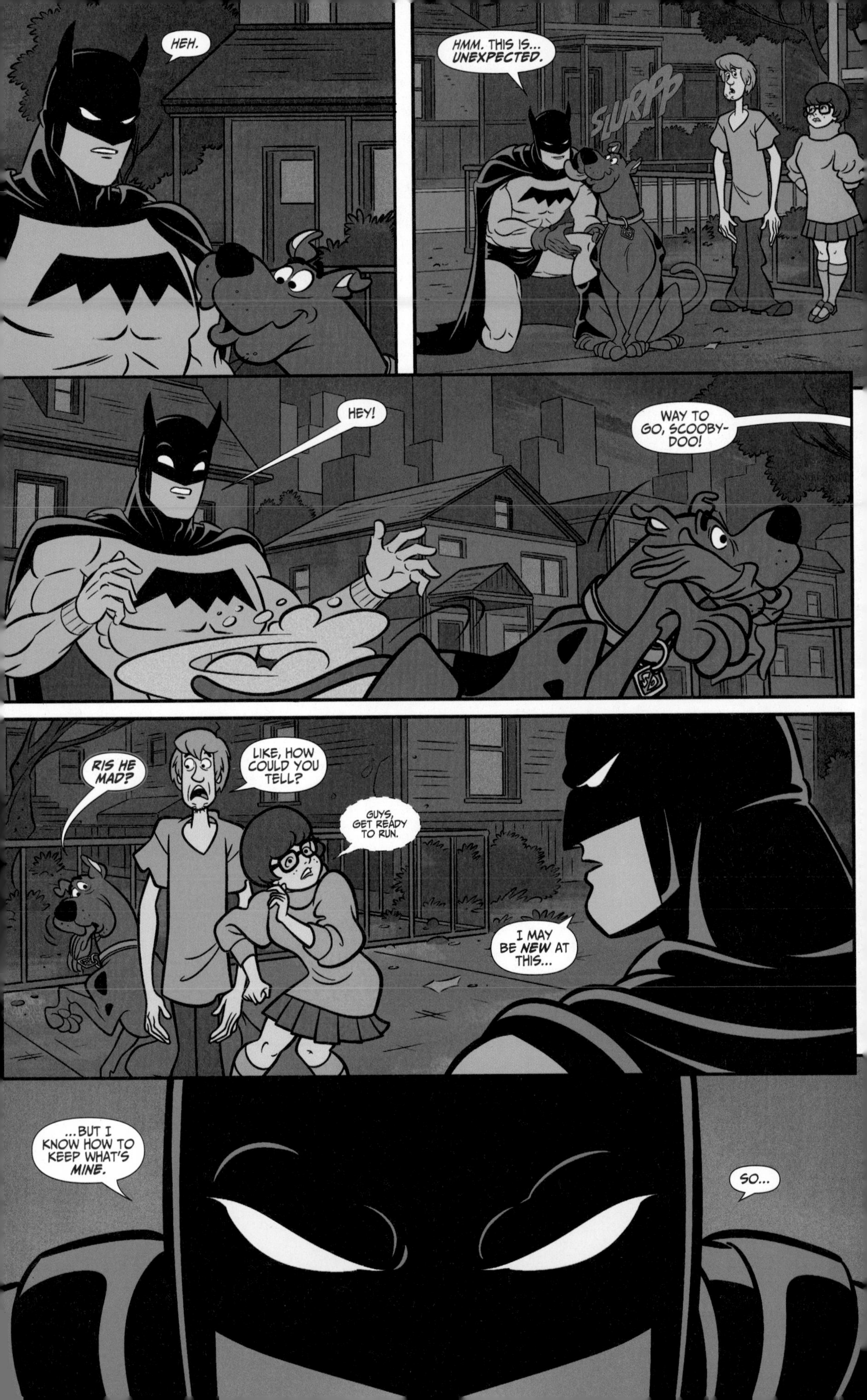
HEH.
HMM. THIS IS... UNEXPECTED.
SLURPP
HEY!
WAY TO GO, SCOOBY-DOO!
RIS HE MAD?
LIKE, HOW COULD YOU TELL?
GUYS, GET READY TO RUN.
I MAY BE NEW AT THIS...
...BUT I KNOW HOW TO KEEP WHAT'S MINE.
SO...

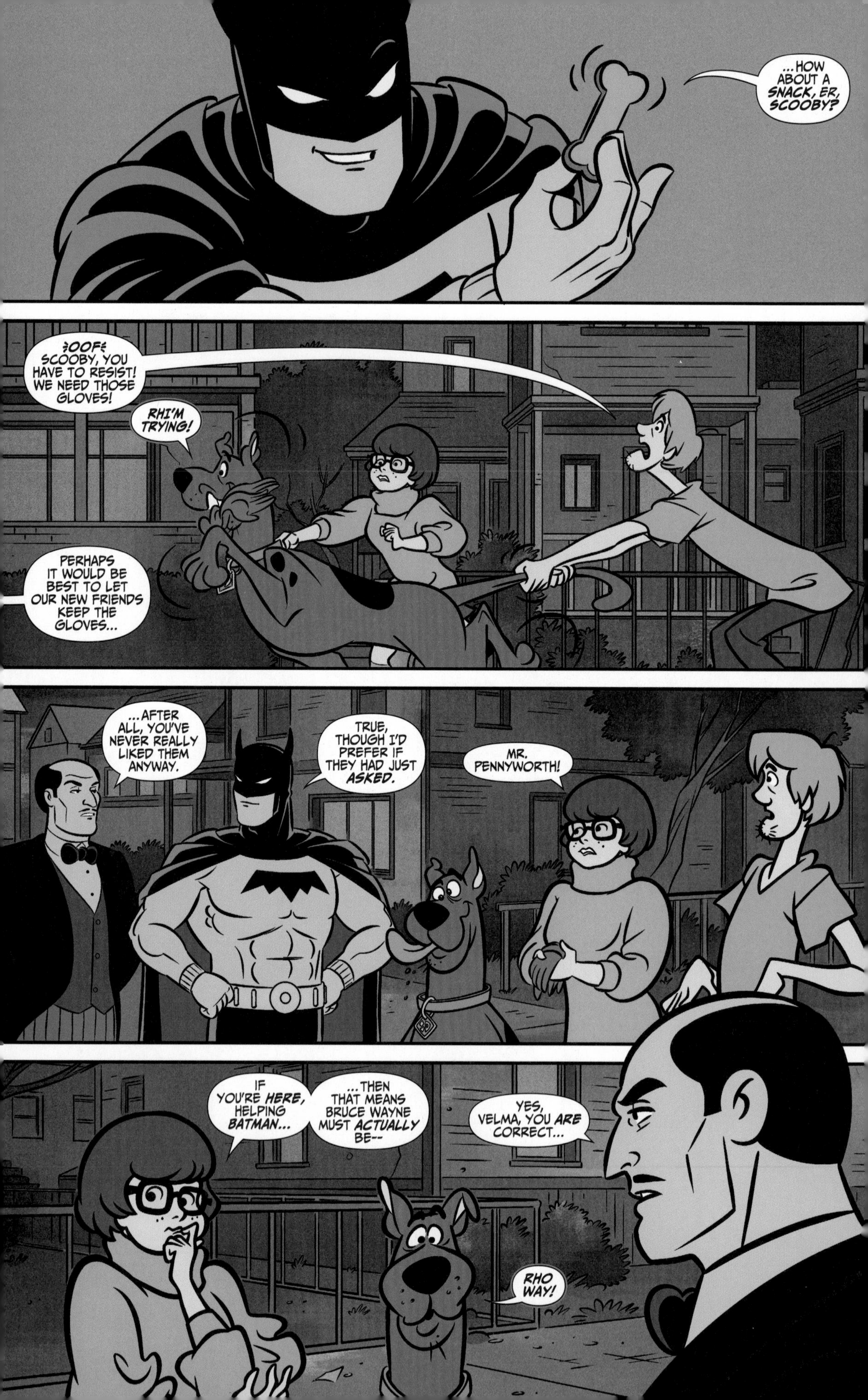
...HOW ABOUT A SNACK, ER, SCOOBY?
OOF SCOOBY, YOU HAVE TO RESIST! WE NEED THOSE GLOVES!
RHI'M TRYING!
PERHAPS IT WOULD BE BEST TO LET OUR NEW FRIENDS KEEP THE GLOVES...
...AFTER ALL, YOU'VE NEVER REALLY LIKED THEM ANYWAY.
TRUE, THOUGH I'D PREFER IF THEY HAD JUST ASKED.
MR. PENNYWORTH!
IF YOU'RE HERE, HELPING BATMAN...
...THEN THAT MEANS BRUCE WAYNE MUST ACTUALLY BE--
YES, VELMA, YOU ARE CORRECT...
RHO WAY!

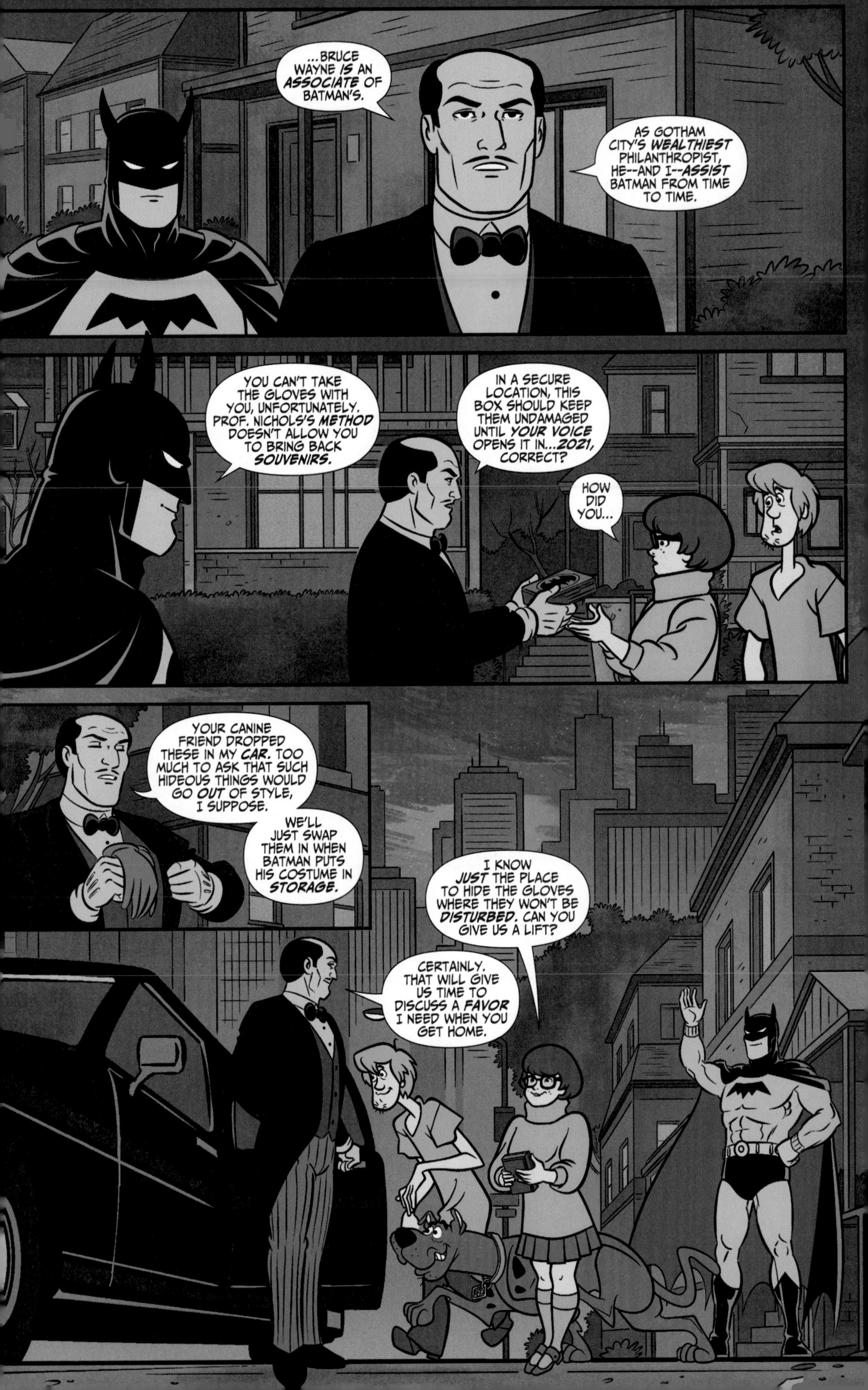
...BRUCE WAYNE IS AN ASSOCIATE OF BATMAN'S.
AS GOTHAM CITY'S WEALTHIEST PHILANTHROPIST, HE--AND I--ASSIST BATMAN FROM TIME TO TIME.
YOU CAN'T TAKE THE GLOVES WITH YOU, UNFORTUNATELY. PROF. NICHOLS'S METHOD DOESN'T ALLOW YOU TO BRING BACK SOUVENIRS.
IN A SECURE LOCATION, THIS BOX SHOULD KEEP THEM UNDAMAGED UNTIL YOUR VOICE OPENS IT IN...2021, CORRECT?
HOW DID YOU...
YOUR CANINE FRIEND DROPPED THESE IN MY CAR. TOO MUCH TO ASK THAT SUCH HIDEOUS THINGS WOULD GO OUT OF STYLE, I SUPPOSE.
WE'LL JUST SWAP THEM IN WHEN BATMAN PUTS HIS COSTUME IN STORAGE.
I KNOW JUST THE PLACE TO HIDE THE GLOVES WHERE THEY WON'T BE DISTURBED. CAN YOU GIVE US A LIFT?
CERTAINLY. THAT WILL GIVE US TIME TO DISCUSS A FAVOR I NEED WHEN YOU GET HOME.

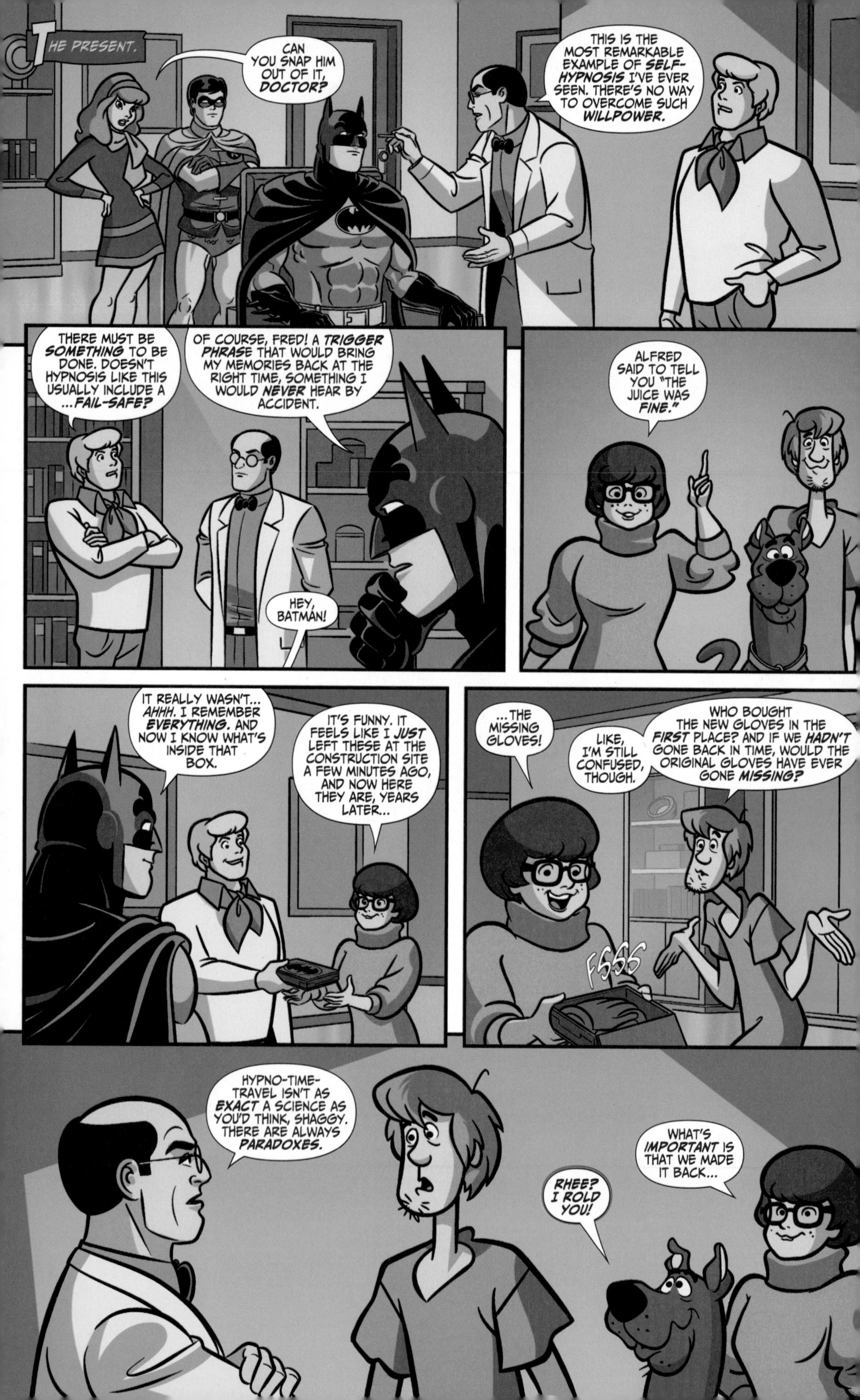
THE PRESENT.
CAN YOU SNAP HIM OUT OF IT, DOCTOR?
THIS IS THE MOST REMARKABLE EXAMPLE OF SELF-HYPNOSIS I'VE EVER SEEN. THERE'S NO WAY TO OVERCOME SUCH WILLPOWER.
THERE MUST BE SOMETHING TO BE DONE. DOESN'T HYPNOSIS LIKE THIS USUALLY INCLUDE A ...FAIL-SAFE?
OF COURSE, FRED! A TRIGGER PHRASE THAT WOULD BRING MY MEMORIES BACK AT THE RIGHT TIME, SOMETHING I WOULD NEVER HEAR BY ACCIDENT.
HEY, BATMAN!
ALFRED SAID TO TELL YOU "THE JUICE WAS FINE."
IT REALLY WASN'T... AHHH. I REMEMBER EVERYTHING. AND NOW I KNOW WHAT'S INSIDE THAT BOX.
IT'S FUNNY. IT FEELS LIKE I JUST LEFT THESE AT THE CONSTRUCTION SITE A FEW MINUTES AGO, AND NOW HERE THEY ARE, YEARS LATER...
...THE MISSING GLOVES!
FSSS
LIKE, I'M STILL CONFUSED, THOUGH.
WHO BOUGHT THE NEW GLOVES IN THE FIRST PLACE? AND IF WE HADN'T GONE BACK IN TIME, WOULD THE ORIGINAL GLOVES HAVE EVER GONE MISSING?
HYPNO-TIME-TRAVEL ISN'T AS EXACT A SCIENCE AS YOU'D THINK, SHAGGY. THERE ARE ALWAYS PARADOXES.
WHAT'S IMPORTANT IS THAT WE MADE IT BACK...
RHEE? I ROLD YOU!

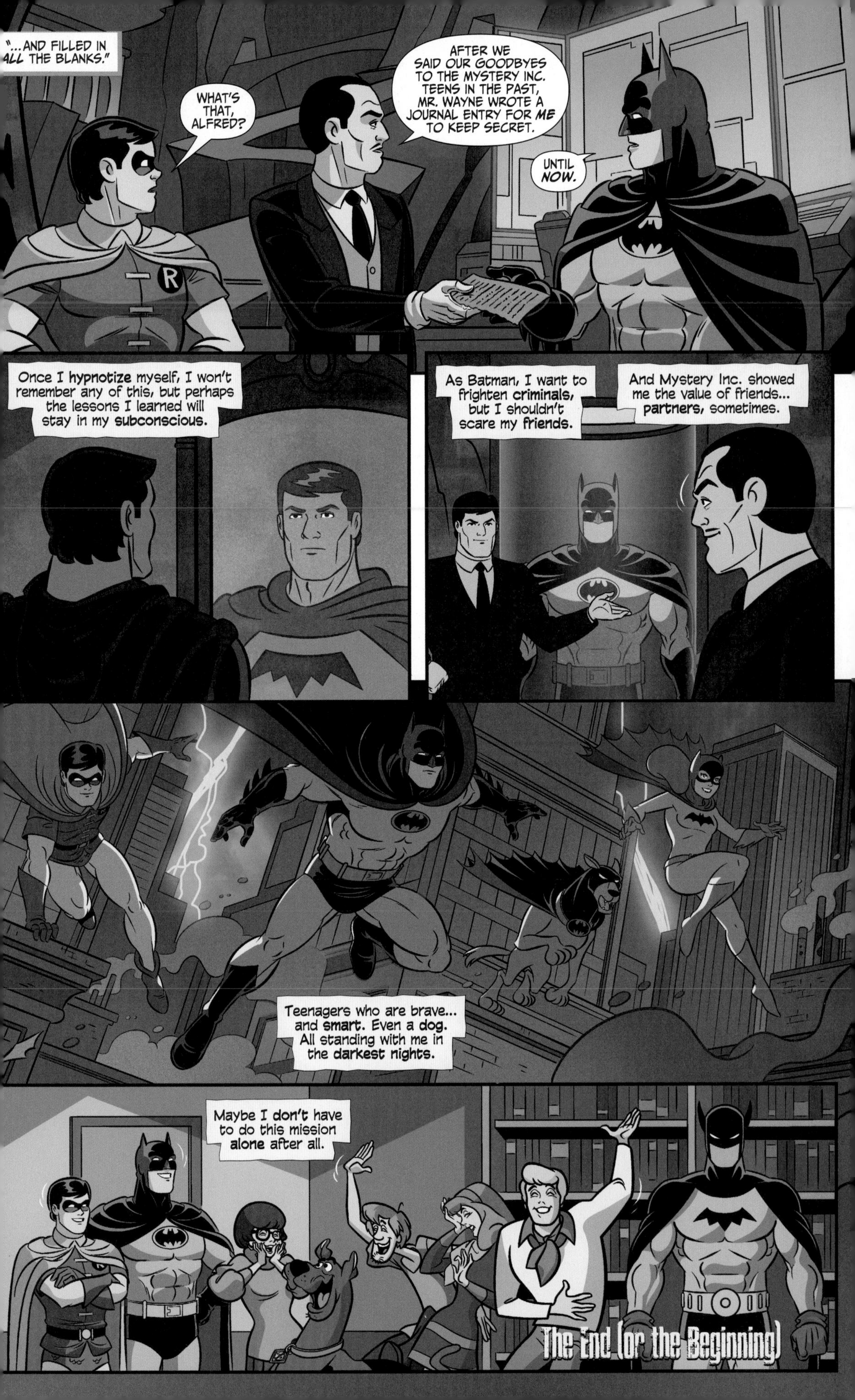
"...AND FILLED IN ALL THE BLANKS."
WHAT'S THAT, ALFRED?
AFTER WE SAID OUR GOODBYES TO THE MYSTERY INC. TEENS IN THE PAST, MR. WAYNE WROTE A JOURNAL ENTRY FOR ME TO KEEP SECRET.
UNTIL NOW.
Once I hypnotize myself, I won't remember any of this, but perhaps the lessons I learned will stay in my subconscious.
As Batman, I want to frighten criminals, but I shouldn't scare my friends.
And Mystery Inc. showed me the value of friends... partners, sometimes.
Teenagers who are brave... and smart. Even a dog. All standing with me in the darkest nights.
Maybe I don't have to do this mission alone after all.
The End (or the Beginning)

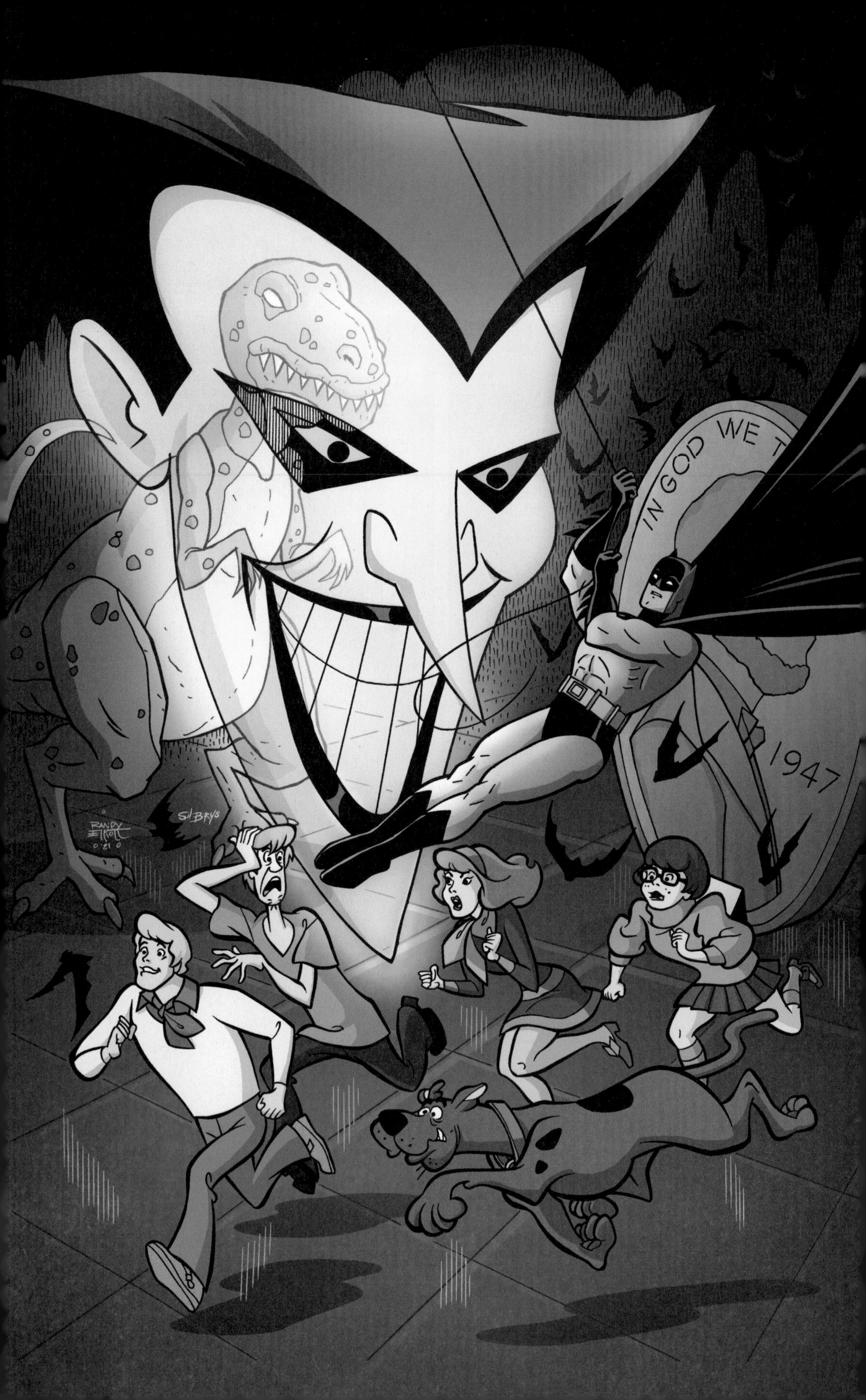
IN GOD WE T
1947

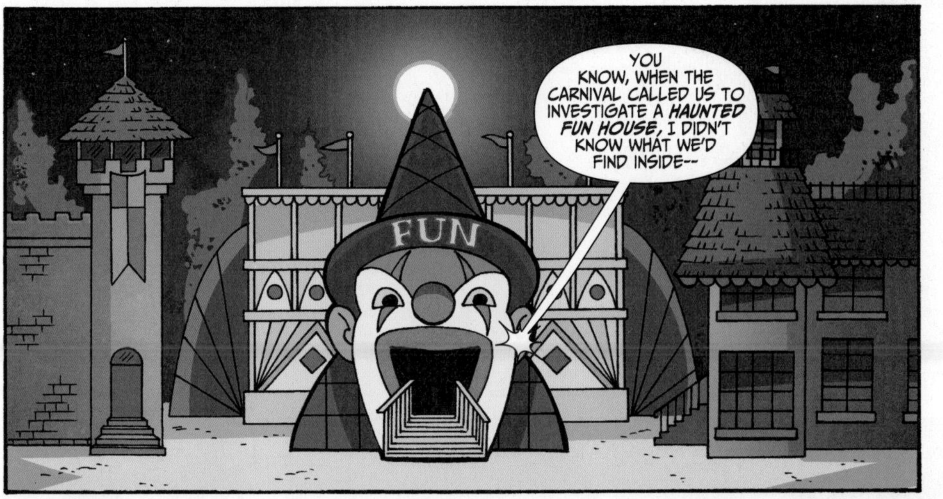
FUN
YOU KNOW, WHEN THE CARNIVAL CALLED US TO INVESTIGATE A HAUNTED FUN HOUSE, I DIDN'T KNOW WHAT WE'D FIND INSIDE--

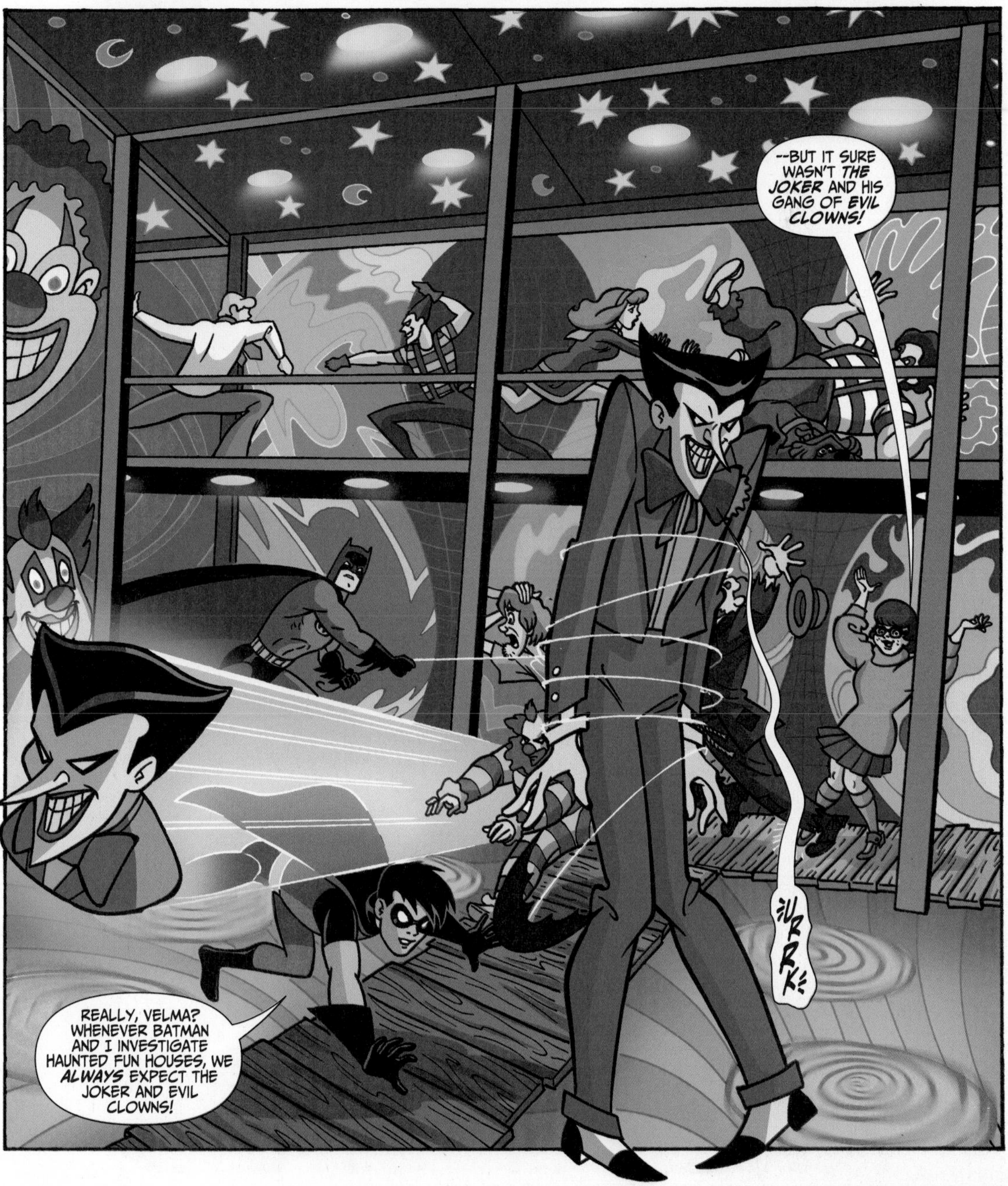
--BUT IT SURE WASN'T THE JOKER AND HIS GANG OF EVIL CLOWNS!
URRK
REALLY, VELMA? WHENEVER BATMAN AND I INVESTIGATE HAUNTED FUN HOUSES, WE ALWAYS EXPECT THE JOKER AND EVIL CLOWNS!

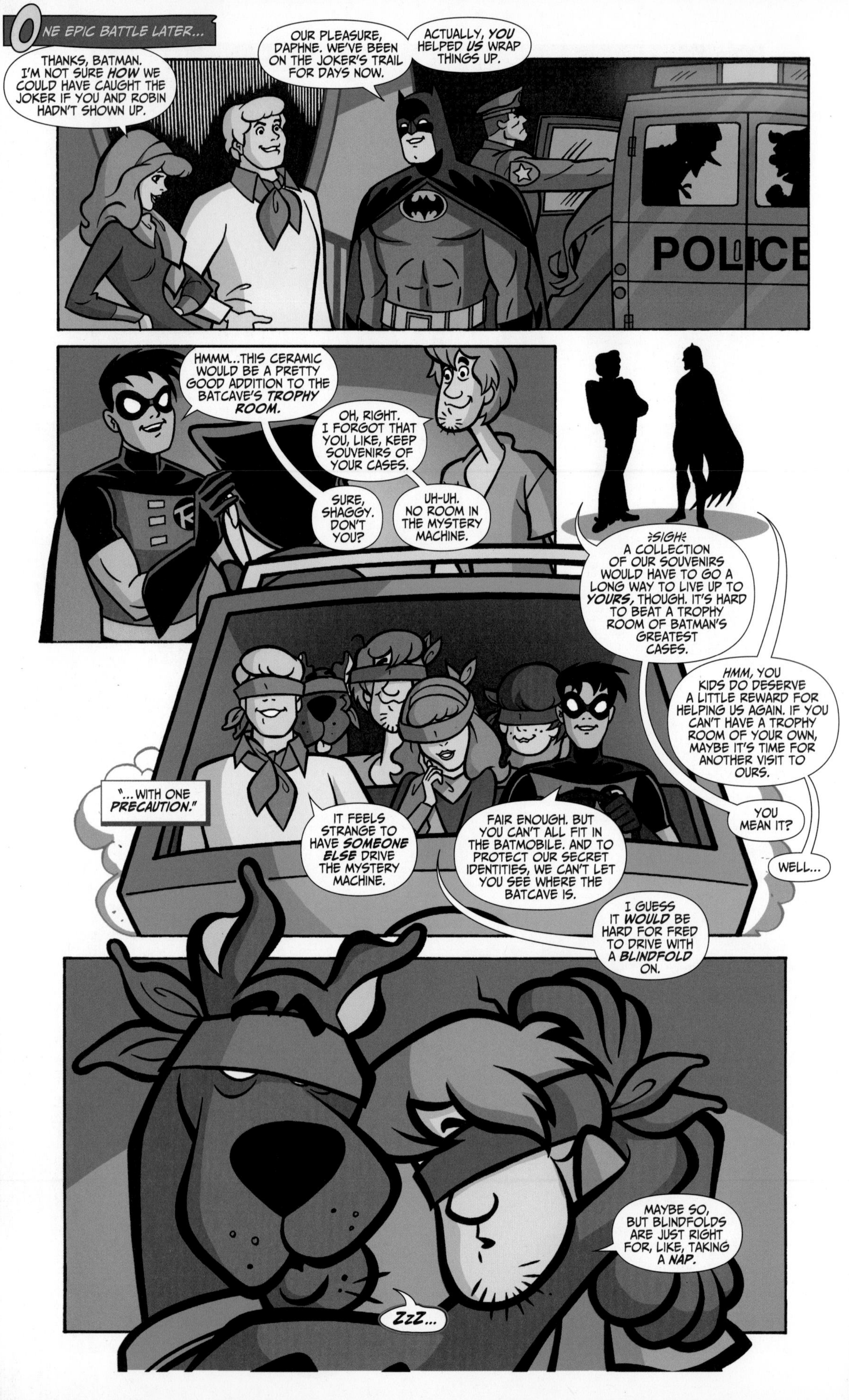
ONE EPIC BATTLE LATER...
THANKS, BATMAN. I'M NOT SURE HOW WE COULD HAVE CAUGHT THE JOKER IF YOU AND ROBIN HADN'T SHOWN UP.
OUR PLEASURE, DAPHNE. WE'VE BEEN ON THE JOKER'S TRAIL FOR DAYS NOW.
ACTUALLY, YOU HELPED US WRAP THINGS UP.
POLICE
HMMM...THIS CERAMIC WOULD BE A PRETTY GOOD ADDITION TO THE BATCAVE'S TROPHY ROOM.
OH, RIGHT. I FORGOT THAT YOU, LIKE, KEEP SOUVENIRS OF YOUR CASES.
SURE, SHAGGY. DON'T YOU?
UH-UH. NO ROOM IN THE MYSTERY MACHINE.
SIGH A COLLECTION OF OUR SOUVENIRS WOULD HAVE TO GO A LONG WAY TO LIVE UP TO YOURS, THOUGH. IT'S HARD TO BEAT A TROPHY ROOM OF BATMAN'S GREATEST CASES.
HMM, YOU KIDS DO DESERVE A LITTLE REWARD FOR HELPING US AGAIN. IF YOU CAN'T HAVE A TROPHY ROOM OF YOUR OWN, MAYBE IT'S TIME FOR ANOTHER VISIT TO OURS.
YOU MEAN IT?
WELL...
"...WITH ONE PRECAUTION."
IT FEELS STRANGE TO HAVE SOMEONE ELSE DRIVE THE MYSTERY MACHINE.
FAIR ENOUGH. BUT YOU CAN'T ALL FIT IN THE BATMOBILE. AND TO PROTECT OUR SECRET IDENTITIES, WE CAN'T LET YOU SEE WHERE THE BATCAVE IS.
I GUESS IT WOULD BE HARD FOR FRED TO DRIVE WITH A BLINDFOLD ON.
MAYBE SO, BUT BLINDFOLDS ARE JUST RIGHT FOR, LIKE, TAKING A NAP.
ZzZ...

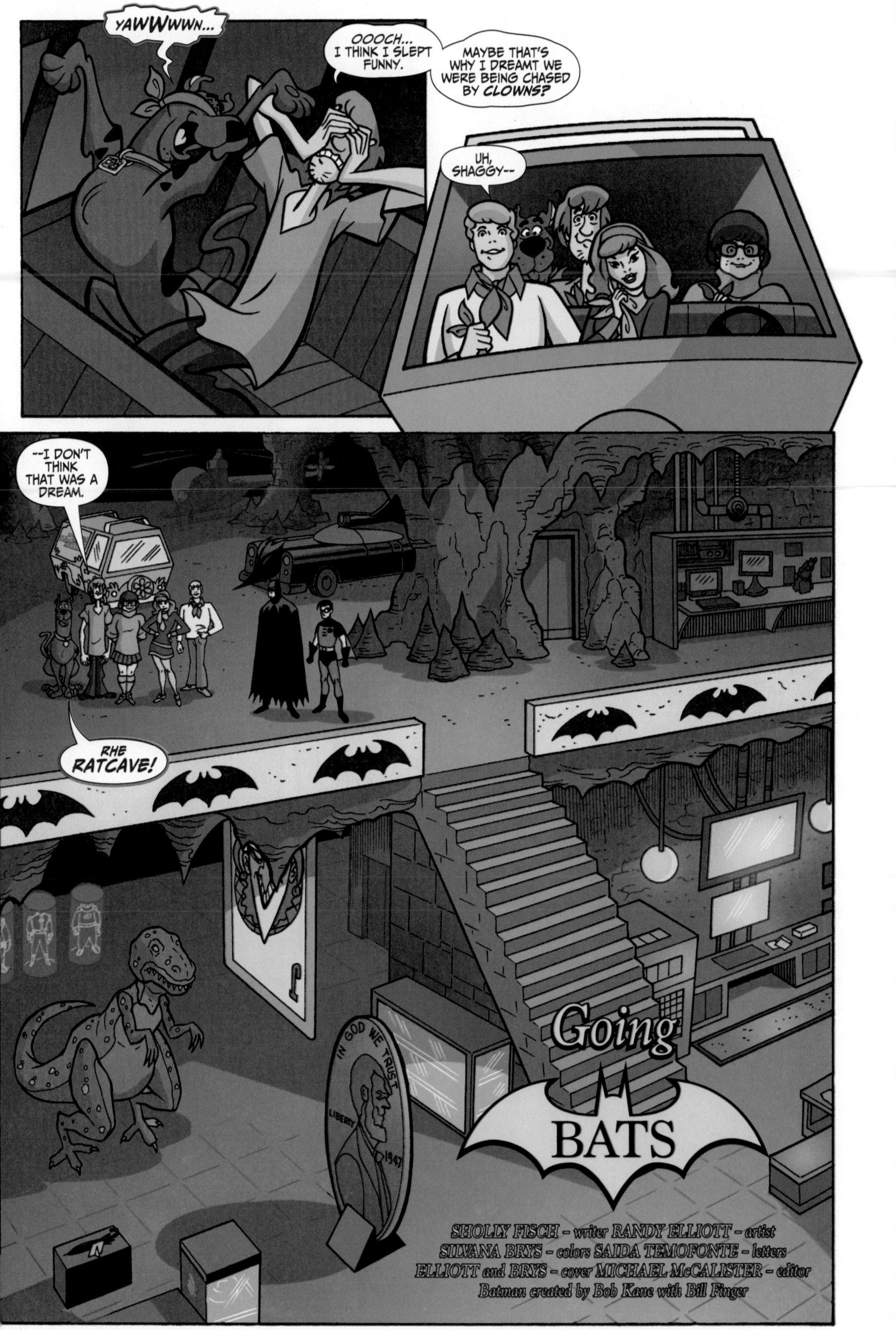
YAWWWWN...
OOOCH... I THINK I SLEPT FUNNY.
MAYBE THAT'S WHY I DREAMT WE WERE BEING CHASED BY CLOWNS?
UH, SHAGGY--
--I DON'T THINK THAT WAS A DREAM.
RHE RATCAVE!
Going
BATS
IN GOD WE TRUST
LIBERTY
1947
SHOLLY FISCH - writer RANDY ELLIOTT - artist
SILVANA BRYS - colors SAIDA TEMOFONTE - letters
ELLIOTT and BRYS - cover MICHAEL McCALISTER - editor
Batman created by Bob Kane with Bill Finger

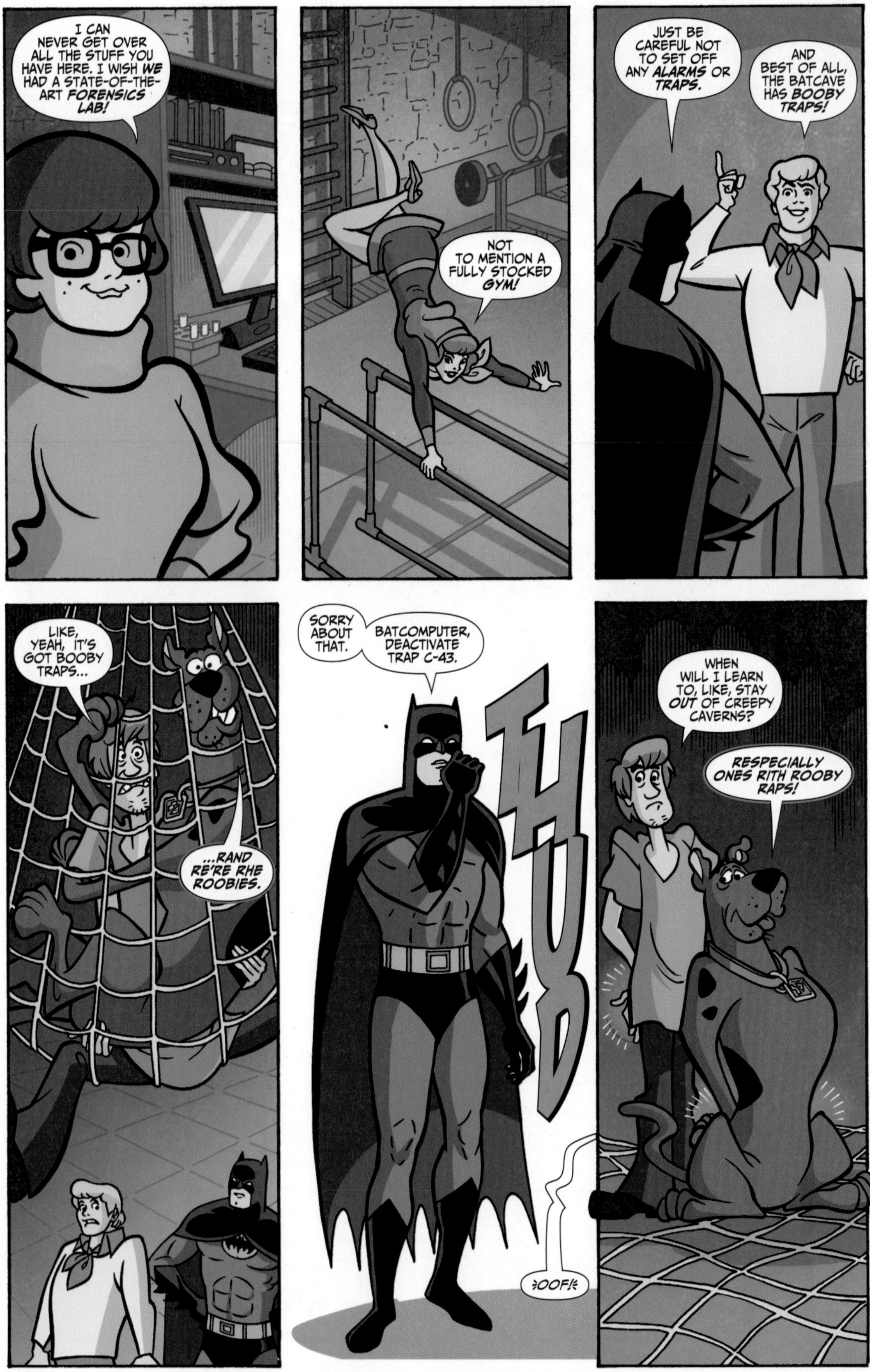
I CAN NEVER GET OVER ALL THE STUFF YOU HAVE HERE. I WISH *WE* HAD A STATE-OF-THE-ART *FORENSICS LAB!*
NOT TO MENTION A FULLY STOCKED *GYM!*
AND BEST OF ALL, THE BATCAVE HAS *BOOBY TRAPS!*
JUST BE CAREFUL NOT TO SET OFF ANY *ALARMS* OR *TRAPS.*
LIKE, YEAH, IT'S GOT BOOBY TRAPS...
...RAND RE'RE RHE ROOBIES.
SORRY ABOUT THAT.
BATCOMPUTER, DEACTIVATE TRAP C-43.
THUD
OOF!
WHEN WILL I LEARN TO, LIKE, STAY *OUT* OF CREEPY CAVERNS?
RESPECIALLY ONES RITH ROOBY RAPS!

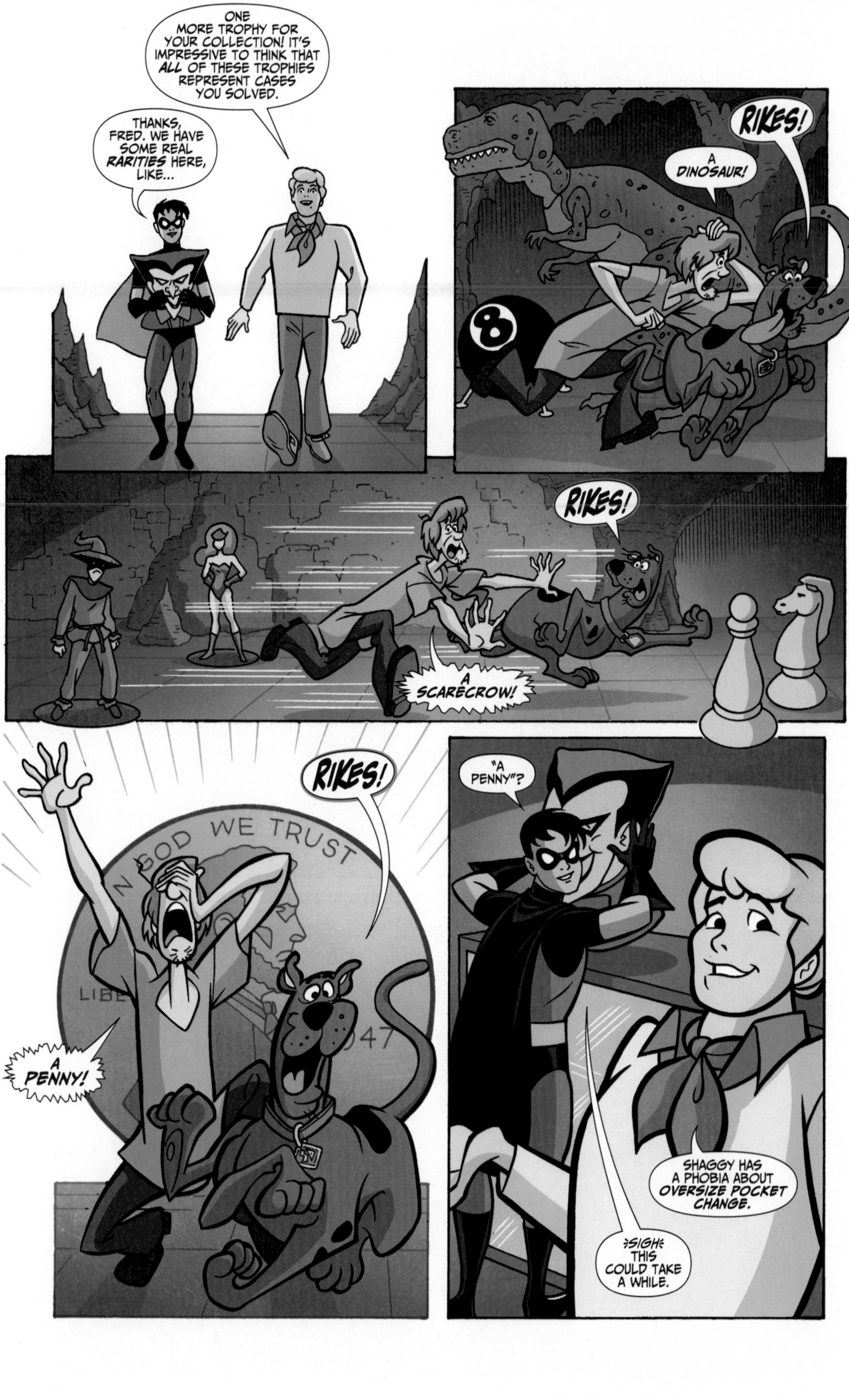
ONE MORE TROPHY FOR YOUR COLLECTION! IT'S IMPRESSIVE TO THINK THAT ALL OF THESE TROPHIES REPRESENT CASES YOU SOLVED.
THANKS, FRED. WE HAVE SOME REAL RARITIES HERE, LIKE...
A DINOSAUR!
RIKES!
RIKES!
A SCARECROW!
IN GOD WE TRUST
LIBE
1947
A PENNY!
RIKES!
"A PENNY"?
SHAGGY HAS A PHOBIA ABOUT OVERSIZE POCKET CHANGE.
SIGH THIS COULD TAKE A WHILE.

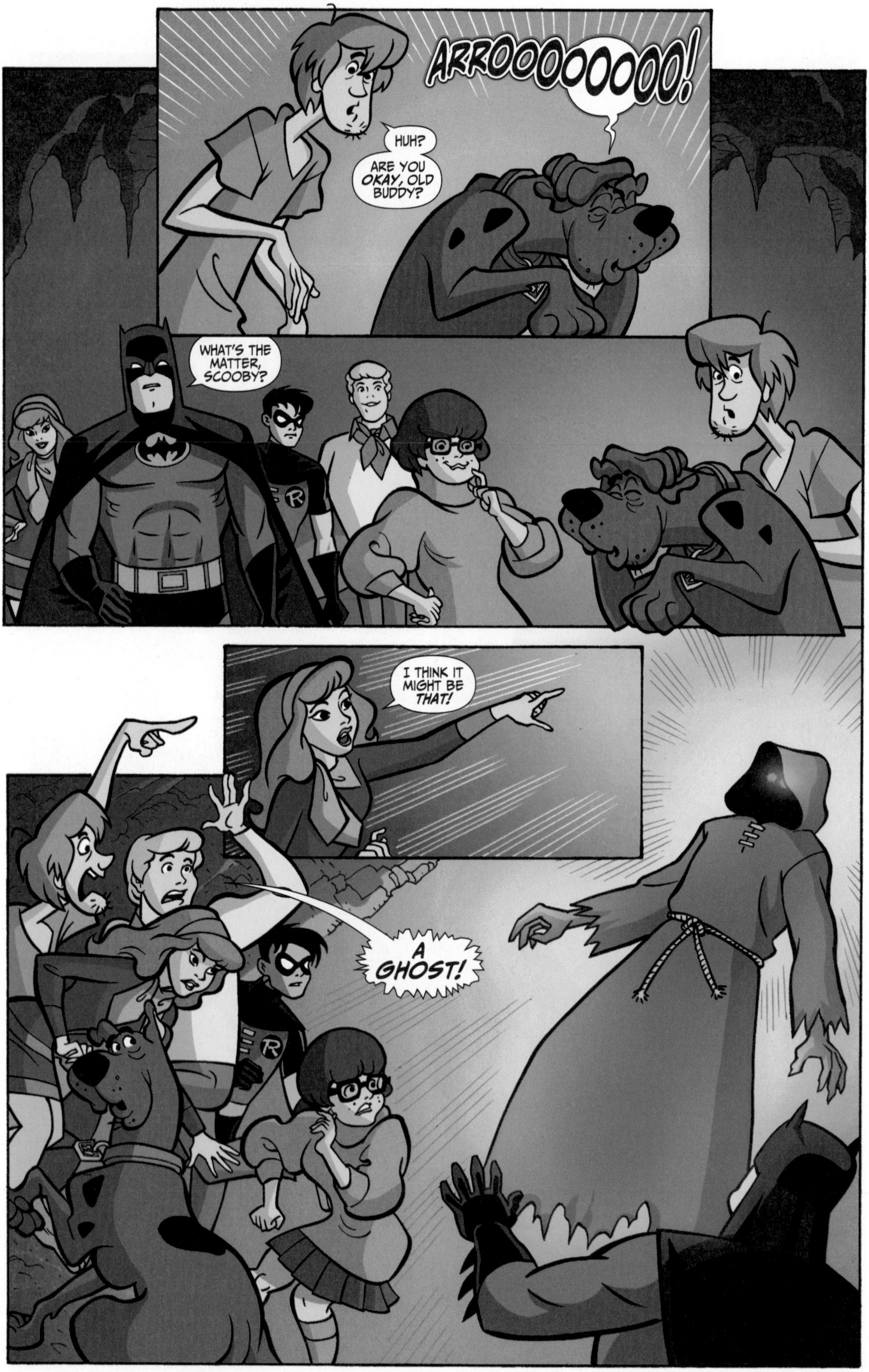
ARROOOOOOOOO!
HUH?
ARE YOU OKAY, OLD BUDDY?
WHAT'S THE MATTER, SCOOBY?
I THINK IT MIGHT BE THAT!
A GHOST!

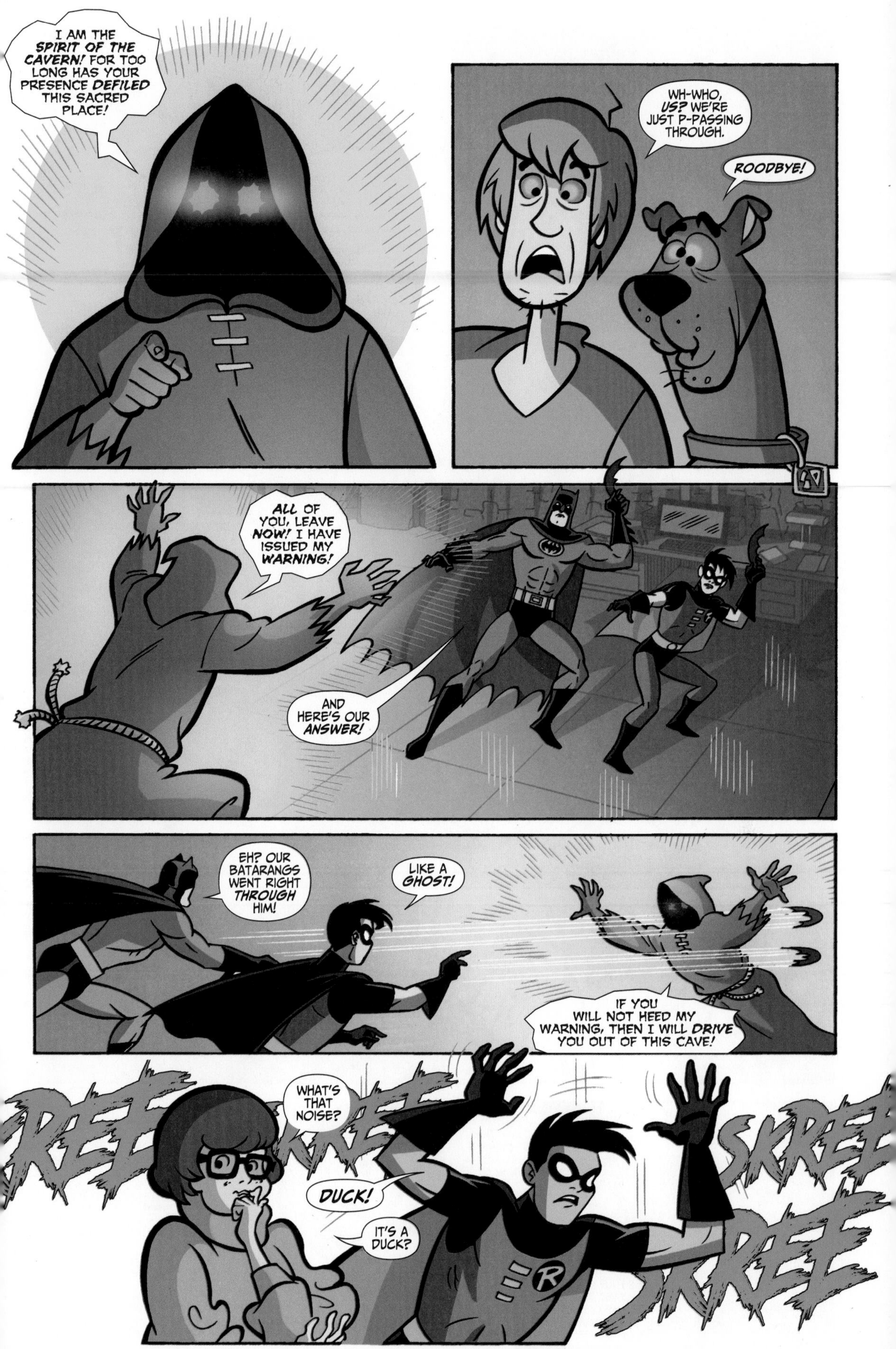
I AM THE SPIRIT OF THE CAVERN! FOR TOO LONG HAS YOUR PRESENCE DEFILED THIS SACRED PLACE!
WH-WHO, US? WE'RE JUST P-PASSING THROUGH.
ROODBYE!
ALL OF YOU, LEAVE NOW! I HAVE ISSUED MY WARNING!
AND HERE'S OUR ANSWER!
EH? OUR BATARANGS WENT RIGHT THROUGH HIM!
LIKE A GHOST!
IF YOU WILL NOT HEED MY WARNING, THEN I WILL DRIVE YOU OUT OF THIS CAVE!
WHAT'S THAT NOISE?
DUCK!
IT'S A DUCK?
SKREE
SKREE

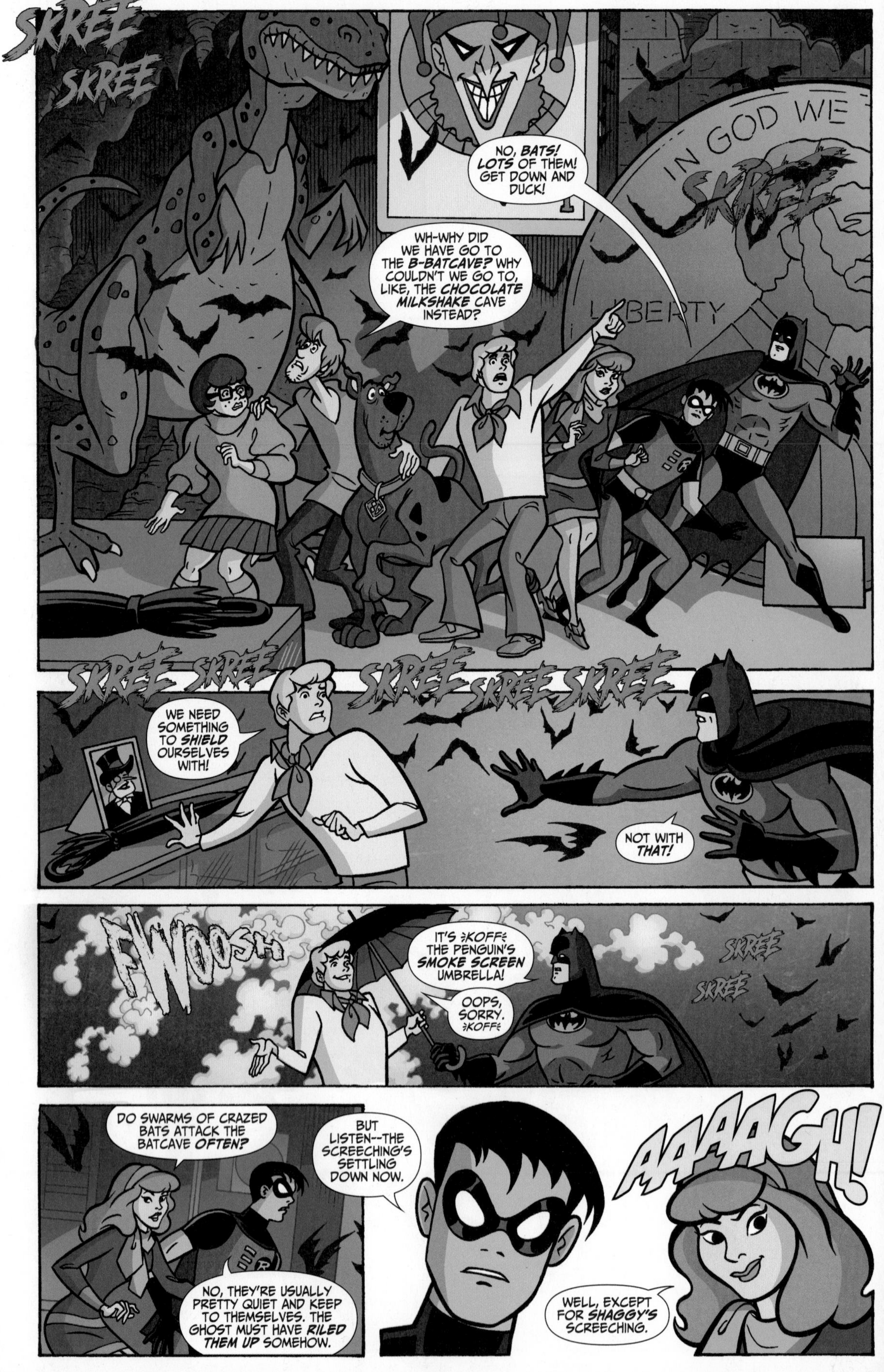
SKREE
SKREE
NO, BATS! LOTS OF THEM! GET DOWN AND DUCK!
WH-WHY DID WE HAVE GO TO THE B-BATCAVE? WHY COULDN'T WE GO TO, LIKE, THE CHOCOLATE MILKSHAKE CAVE INSTEAD?
IN GOD WE
LIBERTY
SKREE
SKREE SKREE
SKREE SKREE SKREE
WE NEED SOMETHING TO SHIELD OURSELVES WITH!
NOT WITH THAT!
FWOOSH
IT'S KOFF THE PENGUIN'S SMOKE SCREEN UMBRELLA!
OOPS, SORRY. KOFF
SKREE
SKREE
DO SWARMS OF CRAZED BATS ATTACK THE BATCAVE OFTEN?
NO, THEY'RE USUALLY PRETTY QUIET AND KEEP TO THEMSELVES. THE GHOST MUST HAVE RILED THEM UP SOMEHOW.
BUT LISTEN--THE SCREECHING'S SETTLING DOWN NOW.
AAAAGH!
WELL, EXCEPT FOR SHAGGY'S SCREECHING.

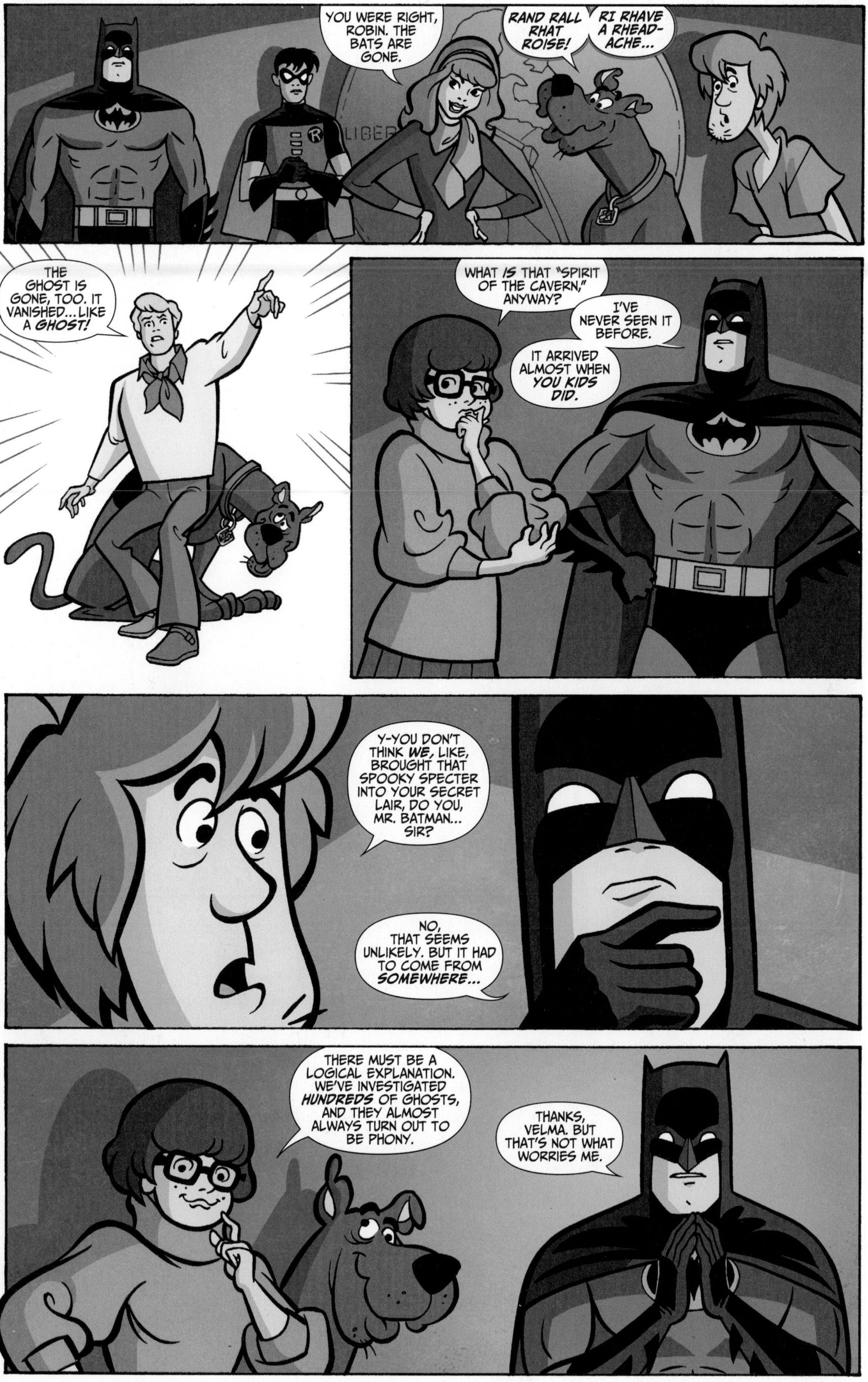

YOU WERE RIGHT, ROBIN. THE BATS ARE GONE.
RAND RALL RHAT ROISE!
RI RHAVE A RHEAD-ACHE...
THE GHOST IS GONE, TOO. IT VANISHED...LIKE A *GHOST!*
WHAT *IS* THAT "SPIRIT OF THE CAVERN," ANYWAY?
I'VE NEVER SEEN IT BEFORE.
IT ARRIVED ALMOST WHEN *YOU KIDS DID.*
Y-YOU DON'T THINK *WE,* LIKE, BROUGHT THAT SPOOKY SPECTER INTO YOUR SECRET LAIR, DO YOU, MR. BATMAN... SIR?
NO, THAT SEEMS UNLIKELY. BUT IT HAD TO COME FROM *SOMEWHERE...*
THERE MUST BE A LOGICAL EXPLANATION. WE'VE INVESTIGATED *HUNDREDS* OF GHOSTS, AND THEY ALMOST ALWAYS TURN OUT TO BE PHONY.
THANKS, VELMA. BUT THAT'S NOT WHAT WORRIES ME.

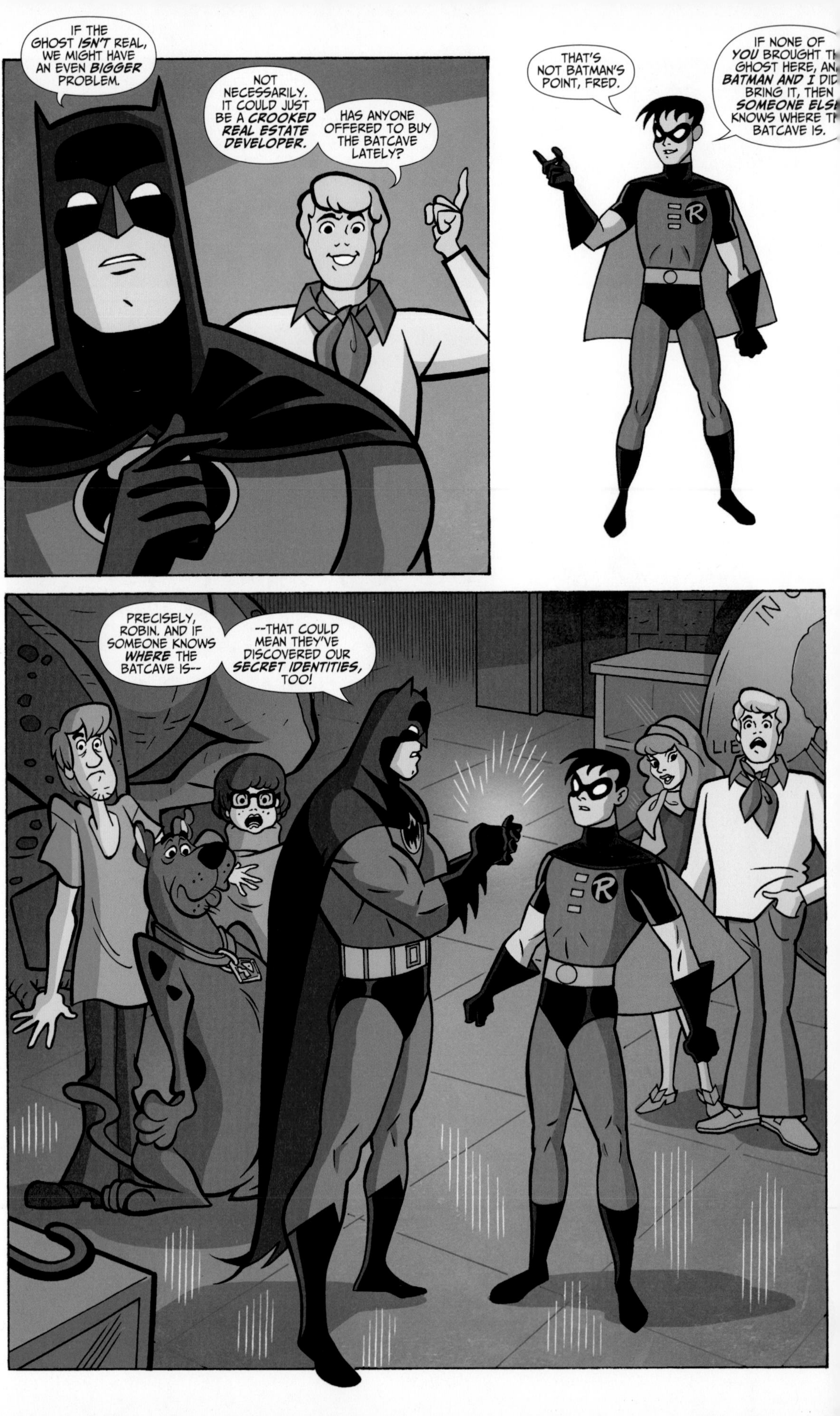
IF THE GHOST ISN'T REAL, WE MIGHT HAVE AN EVEN BIGGER PROBLEM.
NOT NECESSARILY. IT COULD JUST BE A CROOKED REAL ESTATE DEVELOPER.
HAS ANYONE OFFERED TO BUY THE BATCAVE LATELY?
THAT'S NOT BATMAN'S POINT, FRED.
IF NONE OF YOU BROUGHT T GHOST HERE, AN BATMAN AND I DI BRING IT, THEN SOMEONE ELS KNOWS WHERE T BATCAVE IS.
PRECISELY, ROBIN. AND IF SOMEONE KNOWS WHERE THE BATCAVE IS--
--THAT COULD MEAN THEY'VE DISCOVERED OUR SECRET IDENTITIES, TOO!

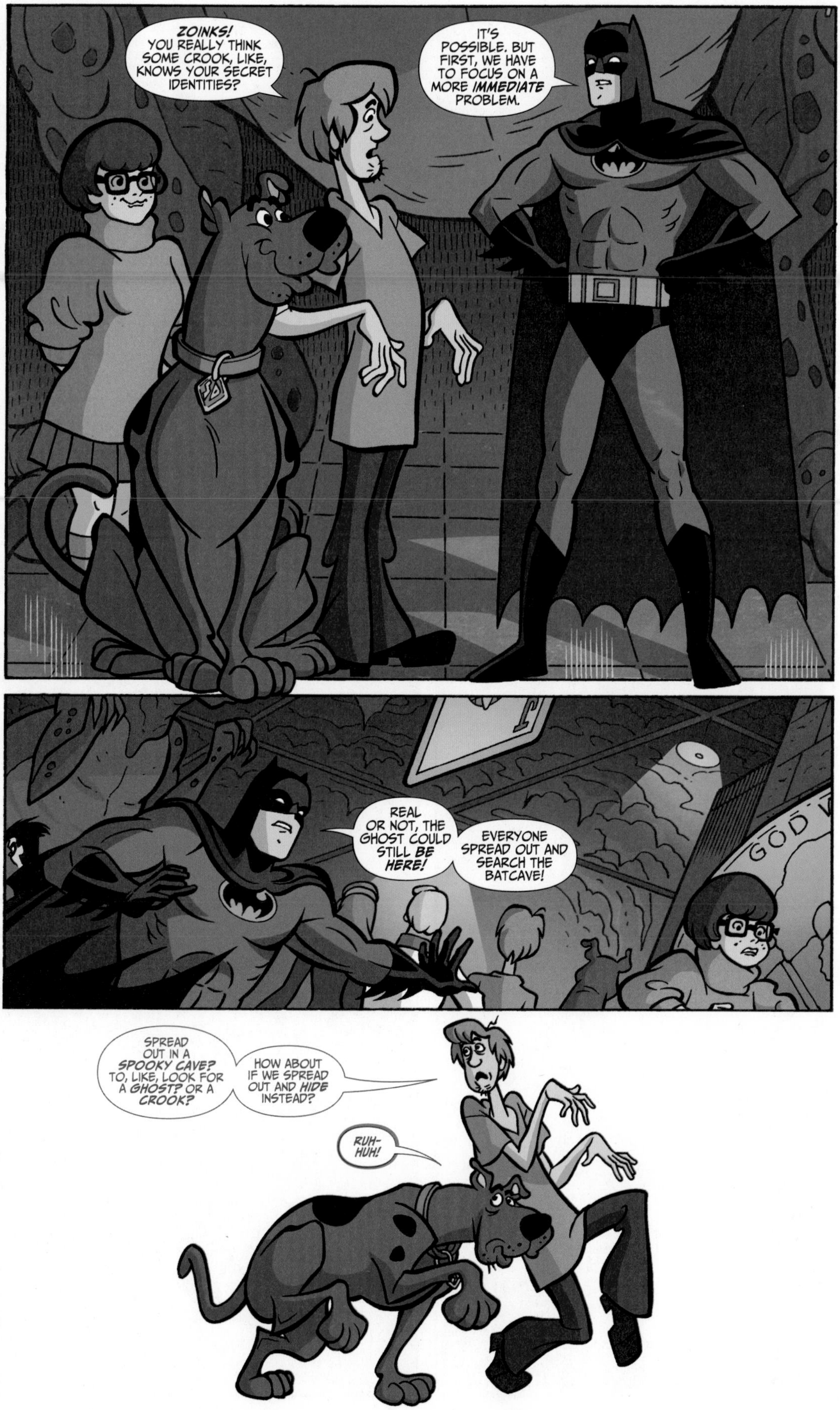

ZOINKS! YOU REALLY THINK SOME CROOK, LIKE, KNOWS YOUR SECRET IDENTITIES?
IT'S POSSIBLE. BUT FIRST, WE HAVE TO FOCUS ON A MORE IMMEDIATE PROBLEM.
REAL OR NOT, THE GHOST COULD STILL BE HERE!
EVERYONE SPREAD OUT AND SEARCH THE BATCAVE!
SPREAD OUT IN A SPOOKY CAVE? TO, LIKE, LOOK FOR A GHOST? OR A CROOK?
HOW ABOUT IF WE SPREAD OUT AND HIDE INSTEAD?
RUH-HUH!

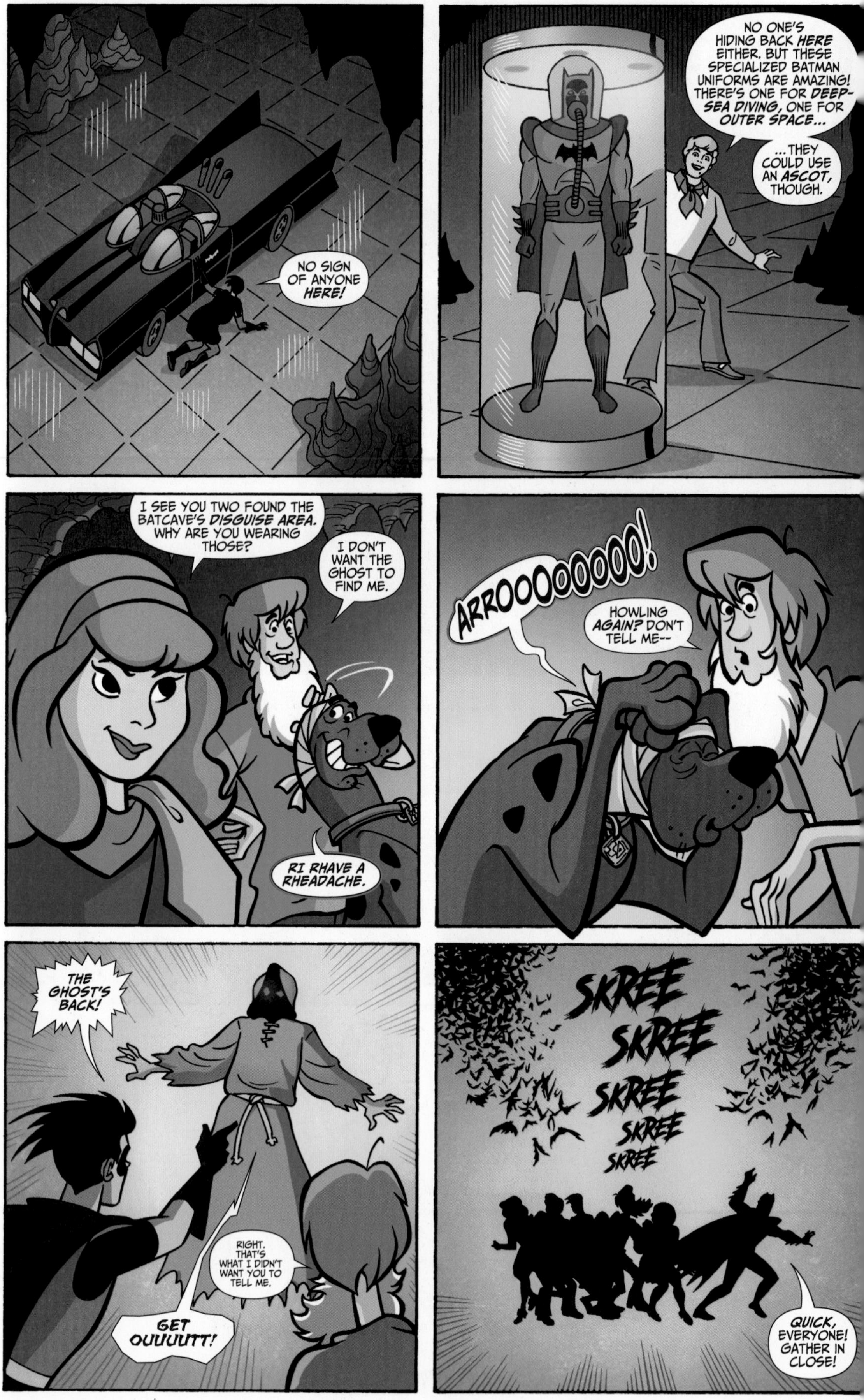
NO SIGN OF ANYONE HERE!
NO ONE'S HIDING BACK HERE EITHER. BUT THESE SPECIALIZED BATMAN UNIFORMS ARE AMAZING! THERE'S ONE FOR DEEP-SEA DIVING, ONE FOR OUTER SPACE...
...THEY COULD USE AN ASCOT, THOUGH.
I SEE YOU TWO FOUND THE BATCAVE'S DISGUISE AREA. WHY ARE YOU WEARING THOSE?
I DON'T WANT THE GHOST TO FIND ME.
RI RHAVE A RHEADACHE.
ARROOOOOOOOO!
HOWLING AGAIN? DON'T TELL ME--
THE GHOST'S BACK!
RIGHT. THAT'S WHAT I DIDN'T WANT YOU TO TELL ME.
GET OUUUUTT!
SKREE SKREE SKREE SKREE SKREE
QUICK, EVERYONE! GATHER IN CLOSE!

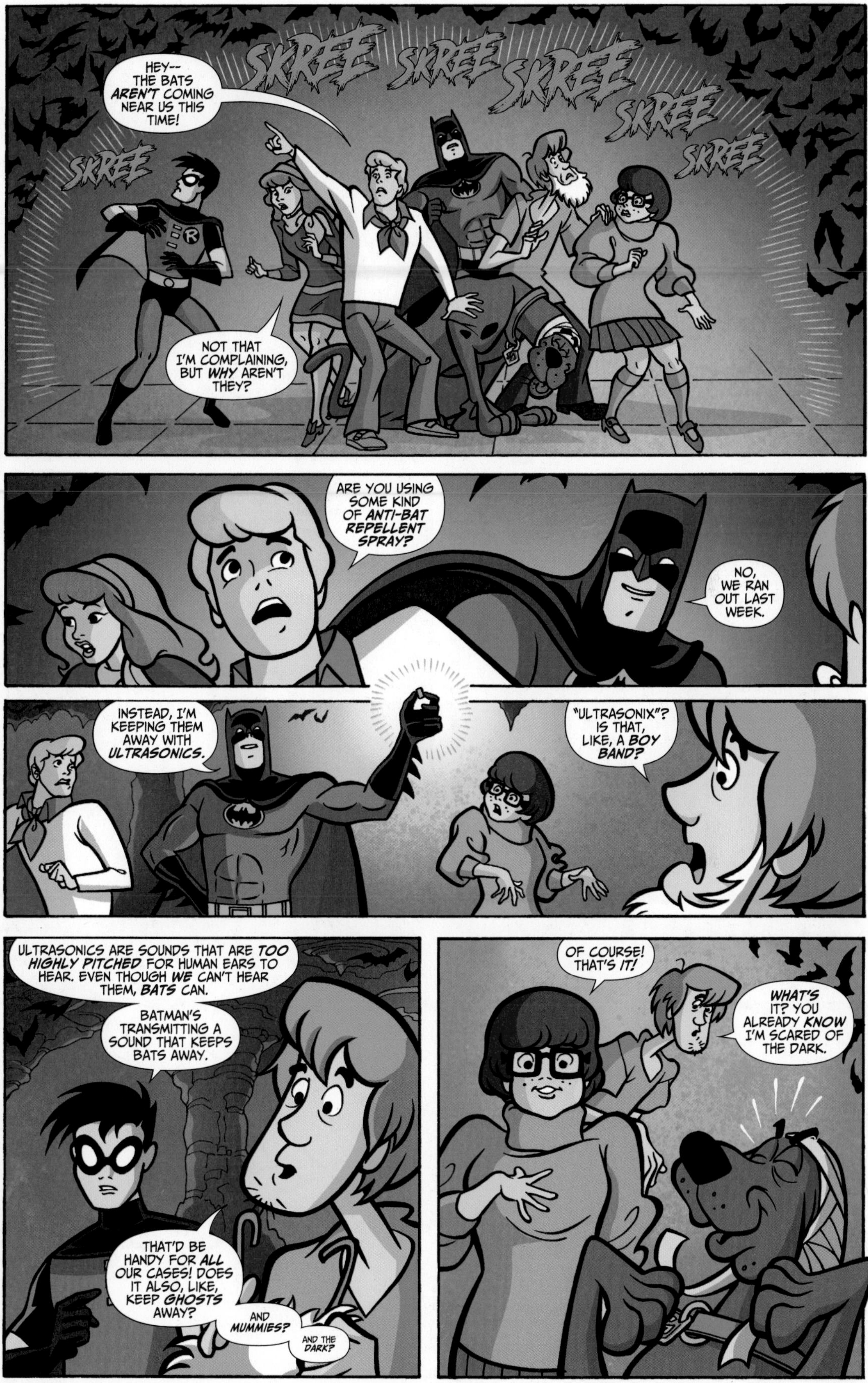
SKREE SKREE SKREE
SKREE
SKREE
SKREE
HEY-- THE BATS AREN'T COMING NEAR US THIS TIME!
NOT THAT I'M COMPLAINING, BUT WHY AREN'T THEY?
ARE YOU USING SOME KIND OF ANTI-BAT REPELLENT SPRAY?
NO, WE RAN OUT LAST WEEK.
INSTEAD, I'M KEEPING THEM AWAY WITH ULTRASONICS.
"ULTRASONIX"? IS THAT, LIKE, A BOY BAND?
ULTRASONICS ARE SOUNDS THAT ARE TOO HIGHLY PITCHED FOR HUMAN EARS TO HEAR. EVEN THOUGH WE CAN'T HEAR THEM, BATS CAN.
BATMAN'S TRANSMITTING A SOUND THAT KEEPS BATS AWAY.
THAT'D BE HANDY FOR ALL OUR CASES! DOES IT ALSO, LIKE, KEEP GHOSTS AWAY?
AND MUMMIES?
AND THE DARK?
OF COURSE! THAT'S IT!
WHAT'S IT? YOU ALREADY KNOW I'M SCARED OF THE DARK.

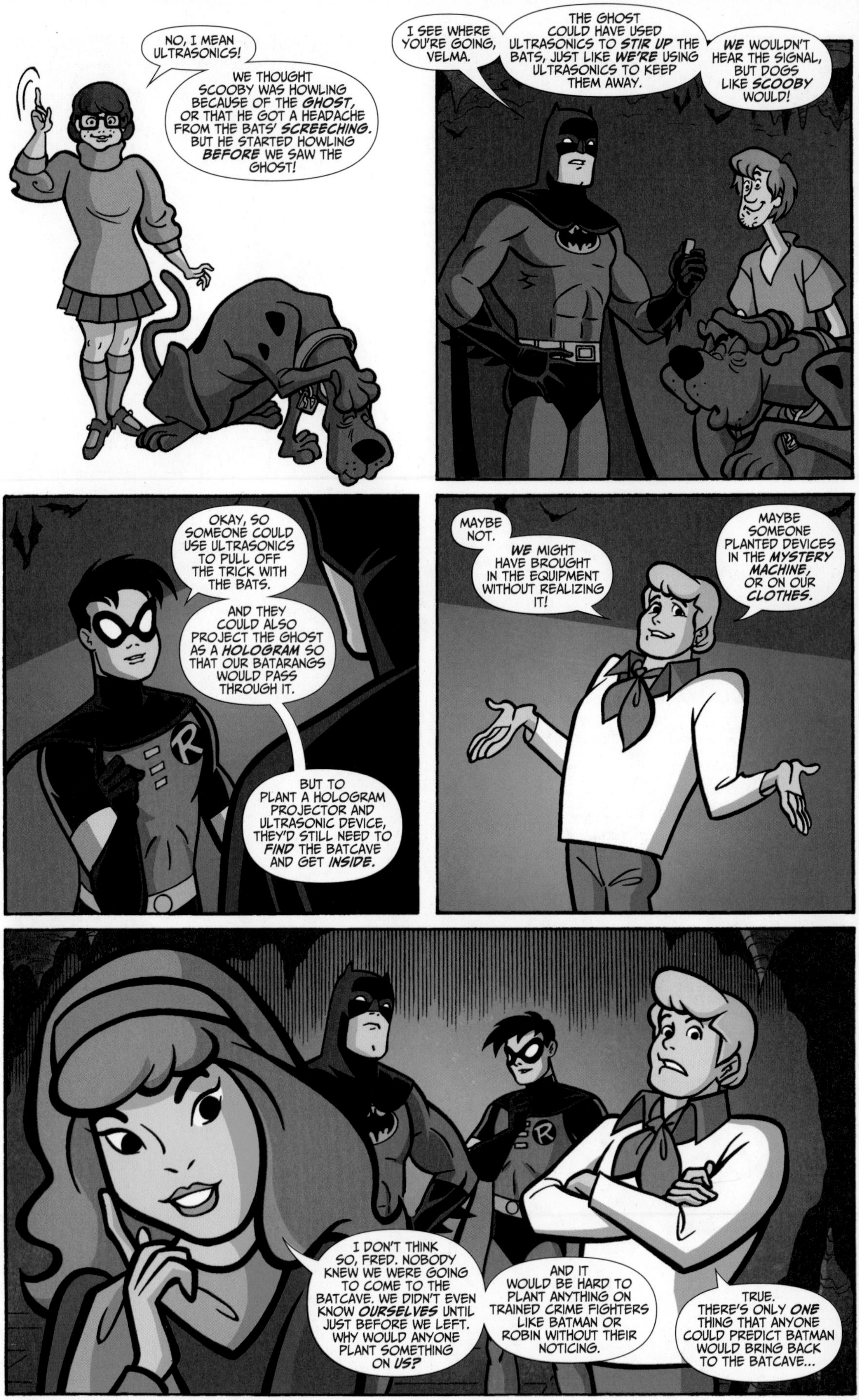
NO, I MEAN ULTRASONICS!
WE THOUGHT SCOOBY WAS HOWLING BECAUSE OF THE *GHOST*, OR THAT HE GOT A HEADACHE FROM THE BATS' *SCREECHING*. BUT HE STARTED HOWLING *BEFORE* WE SAW THE GHOST!
I SEE WHERE YOU'RE GOING, VELMA.
THE GHOST COULD HAVE USED ULTRASONICS TO *STIR UP* THE BATS, JUST LIKE *WE'RE* USING ULTRASONICS TO KEEP THEM AWAY.
WE WOULDN'T HEAR THE SIGNAL, BUT DOGS LIKE *SCOOBY* WOULD!
OKAY, SO SOMEONE COULD USE ULTRASONICS TO PULL OFF THE TRICK WITH THE BATS.
AND THEY COULD ALSO PROJECT THE GHOST AS A *HOLOGRAM* SO THAT OUR BATARANGS WOULD PASS THROUGH IT.
BUT TO PLANT A HOLOGRAM PROJECTOR AND ULTRASONIC DEVICE, THEY'D STILL NEED TO *FIND* THE BATCAVE AND GET *INSIDE*.
MAYBE NOT.
WE MIGHT HAVE BROUGHT IN THE EQUIPMENT WITHOUT REALIZING IT!
MAYBE SOMEONE PLANTED DEVICES IN THE *MYSTERY MACHINE*, OR ON OUR *CLOTHES*.
I DON'T THINK SO, FRED. NOBODY KNEW WE WERE GOING TO COME TO THE BATCAVE. WE DIDN'T EVEN KNOW *OURSELVES* UNTIL JUST BEFORE WE LEFT. WHY WOULD ANYONE PLANT SOMETHING ON *US?*
AND IT WOULD BE HARD TO PLANT ANYTHING ON TRAINED CRIME FIGHTERS LIKE BATMAN OR ROBIN WITHOUT THEIR NOTICING.
TRUE. THERE'S ONLY *ONE* THING THAT ANYONE COULD PREDICT BATMAN WOULD BRING BACK TO THE BATCAVE...

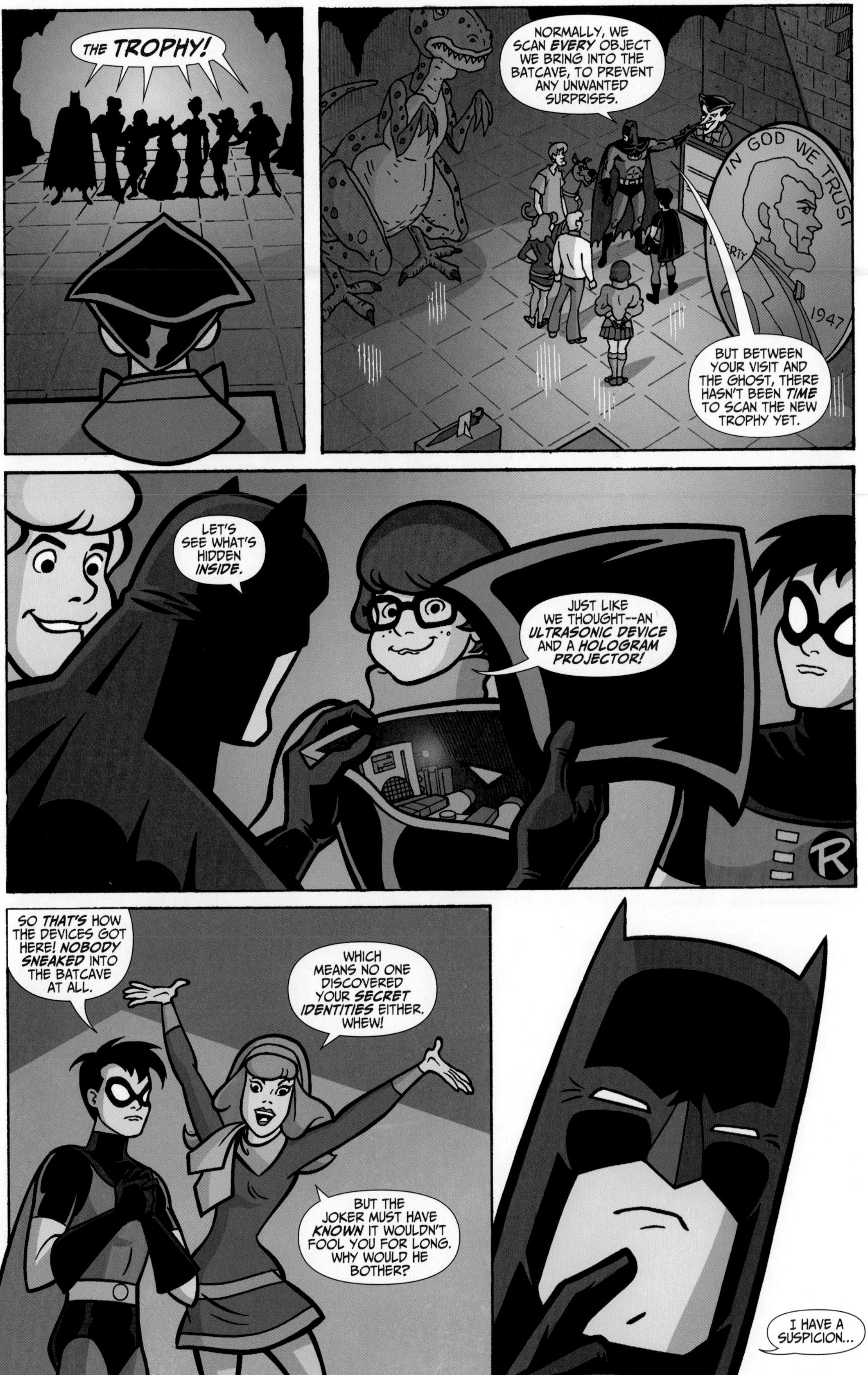
THE TROPHY!
NORMALLY, WE SCAN EVERY OBJECT WE BRING INTO THE BATCAVE, TO PREVENT ANY UNWANTED SURPRISES.
IN GOD WE TRUST
LIBERTY
1947
BUT BETWEEN YOUR VISIT AND THE GHOST, THERE HASN'T BEEN TIME TO SCAN THE NEW TROPHY YET.
LET'S SEE WHAT'S HIDDEN INSIDE.
JUST LIKE WE THOUGHT--AN ULTRASONIC DEVICE AND A HOLOGRAM PROJECTOR!
SO THAT'S HOW THE DEVICES GOT HERE! NOBODY SNEAKED INTO THE BATCAVE AT ALL.
WHICH MEANS NO ONE DISCOVERED YOUR SECRET IDENTITIES EITHER. WHEW!
BUT THE JOKER MUST HAVE KNOWN IT WOULDN'T FOOL YOU FOR LONG. WHY WOULD HE BOTHER?
I HAVE A SUSPICION...

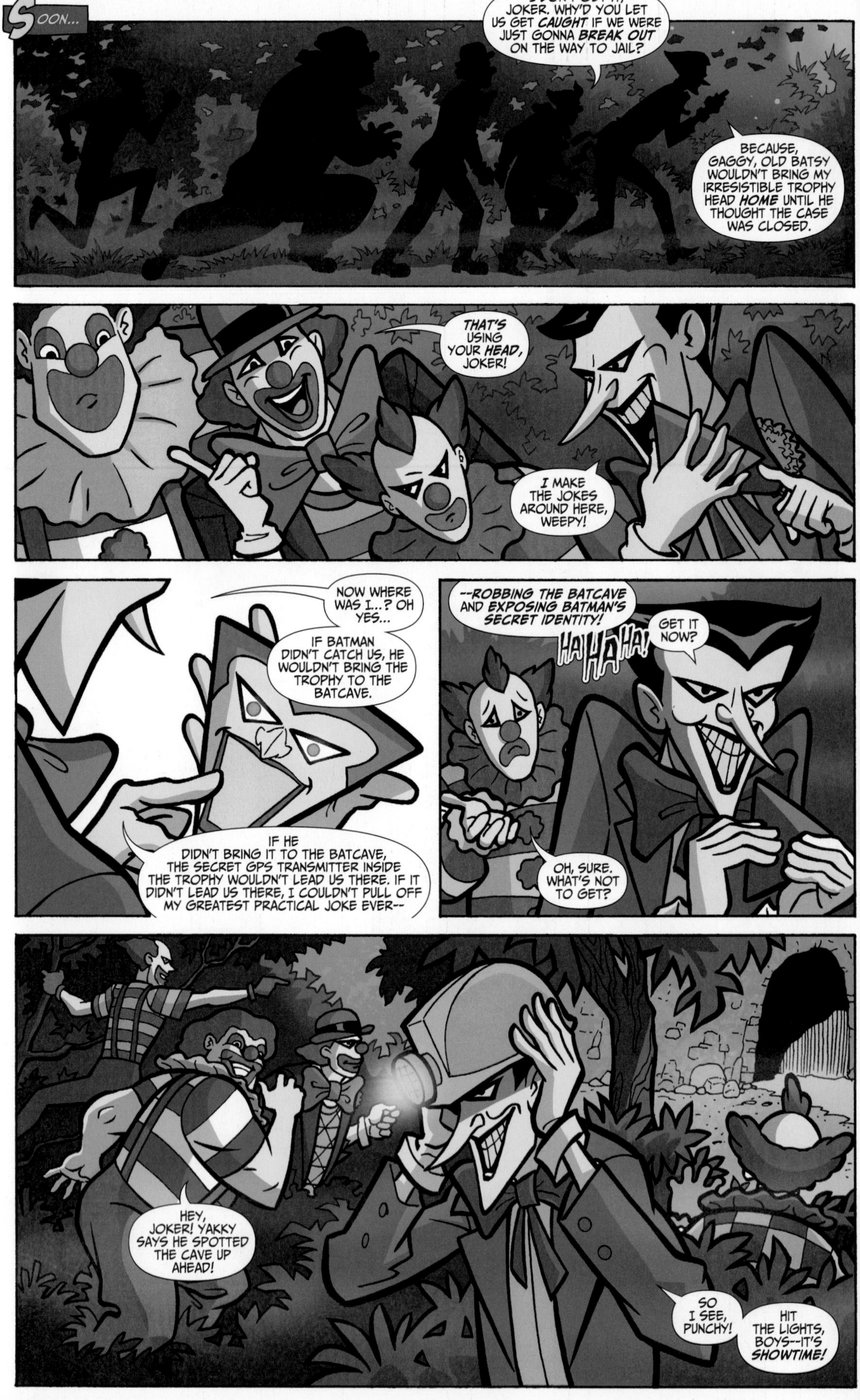
SOON...
I DON'T GET IT, JOKER. WHY'D YOU LET US GET *CAUGHT* IF WE WERE JUST GONNA *BREAK OUT* ON THE WAY TO JAIL?
BECAUSE, GAGGY, OLD BATSY WOULDN'T BRING MY IRRESISTIBLE TROPHY HEAD *HOME* UNTIL HE THOUGHT THE CASE WAS CLOSED.
THAT'S USING YOUR *HEAD*, JOKER!
I MAKE THE JOKES AROUND HERE, WEEPY!
NOW WHERE WAS I...? OH YES...
IF BATMAN DIDN'T CATCH US, HE WOULDN'T BRING THE TROPHY TO THE BATCAVE.
IF HE DIDN'T BRING IT TO THE BATCAVE, THE SECRET GPS TRANSMITTER INSIDE THE TROPHY WOULDN'T LEAD US THERE. IF IT DIDN'T LEAD US THERE, I COULDN'T PULL OFF MY GREATEST PRACTICAL JOKE EVER--
--*ROBBING THE BATCAVE* AND *EXPOSING BATMAN'S SECRET IDENTITY!*
HA HA HA!
GET IT NOW?
OH, SURE. WHAT'S NOT TO GET?
HEY, JOKER! YAKKY SAYS HE SPOTTED THE CAVE UP AHEAD!
SO I SEE, PUNCHY!
HIT THE LIGHTS, BOYS--IT'S *SHOWTIME!*

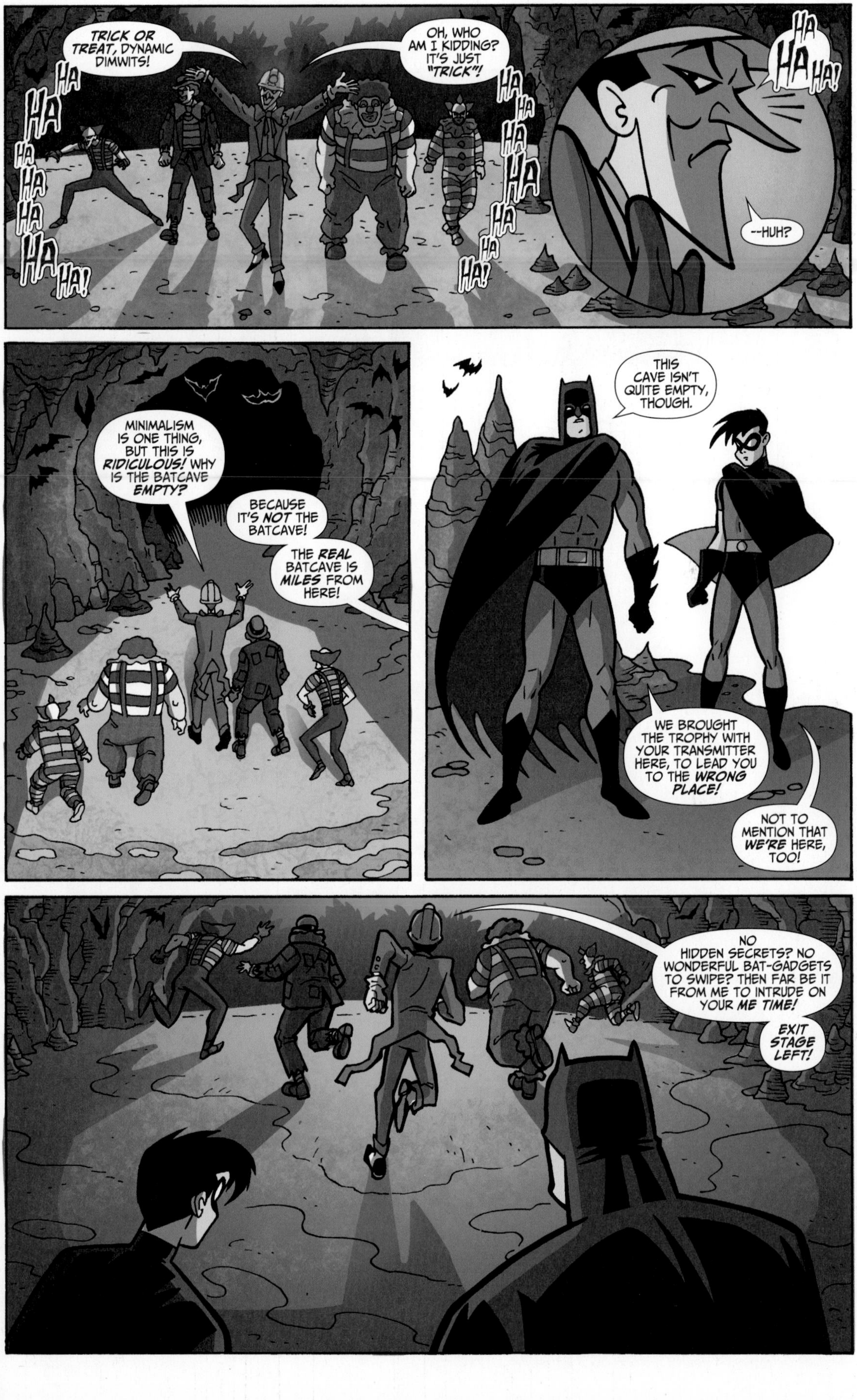

TRICK OR TREAT, DYNAMIC DIMWITS!
HA HA HA HA HA HA HA HA HA!
OH, WHO AM I KIDDING? IT'S JUST "TRICK"!
HA HA HA HA HA HA HA HA HA!
HA HA HA!
--HUH?
MINIMALISM IS ONE THING, BUT THIS IS RIDICULOUS! WHY IS THE BATCAVE EMPTY?
BECAUSE IT'S NOT THE BATCAVE!
THE REAL BATCAVE IS MILES FROM HERE!
THIS CAVE ISN'T QUITE EMPTY, THOUGH.
WE BROUGHT THE TROPHY WITH YOUR TRANSMITTER HERE, TO LEAD YOU TO THE WRONG PLACE!
NOT TO MENTION THAT WE'RE HERE, TOO!
NO HIDDEN SECRETS? NO WONDERFUL BAT-GADGETS TO SWIPE? THEN FAR BE IT FROM ME TO INTRUDE ON YOUR ME TIME!
EXIT STAGE LEFT!

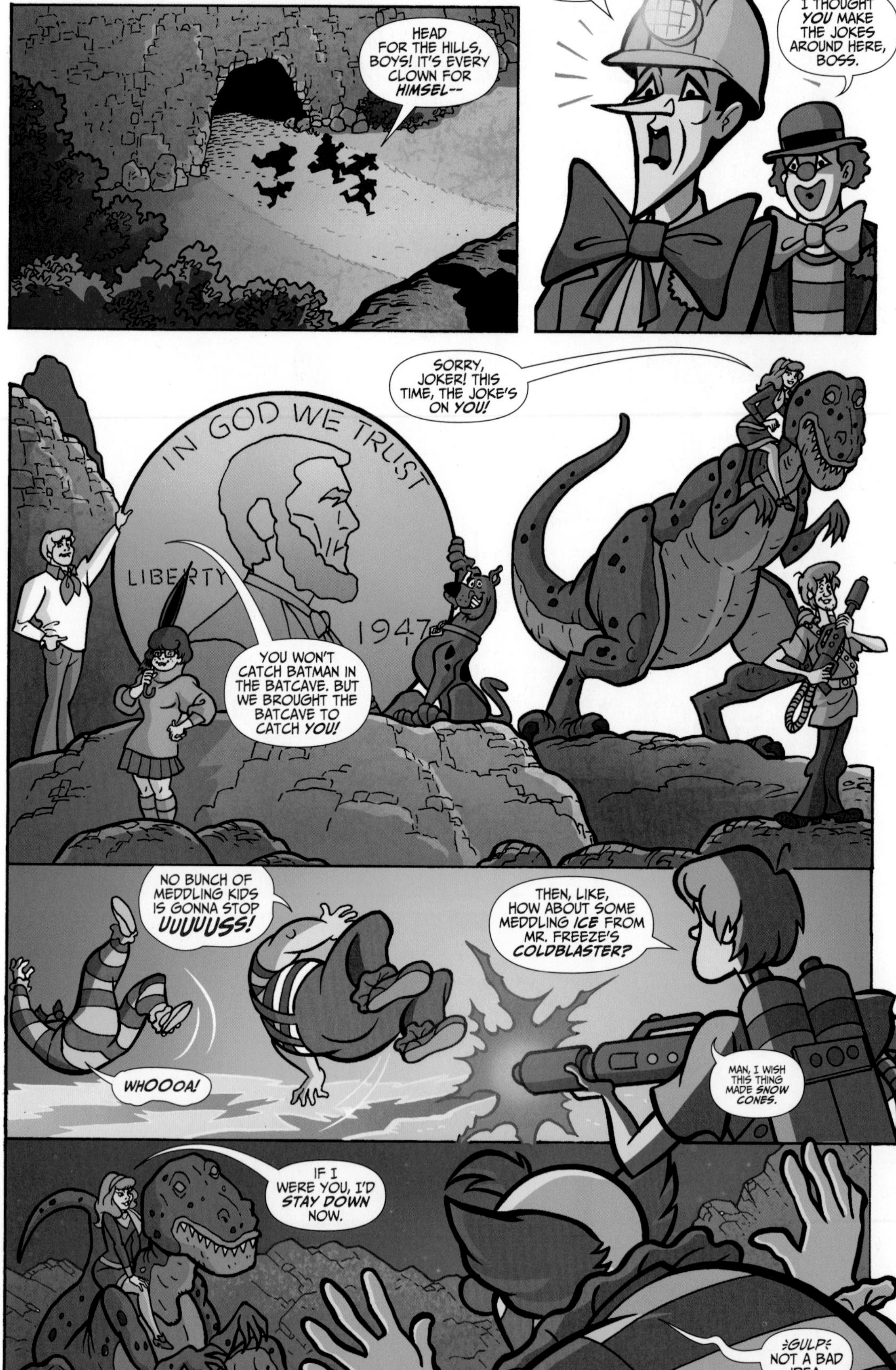
HEAD FOR THE HILLS, BOYS! IT'S EVERY CLOWN FOR HIMSEL--
IS THIS SOMEBODY'S IDEA OF A JOKE?
I THOUGHT YOU MAKE THE JOKES AROUND HERE, BOSS.
SORRY, JOKER! THIS TIME, THE JOKE'S ON YOU!
IN GOD WE TRUST
LIBERTY
1947
YOU WON'T CATCH BATMAN IN THE BATCAVE. BUT WE BROUGHT THE BATCAVE TO CATCH YOU!
NO BUNCH OF MEDDLING KIDS IS GONNA STOP UUUUUSS!
THEN, LIKE, HOW ABOUT SOME MEDDLING ICE FROM MR. FREEZE'S COLDBLASTER?
WHOOOA!
MAN, I WISH THIS THING MADE SNOW CONES.
IF I WERE YOU, I'D STAY DOWN NOW.
GULP NOT A BAD IDEA.

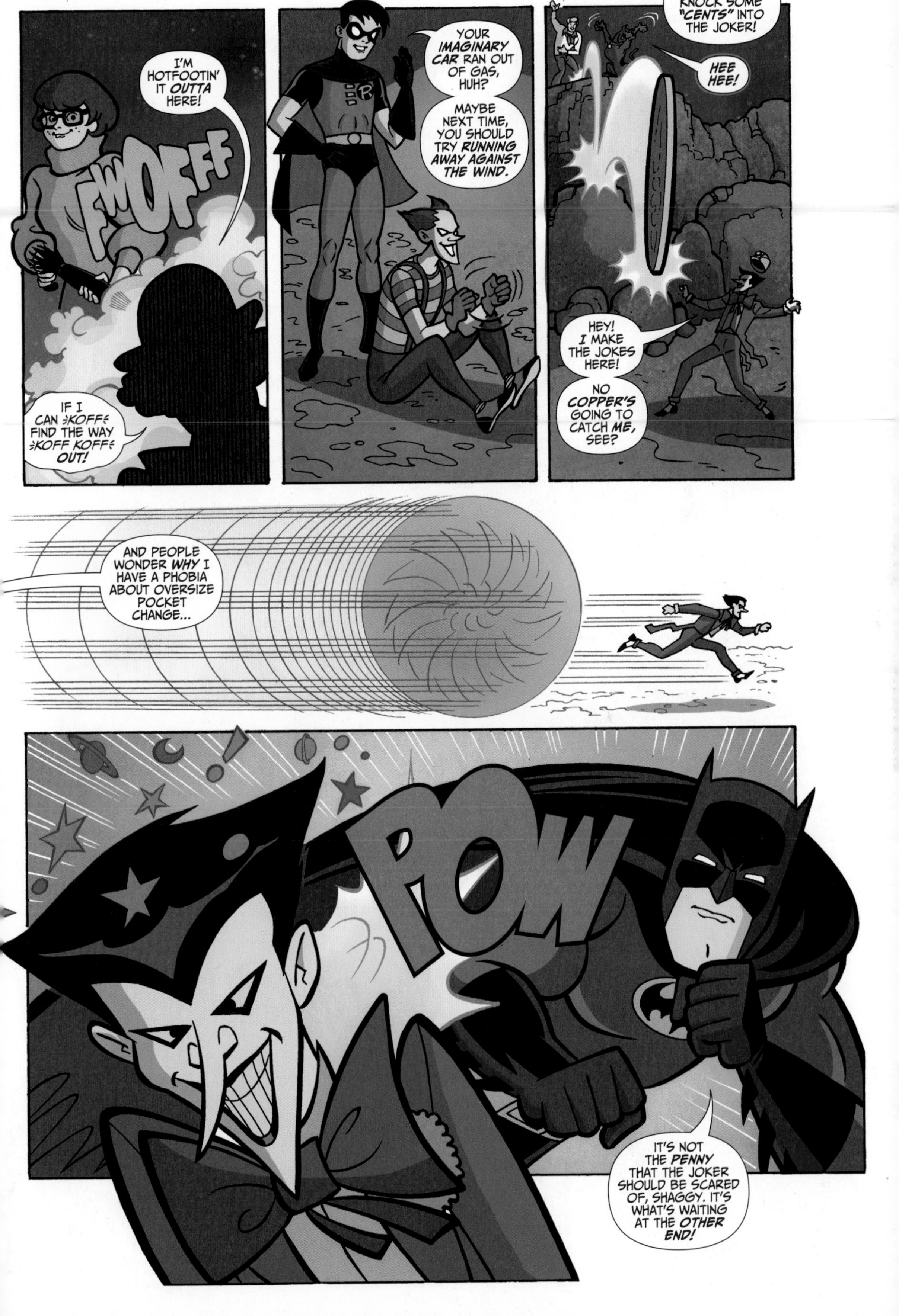

I'M HOTFOOTIN' IT OUTTA HERE!
FWOFFF
IF I CAN ≷KOFF≶ FIND THE WAY ≷KOFF KOFF≶ OUT!
YOUR IMAGINARY CAR RAN OUT OF GAS, HUH?
MAYBE NEXT TIME, YOU SHOULD TRY RUNNING AWAY AGAINST THE WIND.
PUSH, SCOOBY! LET'S KNOCK SOME "CENTS" INTO THE JOKER!
HEE HEE!
HEY! I MAKE THE JOKES HERE!
NO COPPER'S GOING TO CATCH ME, SEE?
AND PEOPLE WONDER WHY I HAVE A PHOBIA ABOUT OVERSIZE POCKET CHANGE...
POW
IT'S NOT THE PENNY THAT THE JOKER SHOULD BE SCARED OF, SHAGGY. IT'S WHAT'S WAITING AT THE OTHER END!

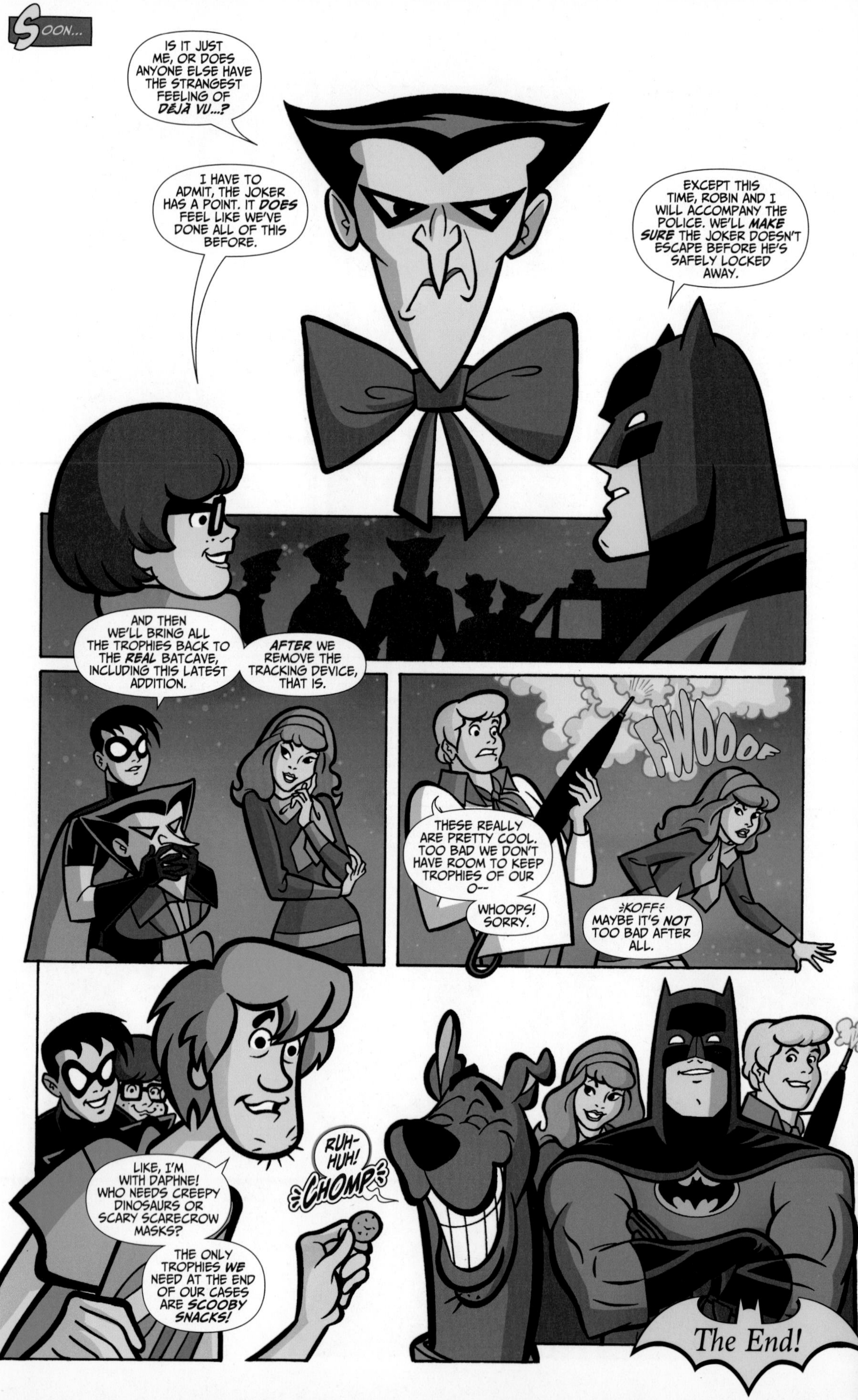
SOON...
IS IT JUST ME, OR DOES ANYONE ELSE HAVE THE STRANGEST FEELING OF DÉJÀ VU...?
I HAVE TO ADMIT, THE JOKER HAS A POINT. IT DOES FEEL LIKE WE'VE DONE ALL OF THIS BEFORE.
EXCEPT THIS TIME, ROBIN AND I WILL ACCOMPANY THE POLICE. WE'LL MAKE SURE THE JOKER DOESN'T ESCAPE BEFORE HE'S SAFELY LOCKED AWAY.
AND THEN WE'LL BRING ALL THE TROPHIES BACK TO THE REAL BATCAVE, INCLUDING THIS LATEST ADDITION.
AFTER WE REMOVE THE TRACKING DEVICE, THAT IS.
FWOOOF
THESE REALLY ARE PRETTY COOL. TOO BAD WE DON'T HAVE ROOM TO KEEP TROPHIES OF OUR O--
WHOOPS! SORRY.
KOFF MAYBE IT'S NOT TOO BAD AFTER ALL.
LIKE, I'M WITH DAPHNE! WHO NEEDS CREEPY DINOSAURS OR SCARY SCARECROW MASKS?
THE ONLY TROPHIES WE NEED AT THE END OF OUR CASES ARE SCOOBY SNACKS!
RUH-HUH!
CHOMP
The End!

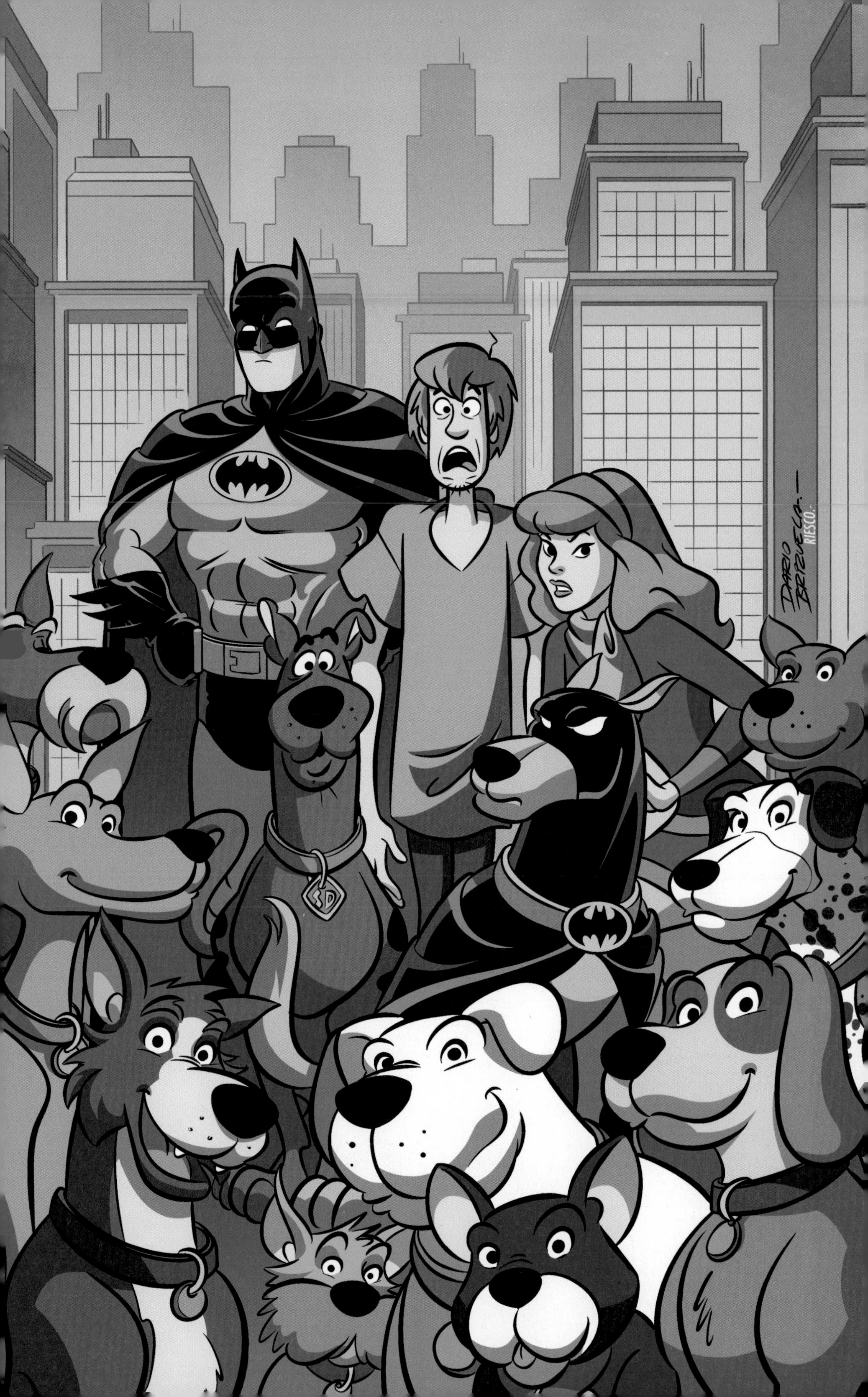
DARIO BRIZUELA
RIESCO.

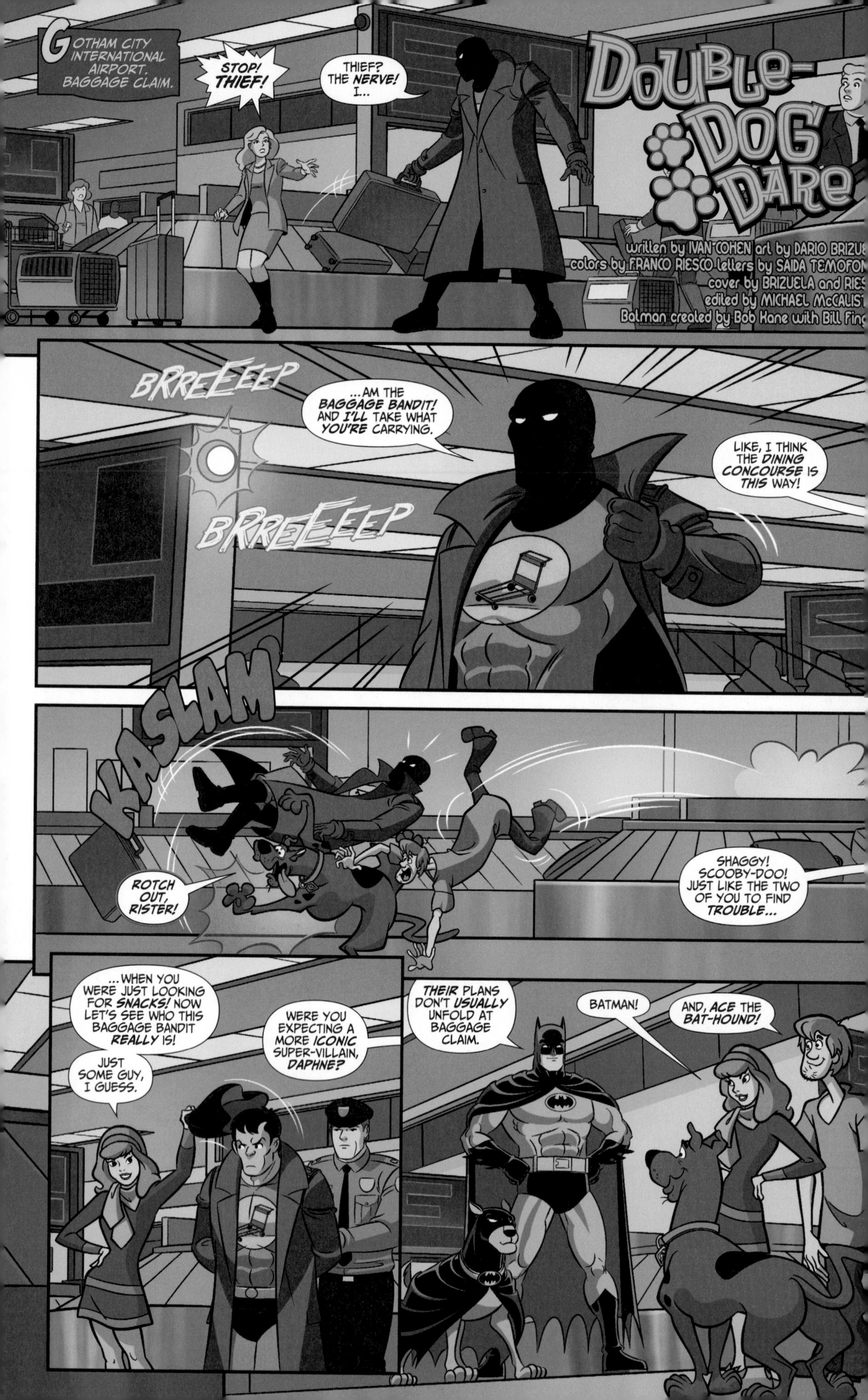
GOTHAM CITY INTERNATIONAL AIRPORT. BAGGAGE CLAIM.
STOP! THIEF!
THIEF? THE NERVE! I...
DOUBLE-DOG DARE
written by IVAN COHEN art by DARIO BRIZUE
colors by FRANCO RIESCO letters by SAIDA TEMOFON
cover by BRIZUELA and RIES
edited by MICHAEL McCALIS
Batman created by Bob Kane with Bill Fing
BRREEEEP
...AM THE BAGGAGE BANDIT! AND I'LL TAKE WHAT YOU'RE CARRYING.
BRREEEEP
LIKE, I THINK THE DINING CONCOURSE IS THIS WAY!
KASLAM
ROTCH OUT, RISTER!
SHAGGY! SCOOBY-DOO! JUST LIKE THE TWO OF YOU TO FIND TROUBLE...
...WHEN YOU WERE JUST LOOKING FOR SNACKS! NOW LET'S SEE WHO THIS BAGGAGE BANDIT REALLY IS!
JUST SOME GUY, I GUESS.
WERE YOU EXPECTING A MORE ICONIC SUPER-VILLAIN, DAPHNE?
THEIR PLANS DON'T USUALLY UNFOLD AT BAGGAGE CLAIM.
BATMAN!
AND, ACE THE BAT-HOUND!

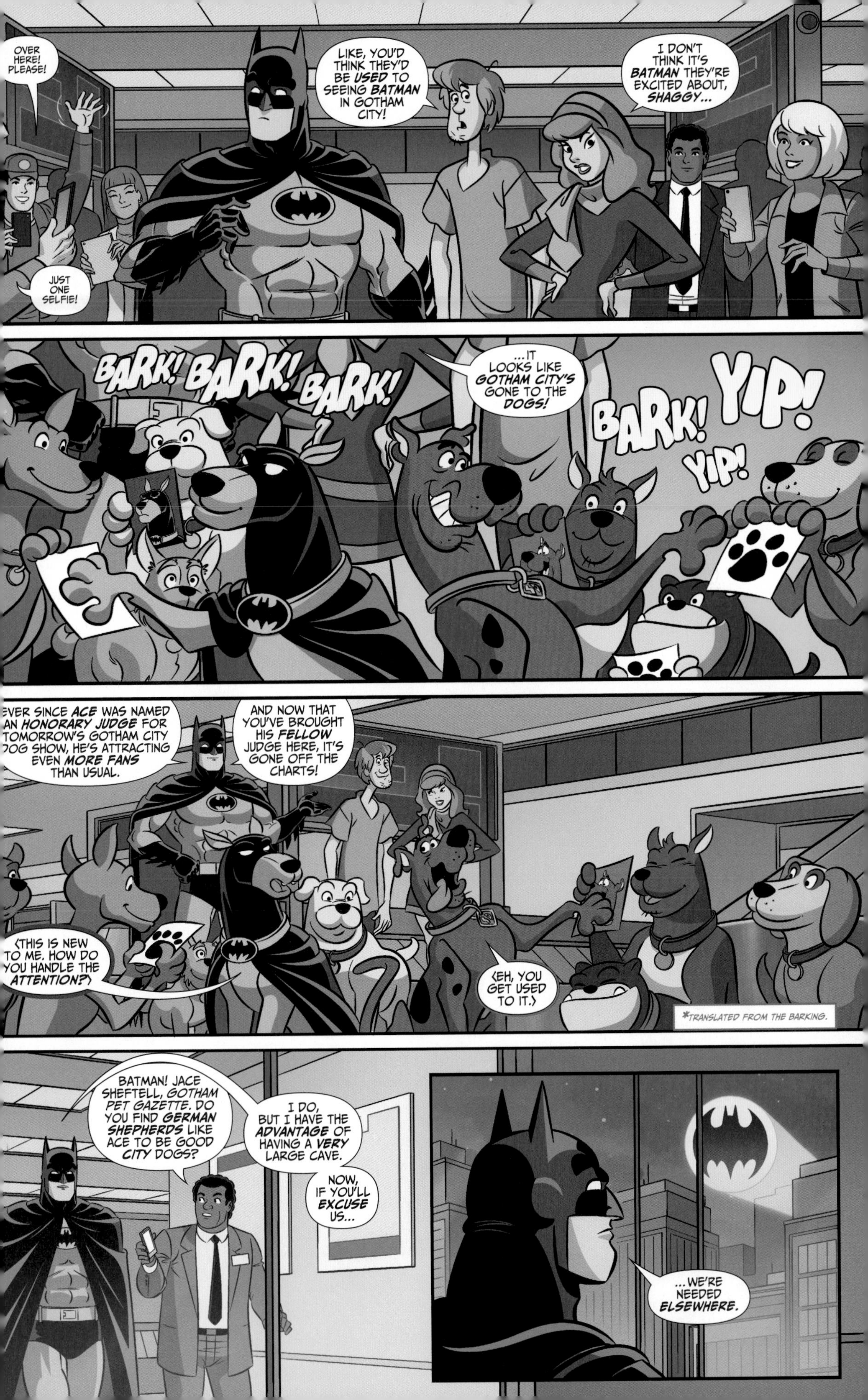
OVER HERE! PLEASE!
LIKE, YOU'D THINK THEY'D BE USED TO SEEING BATMAN IN GOTHAM CITY!
I DON'T THINK IT'S BATMAN THEY'RE EXCITED ABOUT, SHAGGY...
JUST ONE SELFIE!
BARK! BARK! BARK!
...IT LOOKS LIKE GOTHAM CITY'S GONE TO THE DOGS!
BARK! YIP!
YIP!
EVER SINCE ACE WAS NAMED AN HONORARY JUDGE FOR TOMORROW'S GOTHAM CITY DOG SHOW, HE'S ATTRACTING EVEN MORE FANS THAN USUAL.
AND NOW THAT YOU'VE BROUGHT HIS FELLOW JUDGE HERE, IT'S GONE OFF THE CHARTS!
‹THIS IS NEW TO ME. HOW DO YOU HANDLE THE ATTENTION?›
‹EH, YOU GET USED TO IT.›
*TRANSLATED FROM THE BARKING.
BATMAN! JACE SHEFTELL, GOTHAM PET GAZETTE. DO YOU FIND GERMAN SHEPHERDS LIKE ACE TO BE GOOD CITY DOGS?
I DO, BUT I HAVE THE ADVANTAGE OF HAVING A VERY LARGE CAVE.
NOW, IF YOU'LL EXCUSE US...
...WE'RE NEEDED ELSEWHERE.

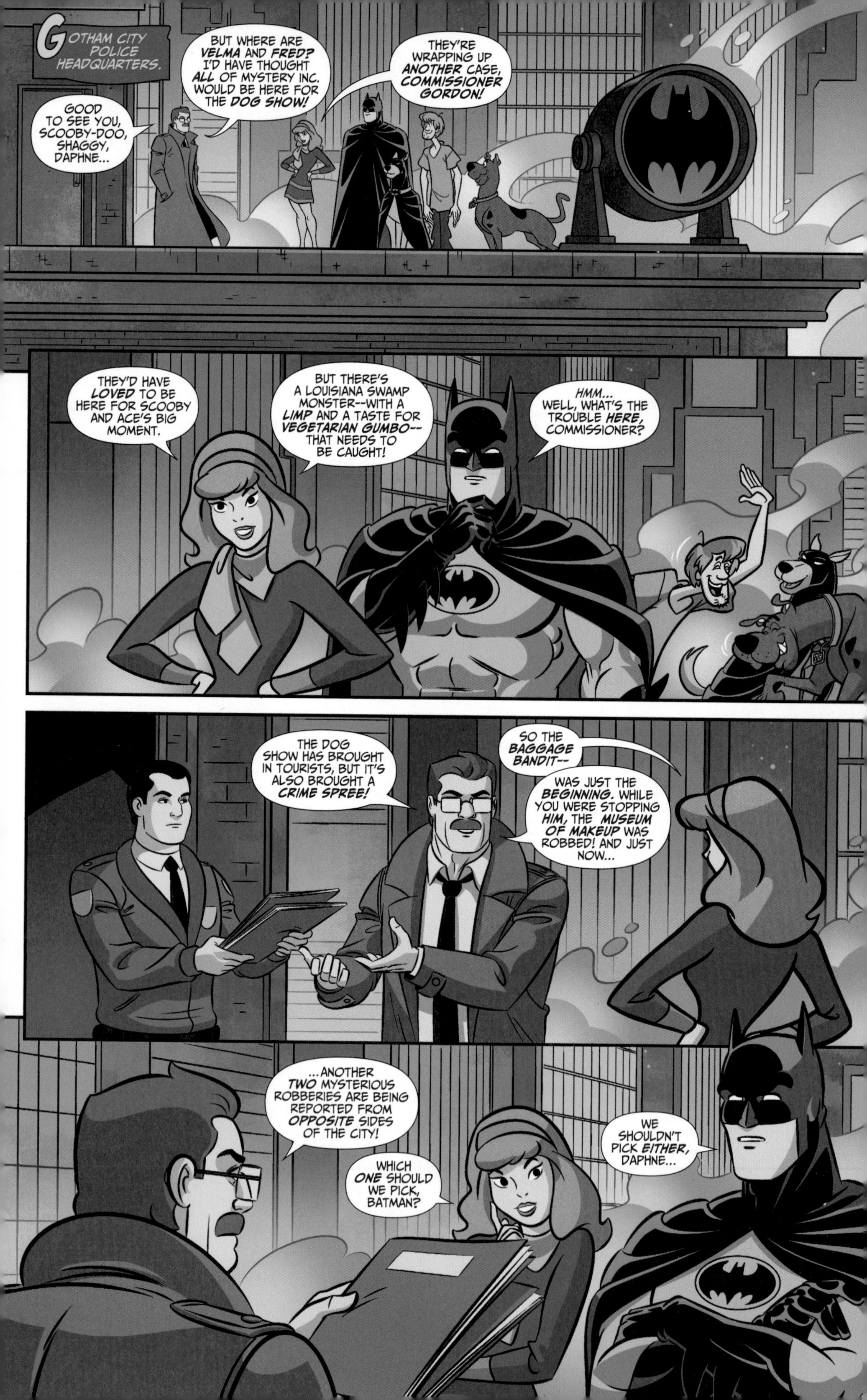
GOTHAM CITY POLICE HEADQUARTERS.
GOOD TO SEE YOU, SCOOBY-DOO, SHAGGY, DAPHNE...
BUT WHERE ARE VELMA AND FRED? I'D HAVE THOUGHT ALL OF MYSTERY INC. WOULD BE HERE FOR THE DOG SHOW!
THEY'RE WRAPPING UP ANOTHER CASE, COMMISSIONER GORDON!
THEY'D HAVE LOVED TO BE HERE FOR SCOOBY AND ACE'S BIG MOMENT.
BUT THERE'S A LOUISIANA SWAMP MONSTER--WITH A LIMP AND A TASTE FOR VEGETARIAN GUMBO--THAT NEEDS TO BE CAUGHT!
HMM... WELL, WHAT'S THE TROUBLE HERE, COMMISSIONER?
THE DOG SHOW HAS BROUGHT IN TOURISTS, BUT IT'S ALSO BROUGHT A CRIME SPREE!
SO THE BAGGAGE BANDIT--
WAS JUST THE BEGINNING. WHILE YOU WERE STOPPING HIM, THE MUSEUM OF MAKEUP WAS ROBBED! AND JUST NOW...
...ANOTHER TWO MYSTERIOUS ROBBERIES ARE BEING REPORTED FROM OPPOSITE SIDES OF THE CITY!
WHICH ONE SHOULD WE PICK, BATMAN?
WE SHOULDN'T PICK EITHER, DAPHNE...

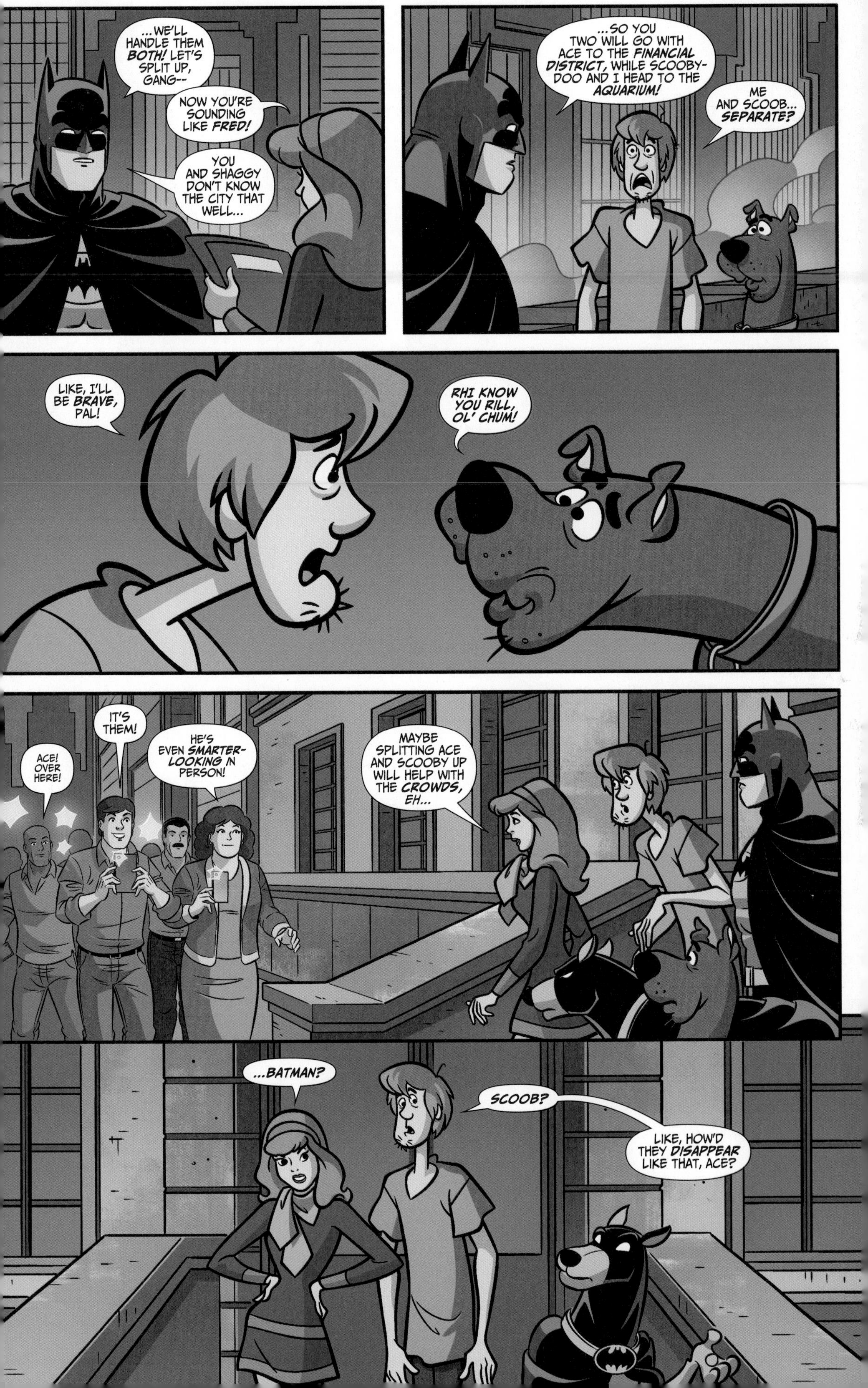
...WE'LL HANDLE THEM BOTH! LET'S SPLIT UP, GANG--
NOW YOU'RE SOUNDING LIKE FRED!
YOU AND SHAGGY DON'T KNOW THE CITY THAT WELL...
...SO YOU TWO WILL GO WITH ACE TO THE FINANCIAL DISTRICT, WHILE SCOOBY-DOO AND I HEAD TO THE AQUARIUM!
ME AND SCOOB... SEPARATE?
LIKE, I'LL BE BRAVE, PAL!
RHI KNOW YOU RILL, OL' CHUM!
ACE! OVER HERE!
IT'S THEM!
HE'S EVEN SMARTER-LOOKING IN PERSON!
MAYBE SPLITTING ACE AND SCOOBY UP WILL HELP WITH THE CROWDS, EH...
...BATMAN?
SCOOB?
LIKE, HOW'D THEY DISAPPEAR LIKE THAT, ACE?

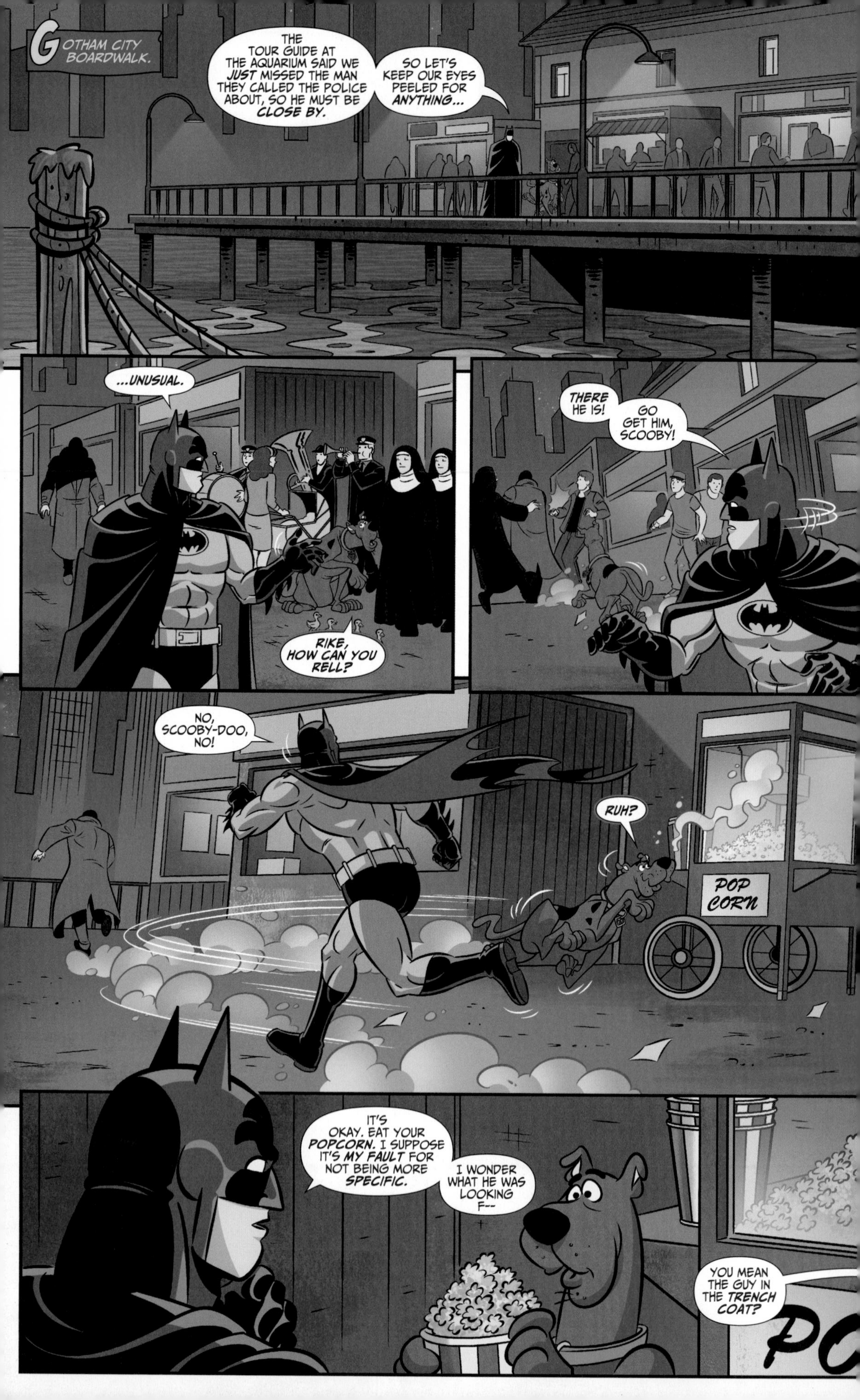
GOTHAM CITY BOARDWALK.
THE TOUR GUIDE AT THE AQUARIUM SAID WE JUST MISSED THE MAN THEY CALLED THE POLICE ABOUT, SO HE MUST BE CLOSE BY.
SO LET'S KEEP OUR EYES PEELED FOR ANYTHING...
...UNUSUAL.
RIKE, HOW CAN YOU RELL?
THERE HE IS!
GO GET HIM, SCOOBY!
NO, SCOOBY-DOO, NO!
RUH?
POP CORN
IT'S OKAY. EAT YOUR POPCORN. I SUPPOSE IT'S MY FAULT FOR NOT BEING MORE SPECIFIC.
I WONDER WHAT HE WAS LOOKING F--
YOU MEAN THE GUY IN THE TRENCH COAT?

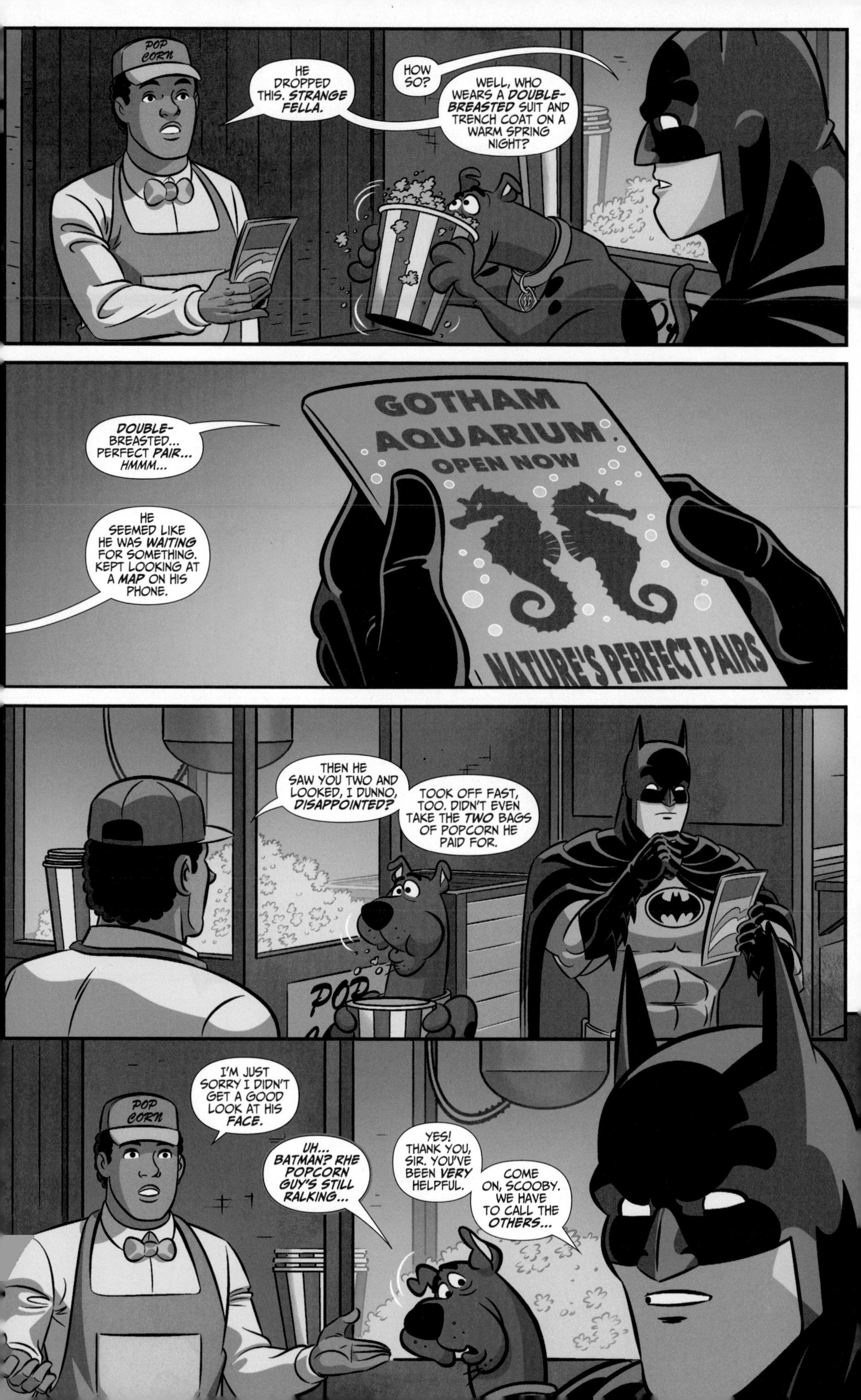
POP CORN
HE DROPPED THIS. STRANGE FELLA.
HOW SO?
WELL, WHO WEARS A DOUBLE-BREASTED SUIT AND TRENCH COAT ON A WARM SPRING NIGHT?
GOTHAM AQUARIUM
OPEN NOW
NATURE'S PERFECT PAIRS
DOUBLE-BREASTED... PERFECT PAIR... HMMM...
HE SEEMED LIKE HE WAS WAITING FOR SOMETHING. KEPT LOOKING AT A MAP ON HIS PHONE.
THEN HE SAW YOU TWO AND LOOKED, I DUNNO, DISAPPOINTED?
TOOK OFF FAST, TOO. DIDN'T EVEN TAKE THE TWO BAGS OF POPCORN HE PAID FOR.
POP CORN
I'M JUST SORRY I DIDN'T GET A GOOD LOOK AT HIS FACE.
UH... BATMAN? RHE POPCORN GUY'S STILL RALKING...
YES! THANK YOU, SIR. YOU'VE BEEN VERY HELPFUL.
COME ON, SCOOBY. WE HAVE TO CALL THE OTHERS...

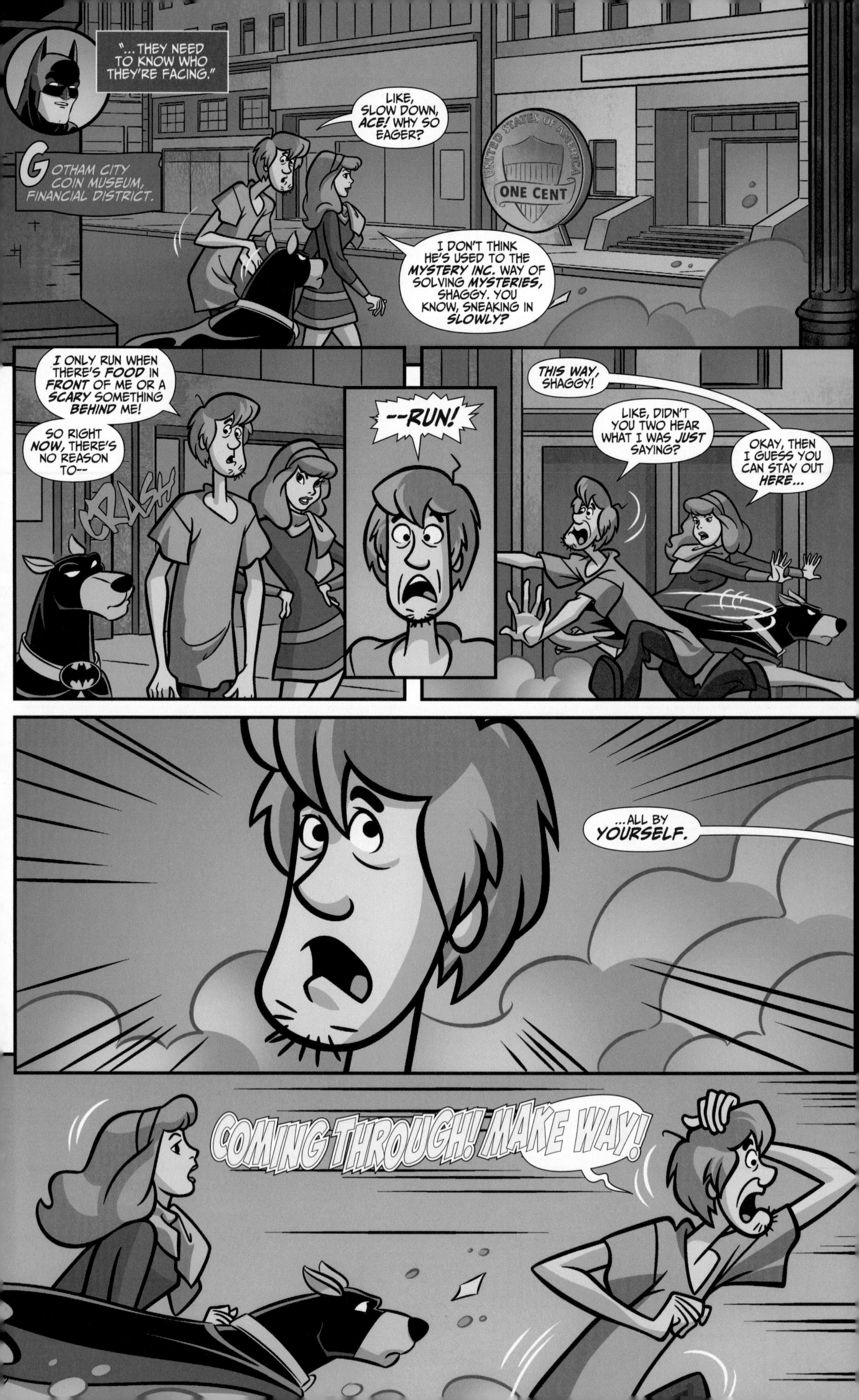
"...THEY NEED TO KNOW WHO THEY'RE FACING."
GOTHAM CITY COIN MUSEUM, FINANCIAL DISTRICT.
LIKE, SLOW DOWN, ACE! WHY SO EAGER?
ONE CENT
I DON'T THINK HE'S USED TO THE MYSTERY INC. WAY OF SOLVING MYSTERIES, SHAGGY. YOU KNOW, SNEAKING IN SLOWLY?
I ONLY RUN WHEN THERE'S FOOD IN FRONT OF ME OR A SCARY SOMETHING BEHIND ME!
SO RIGHT NOW, THERE'S NO REASON TO--
CRASH
--RUN!
THIS WAY, SHAGGY!
LIKE, DIDN'T YOU TWO HEAR WHAT I WAS JUST SAYING?
OKAY, THEN I GUESS YOU CAN STAY OUT HERE...
...ALL BY YOURSELF.
COMING THROUGH! MAKE WAY!

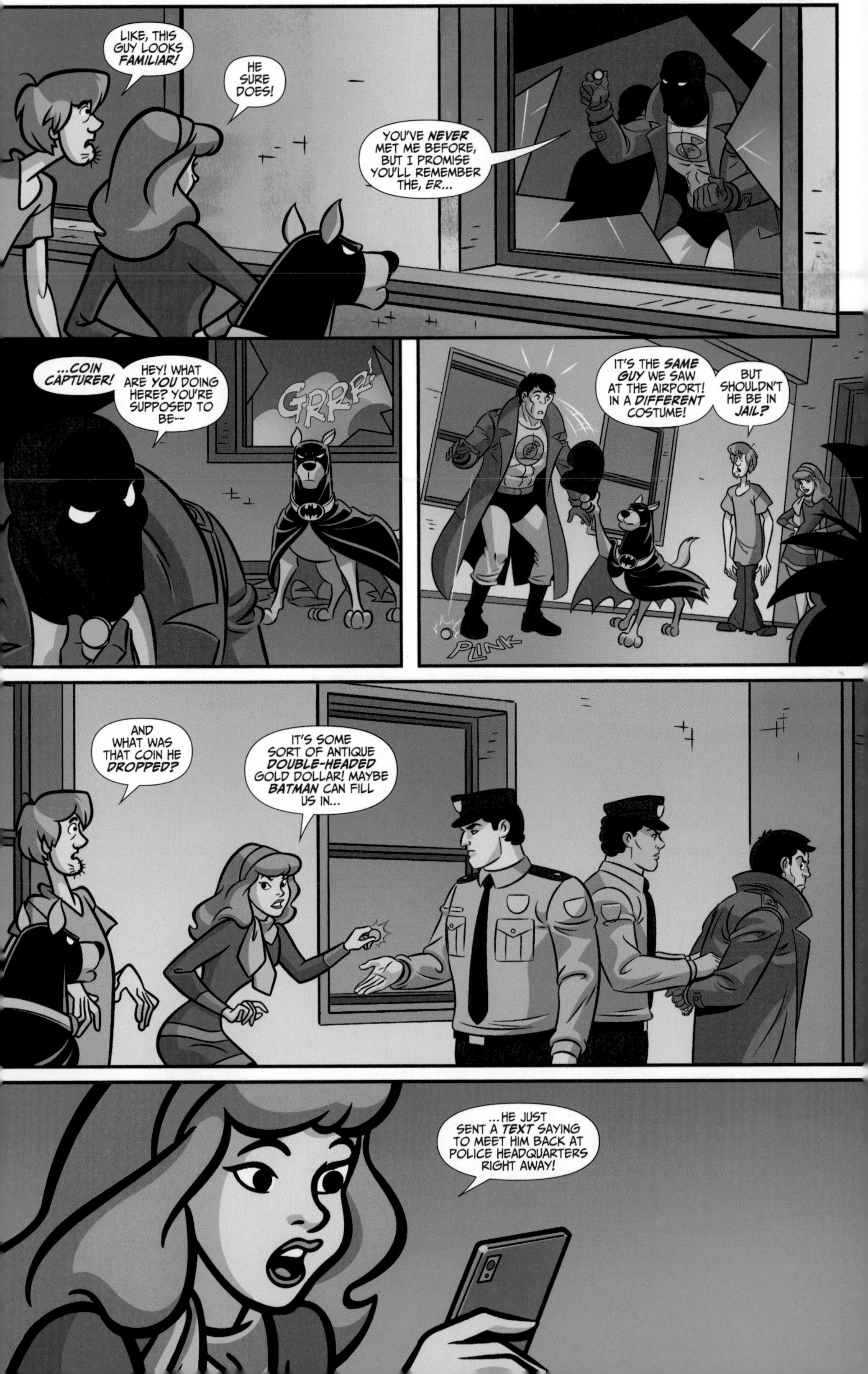
LIKE, THIS GUY LOOKS FAMILIAR!
HE SURE DOES!
YOU'VE NEVER MET ME BEFORE, BUT I PROMISE YOU'LL REMEMBER THE, ER...
...COIN CAPTURER!
HEY! WHAT ARE YOU DOING HERE? YOU'RE SUPPOSED TO BE--
GRRR!
IT'S THE SAME GUY WE SAW AT THE AIRPORT! IN A DIFFERENT COSTUME!
BUT SHOULDN'T HE BE IN JAIL?
PLINK
AND WHAT WAS THAT COIN HE DROPPED?
IT'S SOME SORT OF ANTIQUE DOUBLE-HEADED GOLD DOLLAR! MAYBE BATMAN CAN FILL US IN...
...HE JUST SENT A TEXT SAYING TO MEET HIM BACK AT POLICE HEADQUARTERS RIGHT AWAY!

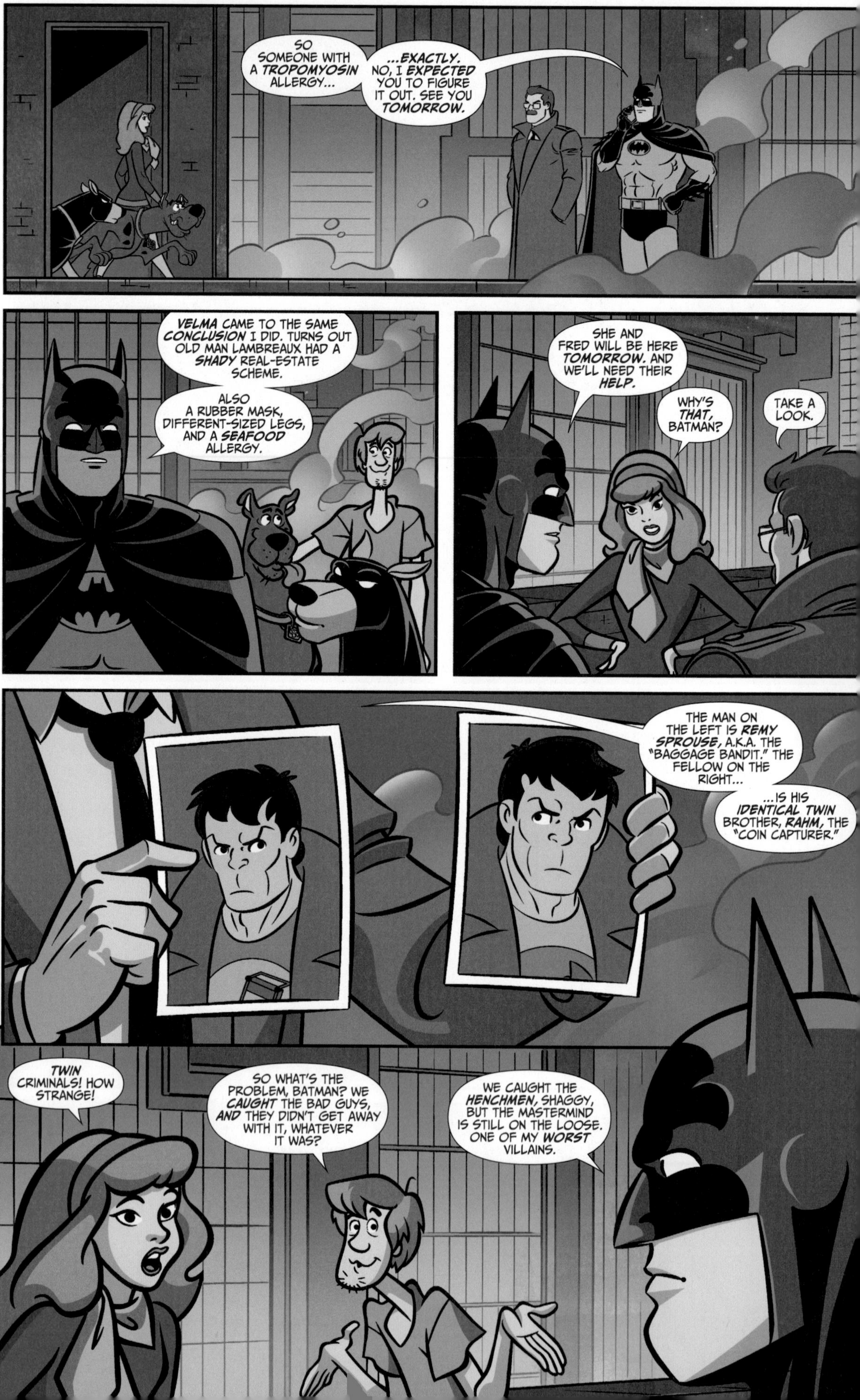
SO SOMEONE WITH A TROPOMYOSIN ALLERGY...
...EXACTLY. NO, I EXPECTED YOU TO FIGURE IT OUT. SEE YOU TOMORROW.
VELMA CAME TO THE SAME CONCLUSION I DID. TURNS OUT OLD MAN LAMBREAUX HAD A SHADY REAL-ESTATE SCHEME.
ALSO A RUBBER MASK, DIFFERENT-SIZED LEGS, AND A SEAFOOD ALLERGY.
SHE AND FRED WILL BE HERE TOMORROW. AND WE'LL NEED THEIR HELP.
WHY'S THAT, BATMAN?
TAKE A LOOK.
THE MAN ON THE LEFT IS REMY SPROUSE, A.K.A. THE "BAGGAGE BANDIT." THE FELLOW ON THE RIGHT...
...IS HIS IDENTICAL TWIN BROTHER, RAHM, THE "COIN CAPTURER."
TWIN CRIMINALS! HOW STRANGE!
SO WHAT'S THE PROBLEM, BATMAN? WE CAUGHT THE BAD GUYS, AND THEY DIDN'T GET AWAY WITH IT, WHATEVER IT WAS?
WE CAUGHT THE HENCHMEN, SHAGGY, BUT THE MASTERMIND IS STILL ON THE LOOSE. ONE OF MY WORST VILLAINS.

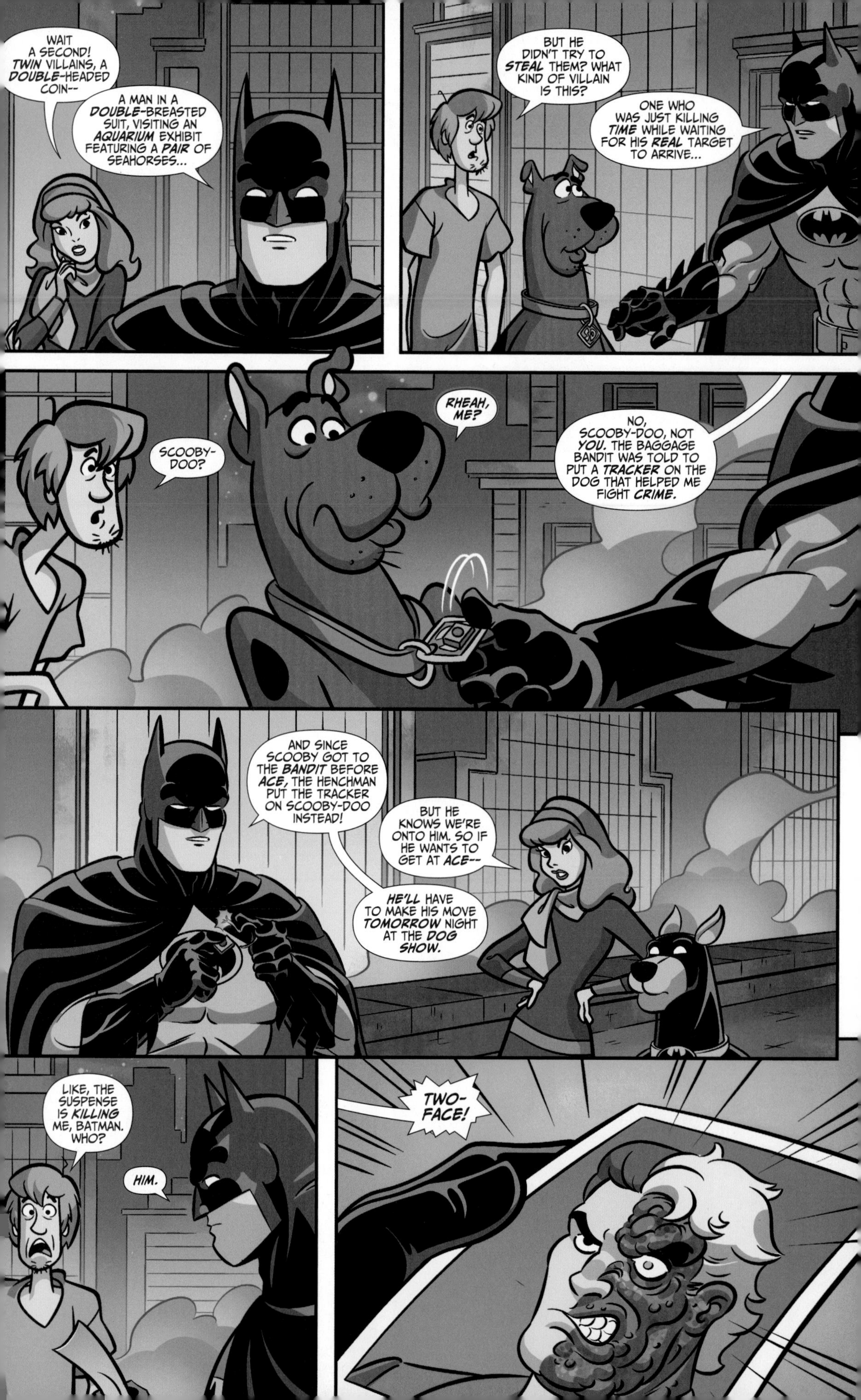
WAIT A SECOND! TWIN VILLAINS, A DOUBLE-HEADED COIN--
A MAN IN A DOUBLE-BREASTED SUIT, VISITING AN AQUARIUM EXHIBIT FEATURING A PAIR OF SEAHORSES...
BUT HE DIDN'T TRY TO STEAL THEM? WHAT KIND OF VILLAIN IS THIS?
ONE WHO WAS JUST KILLING TIME WHILE WAITING FOR HIS REAL TARGET TO ARRIVE...
SCOOBY-DOO?
RHEAH, ME?
NO, SCOOBY-DOO, NOT YOU. THE BAGGAGE BANDIT WAS TOLD TO PUT A TRACKER ON THE DOG THAT HELPED ME FIGHT CRIME.
AND SINCE SCOOBY GOT TO THE BANDIT BEFORE ACE, THE HENCHMAN PUT THE TRACKER ON SCOOBY-DOO INSTEAD!
BUT HE KNOWS WE'RE ONTO HIM. SO IF HE WANTS TO GET AT ACE--
HE'LL HAVE TO MAKE HIS MOVE TOMORROW NIGHT AT THE DOG SHOW.
LIKE, THE SUSPENSE IS KILLING ME, BATMAN. WHO?
HIM.
TWO-FACE!

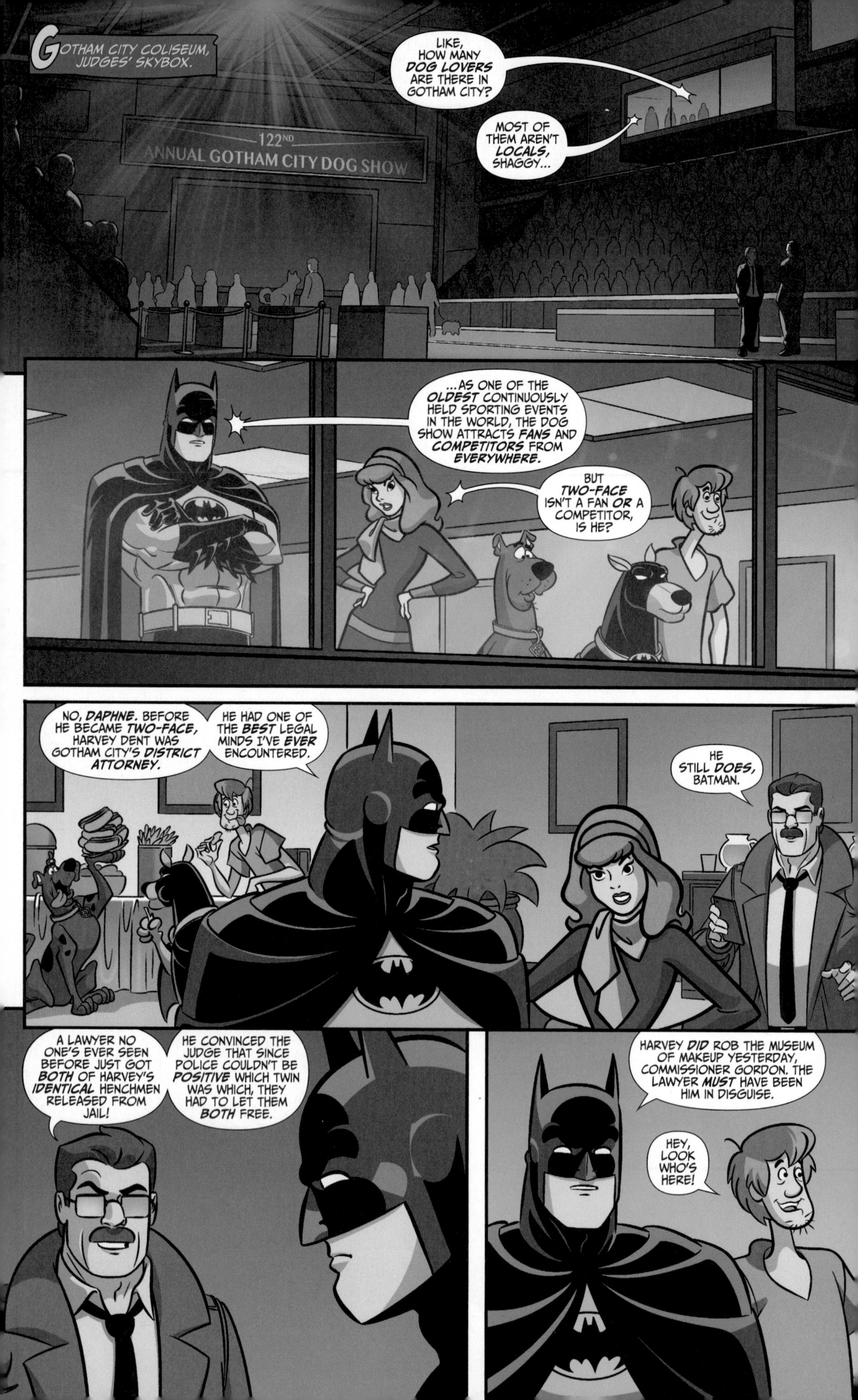
GOTHAM CITY COLISEUM, JUDGES' SKYBOX.
122ND ANNUAL GOTHAM CITY DOG SHOW
LIKE, HOW MANY DOG LOVERS ARE THERE IN GOTHAM CITY?
MOST OF THEM AREN'T LOCALS, SHAGGY...
...AS ONE OF THE OLDEST CONTINUOUSLY HELD SPORTING EVENTS IN THE WORLD, THE DOG SHOW ATTRACTS FANS AND COMPETITORS FROM EVERYWHERE.
BUT TWO-FACE ISN'T A FAN OR A COMPETITOR, IS HE?
NO, DAPHNE. BEFORE HE BECAME TWO-FACE, HARVEY DENT WAS GOTHAM CITY'S DISTRICT ATTORNEY.
HE HAD ONE OF THE BEST LEGAL MINDS I'VE EVER ENCOUNTERED.
HE STILL DOES, BATMAN.
A LAWYER NO ONE'S EVER SEEN BEFORE JUST GOT BOTH OF HARVEY'S IDENTICAL HENCHMEN RELEASED FROM JAIL!
HE CONVINCED THE JUDGE THAT SINCE POLICE COULDN'T BE POSITIVE WHICH TWIN WAS WHICH, THEY HAD TO LET THEM BOTH FREE.
HARVEY DID ROB THE MUSEUM OF MAKEUP YESTERDAY, COMMISSIONER GORDON. THE LAWYER MUST HAVE BEEN HIM IN DISGUISE.
HEY, LOOK WHO'S HERE!

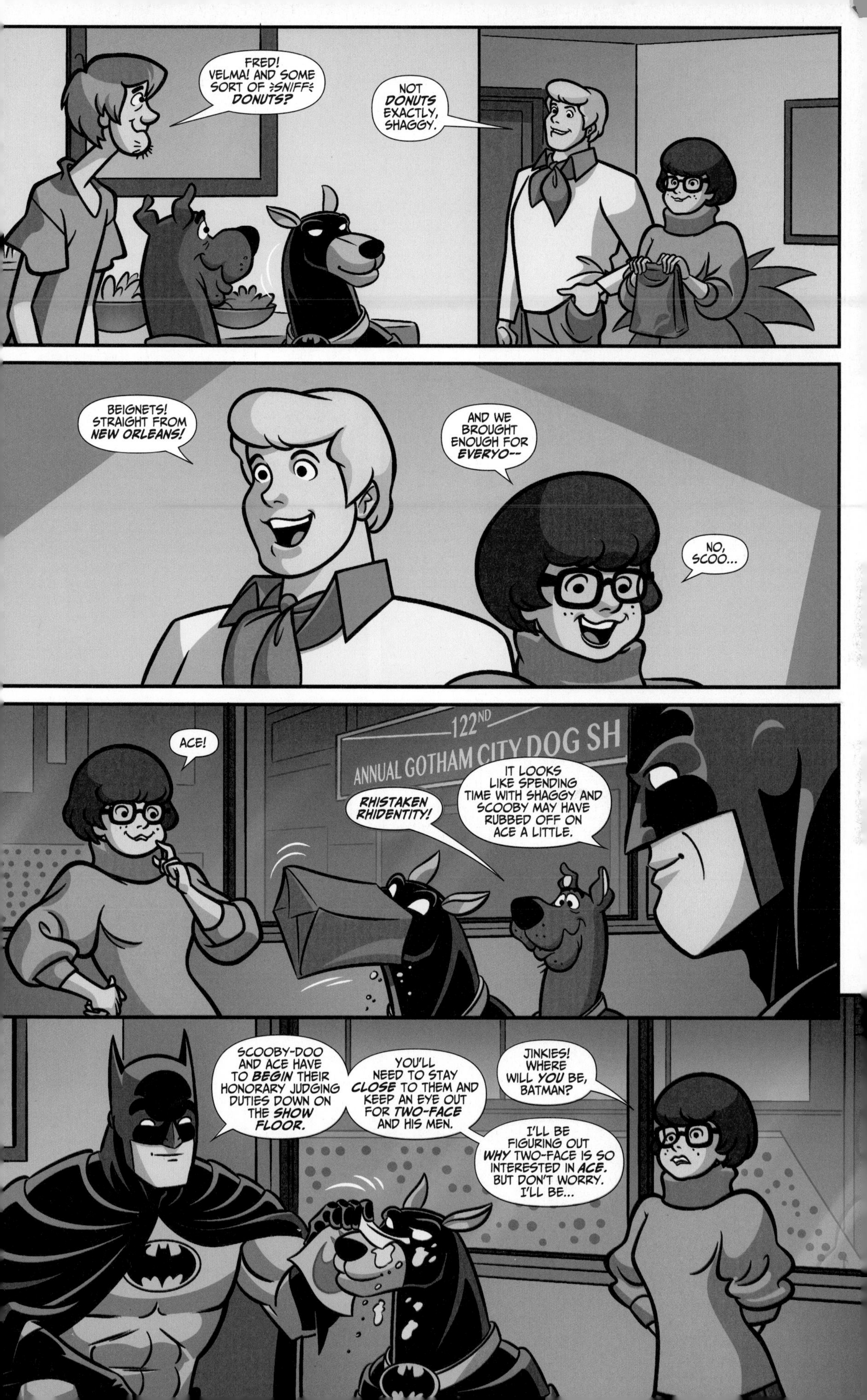
FRED! VELMA! AND SOME SORT OF ≶SNIFF≶ DONUTS?
NOT DONUTS EXACTLY, SHAGGY.
BEIGNETS! STRAIGHT FROM NEW ORLEANS!
AND WE BROUGHT ENOUGH FOR EVERYO--
NO, SCOO...
ACE!
122ND ANNUAL GOTHAM CITY DOG SH
RHISTAKEN RHIDENTITY!
IT LOOKS LIKE SPENDING TIME WITH SHAGGY AND SCOOBY MAY HAVE RUBBED OFF ON ACE A LITTLE.
SCOOBY-DOO AND ACE HAVE TO BEGIN THEIR HONORARY JUDGING DUTIES DOWN ON THE SHOW FLOOR.
YOU'LL NEED TO STAY CLOSE TO THEM AND KEEP AN EYE OUT FOR TWO-FACE AND HIS MEN.
JINKIES! WHERE WILL YOU BE, BATMAN?
I'LL BE FIGURING OUT WHY TWO-FACE IS SO INTERESTED IN ACE. BUT DON'T WORRY. I'LL BE...

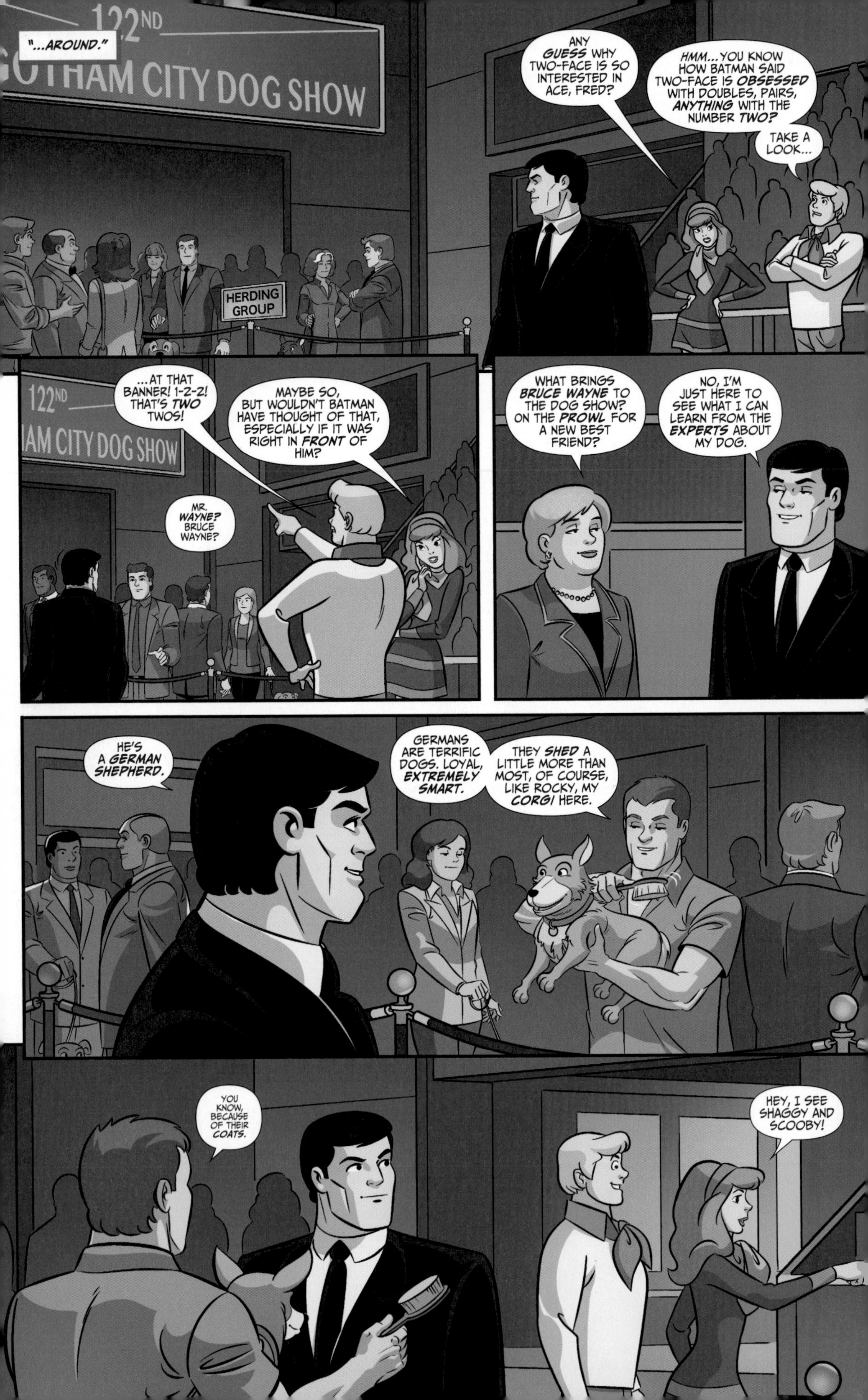
"...AROUND."
122ND
GOTHAM CITY DOG SHOW
HERDING GROUP
ANY GUESS WHY TWO-FACE IS SO INTERESTED IN ACE, FRED?
HMM... YOU KNOW HOW BATMAN SAID TWO-FACE IS OBSESSED WITH DOUBLES, PAIRS, ANYTHING WITH THE NUMBER TWO?
TAKE A LOOK...
...AT THAT BANNER! 1-2-2! THAT'S TWO TWOS!
MAYBE SO, BUT WOULDN'T BATMAN HAVE THOUGHT OF THAT, ESPECIALLY IF IT WAS RIGHT IN FRONT OF HIM?
MR. WAYNE? BRUCE WAYNE?
WHAT BRINGS BRUCE WAYNE TO THE DOG SHOW? ON THE PROWL FOR A NEW BEST FRIEND?
NO, I'M JUST HERE TO SEE WHAT I CAN LEARN FROM THE EXPERTS ABOUT MY DOG.
HE'S A GERMAN SHEPHERD.
GERMANS ARE TERRIFIC DOGS. LOYAL, EXTREMELY SMART.
THEY SHED A LITTLE MORE THAN MOST, OF COURSE, LIKE ROCKY, MY CORGI HERE.
YOU KNOW, BECAUSE OF THEIR COATS.
HEY, I SEE SHAGGY AND SCOOBY!

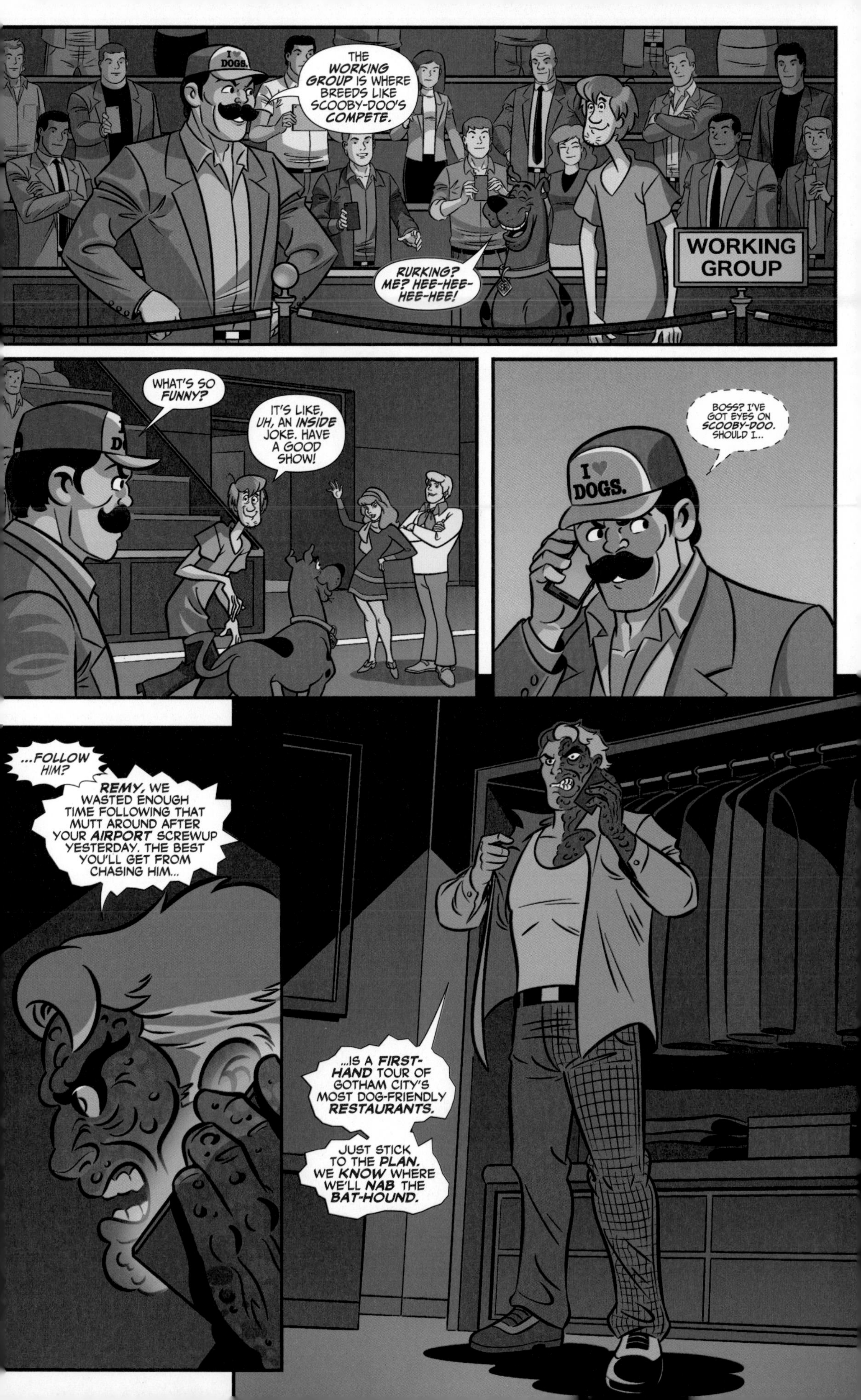

THE WORKING GROUP IS WHERE BREEDS LIKE SCOOBY-DOO'S COMPETE.
RURKING? ME? HEE-HEE-HEE-HEE!
WORKING GROUP
I ♥ DOGS.
WHAT'S SO FUNNY?
IT'S LIKE, UH, AN INSIDE JOKE. HAVE A GOOD SHOW!
BOSS? I'VE GOT EYES ON SCOOBY-DOO. SHOULD I...
...FOLLOW HIM?
REMY, WE WASTED ENOUGH TIME FOLLOWING THAT MUTT AROUND AFTER YOUR AIRPORT SCREWUP YESTERDAY. THE BEST YOU'LL GET FROM CHASING HIM...
...IS A FIRST-HAND TOUR OF GOTHAM CITY'S MOST DOG-FRIENDLY RESTAURANTS.
JUST STICK TO THE PLAN. WE KNOW WHERE WE'LL NAB THE BAT-HOUND.

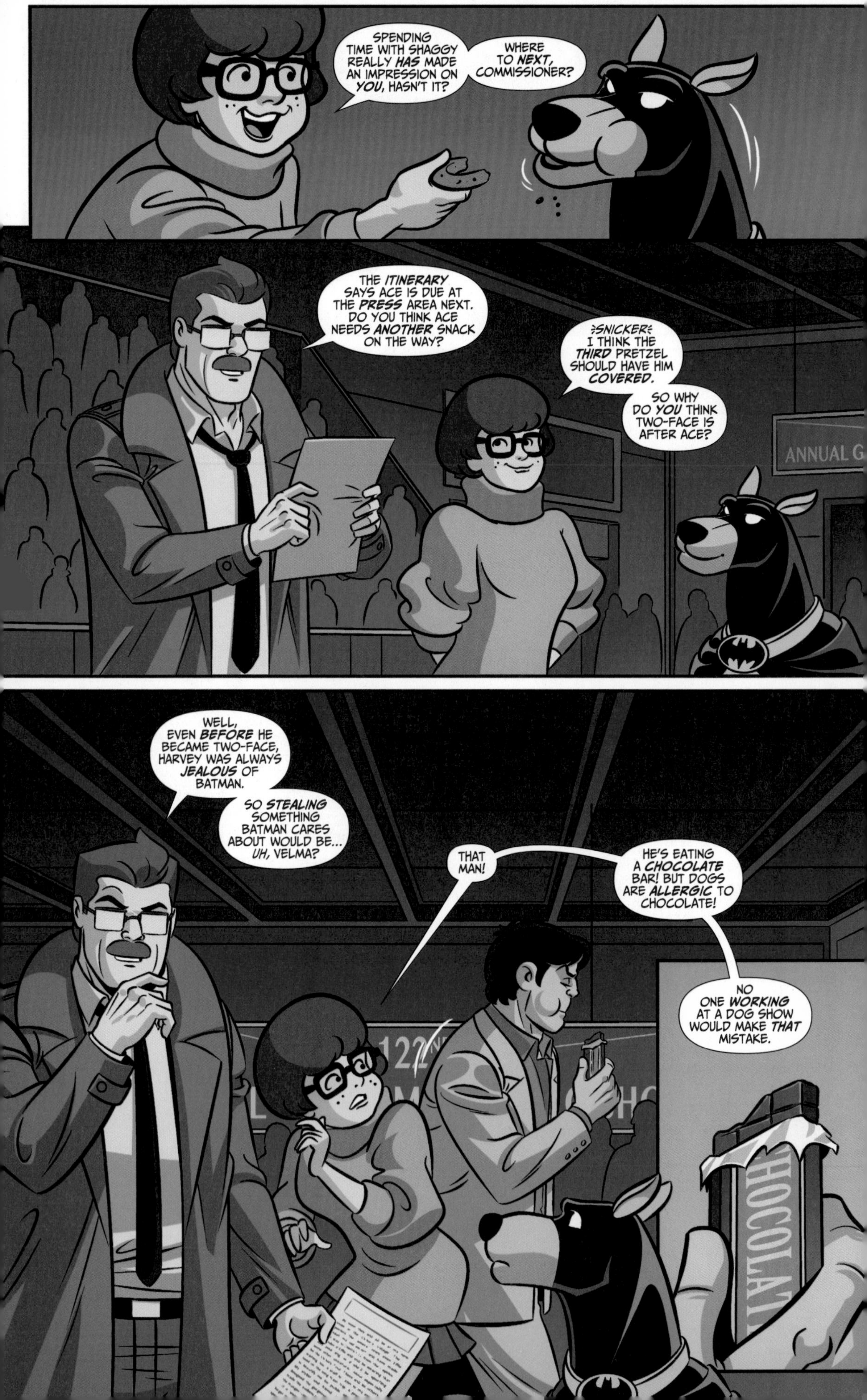
SPENDING TIME WITH SHAGGY REALLY HAS MADE AN IMPRESSION ON YOU, HASN'T IT?
WHERE TO NEXT, COMMISSIONER?
THE ITINERARY SAYS ACE IS DUE AT THE PRESS AREA NEXT. DO YOU THINK ACE NEEDS ANOTHER SNACK ON THE WAY?
SNICKER I THINK THE THIRD PRETZEL SHOULD HAVE HIM COVERED.
SO WHY DO YOU THINK TWO-FACE IS AFTER ACE?
ANNUAL G
WELL, EVEN BEFORE HE BECAME TWO-FACE, HARVEY WAS ALWAYS JEALOUS OF BATMAN.
SO STEALING SOMETHING BATMAN CARES ABOUT WOULD BE... UH, VELMA?
THAT MAN!
HE'S EATING A CHOCOLATE BAR! BUT DOGS ARE ALLERGIC TO CHOCOLATE!
NO ONE WORKING AT A DOG SHOW WOULD MAKE THAT MISTAKE.
122ND
CHOCOLAT

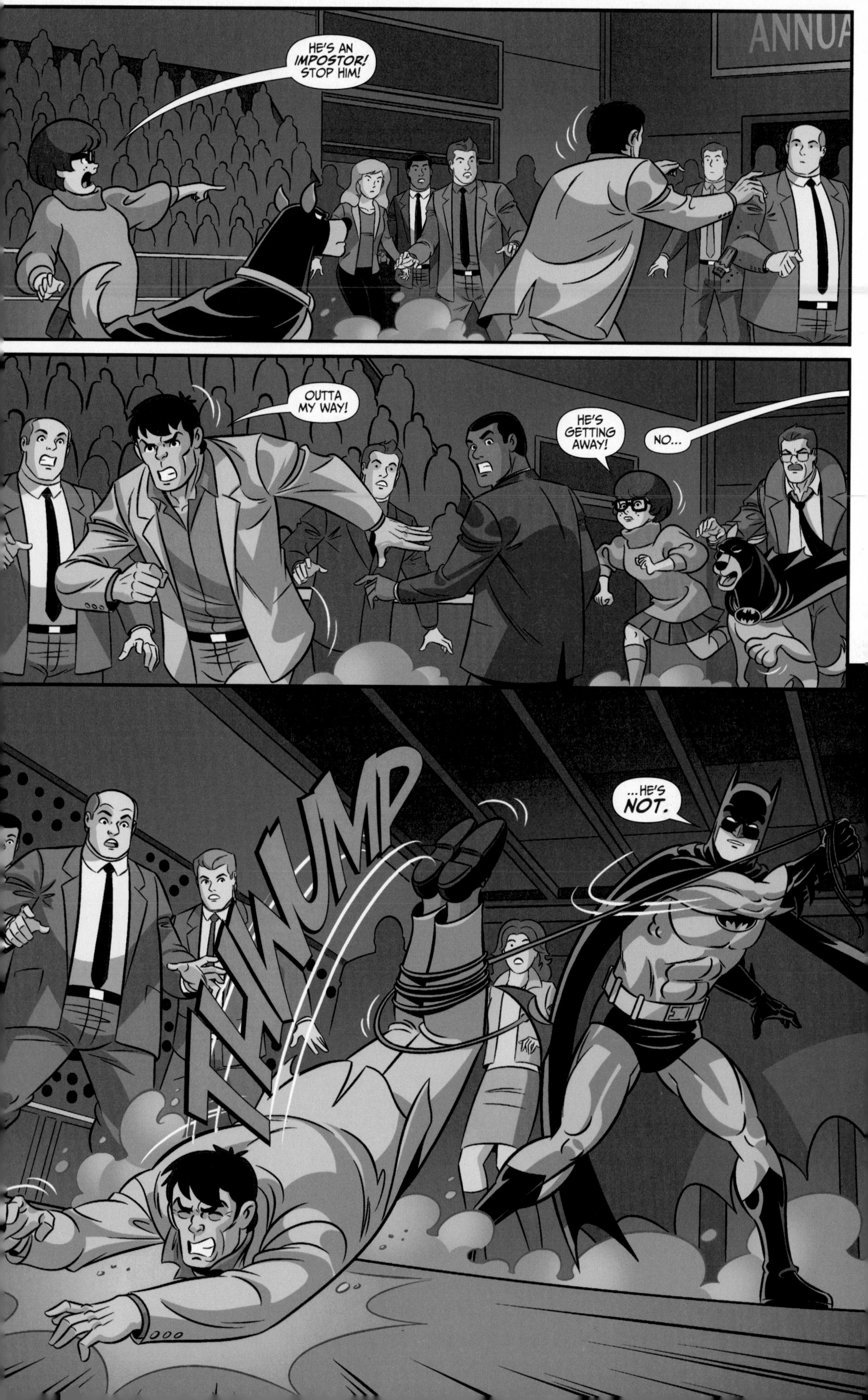
HE'S AN IMPOSTOR! STOP HIM!
ANNUA
OUTTA MY WAY!
HE'S GETTING AWAY!
NO...
...HE'S NOT.
THWUMP

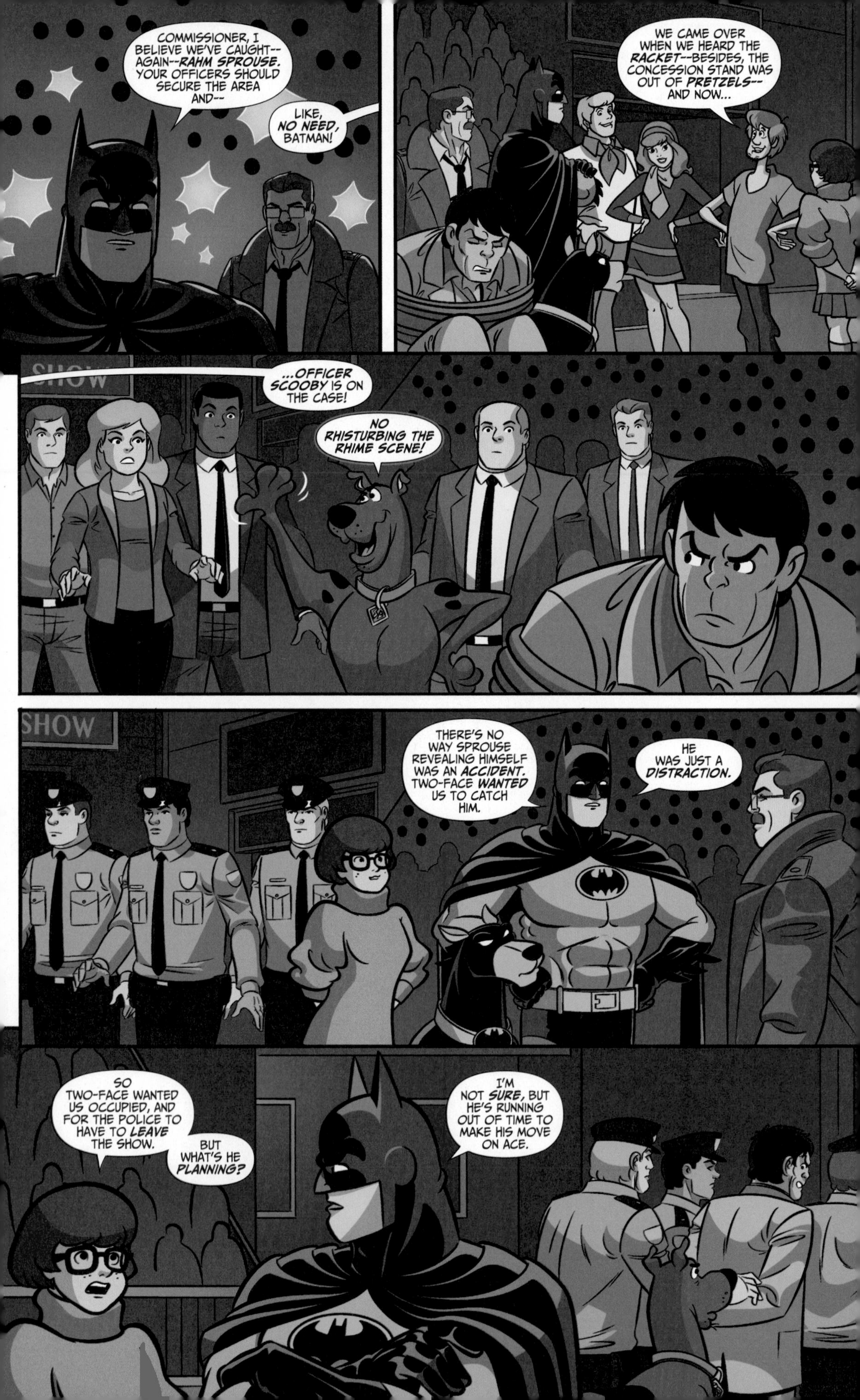

COMMISSIONER, I BELIEVE WE'VE CAUGHT--AGAIN--RAHM SPROUSE. YOUR OFFICERS SHOULD SECURE THE AREA AND--
LIKE, NO NEED, BATMAN!
WE CAME OVER WHEN WE HEARD THE RACKET--BESIDES, THE CONCESSION STAND WAS OUT OF PRETZELS-- AND NOW...
...OFFICER SCOOBY IS ON THE CASE!
NO RHISTURBING THE RHIME SCENE!
SHOW
SHOW
THERE'S NO WAY SPROUSE REVEALING HIMSELF WAS AN ACCIDENT. TWO-FACE WANTED US TO CATCH HIM.
HE WAS JUST A DISTRACTION.
SO TWO-FACE WANTED US OCCUPIED, AND FOR THE POLICE TO HAVE TO LEAVE THE SHOW.
BUT WHAT'S HE PLANNING?
I'M NOT SURE, BUT HE'S RUNNING OUT OF TIME TO MAKE HIS MOVE ON ACE.

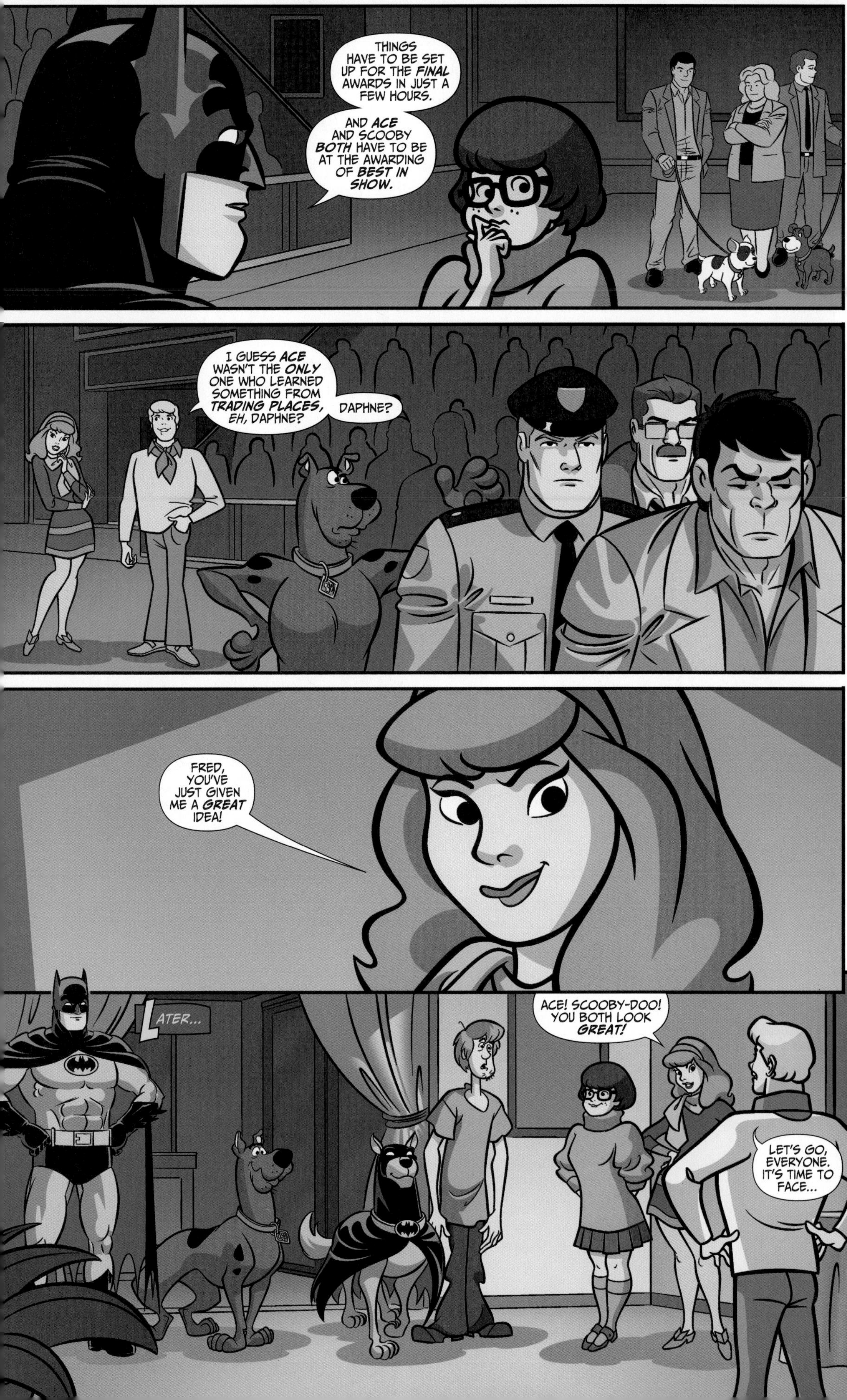
THINGS HAVE TO BE SET UP FOR THE FINAL AWARDS IN JUST A FEW HOURS.
AND ACE AND SCOOBY BOTH HAVE TO BE AT THE AWARDING OF BEST IN SHOW.
I GUESS ACE WASN'T THE ONLY ONE WHO LEARNED SOMETHING FROM TRADING PLACES, EH, DAPHNE?
DAPHNE?
FRED, YOU'VE JUST GIVEN ME A GREAT IDEA!
LATER...
ACE! SCOOBY-DOO! YOU BOTH LOOK GREAT!
LET'S GO, EVERYONE. IT'S TIME TO FACE...

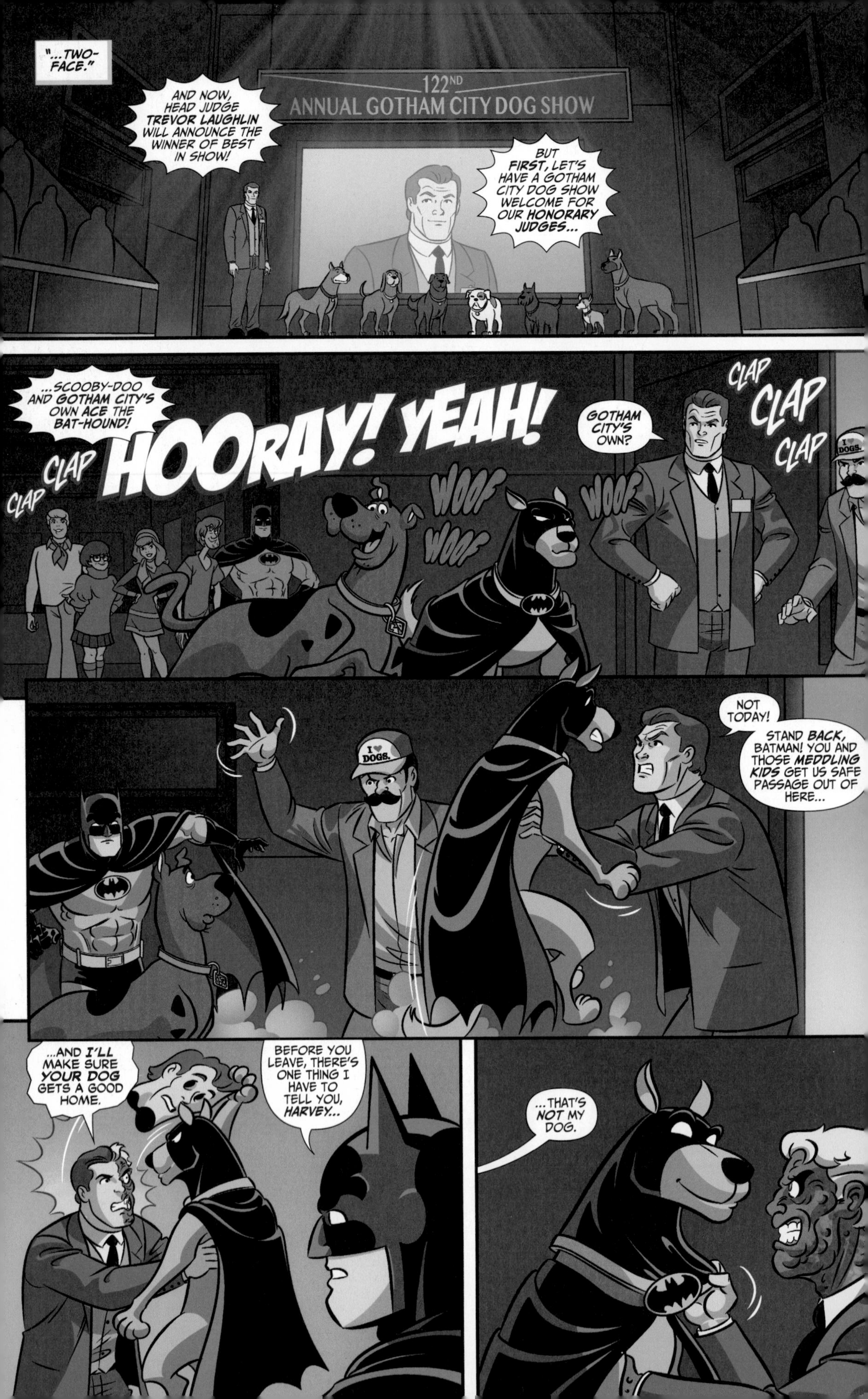

"...TWO-FACE."
122ND ANNUAL GOTHAM CITY DOG SHOW
AND NOW, HEAD JUDGE TREVOR LAUGHLIN WILL ANNOUNCE THE WINNER OF BEST IN SHOW!
BUT FIRST, LET'S HAVE A GOTHAM CITY DOG SHOW WELCOME FOR OUR HONORARY JUDGES...
...SCOOBY-DOO AND GOTHAM CITY'S OWN ACE THE BAT-HOUND!
CLAP CLAP
HOORAY! YEAH!
WOOF WOOF
WOOF
GOTHAM CITY'S OWN?
CLAP CLAP CLAP
I ♥ DOGS.
NOT TODAY!
STAND BACK, BATMAN! YOU AND THOSE MEDDLING KIDS GET US SAFE PASSAGE OUT OF HERE...
...AND I'LL MAKE SURE YOUR DOG GETS A GOOD HOME.
BEFORE YOU LEAVE, THERE'S ONE THING I HAVE TO TELL YOU, HARVEY...
...THAT'S NOT MY DOG.

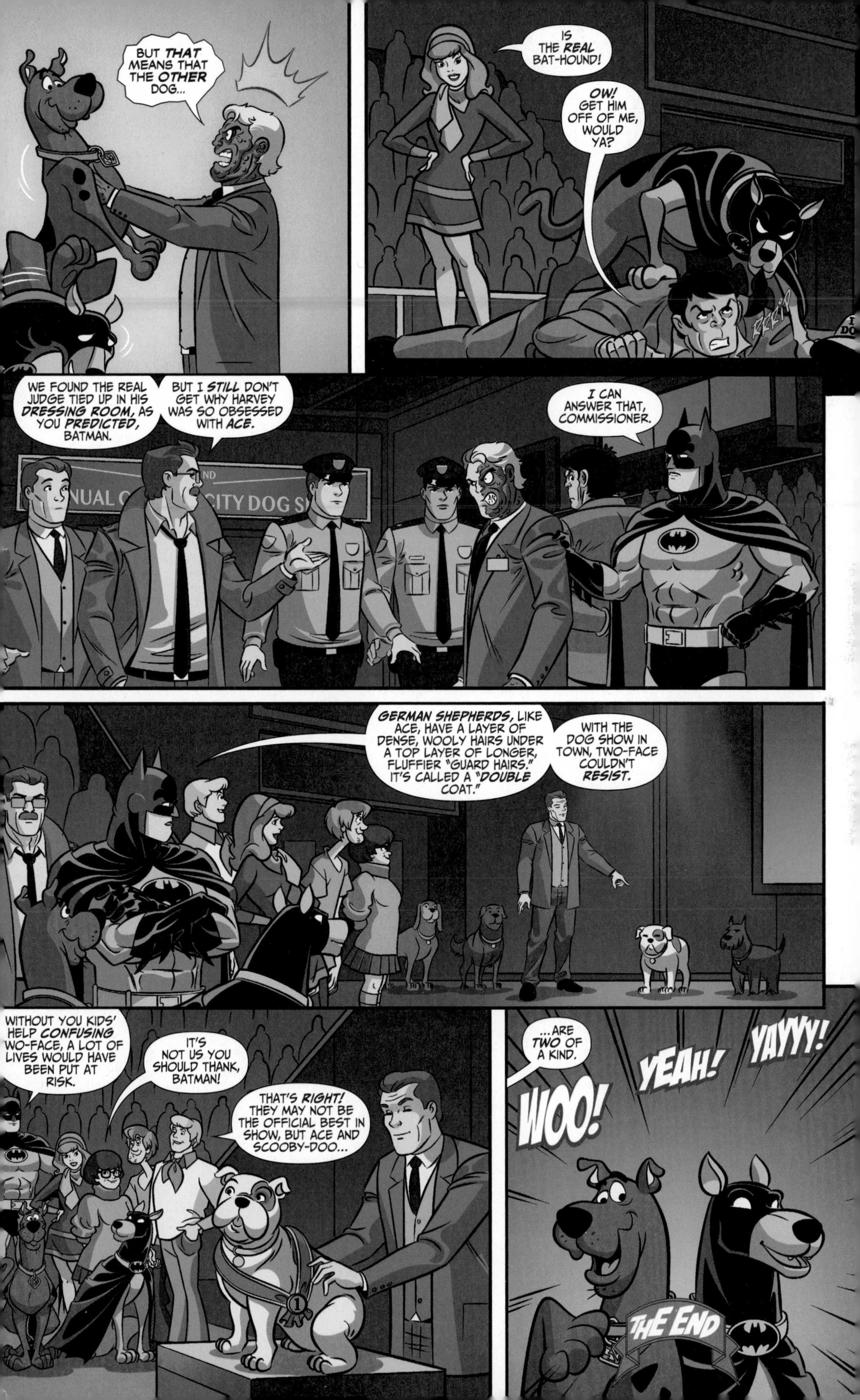

BUT **THAT** MEANS THAT THE **OTHER** DOG...
IS THE **REAL** BAT-HOUND!
OW! GET HIM OFF OF ME, WOULD YA?
RRRIP
WE FOUND THE REAL JUDGE TIED UP IN HIS **DRESSING ROOM,** AS YOU **PREDICTED,** BATMAN.
BUT I **STILL** DON'T GET WHY HARVEY WAS SO OBSESSED WITH **ACE.**
I CAN ANSWER THAT, COMMISSIONER.
GERMAN SHEPHERDS, LIKE ACE, HAVE A LAYER OF DENSE, WOOLY HAIRS UNDER A TOP LAYER OF LONGER, FLUFFIER "GUARD HAIRS." IT'S CALLED A "**DOUBLE** COAT."
WITH THE DOG SHOW IN TOWN, TWO-FACE COULDN'T **RESIST.**
WITHOUT YOU KIDS' HELP **CONFUSING** WO-FACE, A LOT OF LIVES WOULD HAVE BEEN PUT AT RISK.
IT'S NOT US YOU SHOULD THANK, BATMAN!
THAT'S **RIGHT!** THEY MAY NOT BE THE OFFICIAL BEST IN SHOW, BUT ACE AND SCOOBY-DOO...
...ARE **TWO** OF A KIND.
WOO!
YEAH!
YAYYY!
THE END

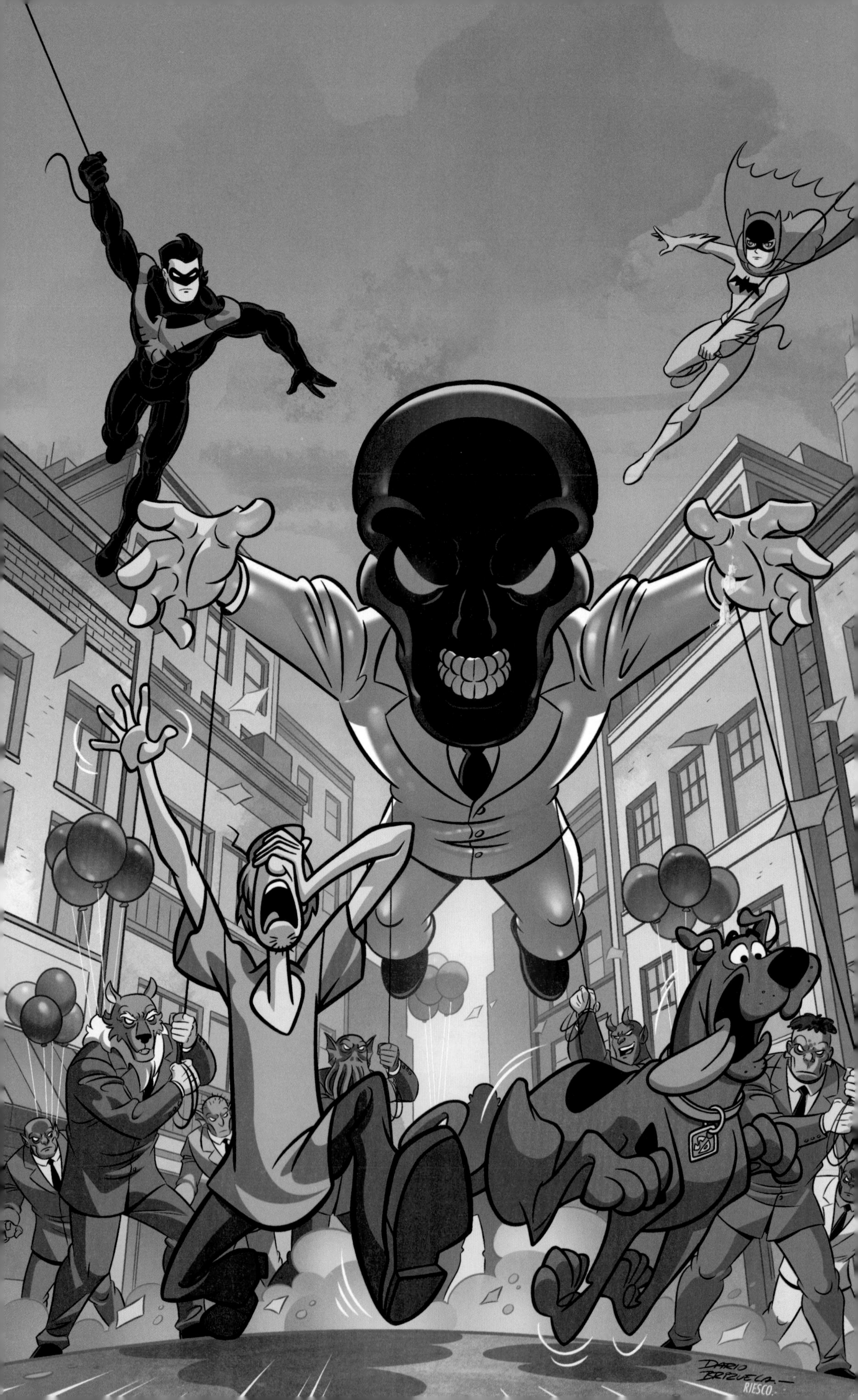
DARIO BRIZUELA
RIESCO.

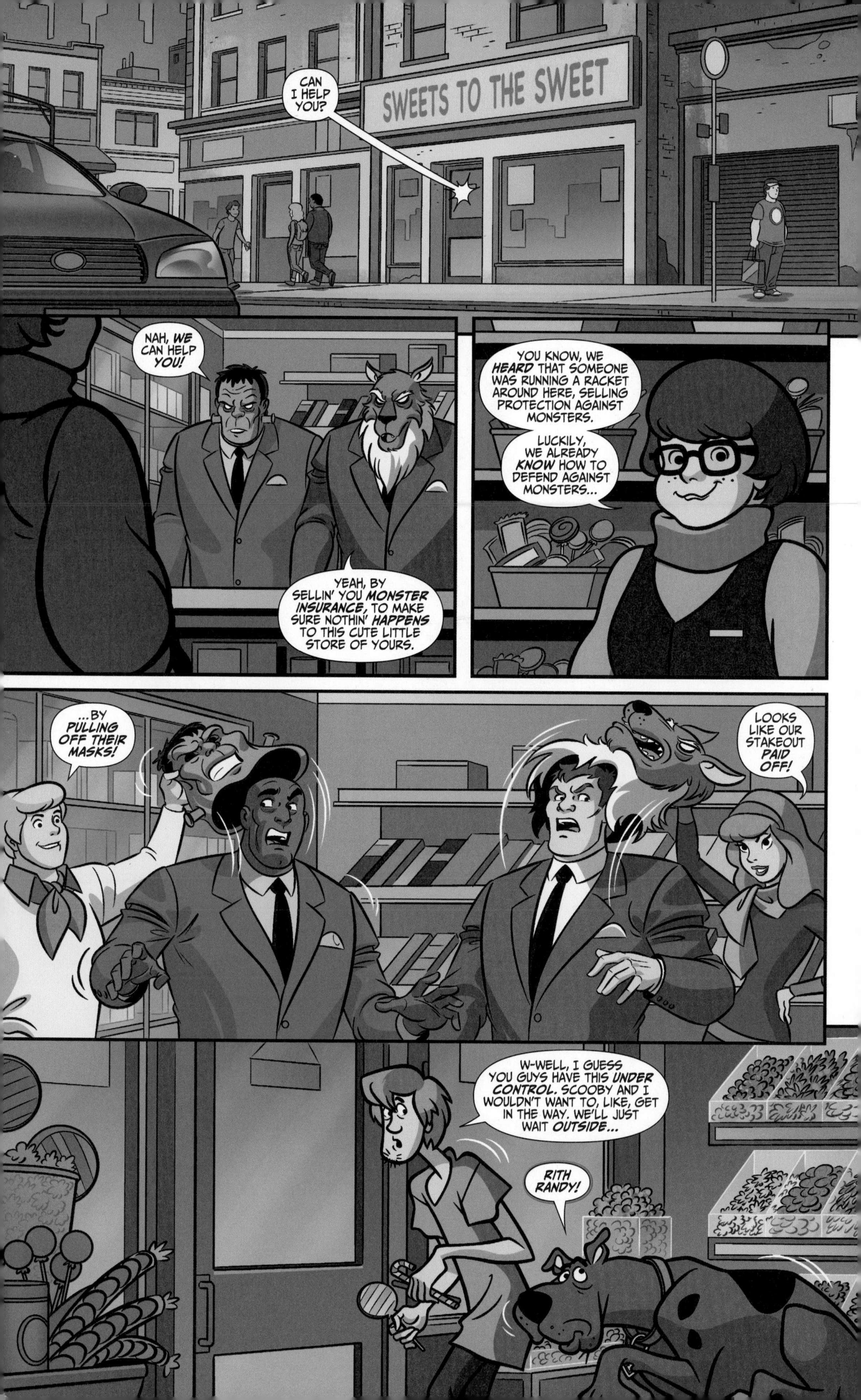
CAN I HELP YOU?
SWEETS TO THE SWEET
NAH, WE CAN HELP YOU!
YEAH, BY SELLIN' YOU MONSTER INSURANCE, TO MAKE SURE NOTHIN' HAPPENS TO THIS CUTE LITTLE STORE OF YOURS.
YOU KNOW, WE HEARD THAT SOMEONE WAS RUNNING A RACKET AROUND HERE, SELLING PROTECTION AGAINST MONSTERS.
LUCKILY, WE ALREADY KNOW HOW TO DEFEND AGAINST MONSTERS...
...BY PULLING OFF THEIR MASKS!
LOOKS LIKE OUR STAKEOUT PAID OFF!
W-WELL, I GUESS YOU GUYS HAVE THIS UNDER CONTROL. SCOOBY AND I WOULDN'T WANT TO, LIKE, GET IN THE WAY. WE'LL JUST WAIT OUTSIDE...
RITH RANDY!

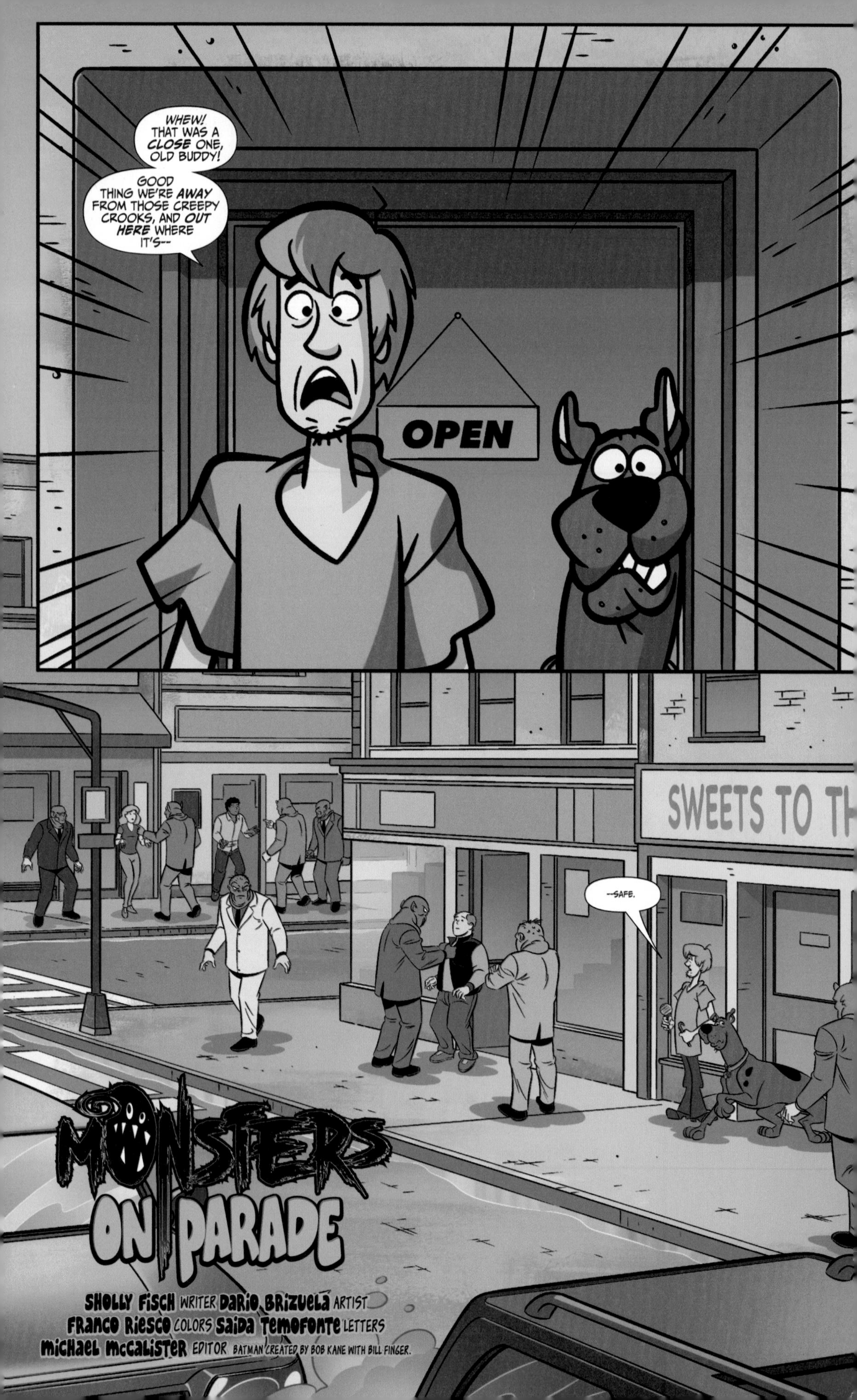
WHEW! THAT WAS A CLOSE ONE, OLD BUDDY!
GOOD THING WE'RE AWAY FROM THOSE CREEPY CROOKS, AND OUT HERE WHERE IT'S--
OPEN
SWEETS TO TH
--SAFE.
MONSTERS ON PARADE
SHOLLY FISCH WRITER DARIO BRIZUELA ARTIST
FRANCO RIESCO COLORS SAIDA TEMOFONTE LETTERS
MICHAEL MCCALISTER EDITOR BATMAN CREATED BY BOB KANE WITH BILL FINGER.

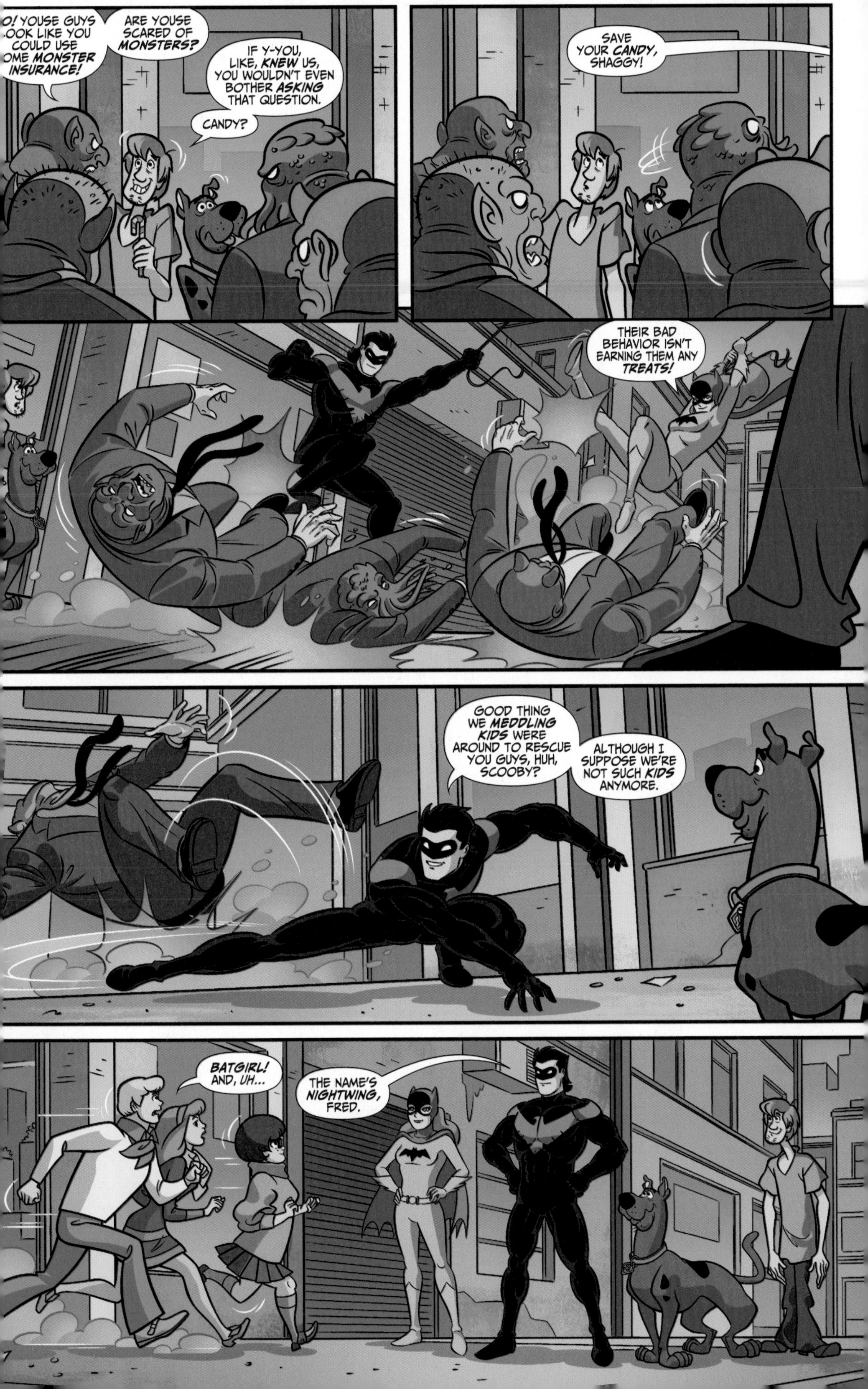
O! YOUSE GUYS OOK LIKE YOU COULD USE OME MONSTER INSURANCE!
ARE YOUSE SCARED OF MONSTERS?
IF Y-YOU, LIKE, KNEW US, YOU WOULDN'T EVEN BOTHER ASKING THAT QUESTION.
CANDY?
SAVE YOUR CANDY, SHAGGY!
THEIR BAD BEHAVIOR ISN'T EARNING THEM ANY TREATS!
GOOD THING WE MEDDLING KIDS WERE AROUND TO RESCUE YOU GUYS, HUH, SCOOBY?
ALTHOUGH I SUPPOSE WE'RE NOT SUCH KIDS ANYMORE.
BATGIRL! AND, UH...
THE NAME'S NIGHTWING, FRED.

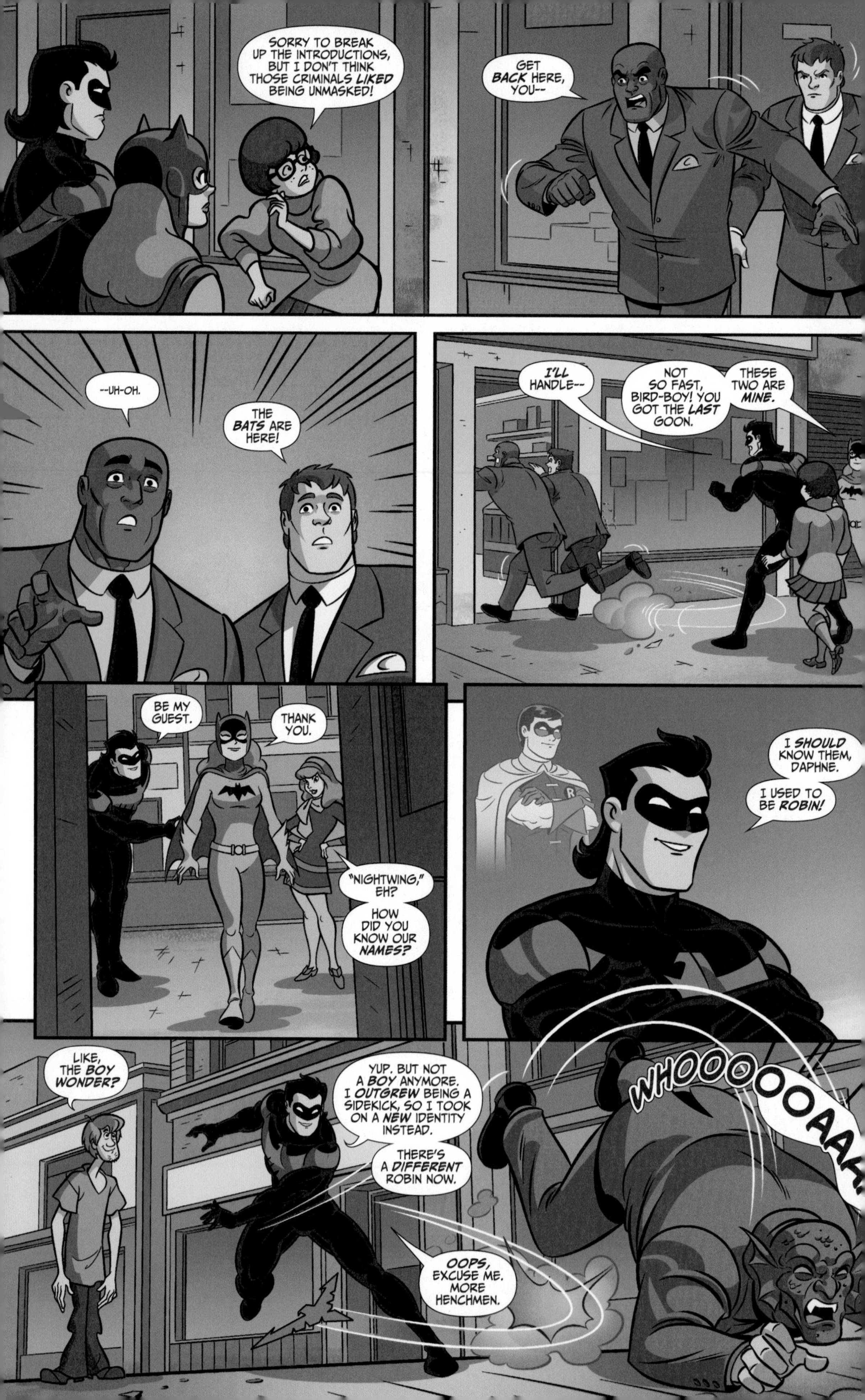
SORRY TO BREAK UP THE INTRODUCTIONS, BUT I DON'T THINK THOSE CRIMINALS LIKED BEING UNMASKED!
GET BACK HERE, YOU--
--UH-OH.
THE BATS ARE HERE!
I'LL HANDLE--
NOT SO FAST, BIRD-BOY! YOU GOT THE LAST GOON.
THESE TWO ARE MINE.
BE MY GUEST.
THANK YOU.
"NIGHTWING," EH?
HOW DID YOU KNOW OUR NAMES?
I SHOULD KNOW THEM, DAPHNE.
I USED TO BE ROBIN!
LIKE, THE BOY WONDER?
YUP. BUT NOT A BOY ANYMORE. I OUTGREW BEING A SIDEKICK, SO I TOOK ON A NEW IDENTITY INSTEAD.
THERE'S A DIFFERENT ROBIN NOW.
WHOOOOOAAK!
OOPS, EXCUSE ME. MORE HENCHMEN.

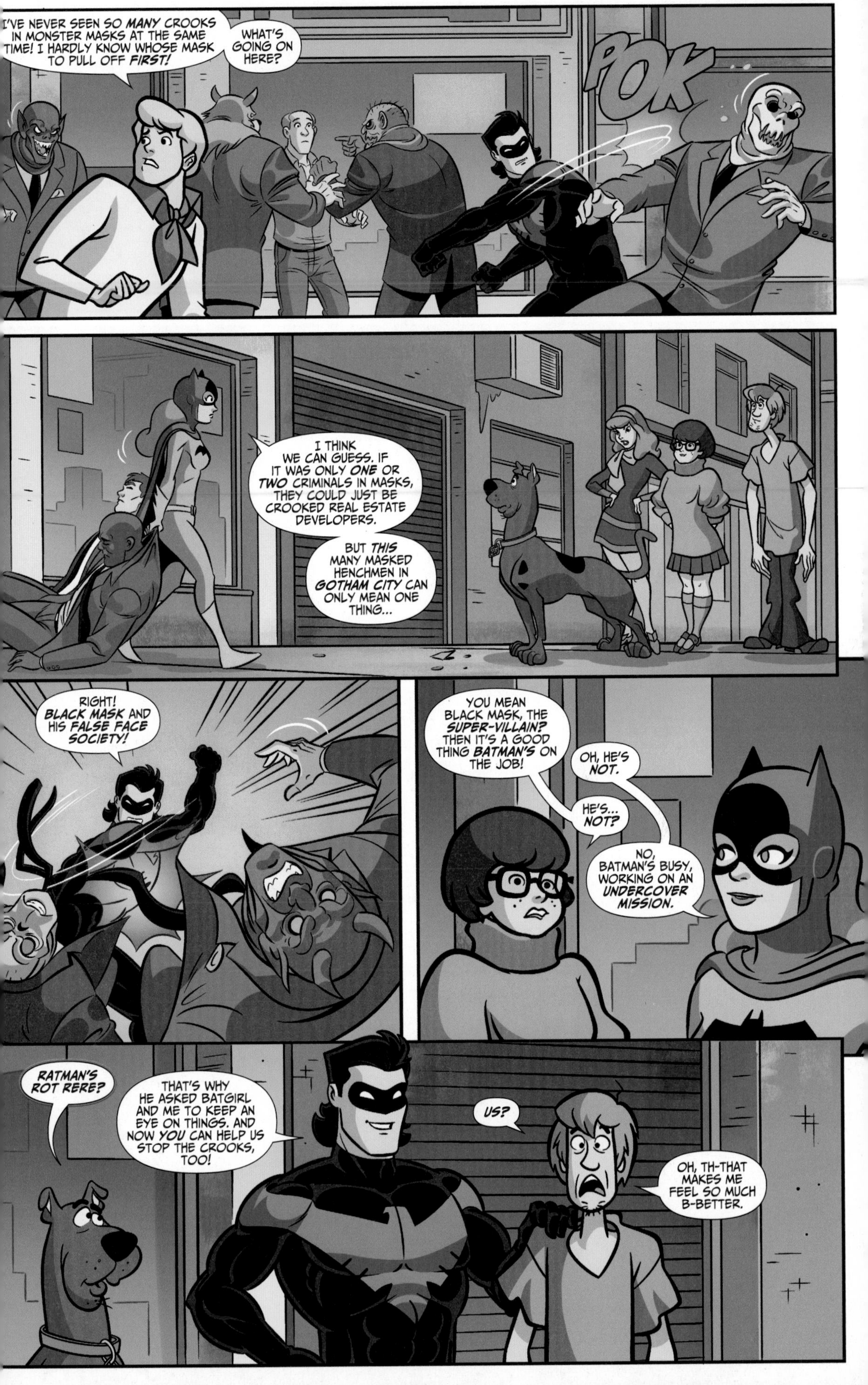
I'VE NEVER SEEN SO MANY CROOKS IN MONSTER MASKS AT THE SAME TIME! I HARDLY KNOW WHOSE MASK TO PULL OFF FIRST!
WHAT'S GOING ON HERE?
POK
I THINK WE CAN GUESS. IF IT WAS ONLY ONE OR TWO CRIMINALS IN MASKS, THEY COULD JUST BE CROOKED REAL ESTATE DEVELOPERS.
BUT THIS MANY MASKED HENCHMEN IN GOTHAM CITY CAN ONLY MEAN ONE THING...
RIGHT! BLACK MASK AND HIS FALSE FACE SOCIETY!
YOU MEAN BLACK MASK, THE SUPER-VILLAIN? THEN IT'S A GOOD THING BATMAN'S ON THE JOB!
OH, HE'S NOT.
HE'S... NOT?
NO, BATMAN'S BUSY, WORKING ON AN UNDERCOVER MISSION.
RATMAN'S ROT RERE?
THAT'S WHY HE ASKED BATGIRL AND ME TO KEEP AN EYE ON THINGS. AND NOW YOU CAN HELP US STOP THE CROOKS, TOO!
US?
OH, TH-THAT MAKES ME FEEL SO MUCH B-BETTER.

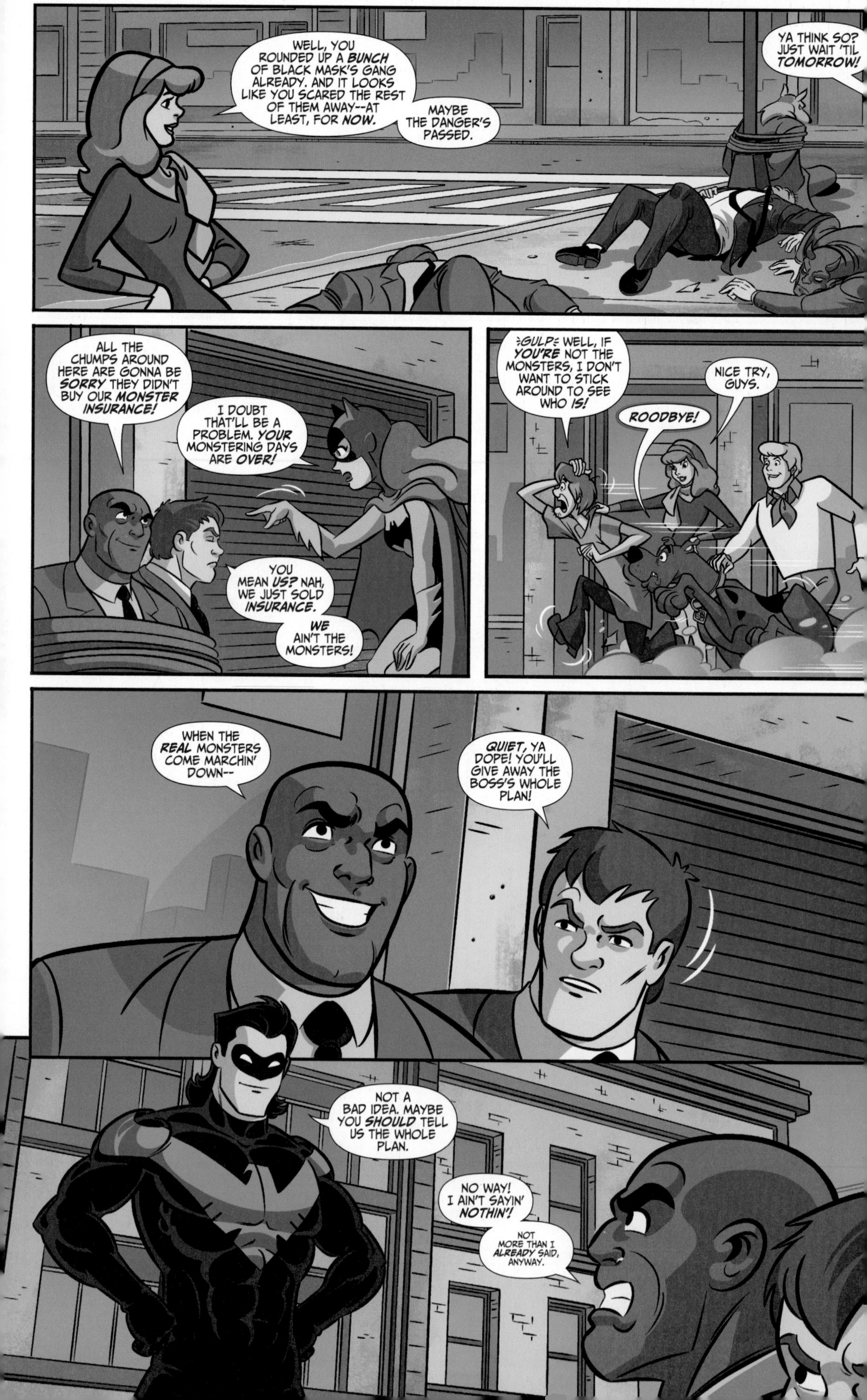

WELL, YOU ROUNDED UP A BUNCH OF BLACK MASK'S GANG ALREADY. AND IT LOOKS LIKE YOU SCARED THE REST OF THEM AWAY--AT LEAST, FOR NOW.
MAYBE THE DANGER'S PASSED.
YA THINK SO? JUST WAIT 'TIL TOMORROW!
ALL THE CHUMPS AROUND HERE ARE GONNA BE SORRY THEY DIDN'T BUY OUR MONSTER INSURANCE!
I DOUBT THAT'LL BE A PROBLEM. YOUR MONSTERING DAYS ARE OVER!
YOU MEAN US? NAH, WE JUST SOLD INSURANCE.
WE AIN'T THE MONSTERS!
GULP WELL, IF YOU'RE NOT THE MONSTERS, I DON'T WANT TO STICK AROUND TO SEE WHO IS!
NICE TRY, GUYS.
ROODBYE!
WHEN THE REAL MONSTERS COME MARCHIN' DOWN--
QUIET, YA DOPE! YOU'LL GIVE AWAY THE BOSS'S WHOLE PLAN!
NOT A BAD IDEA. MAYBE YOU SHOULD TELL US THE WHOLE PLAN.
NO WAY! I AIN'T SAYIN' NOTHIN'!
NOT MORE THAN I ALREADY SAID, ANYWAY.

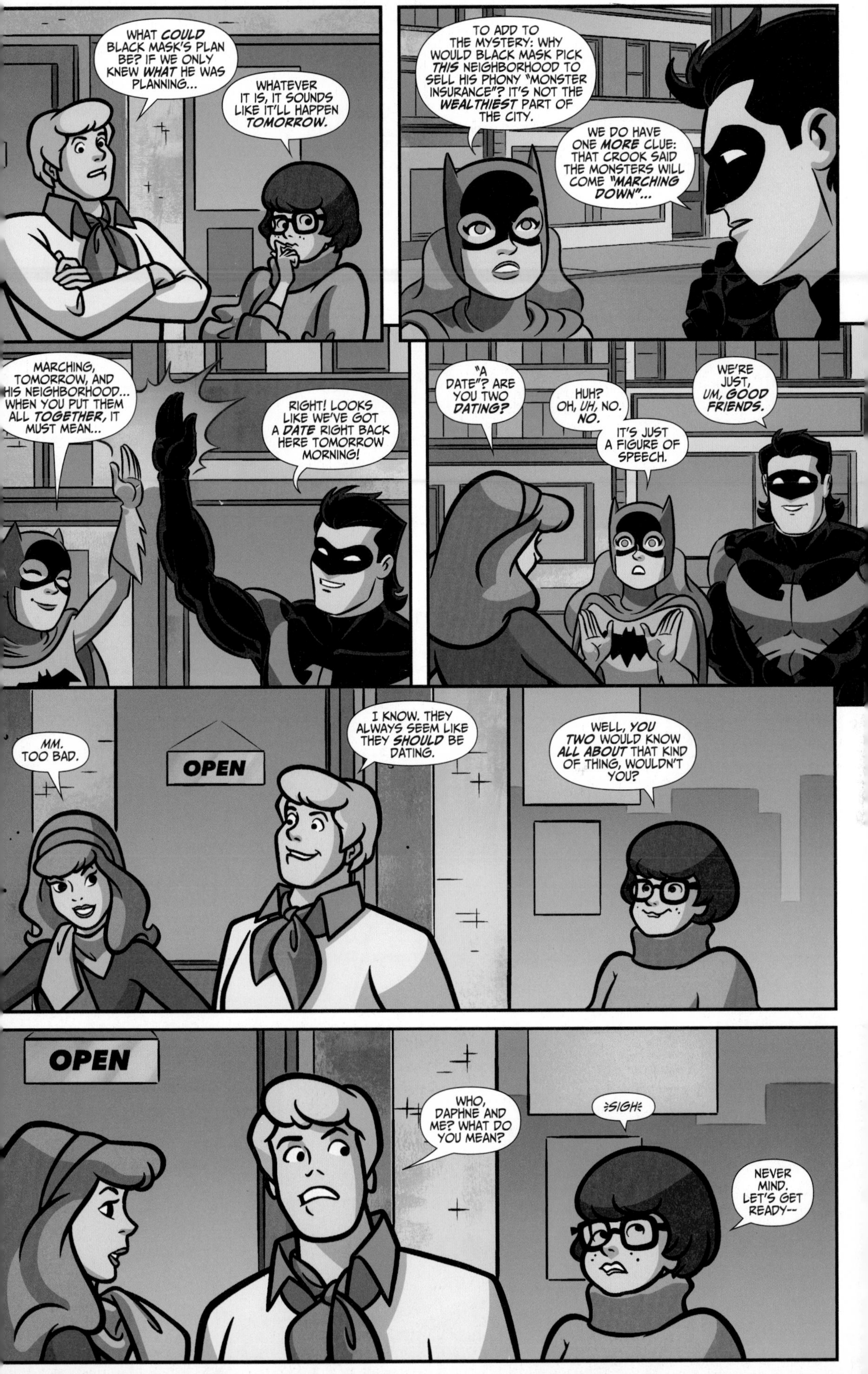

WHAT COULD BLACK MASK'S PLAN BE? IF WE ONLY KNEW WHAT HE WAS PLANNING...
WHATEVER IT IS, IT SOUNDS LIKE IT'LL HAPPEN TOMORROW.
TO ADD TO THE MYSTERY: WHY WOULD BLACK MASK PICK THIS NEIGHBORHOOD TO SELL HIS PHONY "MONSTER INSURANCE"? IT'S NOT THE WEALTHIEST PART OF THE CITY.
WE DO HAVE ONE MORE CLUE: THAT CROOK SAID THE MONSTERS WILL COME "MARCHING DOWN"...
MARCHING, TOMORROW, AND HIS NEIGHBORHOOD... WHEN YOU PUT THEM ALL TOGETHER, IT MUST MEAN...
RIGHT! LOOKS LIKE WE'VE GOT A DATE RIGHT BACK HERE TOMORROW MORNING!
"A DATE"? ARE YOU TWO DATING?
HUH? OH, UH, NO. NO.
IT'S JUST A FIGURE OF SPEECH.
WE'RE JUST, UM, GOOD FRIENDS.
MM. TOO BAD.
OPEN
I KNOW. THEY ALWAYS SEEM LIKE THEY SHOULD BE DATING.
WELL, YOU TWO WOULD KNOW ALL ABOUT THAT KIND OF THING, WOULDN'T YOU?
OPEN
WHO, DAPHNE AND ME? WHAT DO YOU MEAN?
SIGH
NEVER MIND. LET'S GET READY--

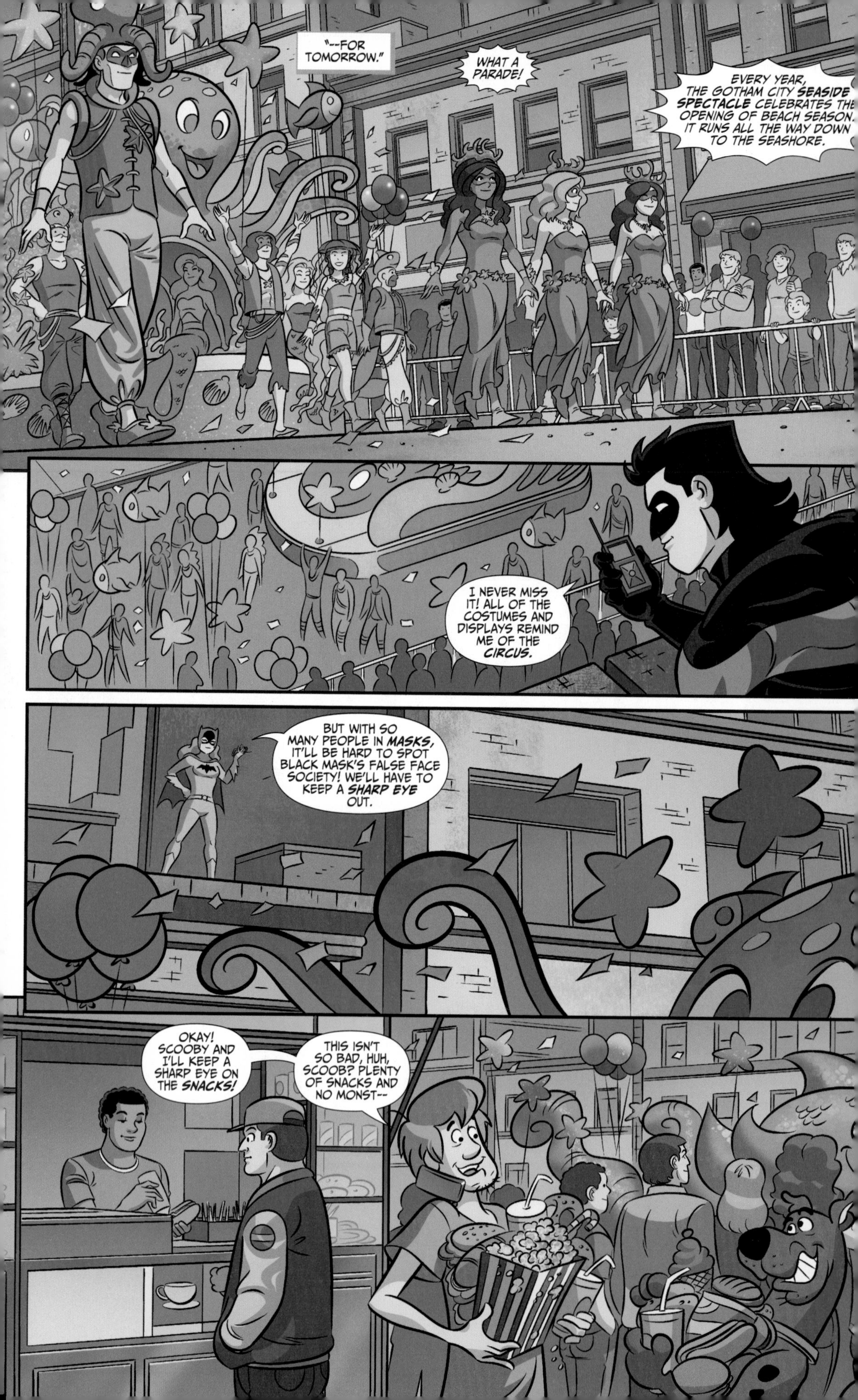
"--FOR TOMORROW."
WHAT A PARADE!
EVERY YEAR, THE GOTHAM CITY SEASIDE SPECTACLE CELEBRATES THE OPENING OF BEACH SEASON. IT RUNS ALL THE WAY DOWN TO THE SEASHORE.
I NEVER MISS IT! ALL OF THE COSTUMES AND DISPLAYS REMIND ME OF THE CIRCUS.
BUT WITH SO MANY PEOPLE IN MASKS, IT'LL BE HARD TO SPOT BLACK MASK'S FALSE FACE SOCIETY! WE'LL HAVE TO KEEP A SHARP EYE OUT.
OKAY! SCOOBY AND I'LL KEEP A SHARP EYE ON THE SNACKS!
THIS ISN'T SO BAD, HUH, SCOOB? PLENTY OF SNACKS AND NO MONST--

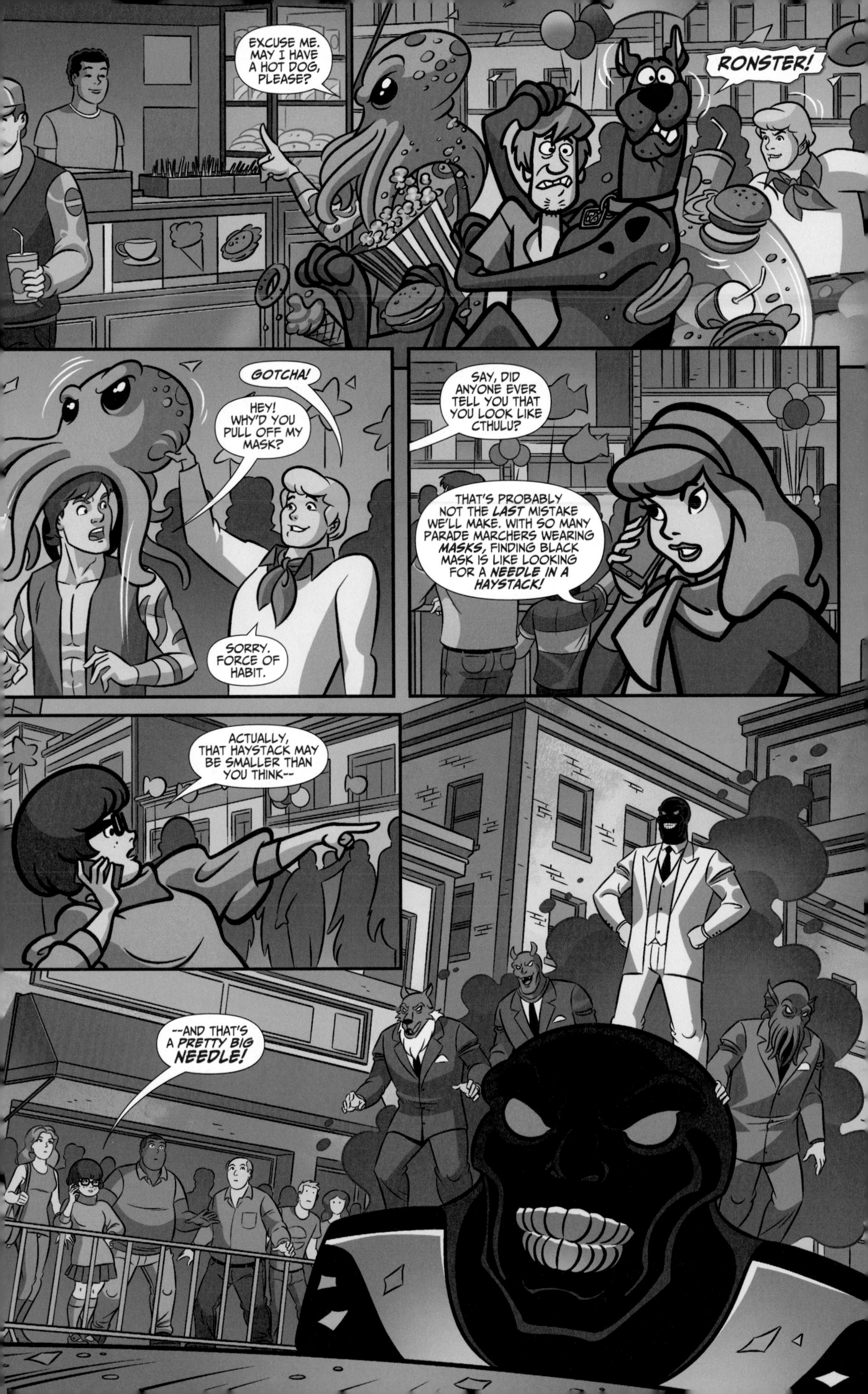
EXCUSE ME. MAY I HAVE A HOT DOG, PLEASE?
RONSTER!
GOTCHA!
HEY! WHY'D YOU PULL OFF MY MASK?
SORRY. FORCE OF HABIT.
SAY, DID ANYONE EVER TELL YOU THAT YOU LOOK LIKE CTHULU?
THAT'S PROBABLY NOT THE LAST MISTAKE WE'LL MAKE. WITH SO MANY PARADE MARCHERS WEARING MASKS, FINDING BLACK MASK IS LIKE LOOKING FOR A NEEDLE IN A HAYSTACK!
ACTUALLY, THAT HAYSTACK MAY BE SMALLER THAN YOU THINK--
--AND THAT'S A PRETTY BIG NEEDLE!

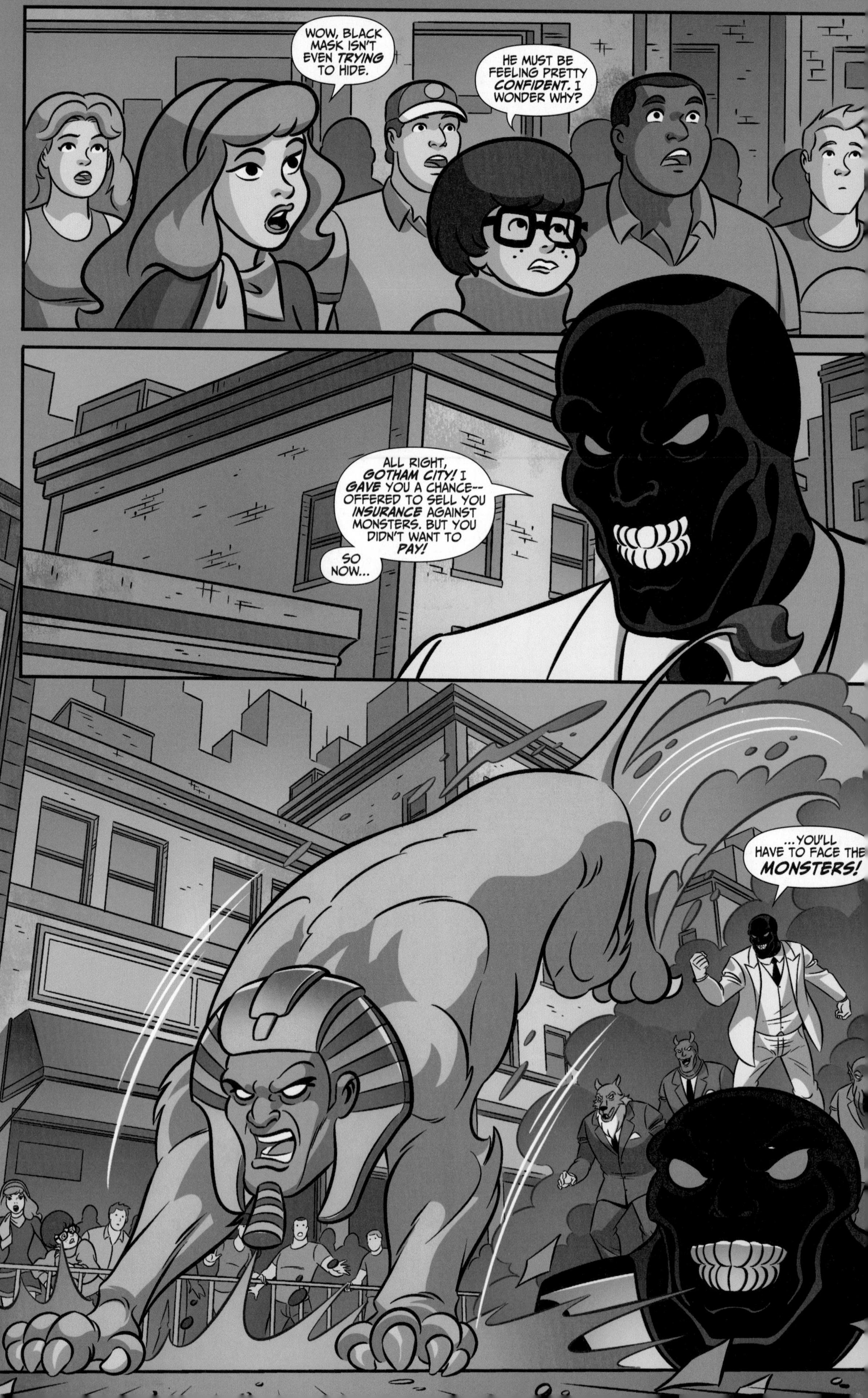
WOW, BLACK MASK ISN'T EVEN TRYING TO HIDE.
HE MUST BE FEELING PRETTY CONFIDENT. I WONDER WHY?
ALL RIGHT, GOTHAM CITY! I GAVE YOU A CHANCE-- OFFERED TO SELL YOU INSURANCE AGAINST MONSTERS. BUT YOU DIDN'T WANT TO PAY!
SO NOW...
...YOU'LL HAVE TO FACE THE MONSTERS!

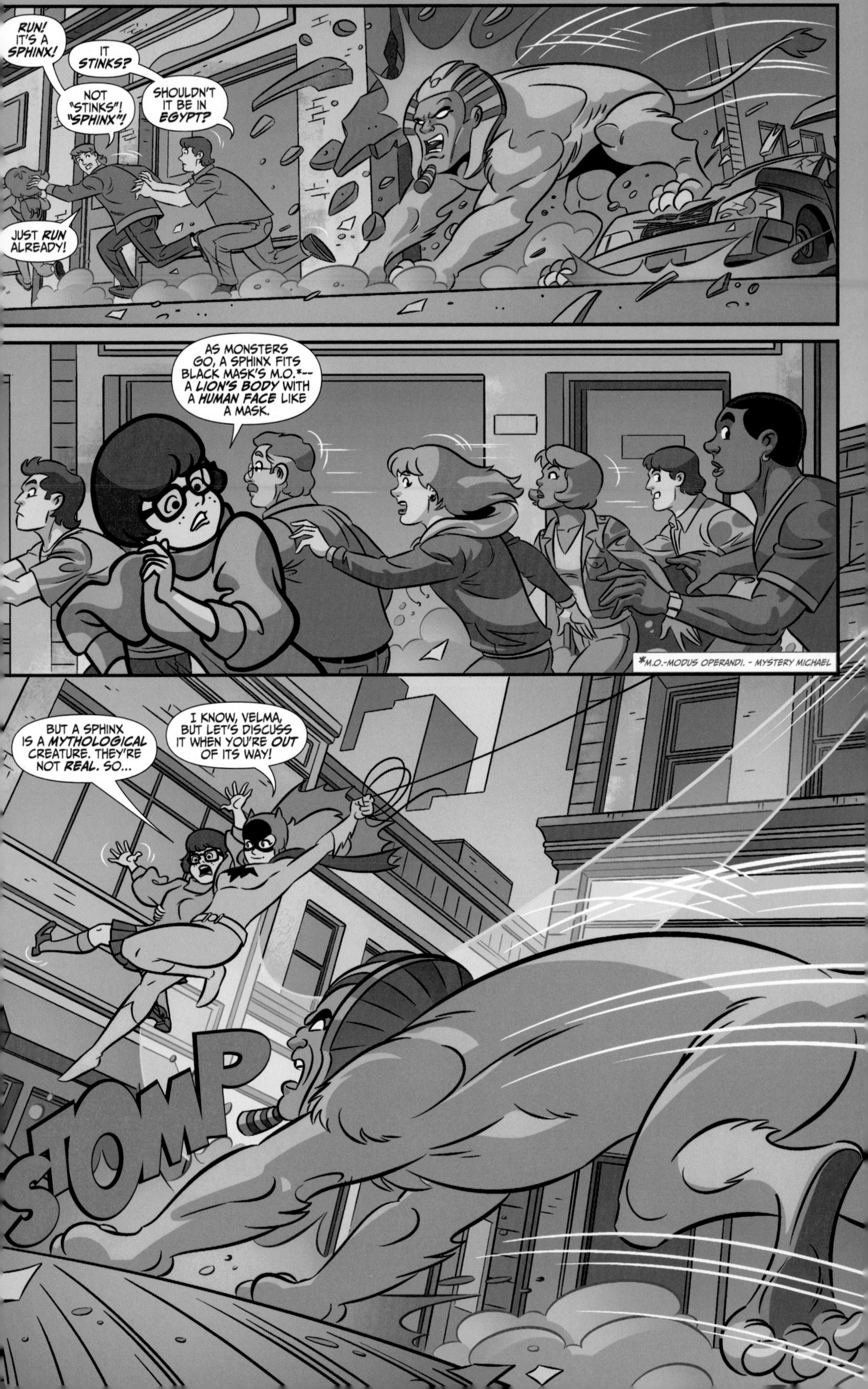
RUN! IT'S A SPHINX!
IT STINKS?
NOT "STINKS"! "SPHINX"!
SHOULDN'T IT BE IN EGYPT?
JUST RUN ALREADY!
AS MONSTERS GO, A SPHINX FITS BLACK MASK'S M.O.*-- A LION'S BODY WITH A HUMAN FACE LIKE A MASK.
*M.O.-MODUS OPERANDI. - MYSTERY MICHAEL
BUT A SPHINX IS A MYTHOLOGICAL CREATURE. THEY'RE NOT REAL. SO...
I KNOW, VELMA, BUT LET'S DISCUSS IT WHEN YOU'RE OUT OF ITS WAY!
STOMP

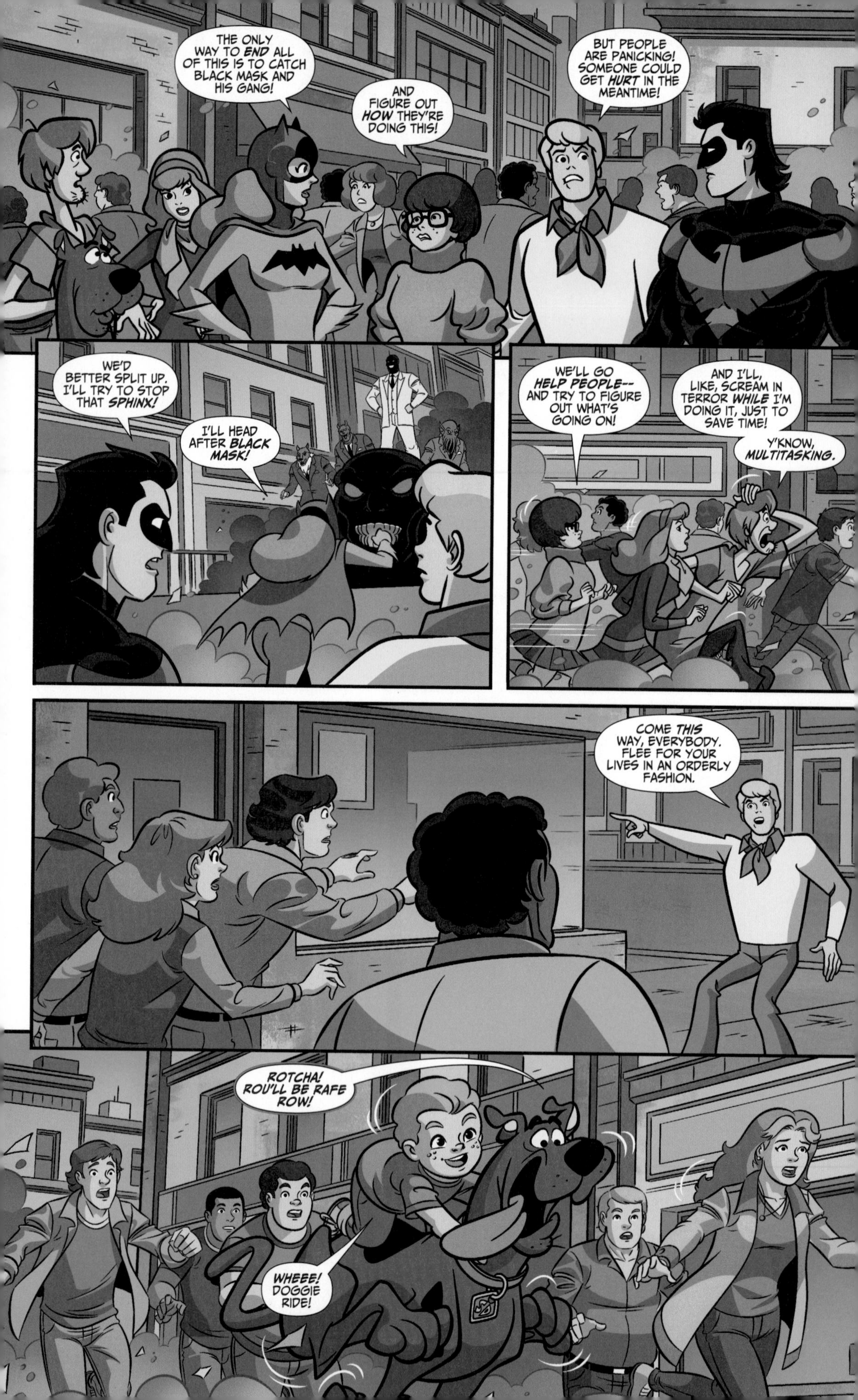
THE ONLY WAY TO END ALL OF THIS IS TO CATCH BLACK MASK AND HIS GANG!
AND FIGURE OUT HOW THEY'RE DOING THIS!
BUT PEOPLE ARE PANICKING! SOMEONE COULD GET HURT IN THE MEANTIME!
WE'D BETTER SPLIT UP. I'LL TRY TO STOP THAT SPHINX!
I'LL HEAD AFTER BLACK MASK!
WE'LL GO HELP PEOPLE-- AND TRY TO FIGURE OUT WHAT'S GOING ON!
AND I'LL, LIKE, SCREAM IN TERROR WHILE I'M DOING IT, JUST TO SAVE TIME!
Y'KNOW, MULTITASKING.
COME THIS WAY, EVERYBODY. FLEE FOR YOUR LIVES IN AN ORDERLY FASHION.
ROTCHA! ROU'LL BE RAFE ROW!
WHEEE! DOGGIE RIDE!

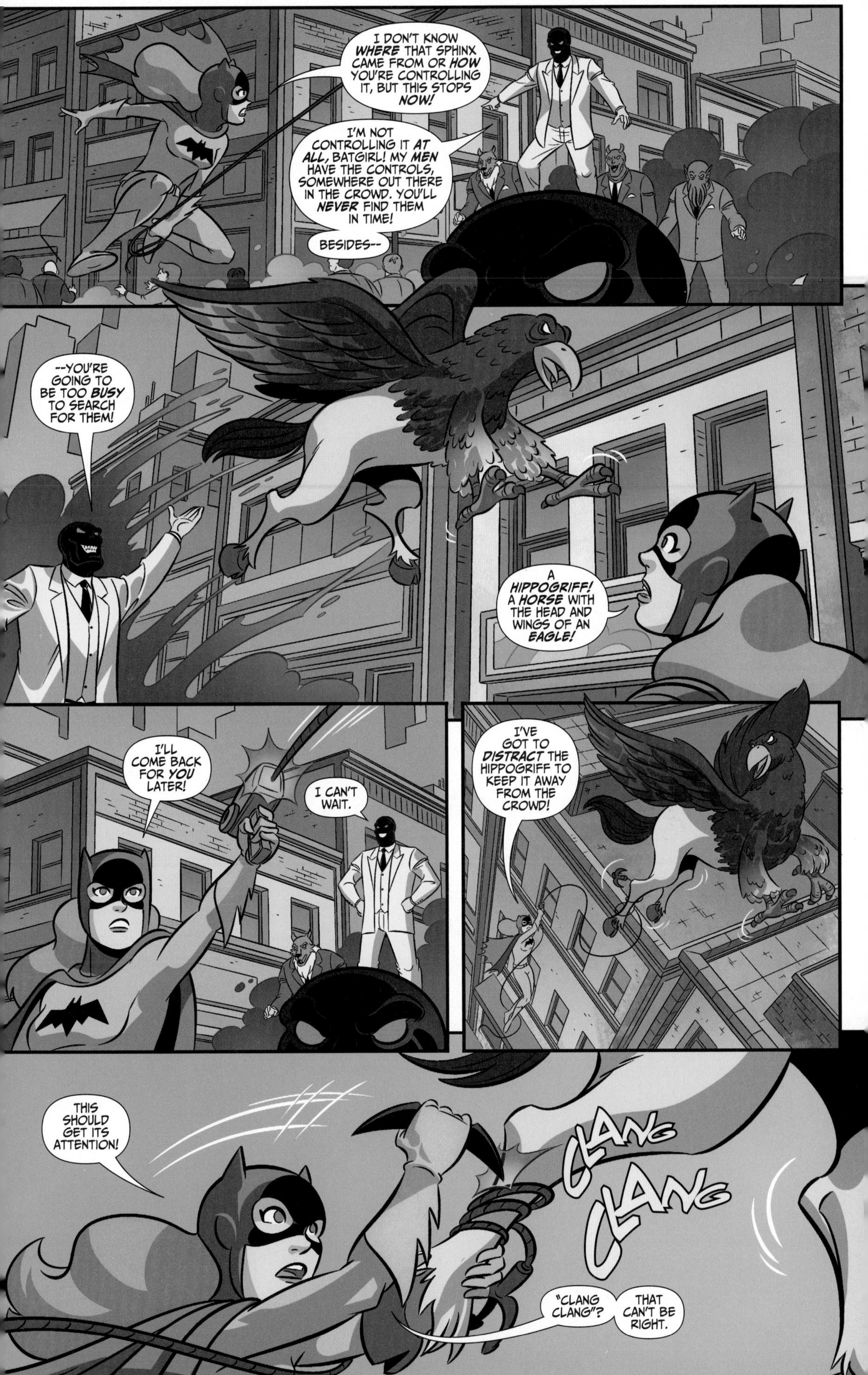
I DON'T KNOW WHERE THAT SPHINX CAME FROM OR HOW YOU'RE CONTROLLING IT, BUT THIS STOPS NOW!
I'M NOT CONTROLLING IT AT ALL, BATGIRL! MY MEN HAVE THE CONTROLS, SOMEWHERE OUT THERE IN THE CROWD. YOU'LL NEVER FIND THEM IN TIME!
BESIDES--
--YOU'RE GOING TO BE TOO BUSY TO SEARCH FOR THEM!
A HIPPOGRIFF! A HORSE WITH THE HEAD AND WINGS OF AN EAGLE!
I'LL COME BACK FOR YOU LATER!
I CAN'T WAIT.
I'VE GOT TO DISTRACT THE HIPPOGRIFF TO KEEP IT AWAY FROM THE CROWD!
THIS SHOULD GET ITS ATTENTION!
CLANG
CLANG
"CLANG CLANG"?
THAT CAN'T BE RIGHT.

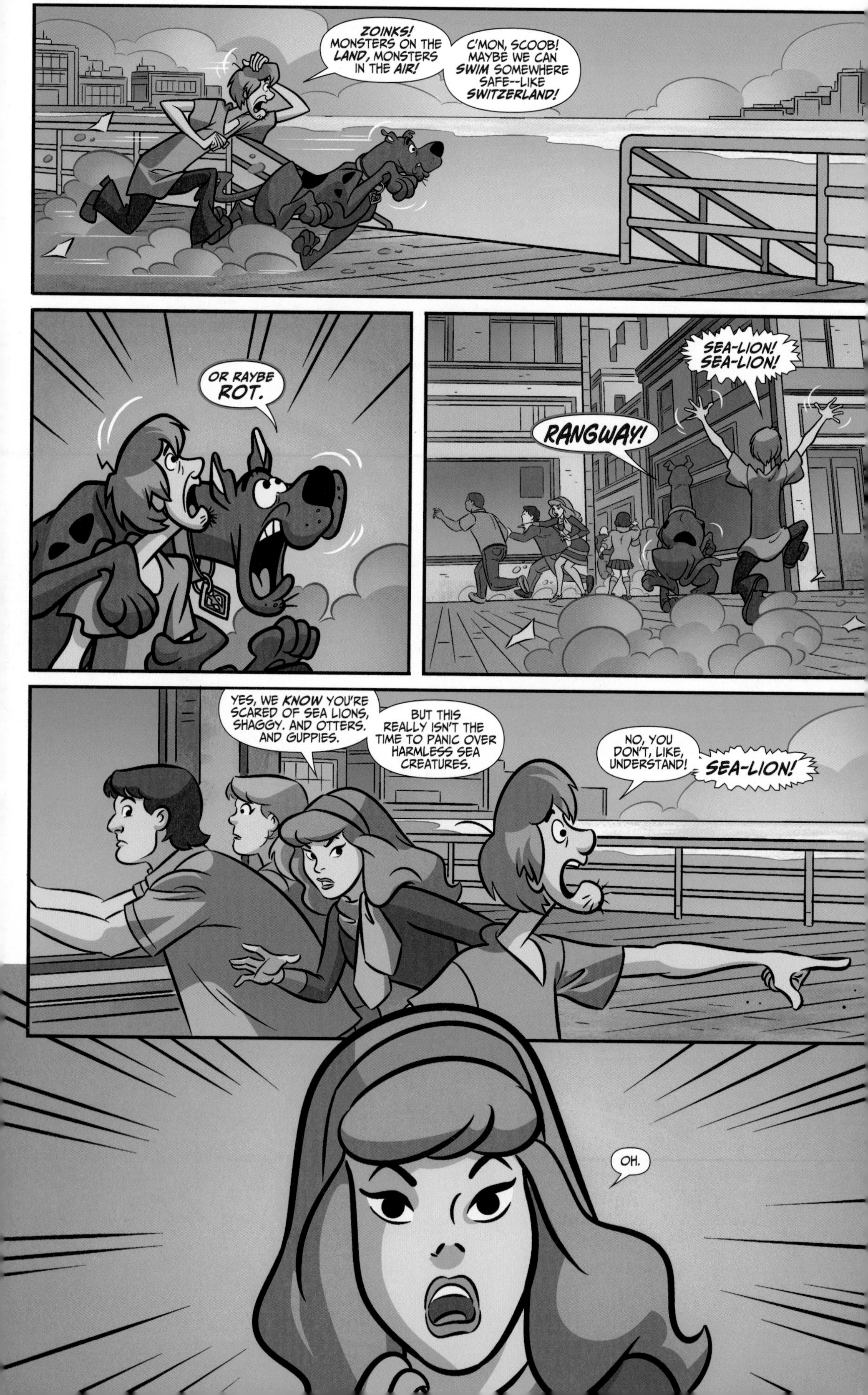
ZOINKS! MONSTERS ON THE LAND, MONSTERS IN THE AIR!
C'MON, SCOOB! MAYBE WE CAN SWIM SOMEWHERE SAFE--LIKE SWITZERLAND!
OR RAYBE ROT.
SEA-LION! SEA-LION!
RANGWAY!
YES, WE KNOW YOU'RE SCARED OF SEA LIONS, SHAGGY. AND OTTERS. AND GUPPIES.
BUT THIS REALLY ISN'T THE TIME TO PANIC OVER HARMLESS SEA CREATURES.
NO, YOU DON'T, LIKE, UNDERSTAND!
SEA-LION!
OH.

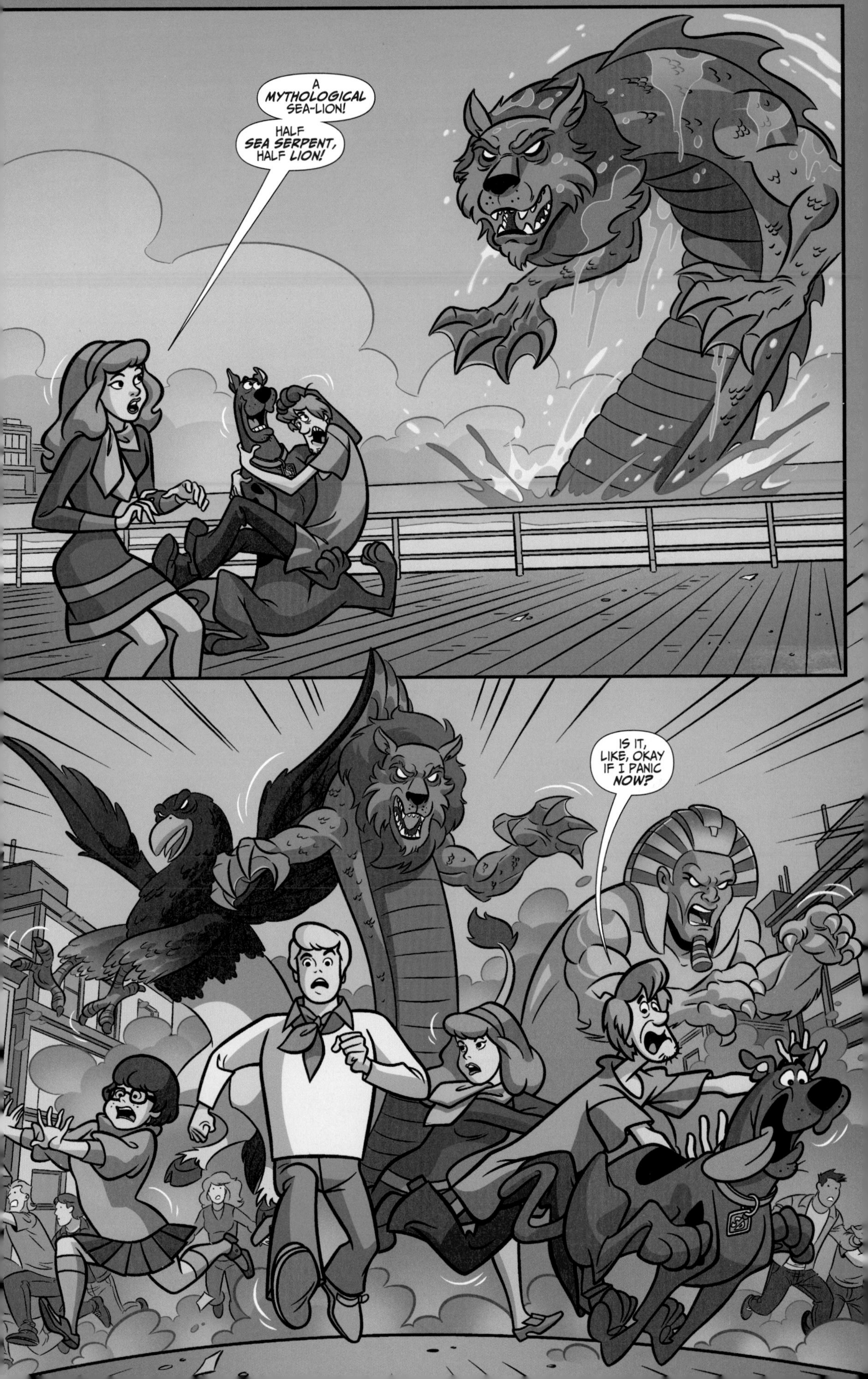
A *MYTHOLOGICAL* SEA-LION!
HALF *SEA SERPENT,* HALF *LION!*
IS IT, LIKE, OKAY IF I PANIC *NOW?*

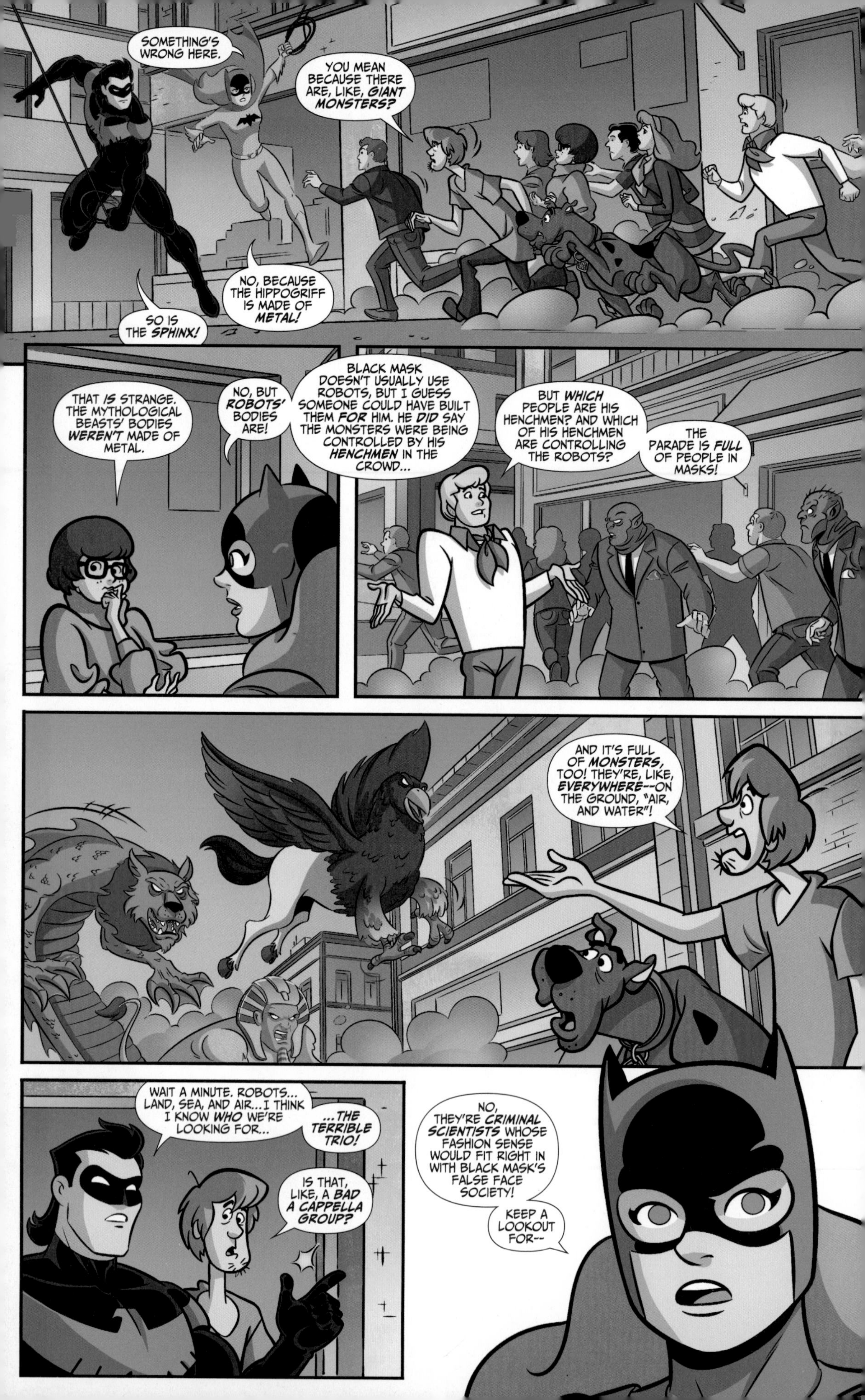
SOMETHING'S WRONG HERE.
YOU MEAN BECAUSE THERE ARE, LIKE, GIANT MONSTERS?
NO, BECAUSE THE HIPPOGRIFF IS MADE OF METAL!
SO IS THE SPHINX!
THAT IS STRANGE. THE MYTHOLOGICAL BEASTS' BODIES WEREN'T MADE OF METAL.
NO, BUT ROBOTS' BODIES ARE!
BLACK MASK DOESN'T USUALLY USE ROBOTS, BUT I GUESS SOMEONE COULD HAVE BUILT THEM FOR HIM. HE DID SAY THE MONSTERS WERE BEING CONTROLLED BY HIS HENCHMEN IN THE CROWD...
BUT WHICH PEOPLE ARE HIS HENCHMEN? AND WHICH OF HIS HENCHMEN ARE CONTROLLING THE ROBOTS?
THE PARADE IS FULL OF PEOPLE IN MASKS!
AND IT'S FULL OF MONSTERS, TOO! THEY'RE, LIKE, EVERYWHERE--ON THE GROUND, "AIR, AND WATER"!
WAIT A MINUTE. ROBOTS... LAND, SEA, AND AIR... I THINK I KNOW WHO WE'RE LOOKING FOR...
...THE TERRIBLE TRIO!
IS THAT, LIKE, A BAD A CAPPELLA GROUP?
NO, THEY'RE CRIMINAL SCIENTISTS WHOSE FASHION SENSE WOULD FIT RIGHT IN WITH BLACK MASK'S FALSE FACE SOCIETY!
KEEP A LOOKOUT FOR--

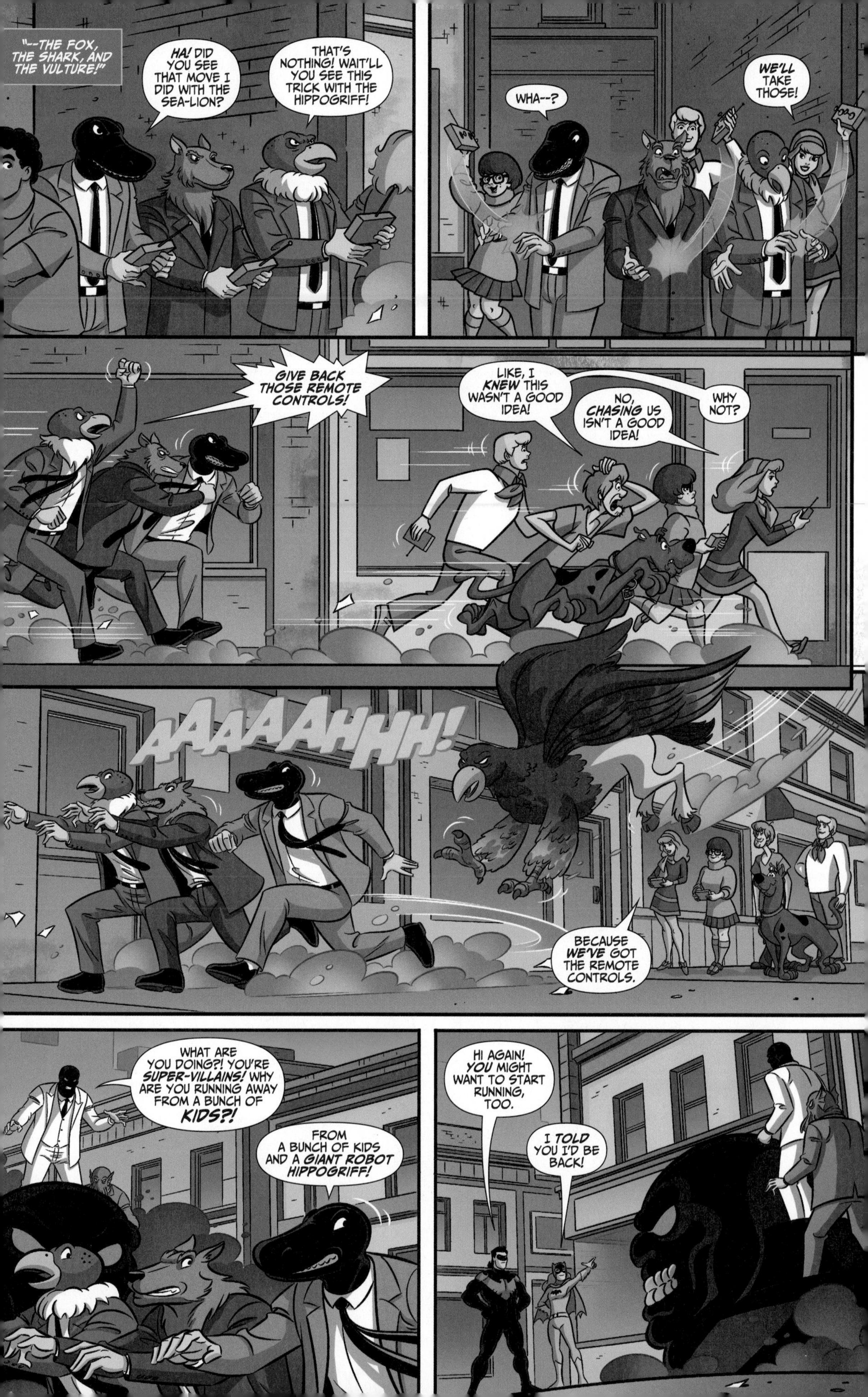
"--THE FOX, THE SHARK, AND THE VULTURE!"
HA! DID YOU SEE THAT MOVE I DID WITH THE SEA-LION?
THAT'S NOTHING! WAIT'LL YOU SEE THIS TRICK WITH THE HIPPOGRIFF!
WHA--?
WE'LL TAKE THOSE!
GIVE BACK THOSE REMOTE CONTROLS!
LIKE, I KNEW THIS WASN'T A GOOD IDEA!
NO, CHASING US ISN'T A GOOD IDEA!
WHY NOT?
AAAAAHHH!
BECAUSE WE'VE GOT THE REMOTE CONTROLS.
WHAT ARE YOU DOING?! YOU'RE SUPER-VILLAINS! WHY ARE YOU RUNNING AWAY FROM A BUNCH OF KIDS?!
FROM A BUNCH OF KIDS AND A GIANT ROBOT HIPPOGRIFF!
HI AGAIN! YOU MIGHT WANT TO START RUNNING, TOO.
I TOLD YOU I'D BE BACK!

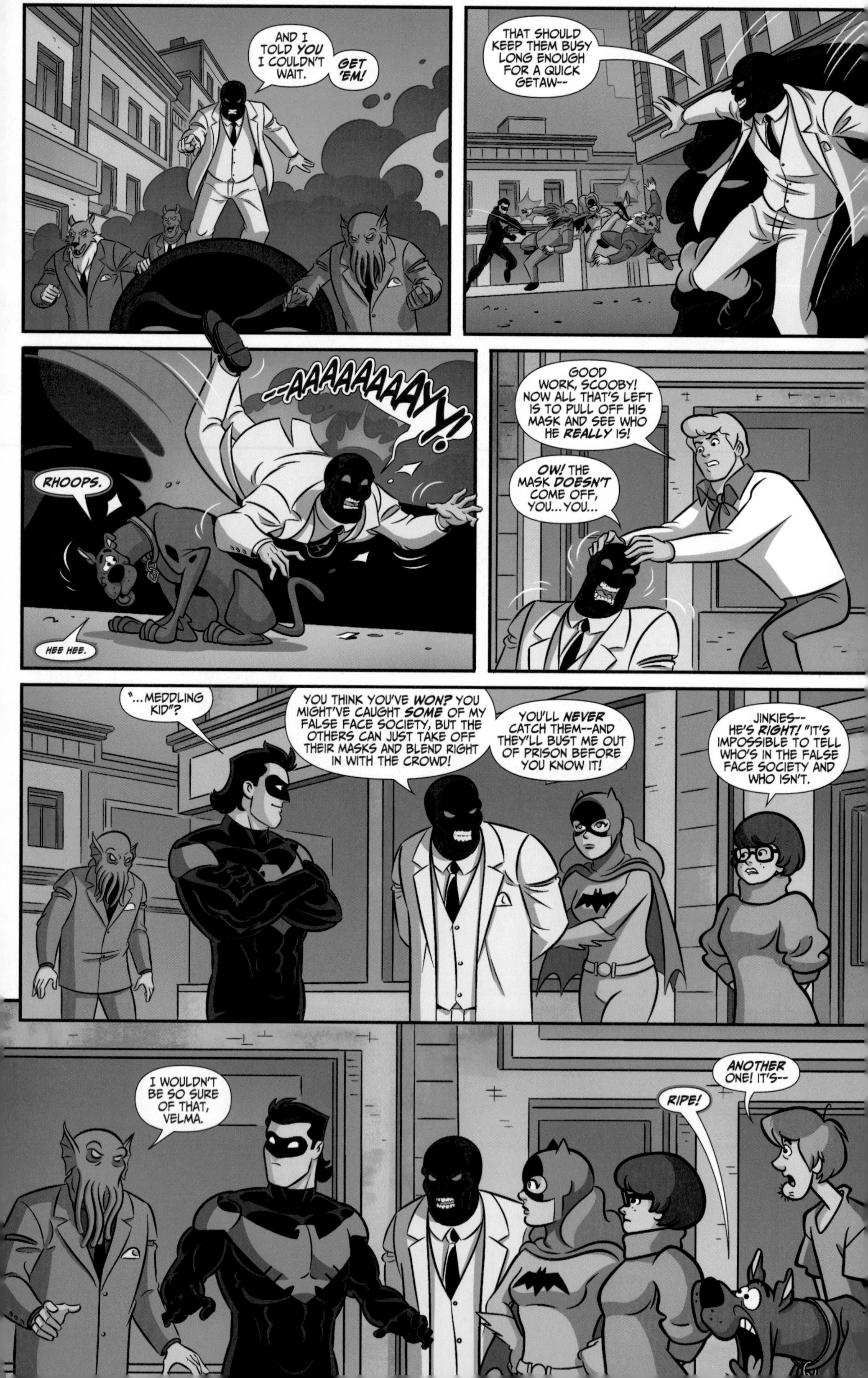
AND I TOLD *YOU* I COULDN'T WAIT.
GET 'EM!
THAT SHOULD KEEP THEM BUSY LONG ENOUGH FOR A QUICK GETAW--
--AAAAAAAAY!!
RHOOPS.
HEE HEE.
GOOD WORK, SCOOBY! NOW ALL THAT'S LEFT IS TO PULL OFF HIS MASK AND SEE WHO HE *REALLY* IS!
OW! THE MASK *DOESN'T* COME OFF, YOU...YOU...
"...MEDDLING KID"?
YOU THINK YOU'VE *WON?* YOU MIGHT'VE CAUGHT *SOME* OF MY FALSE FACE SOCIETY, BUT THE OTHERS CAN JUST TAKE OFF THEIR MASKS AND BLEND RIGHT IN WITH THE CROWD!
YOU'LL *NEVER* CATCH THEM--AND THEY'LL BUST ME OUT OF PRISON BEFORE YOU KNOW IT!
JINKIES-- HE'S *RIGHT!* "IT'S IMPOSSIBLE TO TELL WHO'S IN THE FALSE FACE SOCIETY AND WHO ISN'T.
I WOULDN'T BE SO SURE OF THAT, VELMA.
ANOTHER ONE! IT'S--
RIPE!

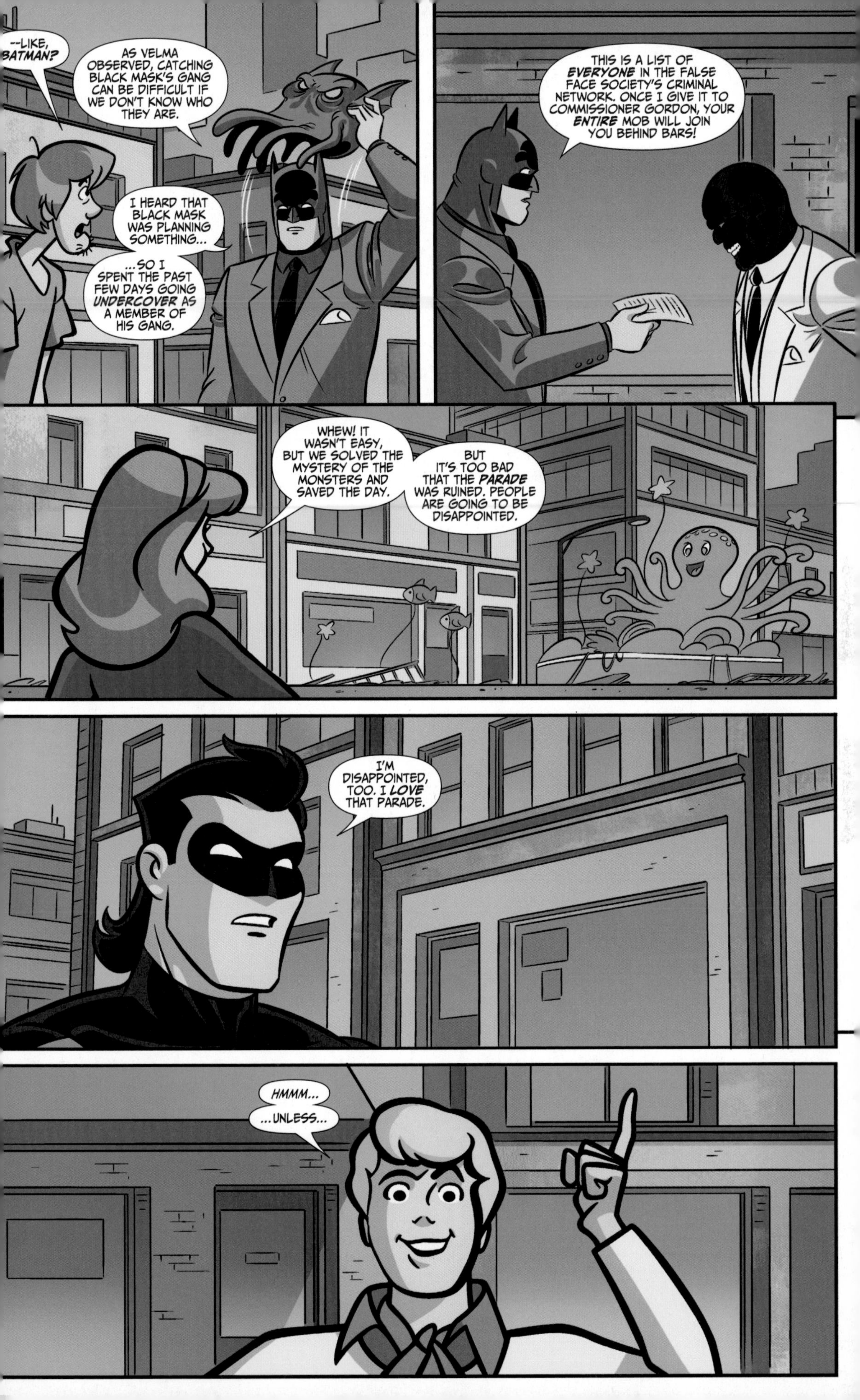
--LIKE, BATMAN?
AS VELMA OBSERVED, CATCHING BLACK MASK'S GANG CAN BE DIFFICULT IF WE DON'T KNOW WHO THEY ARE.
I HEARD THAT BLACK MASK WAS PLANNING SOMETHING...
...SO I SPENT THE PAST FEW DAYS GOING UNDERCOVER AS A MEMBER OF HIS GANG.
THIS IS A LIST OF EVERYONE IN THE FALSE FACE SOCIETY'S CRIMINAL NETWORK. ONCE I GIVE IT TO COMMISSIONER GORDON, YOUR ENTIRE MOB WILL JOIN YOU BEHIND BARS!
WHEW! IT WASN'T EASY, BUT WE SOLVED THE MYSTERY OF THE MONSTERS AND SAVED THE DAY.
BUT IT'S TOO BAD THAT THE PARADE WAS RUINED. PEOPLE ARE GOING TO BE DISAPPOINTED.
I'M DISAPPOINTED, TOO. I LOVE THAT PARADE.
HMMM...
...UNLESS...

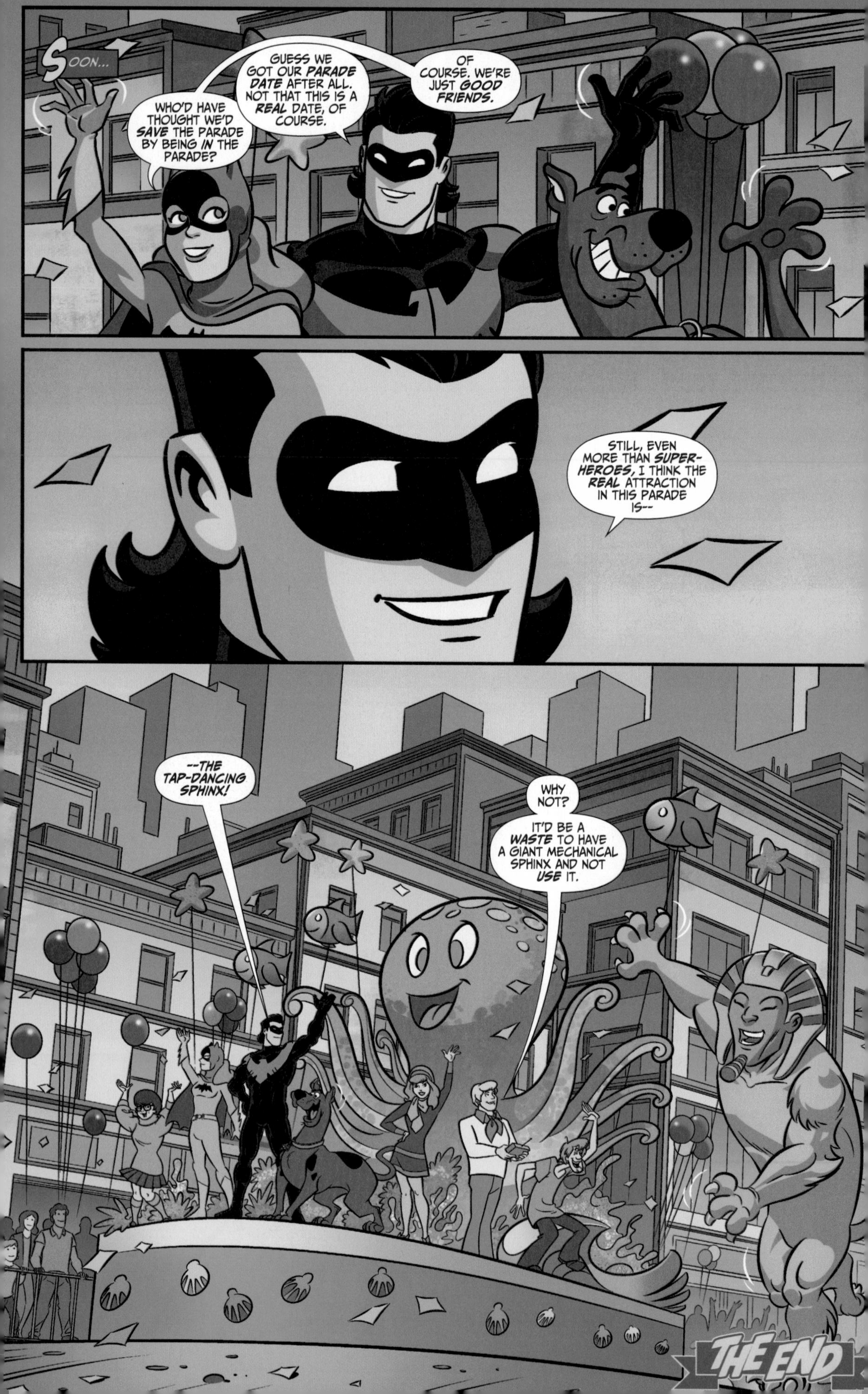
SOON...
WHO'D HAVE THOUGHT WE'D SAVE THE PARADE BY BEING IN THE PARADE?
GUESS WE GOT OUR PARADE DATE AFTER ALL. NOT THAT THIS IS A REAL DATE, OF COURSE.
OF COURSE. WE'RE JUST GOOD FRIENDS.
STILL, EVEN MORE THAN SUPER-HEROES, I THINK THE REAL ATTRACTION IN THIS PARADE IS--
--THE TAP-DANCING SPHINX!
WHY NOT?
IT'D BE A WASTE TO HAVE A GIANT MECHANICAL SPHINX AND NOT USE IT.
THE END

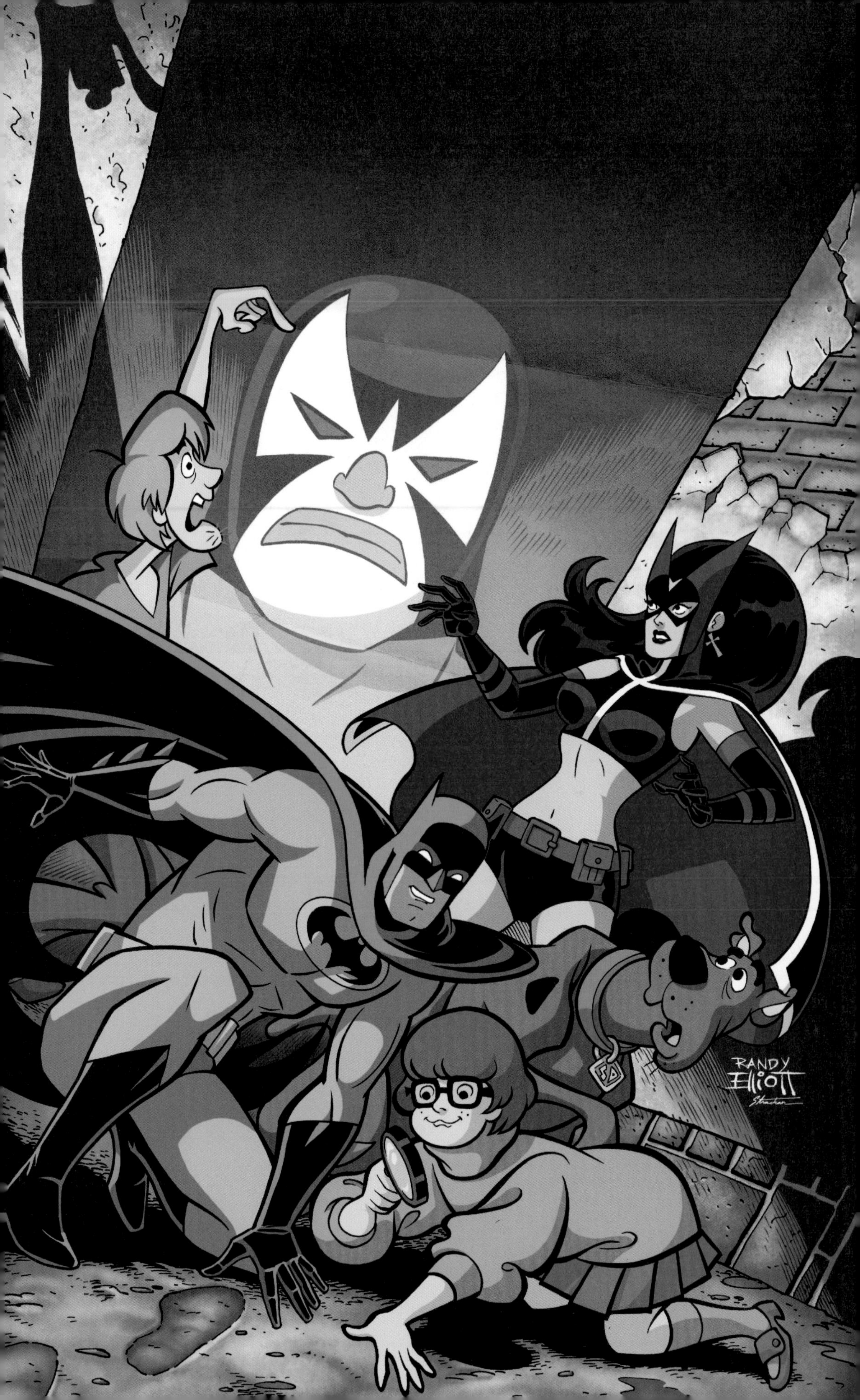
RANDY ELLIOTT

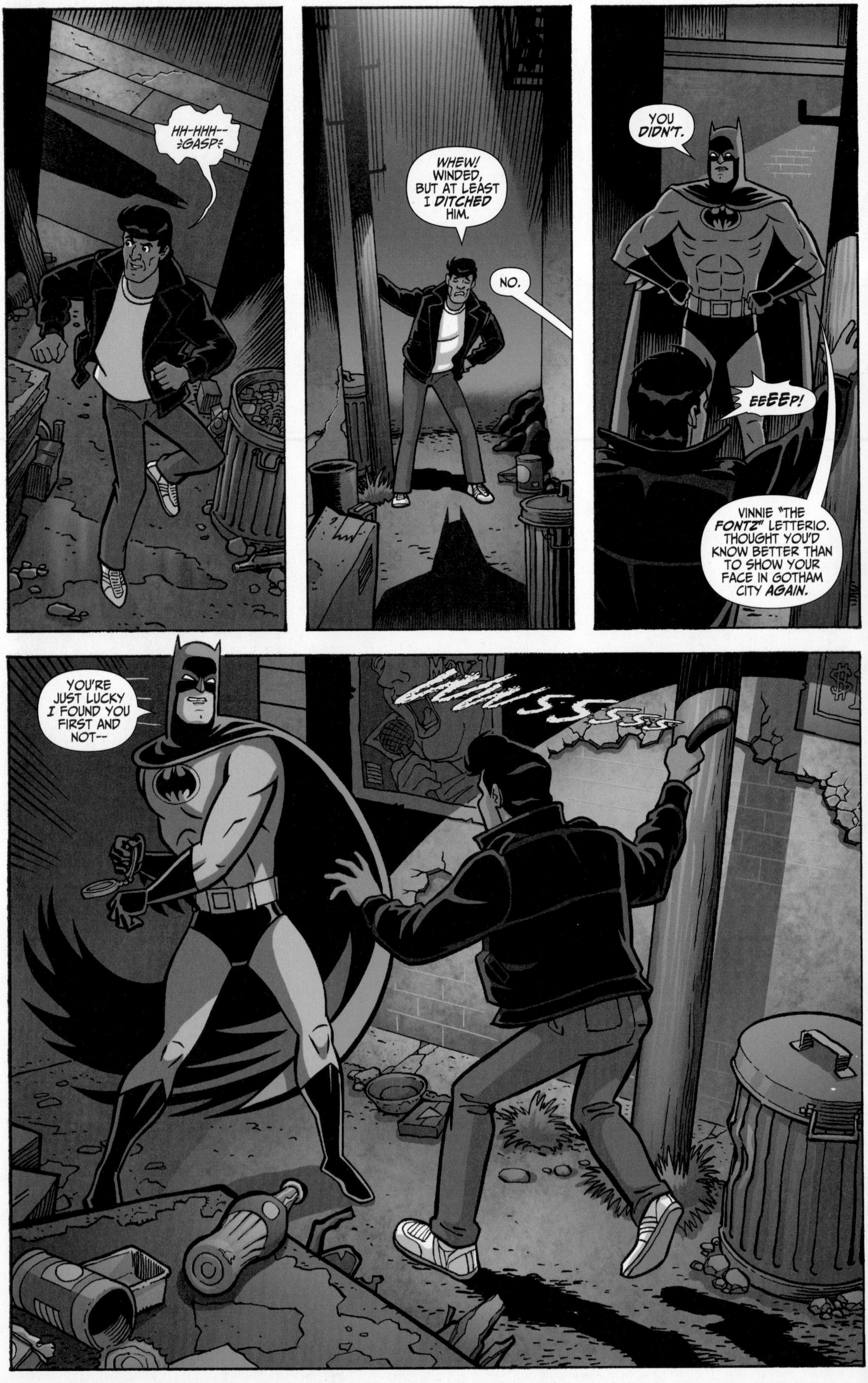
HH-HHH-- *GASP*
WHEW! WINDED, BUT AT LEAST I *DITCHED* HIM.
NO.
YOU *DIDN'T.*
EEEEP!
VINNIE "THE *FONTZ*" LETTERIO. THOUGHT YOU'D KNOW BETTER THAN TO SHOW YOUR FACE IN GOTHAM CITY *AGAIN.*
YOU'RE JUST LUCKY *I* FOUND YOU FIRST AND NOT--

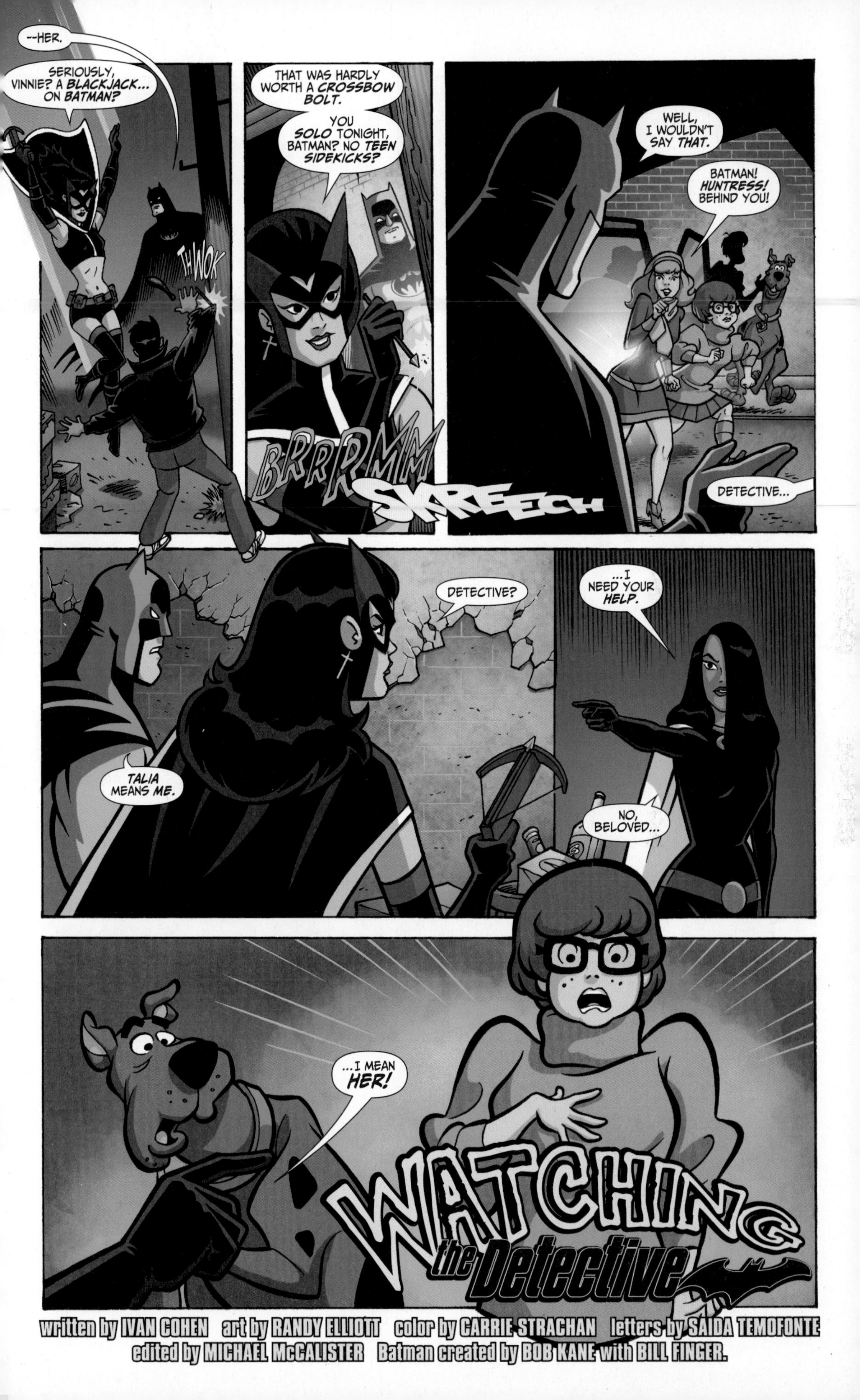
--HER.
SERIOUSLY, VINNIE? A BLACKJACK... ON BATMAN?
THWOK
THAT WAS HARDLY WORTH A CROSSBOW BOLT.
YOU SOLO TONIGHT, BATMAN? NO TEEN SIDEKICKS?
BRRRRMMM
SKREEECH
WELL, I WOULDN'T SAY THAT.
BATMAN! HUNTRESS! BEHIND YOU!
DETECTIVE...
DETECTIVE?
...I NEED YOUR HELP.
TALIA MEANS ME.
NO, BELOVED...
...I MEAN HER!
WATCHING the Detective
written by IVAN COHEN art by RANDY ELLIOTT color by CARRIE STRACHAN letters by SAIDA TEMOFONTE
edited by MICHAEL McCALISTER Batman created by BOB KANE with BILL FINGER.

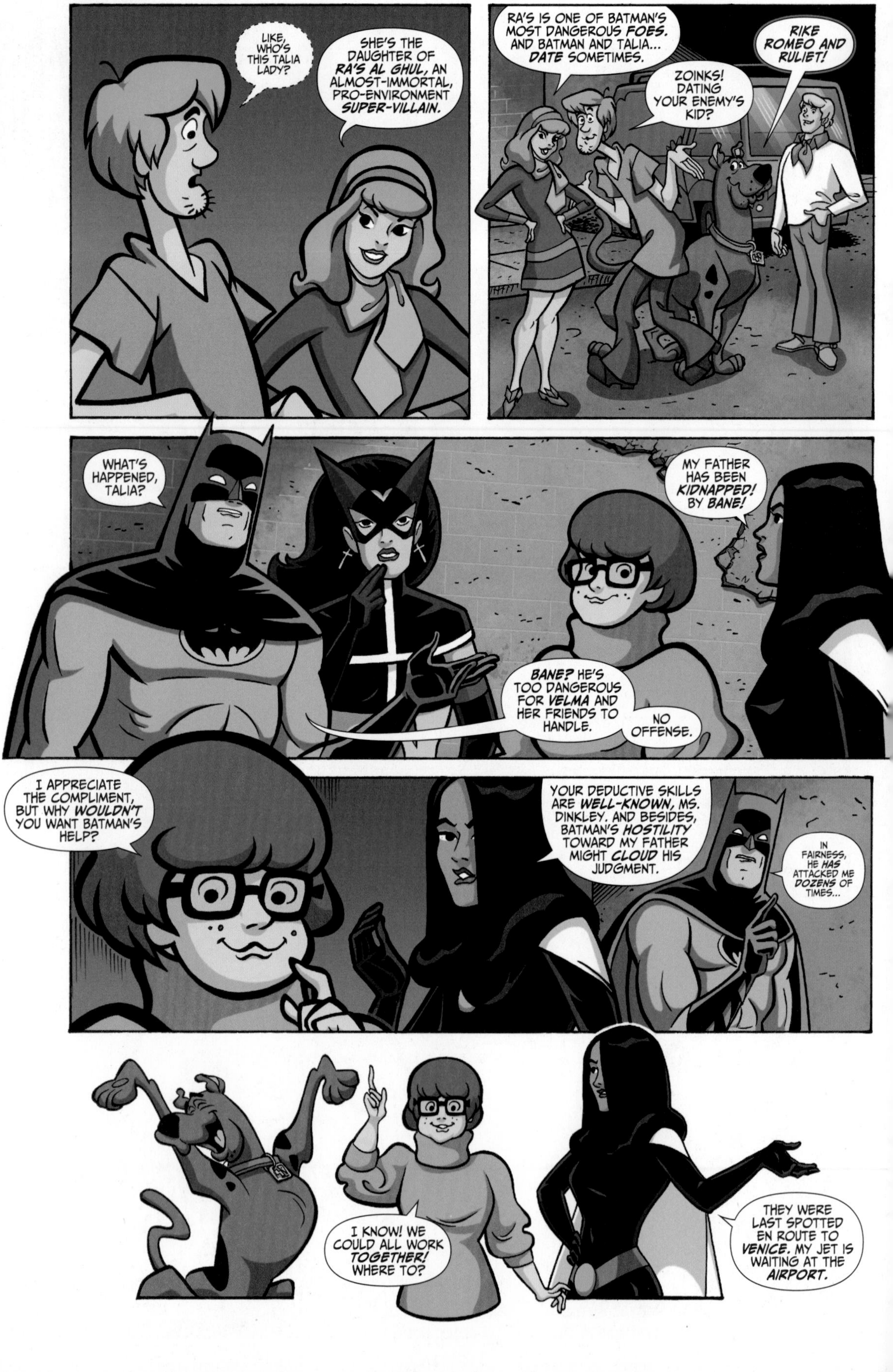
LIKE, WHO'S THIS TALIA LADY?
SHE'S THE DAUGHTER OF RA'S AL GHUL, AN ALMOST-IMMORTAL, PRO-ENVIRONMENT SUPER-VILLAIN.
RA'S IS ONE OF BATMAN'S MOST DANGEROUS FOES. AND BATMAN AND TALIA... DATE SOMETIMES.
ZOINKS! DATING YOUR ENEMY'S KID?
RIKE ROMEO AND RULIET!
WHAT'S HAPPENED, TALIA?
MY FATHER HAS BEEN KIDNAPPED! BY BANE!
BANE? HE'S TOO DANGEROUS FOR VELMA AND HER FRIENDS TO HANDLE.
NO OFFENSE.
I APPRECIATE THE COMPLIMENT, BUT WHY WOULDN'T YOU WANT BATMAN'S HELP?
YOUR DEDUCTIVE SKILLS ARE WELL-KNOWN, MS. DINKLEY. AND BESIDES, BATMAN'S HOSTILITY TOWARD MY FATHER MIGHT CLOUD HIS JUDGMENT.
IN FAIRNESS, HE HAS ATTACKED ME DOZENS OF TIMES...
I KNOW! WE COULD ALL WORK TOGETHER! WHERE TO?
THEY WERE LAST SPOTTED EN ROUTE TO VENICE. MY JET IS WAITING AT THE AIRPORT.

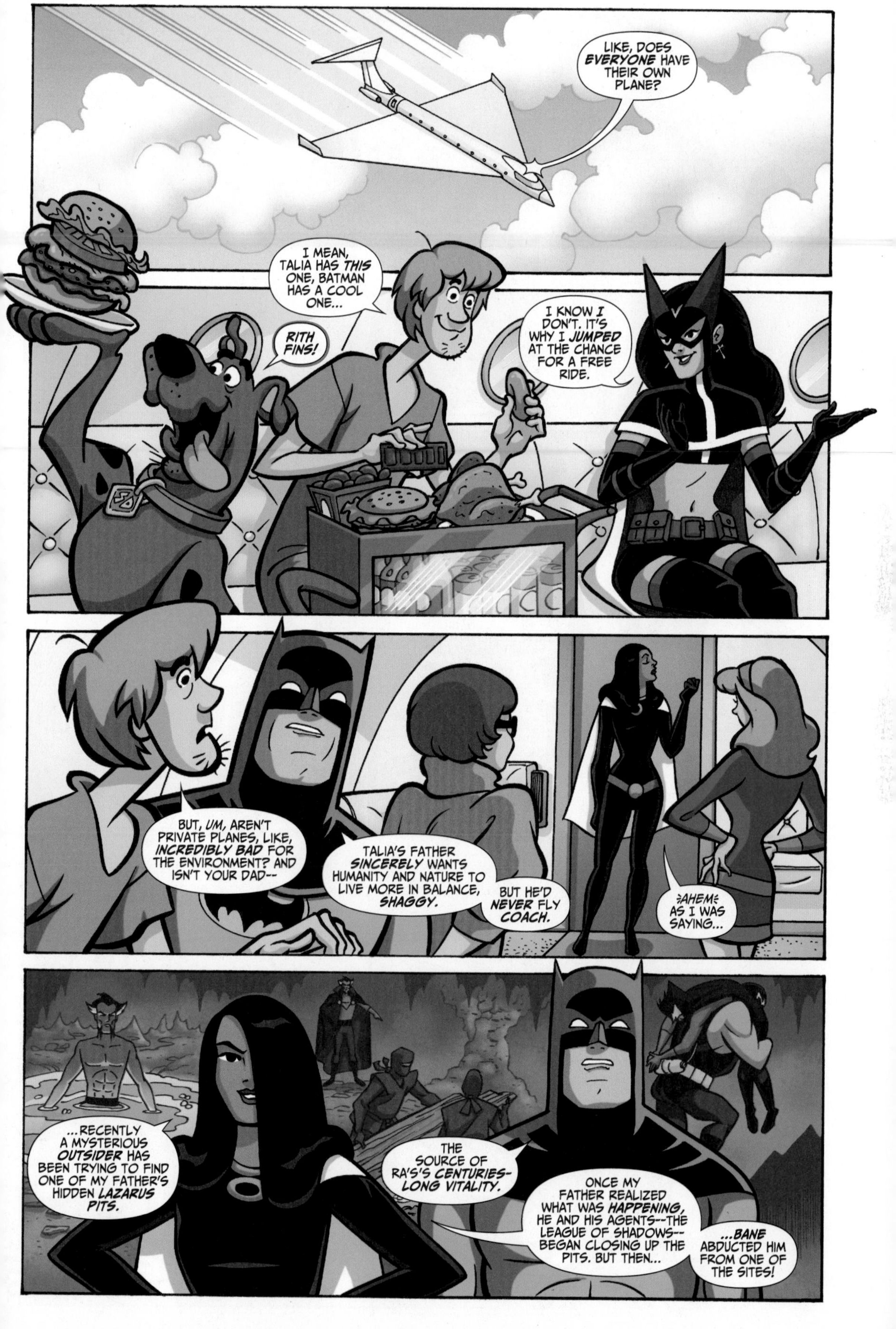
LIKE, DOES EVERYONE HAVE THEIR OWN PLANE?
I MEAN, TALIA HAS THIS ONE, BATMAN HAS A COOL ONE...
RITH FINS!
I KNOW I DON'T. IT'S WHY I JUMPED AT THE CHANCE FOR A FREE RIDE.
BUT, UM, AREN'T PRIVATE PLANES, LIKE, INCREDIBLY BAD FOR THE ENVIRONMENT? AND ISN'T YOUR DAD--
TALIA'S FATHER SINCERELY WANTS HUMANITY AND NATURE TO LIVE MORE IN BALANCE, SHAGGY.
BUT HE'D NEVER FLY COACH.
AHEM AS I WAS SAYING...
...RECENTLY A MYSTERIOUS OUTSIDER HAS BEEN TRYING TO FIND ONE OF MY FATHER'S HIDDEN LAZARUS PITS.
THE SOURCE OF RA'S'S CENTURIES-LONG VITALITY.
ONCE MY FATHER REALIZED WHAT WAS HAPPENING, HE AND HIS AGENTS--THE LEAGUE OF SHADOWS--BEGAN CLOSING UP THE PITS. BUT THEN...
...BANE ABDUCTED HIM FROM ONE OF THE SITES!

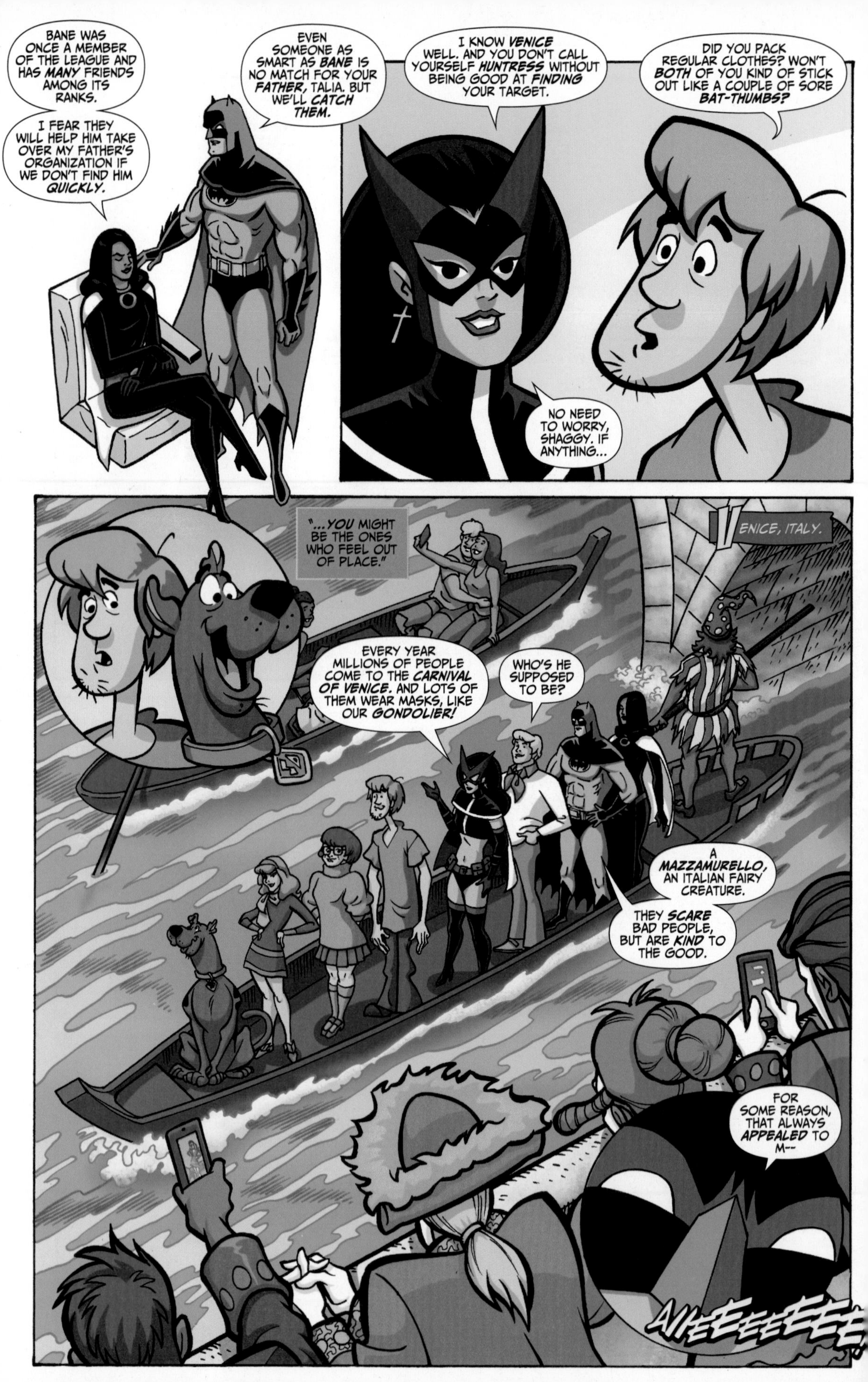
BANE WAS ONCE A MEMBER OF THE LEAGUE AND HAS MANY FRIENDS AMONG ITS RANKS.
I FEAR THEY WILL HELP HIM TAKE OVER MY FATHER'S ORGANIZATION IF WE DON'T FIND HIM QUICKLY.
EVEN SOMEONE AS SMART AS BANE IS NO MATCH FOR YOUR FATHER, TALIA. BUT WE'LL CATCH THEM.
I KNOW VENICE WELL. AND YOU DON'T CALL YOURSELF HUNTRESS WITHOUT BEING GOOD AT FINDING YOUR TARGET.
DID YOU PACK REGULAR CLOTHES? WON'T BOTH OF YOU KIND OF STICK OUT LIKE A COUPLE OF SORE BAT-THUMBS?
NO NEED TO WORRY, SHAGGY. IF ANYTHING...
"...YOU MIGHT BE THE ONES WHO FEEL OUT OF PLACE."
ENICE, ITALY.
EVERY YEAR MILLIONS OF PEOPLE COME TO THE CARNIVAL OF VENICE. AND LOTS OF THEM WEAR MASKS, LIKE OUR GONDOLIER!
WHO'S HE SUPPOSED TO BE?
A MAZZAMURELLO, AN ITALIAN FAIRY CREATURE.
THEY SCARE BAD PEOPLE, BUT ARE KIND TO THE GOOD.
FOR SOME REASON, THAT ALWAYS APPEALED TO M--
AIIEEEEEEEEE

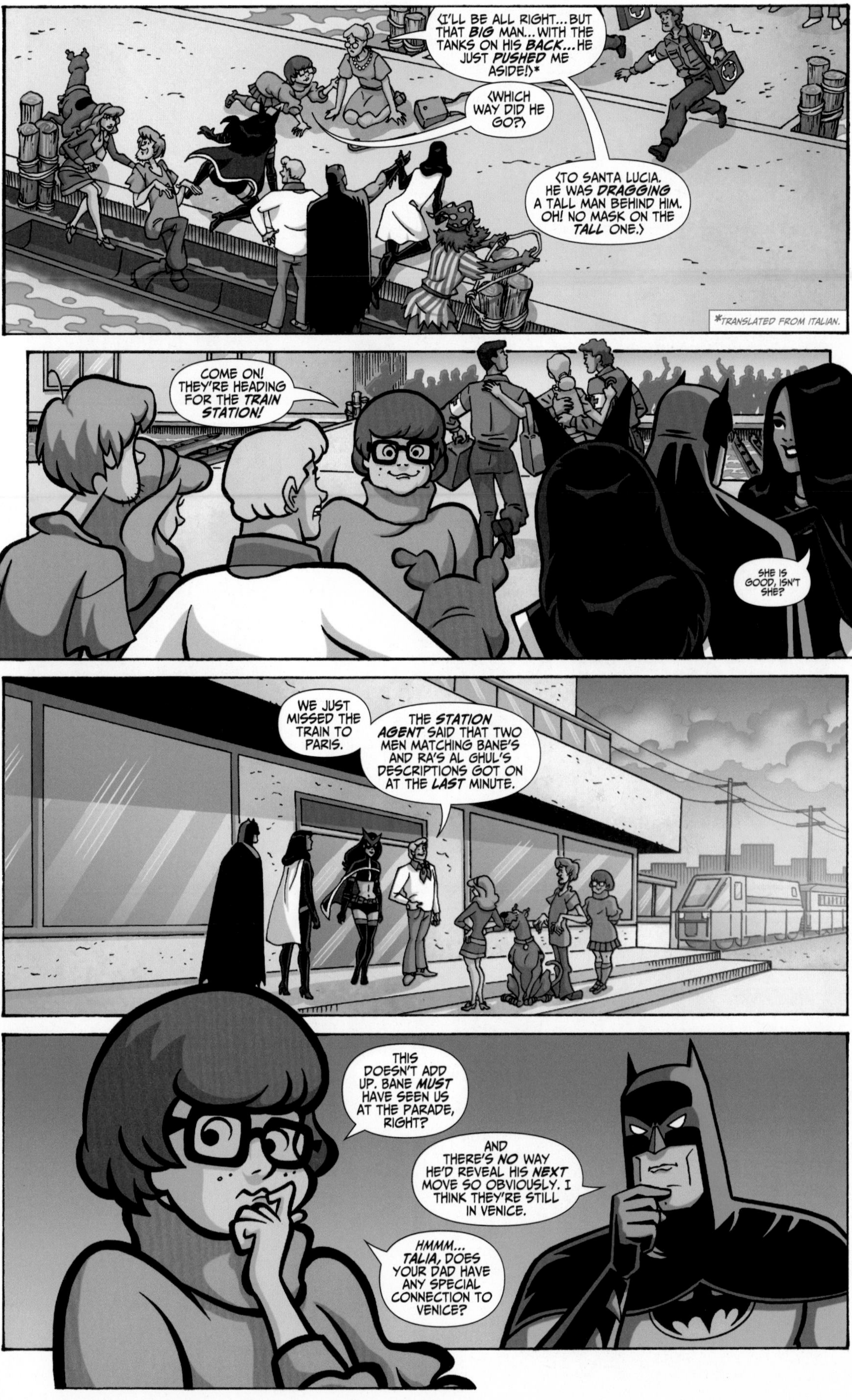
‹I'LL BE ALL RIGHT... BUT THAT BIG MAN... WITH THE TANKS ON HIS BACK... HE JUST PUSHED ME ASIDE!›*
‹WHICH WAY DID HE GO?›
‹TO SANTA LUCIA. HE WAS DRAGGING A TALL MAN BEHIND HIM. OH! NO MASK ON THE TALL ONE.›
*TRANSLATED FROM ITALIAN.
COME ON! THEY'RE HEADING FOR THE TRAIN STATION!
SHE IS GOOD, ISN'T SHE?
WE JUST MISSED THE TRAIN TO PARIS.
THE STATION AGENT SAID THAT TWO MEN MATCHING BANE'S AND RA'S AL GHUL'S DESCRIPTIONS GOT ON AT THE LAST MINUTE.
THIS DOESN'T ADD UP. BANE MUST HAVE SEEN US AT THE PARADE, RIGHT?
AND THERE'S NO WAY HE'D REVEAL HIS NEXT MOVE SO OBVIOUSLY. I THINK THEY'RE STILL IN VENICE.
HMMM... TALIA, DOES YOUR DAD HAVE ANY SPECIAL CONNECTION TO VENICE?

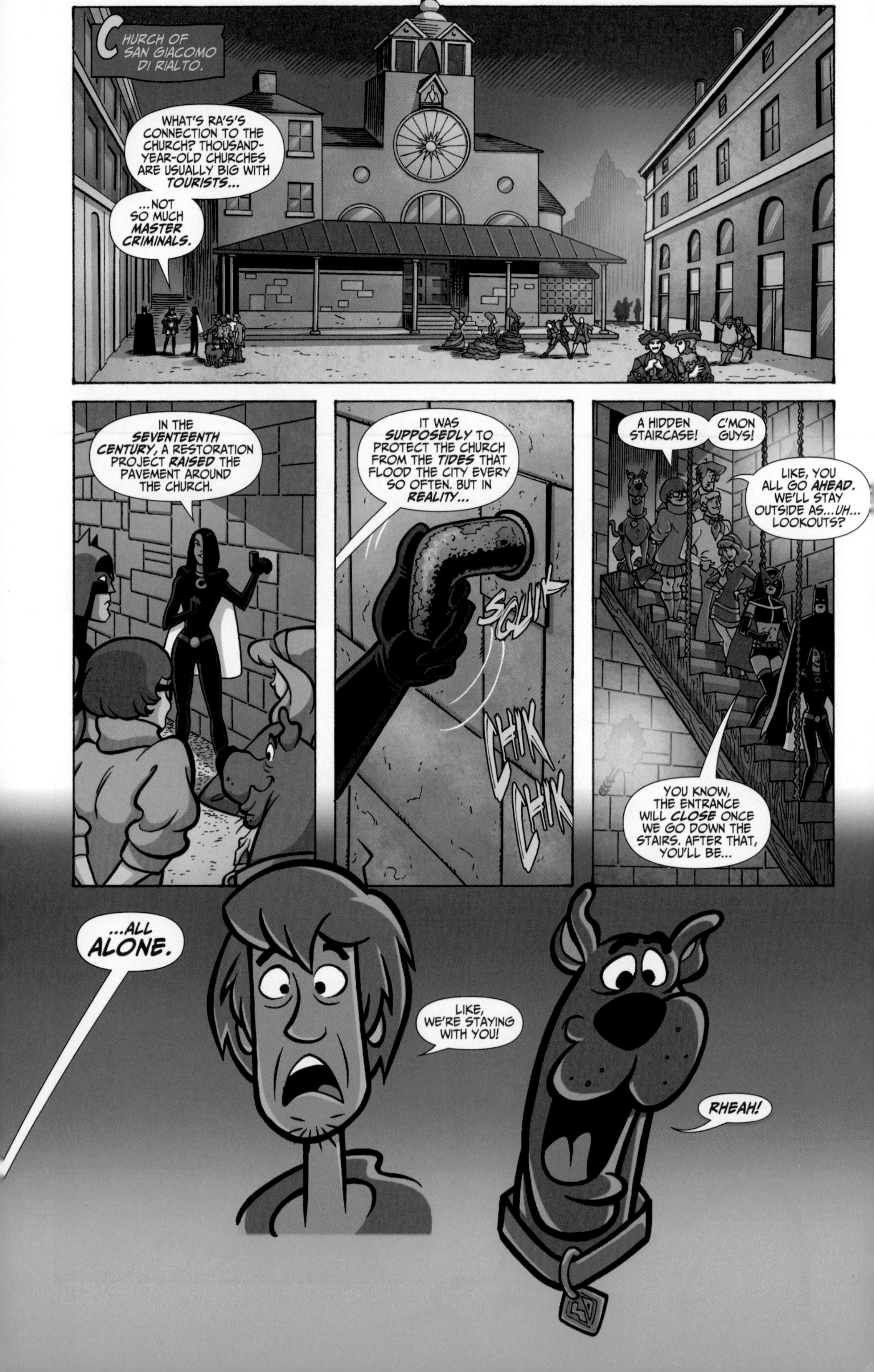
CHURCH OF SAN GIACOMO DI RIALTO.
WHAT'S RA'S'S CONNECTION TO THE CHURCH? THOUSAND-YEAR-OLD CHURCHES ARE USUALLY BIG WITH TOURISTS...
...NOT SO MUCH MASTER CRIMINALS.
IN THE SEVENTEENTH CENTURY, A RESTORATION PROJECT RAISED THE PAVEMENT AROUND THE CHURCH.
IT WAS SUPPOSEDLY TO PROTECT THE CHURCH FROM THE TIDES THAT FLOOD THE CITY EVERY SO OFTEN. BUT IN REALITY...
SQUIK
CHIK CHIK
A HIDDEN STAIRCASE!
C'MON GUYS!
LIKE, YOU ALL GO AHEAD. WE'LL STAY OUTSIDE AS...UH... LOOKOUTS?
YOU KNOW, THE ENTRANCE WILL CLOSE ONCE WE GO DOWN THE STAIRS. AFTER THAT, YOU'LL BE...
...ALL ALONE.
LIKE, WE'RE STAYING WITH YOU!
RHEAH!

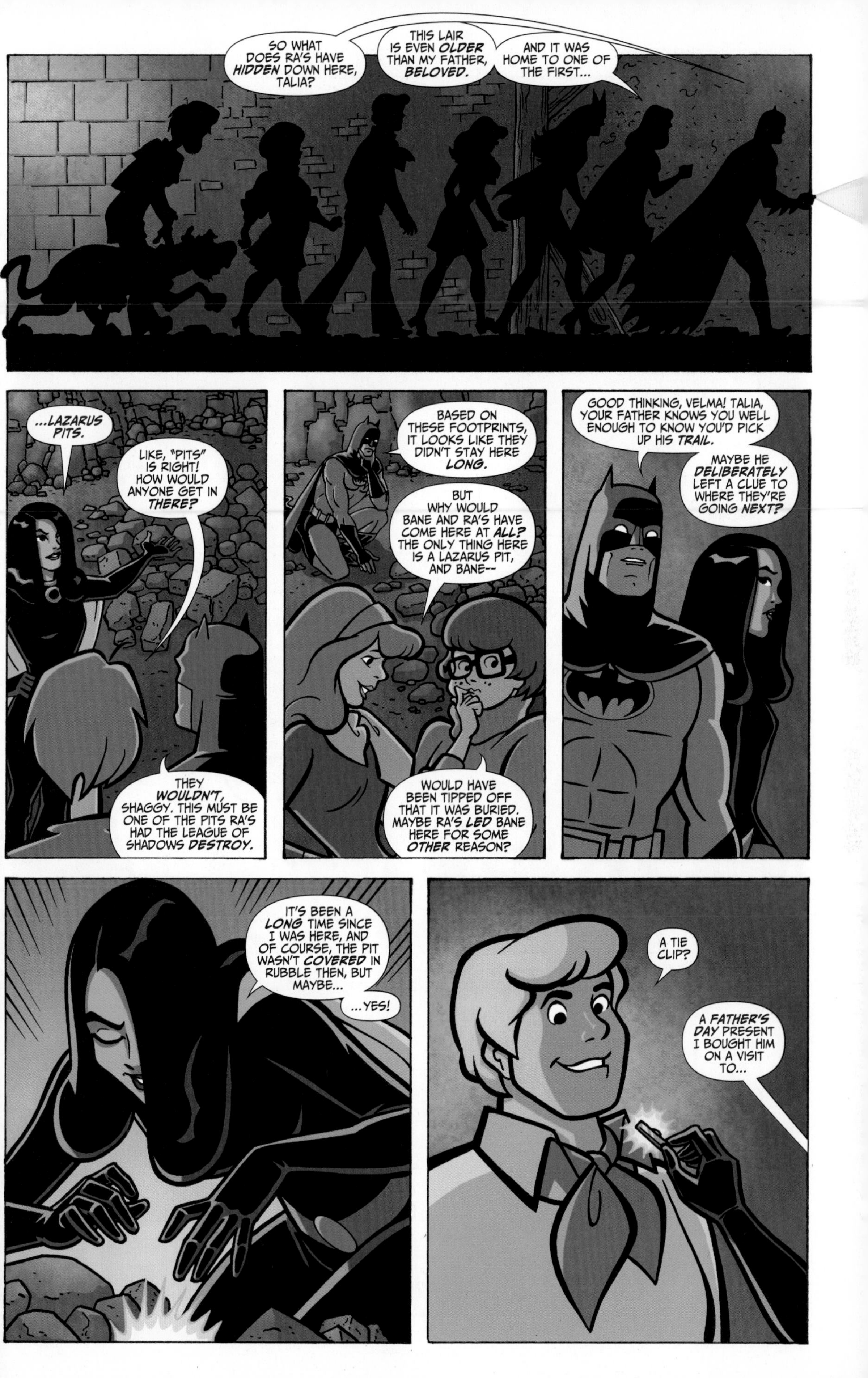
SO WHAT DOES RA'S HAVE HIDDEN DOWN HERE, TALIA?
THIS LAIR IS EVEN OLDER THAN MY FATHER, BELOVED.
AND IT WAS HOME TO ONE OF THE FIRST...
...LAZARUS PITS.
LIKE, "PITS" IS RIGHT! HOW WOULD ANYONE GET IN THERE?
THEY WOULDN'T, SHAGGY. THIS MUST BE ONE OF THE PITS RA'S HAD THE LEAGUE OF SHADOWS DESTROY.
BASED ON THESE FOOTPRINTS, IT LOOKS LIKE THEY DIDN'T STAY HERE LONG.
BUT WHY WOULD BANE AND RA'S HAVE COME HERE AT ALL? THE ONLY THING HERE IS A LAZARUS PIT, AND BANE--
WOULD HAVE BEEN TIPPED OFF THAT IT WAS BURIED. MAYBE RA'S LED BANE HERE FOR SOME OTHER REASON?
GOOD THINKING, VELMA! TALIA, YOUR FATHER KNOWS YOU WELL ENOUGH TO KNOW YOU'D PICK UP HIS TRAIL.
MAYBE HE DELIBERATELY LEFT A CLUE TO WHERE THEY'RE GOING NEXT?
IT'S BEEN A LONG TIME SINCE I WAS HERE, AND OF COURSE, THE PIT WASN'T COVERED IN RUBBLE THEN, BUT MAYBE...
...YES!
A TIE CLIP?
A FATHER'S DAY PRESENT I BOUGHT HIM ON A VISIT TO...

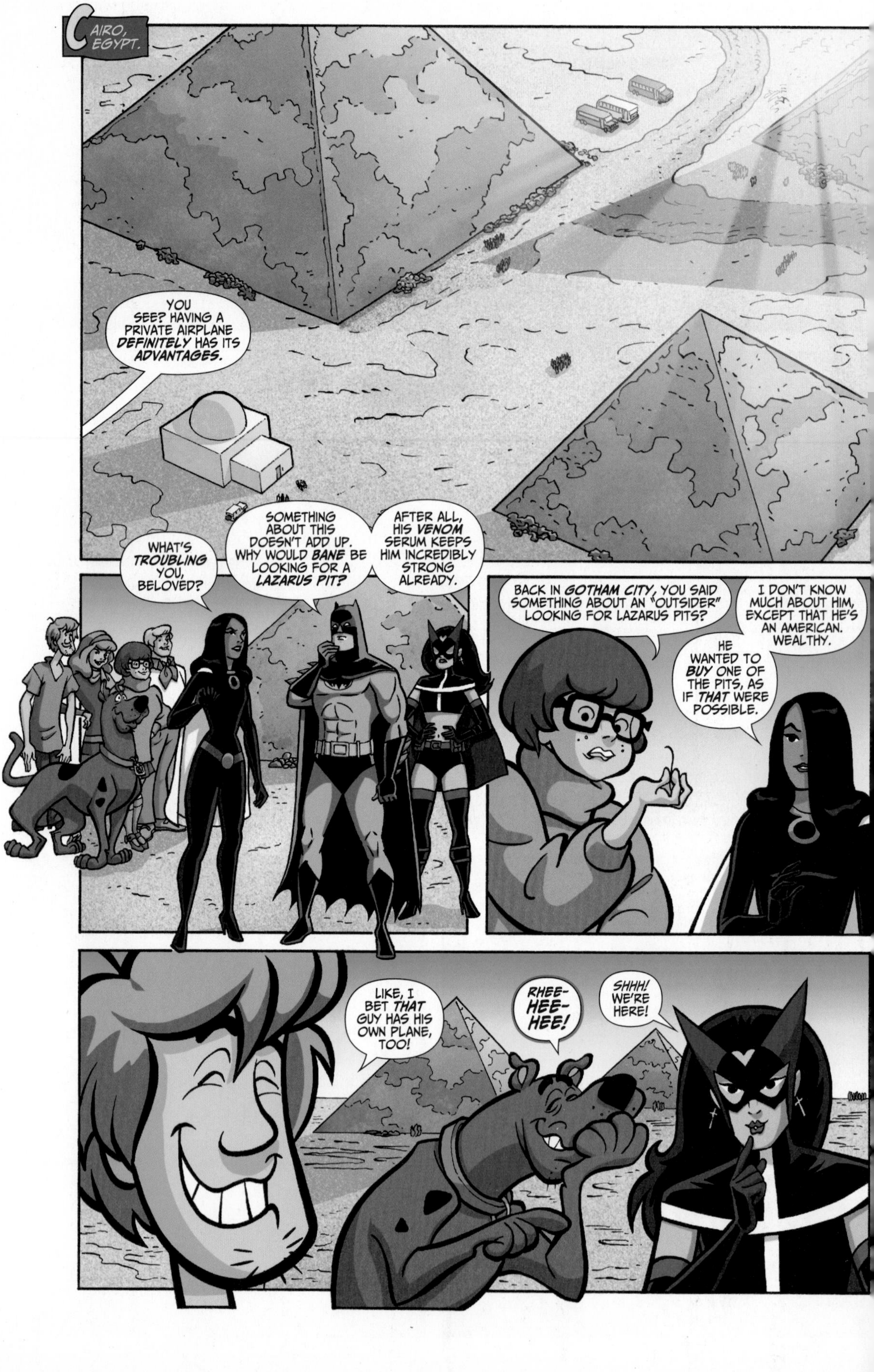
CAIRO, EGYPT.
YOU SEE? HAVING A PRIVATE AIRPLANE DEFINITELY HAS ITS ADVANTAGES.
WHAT'S TROUBLING YOU, BELOVED?
SOMETHING ABOUT THIS DOESN'T ADD UP. WHY WOULD BANE BE LOOKING FOR A LAZARUS PIT?
AFTER ALL, HIS VENOM SERUM KEEPS HIM INCREDIBLY STRONG ALREADY.
BACK IN GOTHAM CITY, YOU SAID SOMETHING ABOUT AN "OUTSIDER" LOOKING FOR LAZARUS PITS?
I DON'T KNOW MUCH ABOUT HIM, EXCEPT THAT HE'S AN AMERICAN. WEALTHY.
HE WANTED TO BUY ONE OF THE PITS, AS IF THAT WERE POSSIBLE.
LIKE, I BET THAT GUY HAS HIS OWN PLANE, TOO!
RHEE-HEE-HEE!
SHHH! WE'RE HERE!

WHAT IS THIS PLACE, TALIA?

CURRENT MAPS SHOW IT AS A *FORMER* MARKOVIAN EMBASSY. BUT OF COURSE...

CLICK CLICK CLICK CLICK

...IT'S *NOT.*

STAND BACK. THE FLOOR OPENS TO THE LAZARUS PIT BELOW. THIS CONTROL PANEL BRINGS UP THE *ELEVATOR PLATFORM.*

T-TAP T-TAP

VRODODO

THERE'S SOMEONE ON THE PLATFORM!

FATHER? IS IT *YOU?*

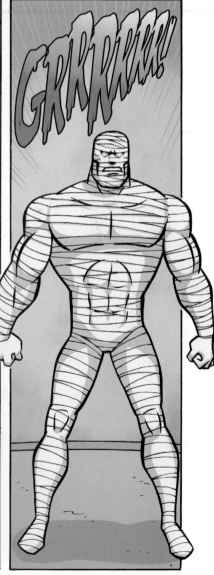

GRRRRRR!

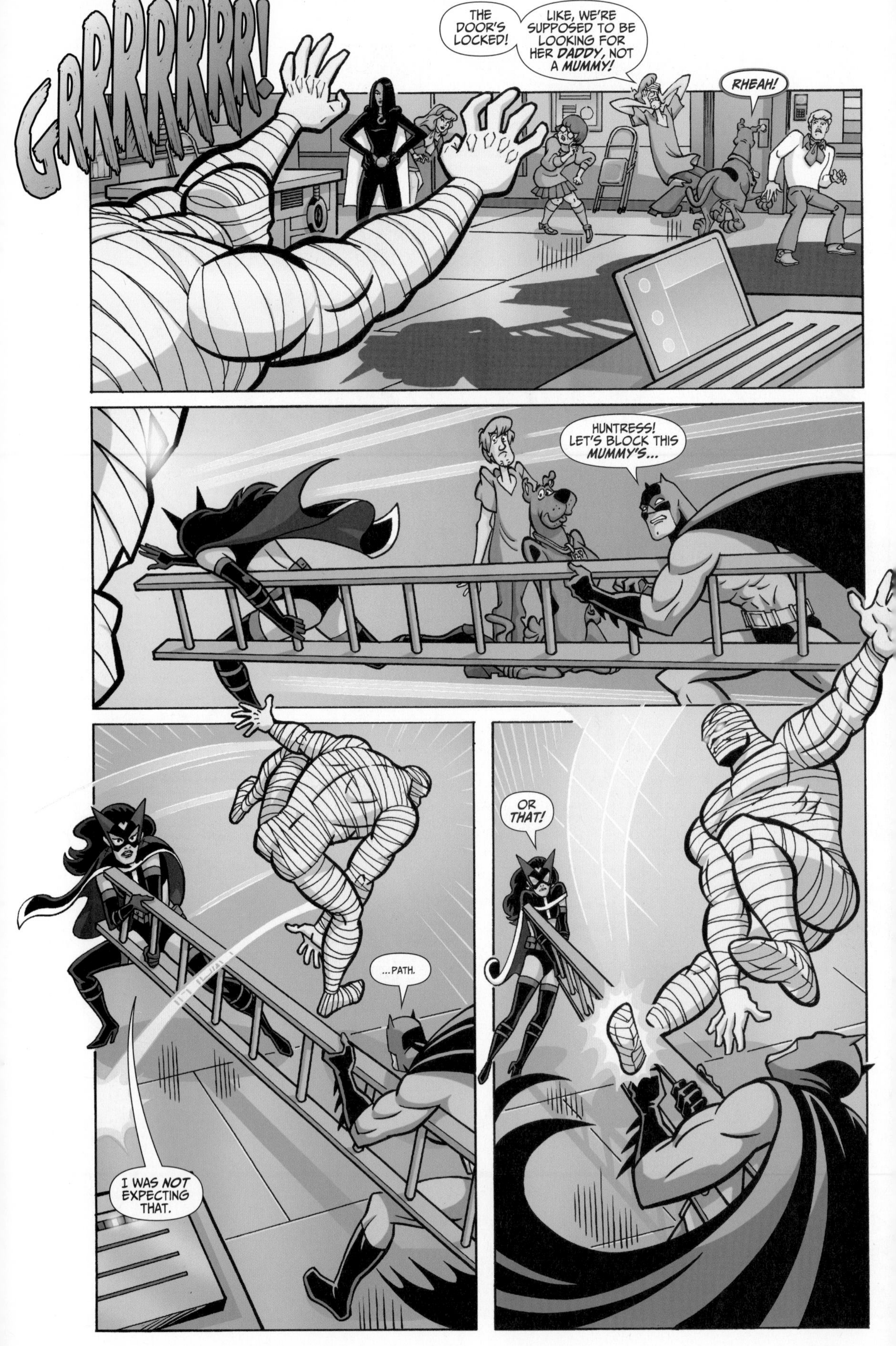
GRRRRRRR!
THE DOOR'S LOCKED!
LIKE, WE'RE SUPPOSED TO BE LOOKING FOR HER DADDY, NOT A MUMMY!
RHEAH!
HUNTRESS! LET'S BLOCK THIS MUMMY'S...
...PATH.
I WAS NOT EXPECTING THAT.
OR THAT!

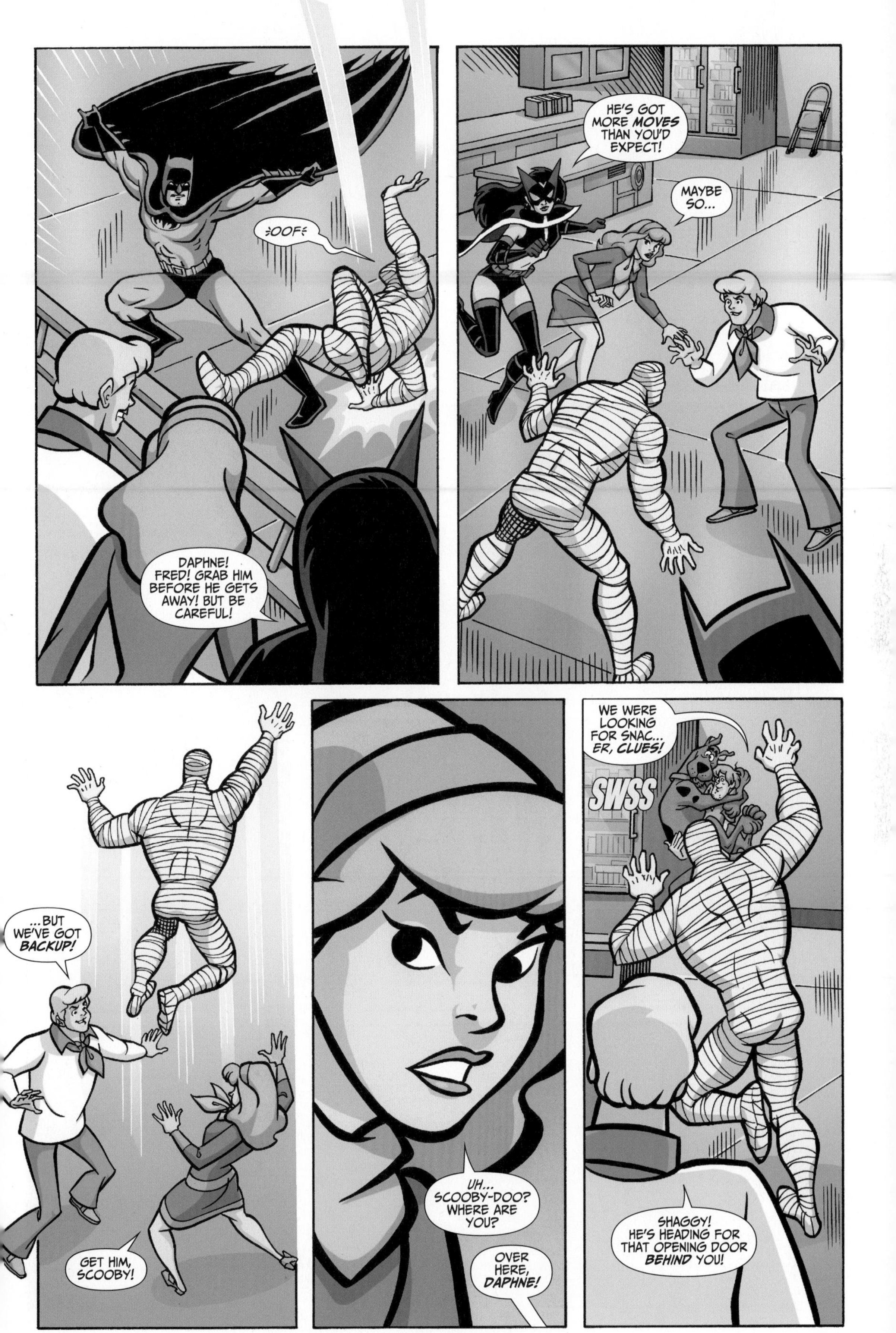

OOF
DAPHNE! FRED! GRAB HIM BEFORE HE GETS AWAY! BUT BE CAREFUL!
HE'S GOT MORE MOVES THAN YOU'D EXPECT!
MAYBE SO...
...BUT WE'VE GOT BACKUP!
GET HIM, SCOOBY!
UH... SCOOBY-DOO? WHERE ARE YOU?
OVER HERE, DAPHNE!
WE WERE LOOKING FOR SNAC... ER, CLUES!
SWSS
SHAGGY! HE'S HEADING FOR THAT OPENING DOOR BEHIND YOU!

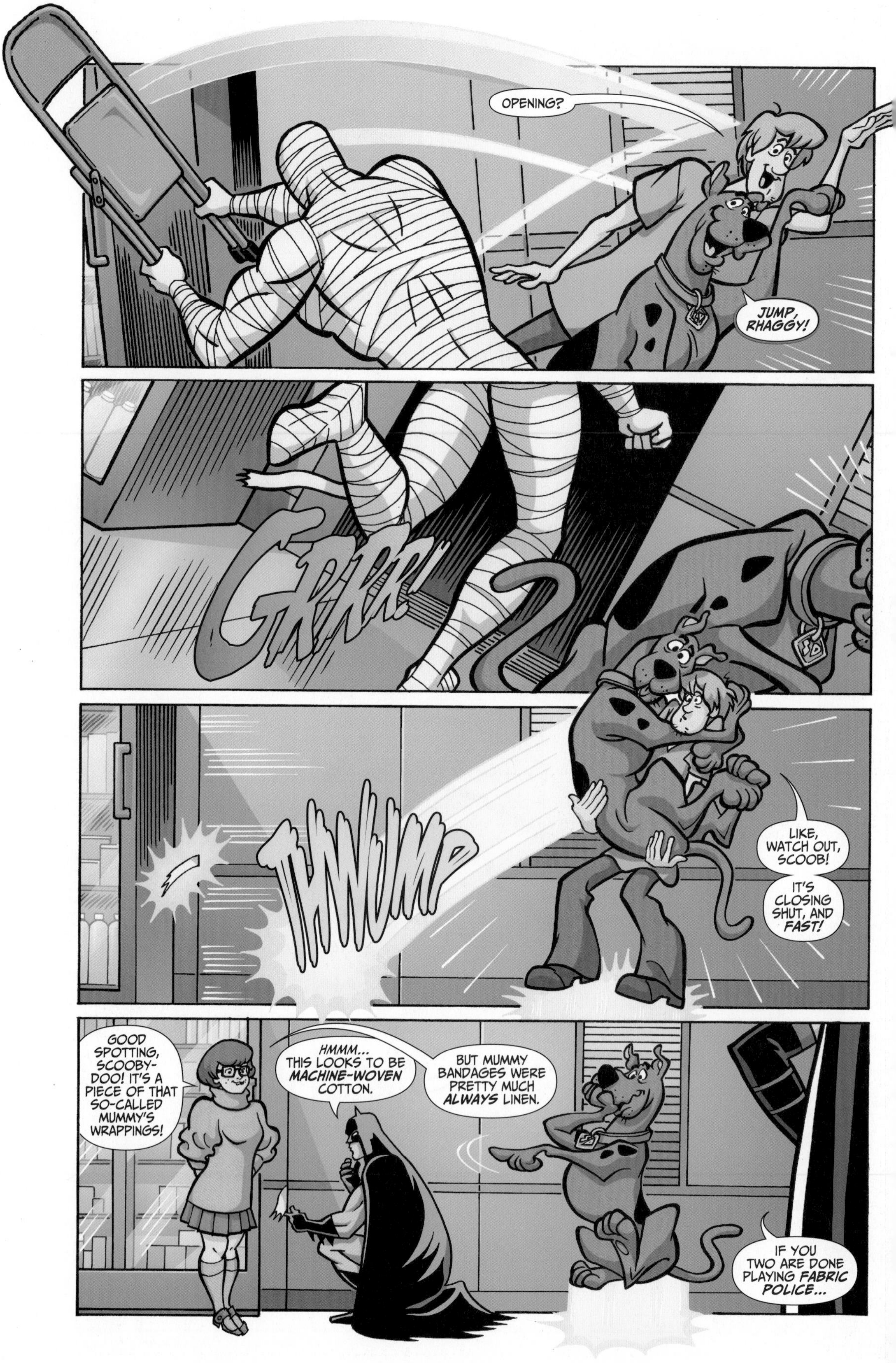
OPENING?
JUMP, RHAGGY!
GRRR!
THWUMP
LIKE, WATCH OUT, SCOOB!
IT'S CLOSING SHUT, AND FAST!
GOOD SPOTTING, SCOOBY-DOO! IT'S A PIECE OF THAT SO-CALLED MUMMY'S WRAPPINGS!
HMMM... THIS LOOKS TO BE MACHINE-WOVEN COTTON.
BUT MUMMY BANDAGES WERE PRETTY MUCH ALWAYS LINEN.
IF YOU TWO ARE DONE PLAYING FABRIC POLICE...

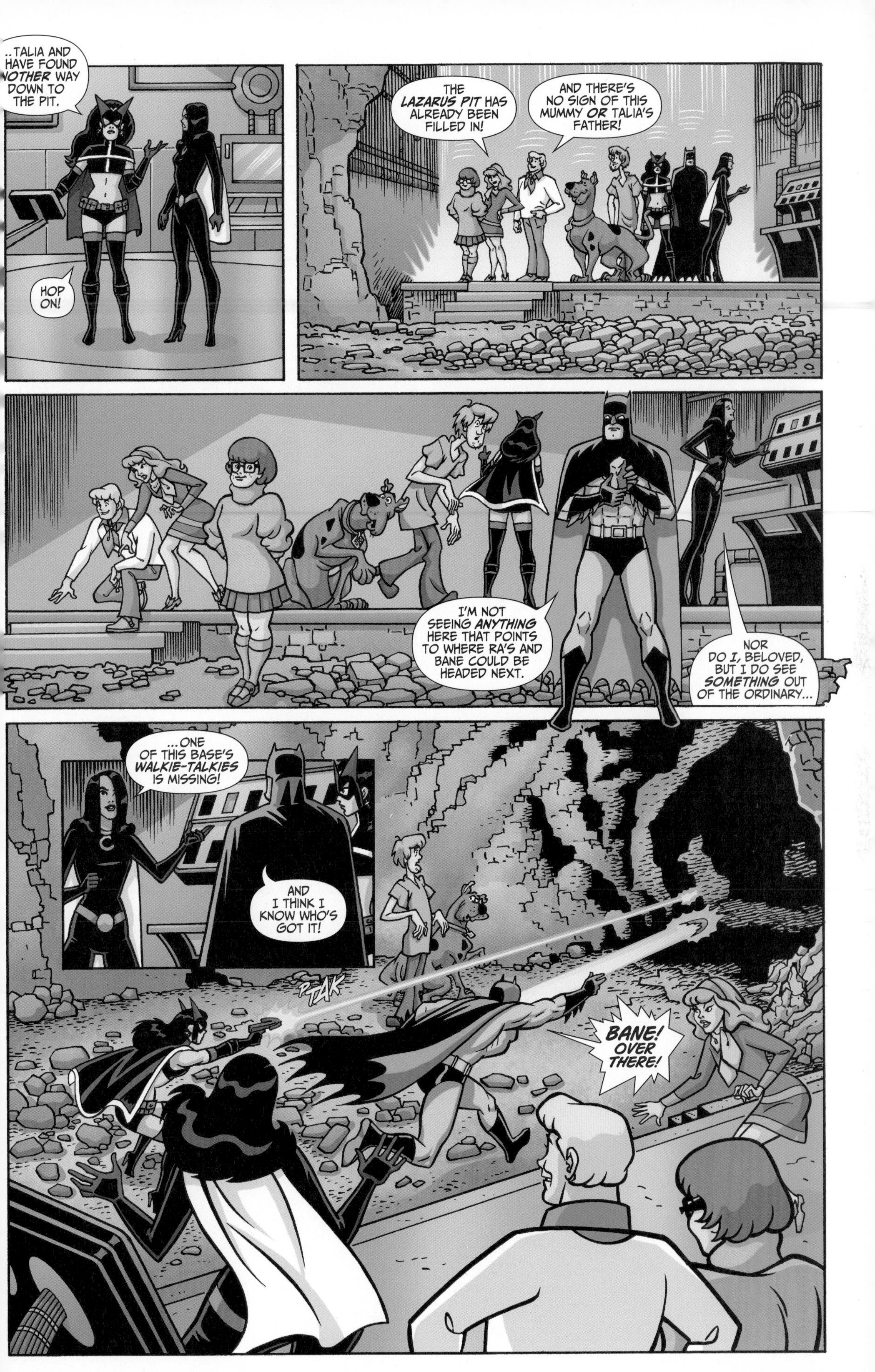
..TALIA AND HAVE FOUND NOTHER WAY DOWN TO THE PIT.
HOP ON!
THE LAZARUS PIT HAS ALREADY BEEN FILLED IN!
AND THERE'S NO SIGN OF THIS MUMMY OR TALIA'S FATHER!
I'M NOT SEEING ANYTHING HERE THAT POINTS TO WHERE RA'S AND BANE COULD BE HEADED NEXT.
NOR DO I, BELOVED, BUT I DO SEE SOMETHING OUT OF THE ORDINARY...
...ONE OF THIS BASE'S WALKIE-TALKIES IS MISSING!
AND I THINK I KNOW WHO'S GOT IT!
PTAK
BANE! OVER THERE!

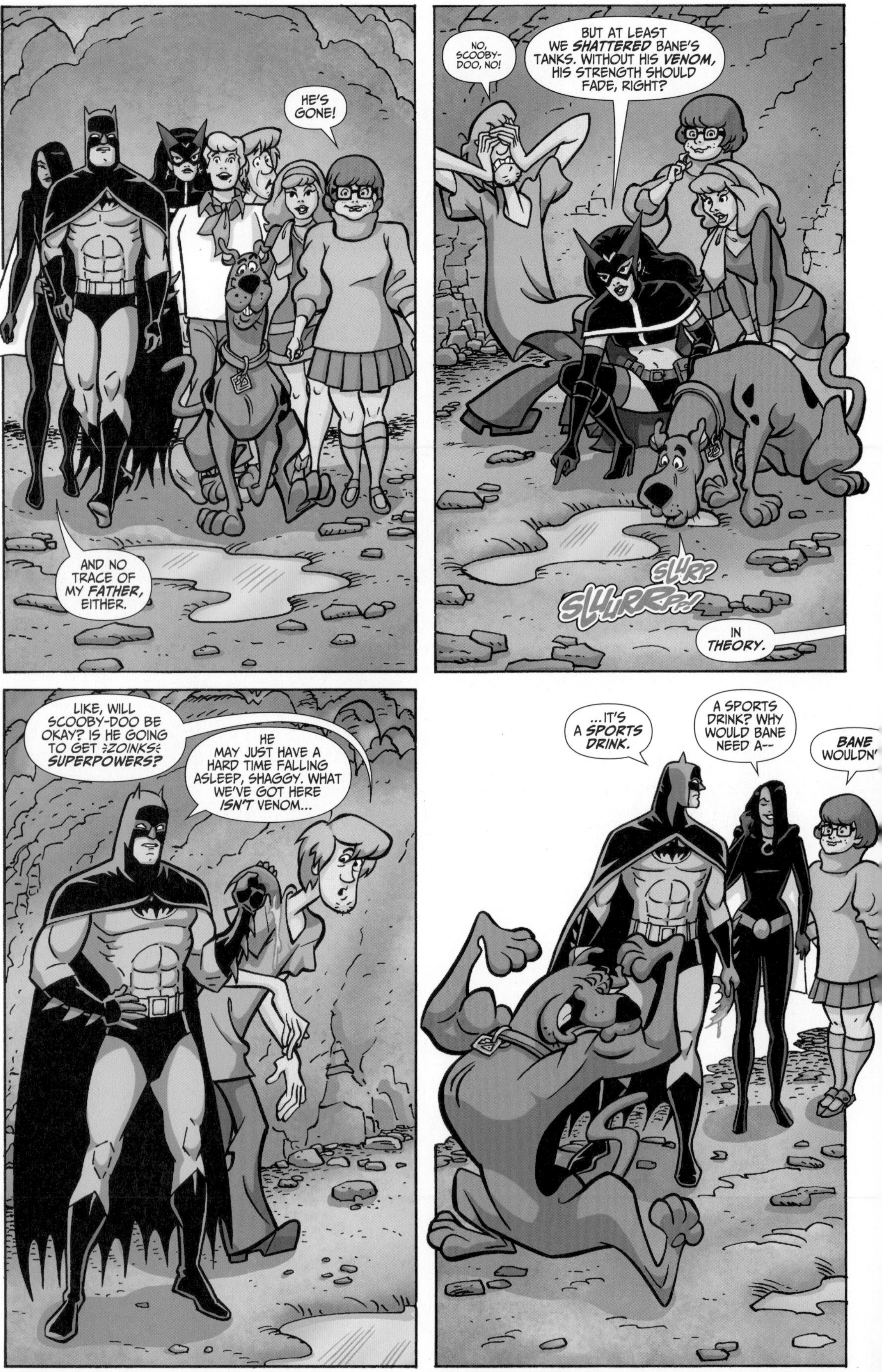
HE'S GONE!
AND NO TRACE OF MY FATHER, EITHER.
NO, SCOOBY-DOO, NO!
BUT AT LEAST WE SHATTERED BANE'S TANKS. WITHOUT HIS VENOM, HIS STRENGTH SHOULD FADE, RIGHT?
SLURP
SLUURRP!
IN THEORY.
LIKE, WILL SCOOBY-DOO BE OKAY? IS HE GOING TO GET ZOINKS SUPERPOWERS?
HE MAY JUST HAVE A HARD TIME FALLING ASLEEP, SHAGGY. WHAT WE'VE GOT HERE ISN'T VENOM...
...IT'S A SPORTS DRINK.
A SPORTS DRINK? WHY WOULD BANE NEED A--
BANE WOULDN'

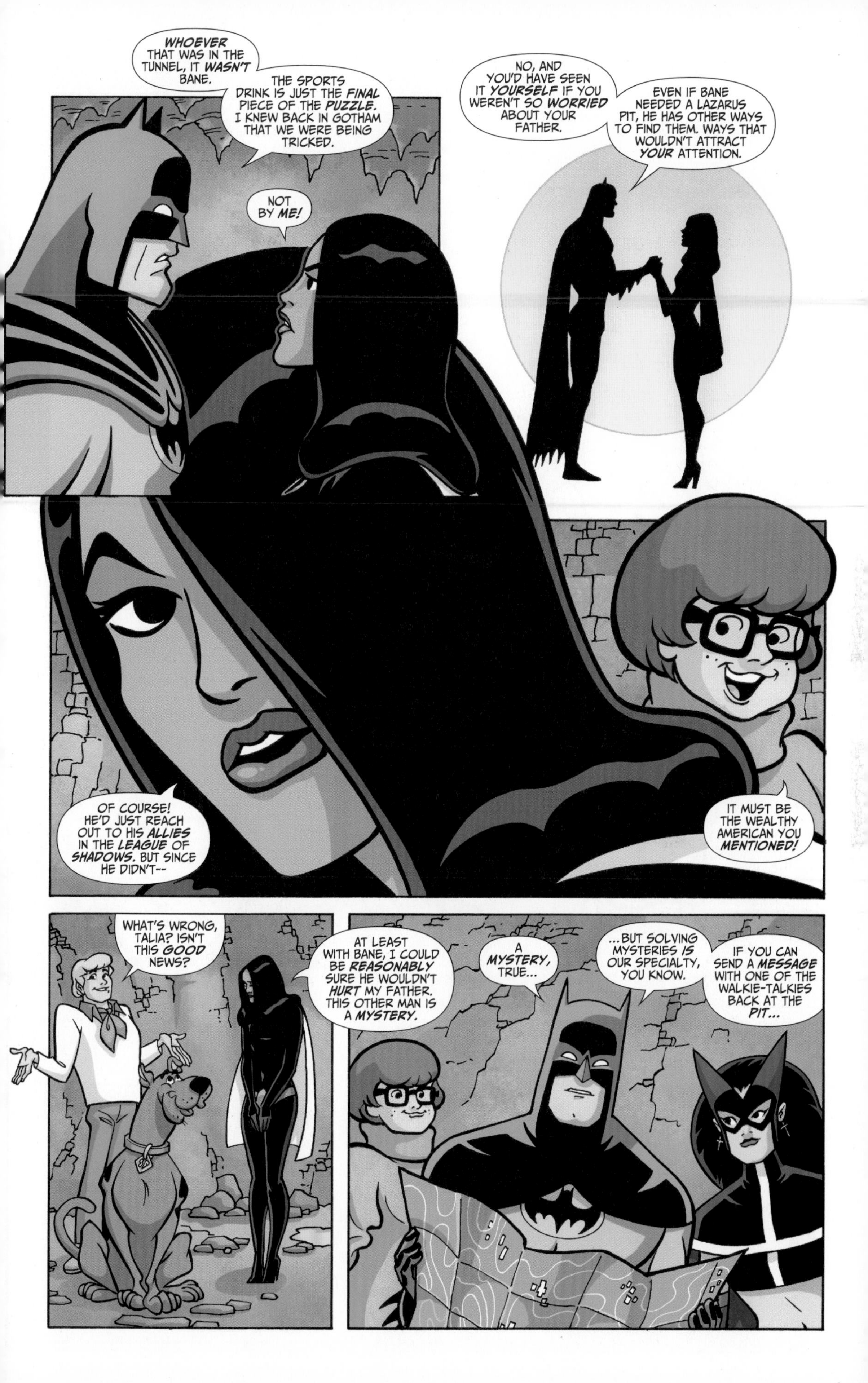
WHOEVER THAT WAS IN THE TUNNEL, IT WASN'T BANE.
THE SPORTS DRINK IS JUST THE FINAL PIECE OF THE PUZZLE. I KNEW BACK IN GOTHAM THAT WE WERE BEING TRICKED.
NOT BY ME!
NO, AND YOU'D HAVE SEEN IT YOURSELF IF YOU WEREN'T SO WORRIED ABOUT YOUR FATHER.
EVEN IF BANE NEEDED A LAZARUS PIT, HE HAS OTHER WAYS TO FIND THEM. WAYS THAT WOULDN'T ATTRACT YOUR ATTENTION.
OF COURSE! HE'D JUST REACH OUT TO HIS ALLIES IN THE LEAGUE OF SHADOWS. BUT SINCE HE DIDN'T--
IT MUST BE THE WEALTHY AMERICAN YOU MENTIONED!
WHAT'S WRONG, TALIA? ISN'T THIS GOOD NEWS?
AT LEAST WITH BANE, I COULD BE REASONABLY SURE HE WOULDN'T HURT MY FATHER. THIS OTHER MAN IS A MYSTERY.
A MYSTERY, TRUE...
...BUT SOLVING MYSTERIES IS OUR SPECIALTY, YOU KNOW.
IF YOU CAN SEND A MESSAGE WITH ONE OF THE WALKIE-TALKIES BACK AT THE PIT...

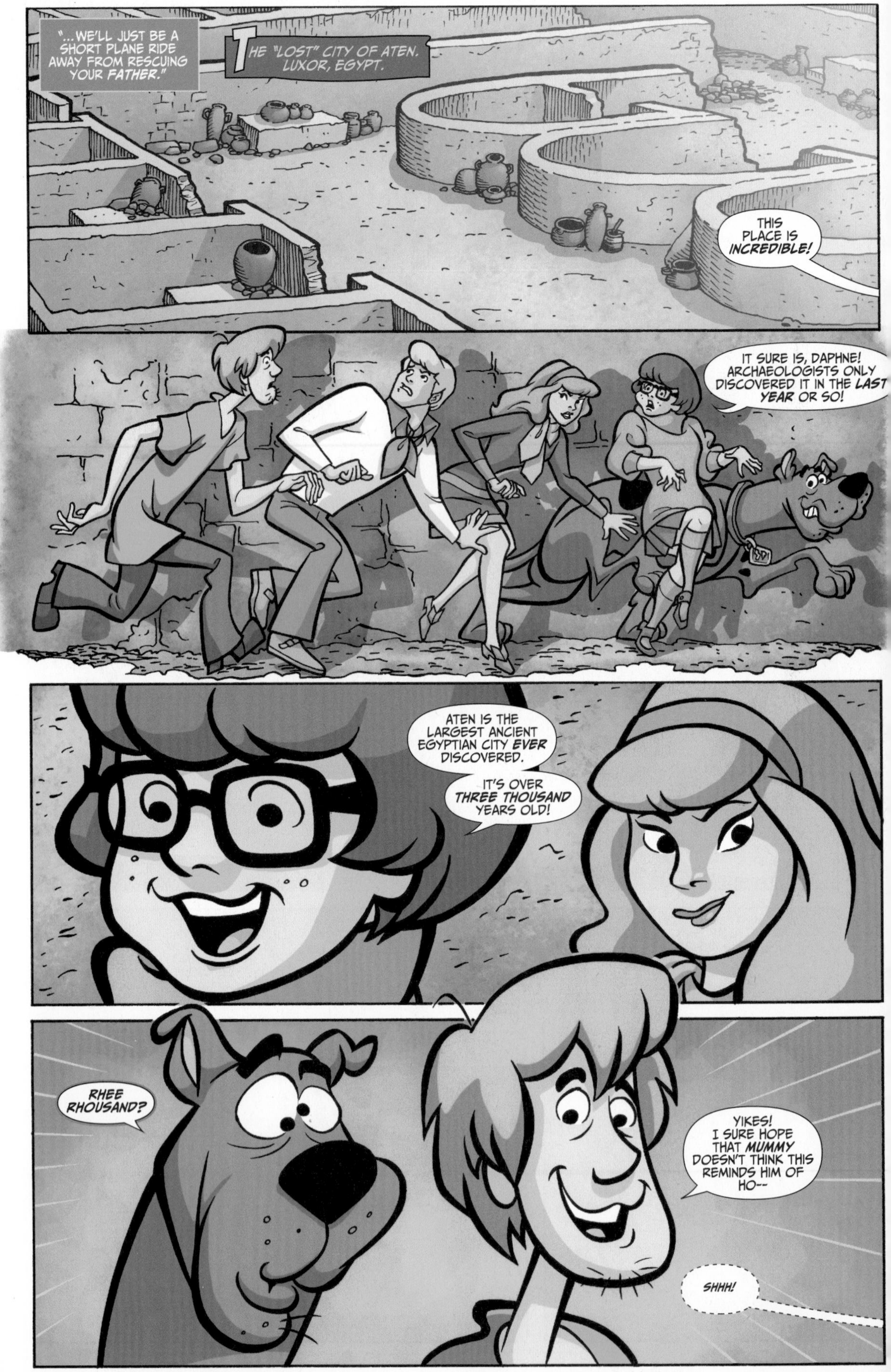
"...WE'LL JUST BE A SHORT PLANE RIDE AWAY FROM RESCUING YOUR FATHER."
THE "LOST" CITY OF ATEN. LUXOR, EGYPT.
THIS PLACE IS INCREDIBLE!
IT SURE IS, DAPHNE! ARCHAEOLOGISTS ONLY DISCOVERED IT IN THE LAST YEAR OR SO!
ATEN IS THE LARGEST ANCIENT EGYPTIAN CITY EVER DISCOVERED.
IT'S OVER THREE THOUSAND YEARS OLD!
RHEE RHOUSAND?
YIKES! I SURE HOPE THAT MUMMY DOESN'T THINK THIS REMINDS HIM OF HO--
SHHH!

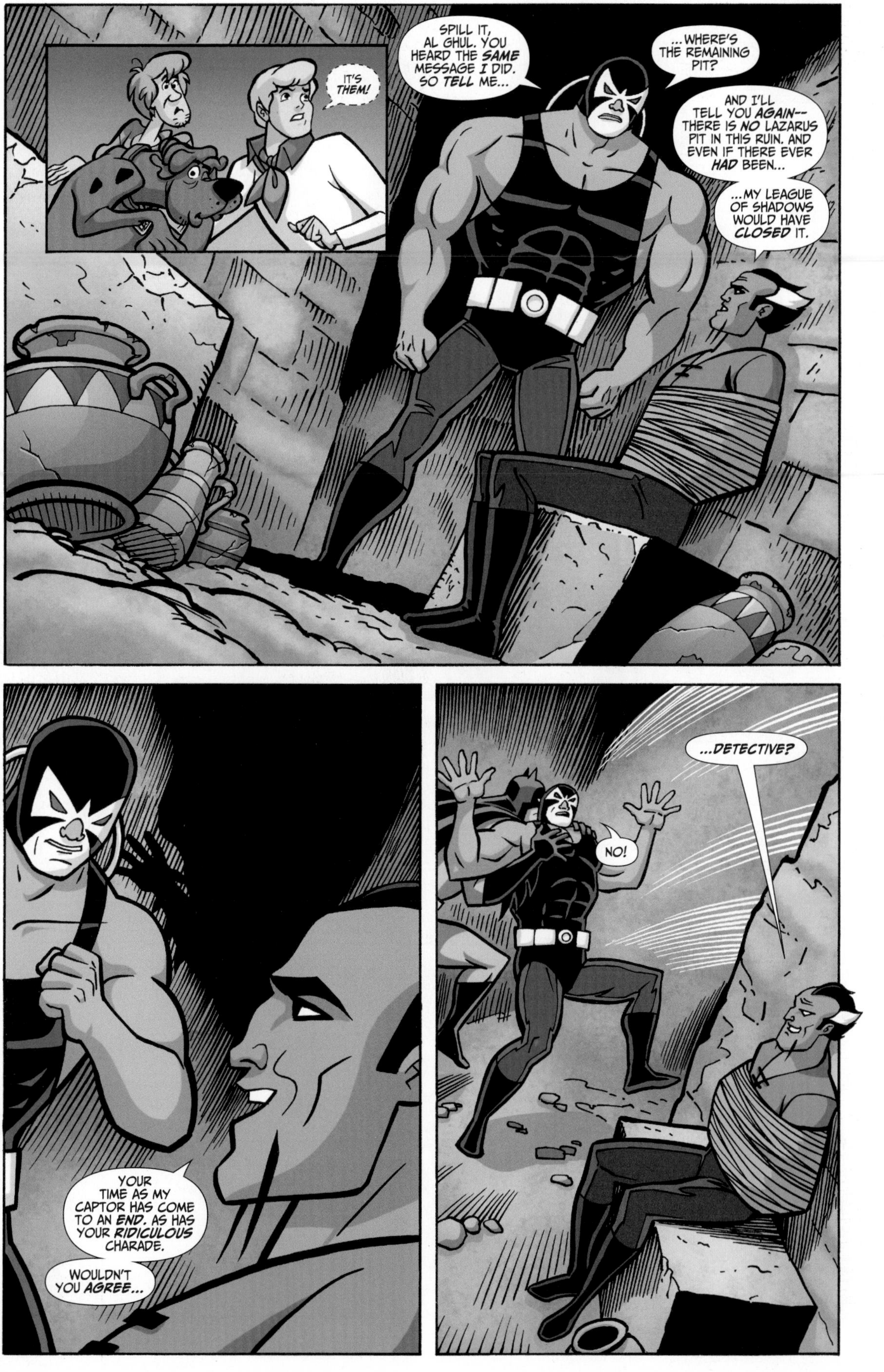
SPILL IT, AL GHUL. YOU HEARD THE SAME MESSAGE I DID. SO TELL ME...
...WHERE'S THE REMAINING PIT?
IT'S THEM!
AND I'LL TELL YOU AGAIN-- THERE IS NO LAZARUS PIT IN THIS RUIN. AND EVEN IF THERE EVER HAD BEEN...
...MY LEAGUE OF SHADOWS WOULD HAVE CLOSED IT.
YOUR TIME AS MY CAPTOR HAS COME TO AN END. AS HAS YOUR RIDICULOUS CHARADE.
WOULDN'T YOU AGREE...
...DETECTIVE?
NO!

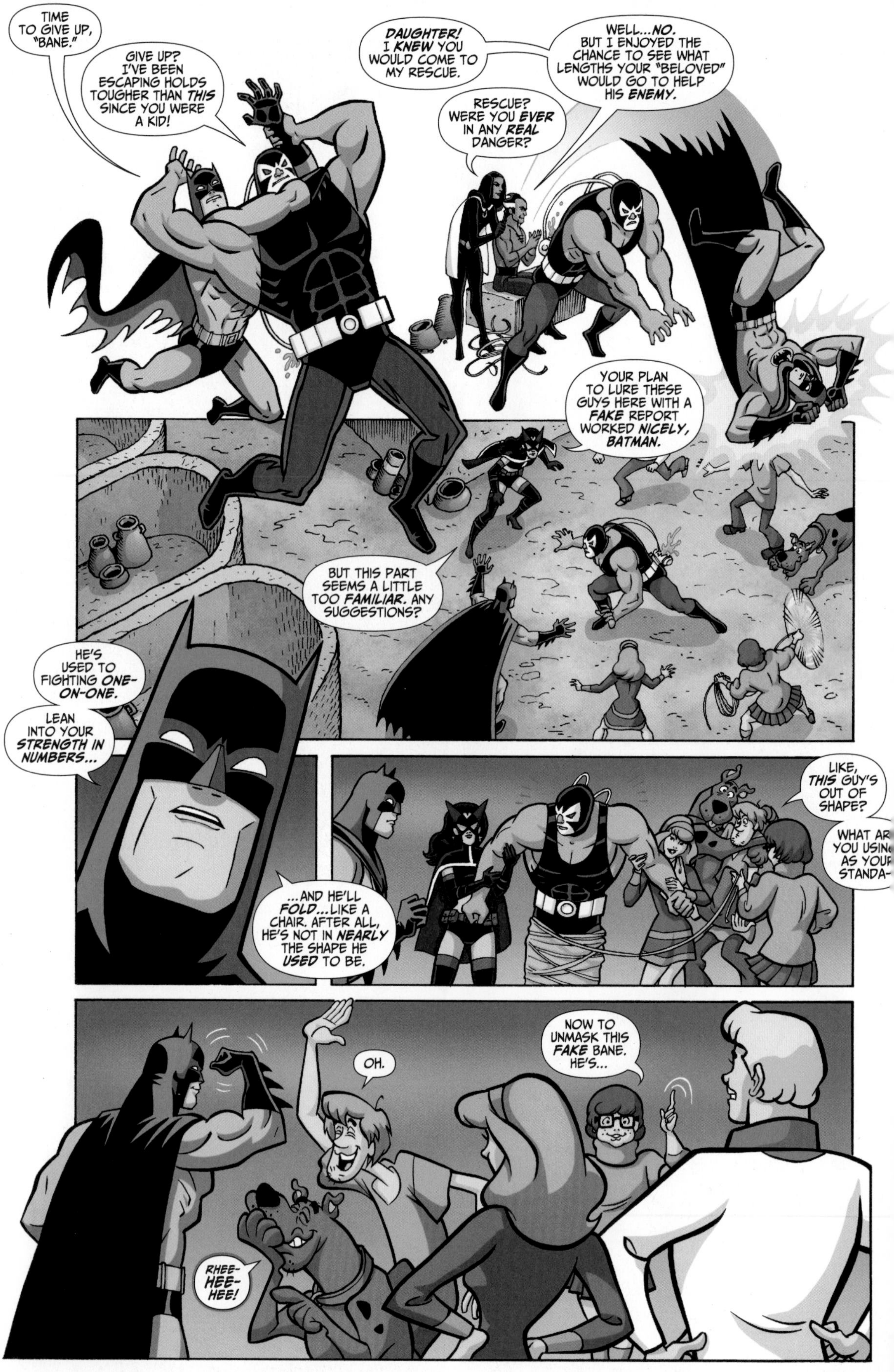
TIME TO GIVE UP, "BANE."
GIVE UP? I'VE BEEN ESCAPING HOLDS TOUGHER THAN THIS SINCE YOU WERE A KID!
DAUGHTER! I KNEW YOU WOULD COME TO MY RESCUE.
WELL...NO. BUT I ENJOYED THE CHANCE TO SEE WHAT LENGTHS YOUR "BELOVED" WOULD GO TO HELP HIS ENEMY.
RESCUE? WERE YOU EVER IN ANY REAL DANGER?
YOUR PLAN TO LURE THESE GUYS HERE WITH A FAKE REPORT WORKED NICELY, BATMAN.
BUT THIS PART SEEMS A LITTLE TOO FAMILIAR. ANY SUGGESTIONS?
HE'S USED TO FIGHTING ONE-ON-ONE.
LEAN INTO YOUR STRENGTH IN NUMBERS...
...AND HE'LL FOLD...LIKE A CHAIR. AFTER ALL, HE'S NOT IN NEARLY THE SHAPE HE USED TO BE.
LIKE, THIS GUY'S OUT OF SHAPE?
OH.
NOW TO UNMASK THIS FAKE BANE. HE'S...
RHEE-HEE-HEE!

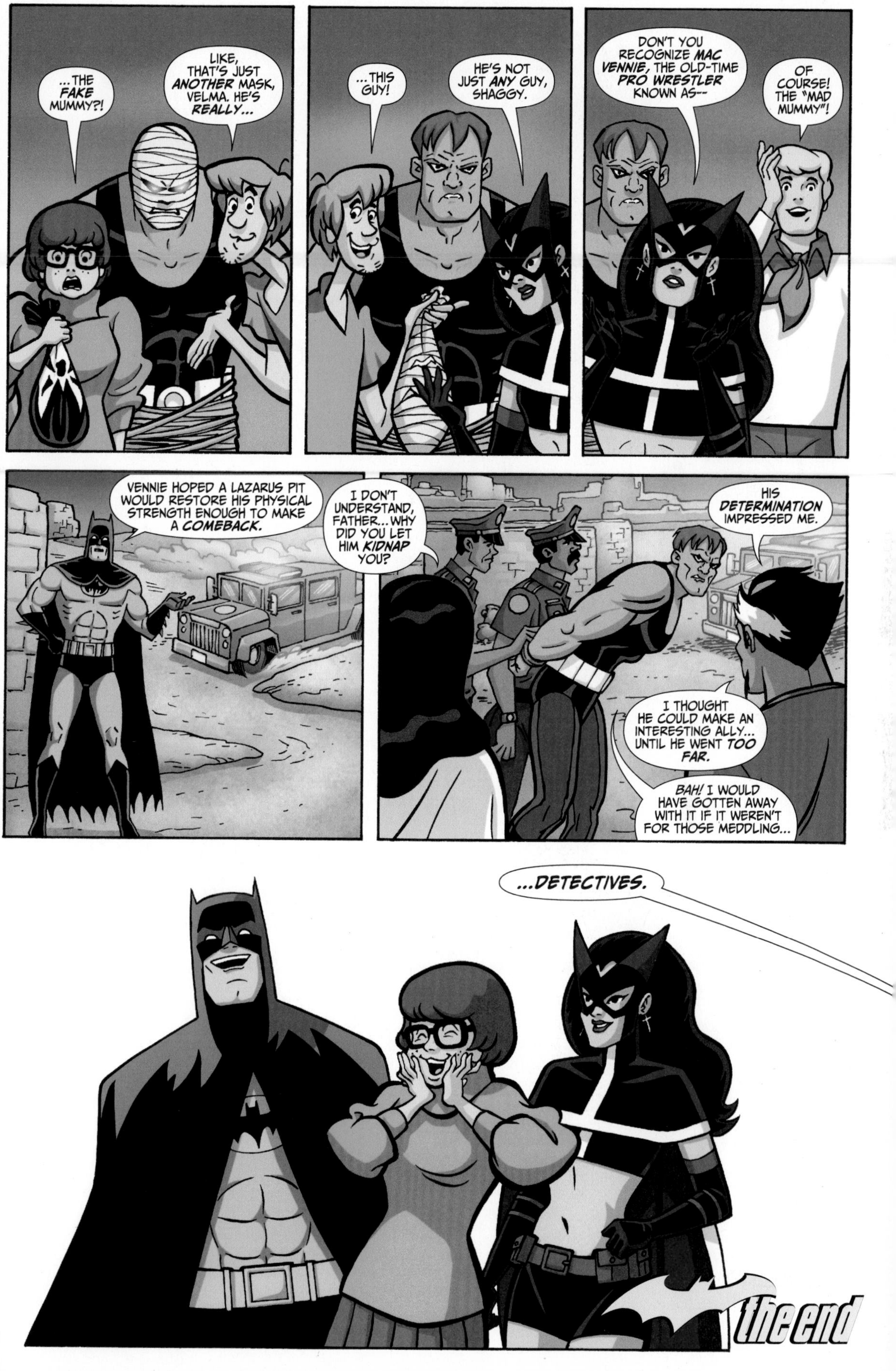
...THE FAKE MUMMY?!
LIKE, THAT'S JUST ANOTHER MASK, VELMA. HE'S REALLY...
...THIS GUY!
HE'S NOT JUST ANY GUY, SHAGGY.
DON'T YOU RECOGNIZE MAC VENNIE, THE OLD-TIME PRO WRESTLER KNOWN AS--
OF COURSE! THE "MAD MUMMY"!
VENNIE HOPED A LAZARUS PIT WOULD RESTORE HIS PHYSICAL STRENGTH ENOUGH TO MAKE A COMEBACK.
I DON'T UNDERSTAND, FATHER... WHY DID YOU LET HIM KIDNAP YOU?
HIS DETERMINATION IMPRESSED ME.
I THOUGHT HE COULD MAKE AN INTERESTING ALLY... UNTIL HE WENT TOO FAR.
BAH! I WOULD HAVE GOTTEN AWAY WITH IT IF IT WEREN'T FOR THOSE MEDDLING...
...DETECTIVES.
the end

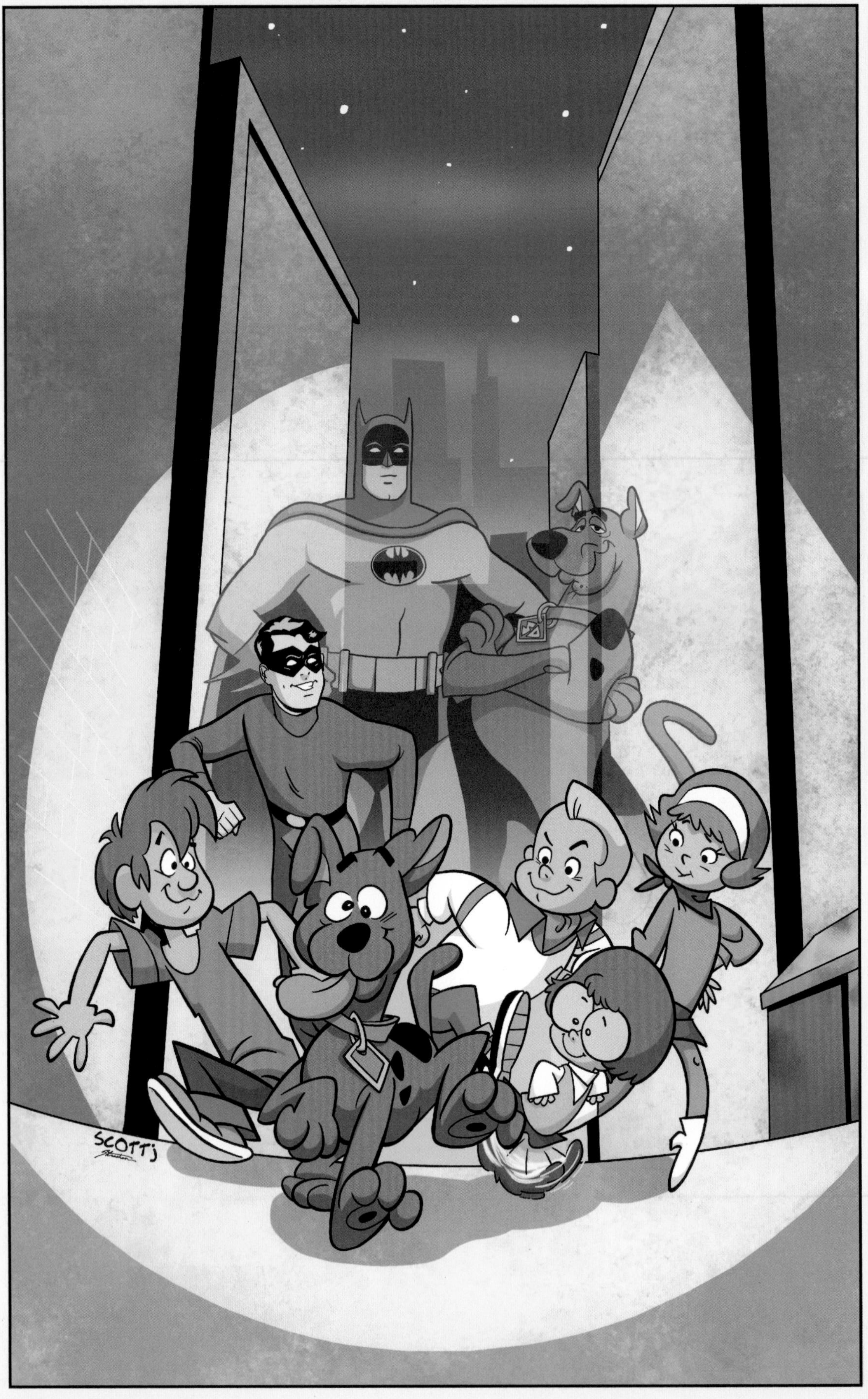
SCOTTj

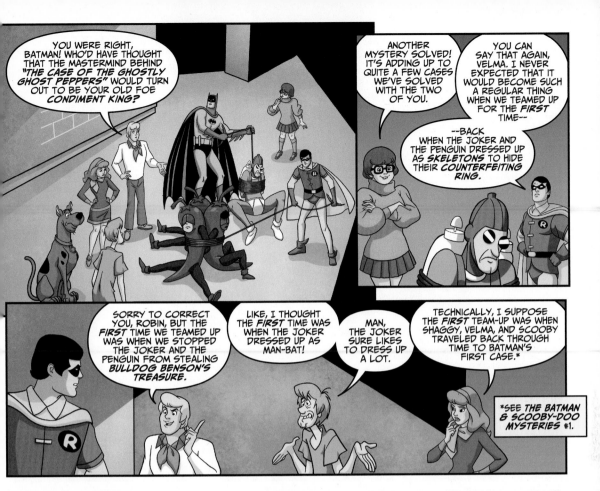

YOU WERE RIGHT, BATMAN! WHO'D HAVE THOUGHT THAT THE MASTERMIND BEHIND *"THE CASE OF THE GHOSTLY GHOST PEPPERS"* WOULD TURN OUT TO BE YOUR OLD FOE *CONDIMENT KING?*

ANOTHER MYSTERY SOLVED! IT'S ADDING UP TO QUITE A FEW CASES WE'VE SOLVED WITH THE TWO OF YOU.

YOU CAN SAY THAT AGAIN, VELMA. I NEVER EXPECTED THAT IT WOULD BECOME SUCH A REGULAR THING WHEN WE TEAMED UP FOR THE *FIRST* TIME--

--BACK WHEN THE JOKER AND THE PENGUIN DRESSED UP AS *SKELETONS* TO HIDE THEIR *COUNTERFEITING RING.*

SORRY TO CORRECT YOU, ROBIN, BUT THE *FIRST* TIME WE TEAMED UP WAS WHEN WE STOPPED THE JOKER AND THE PENGUIN FROM STEALING *BULLDOG BENSON'S TREASURE.*

LIKE, I THOUGHT THE *FIRST* TIME WAS WHEN THE JOKER DRESSED UP AS MAN-BAT!

MAN, THE JOKER SURE LIKES TO DRESS UP A LOT.

TECHNICALLY, I SUPPOSE THE *FIRST* TEAM-UP WAS WHEN SHAGGY, VELMA, AND SCOOBY TRAVELED BACK THROUGH TIME TO BATMAN'S FIRST CASE.*

*SEE *THE BATMAN & SCOOBY-DOO MYSTERIES* #1.

RUH? RHICH *RAS* REALLY RIRST?

ACTUALLY, SCOOBY, THEY'RE *ALL* MISTAKEN.

ALL OF THOSE CASES HAPPENED *AFTER* I GOT THE IDEA TO BECOME BATMAN.

A BAT! THAT'S IT! IT'S AN OMEN! I SHALL BECOME A *BAT!*

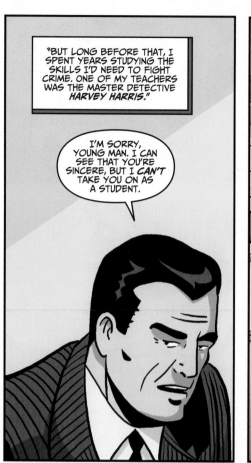

"BUT LONG BEFORE THAT, I SPENT YEARS STUDYING THE SKILLS I'D NEED TO FIGHT CRIME. ONE OF MY TEACHERS WAS THE MASTER DETECTIVE *HARVEY HARRIS*."

I'M SORRY, YOUNG MAN. I CAN SEE THAT YOU'RE SINCERE, BUT I *CAN'T* TAKE YOU ON AS A STUDENT.

PLEASE, MR. HARRIS! I'VE BEEN TRAVELING THE WORLD, SEARCHING FOR THE VERY BEST TEACHERS. YOU'RE THE *WORLD'S GREATEST DETECTIVE!*

THAT'S VERY FLATTERING. BUT I'M AFRAID I DON'T HAVE ANY OPENINGS RIGHT NOW...

...BECAUSE I ALREADY *HAVE* STUDENTS.

THOSE MEDDLING KIDS

SHOLLY FISCH – Writer   SCOTT JERALDS – Artist   CARRIE STRACHAN – Colors
WES ABBOTT – Letters   MICHAEL McCALISTER – Editor
Batman created by BOB KANE with BILL FINGER

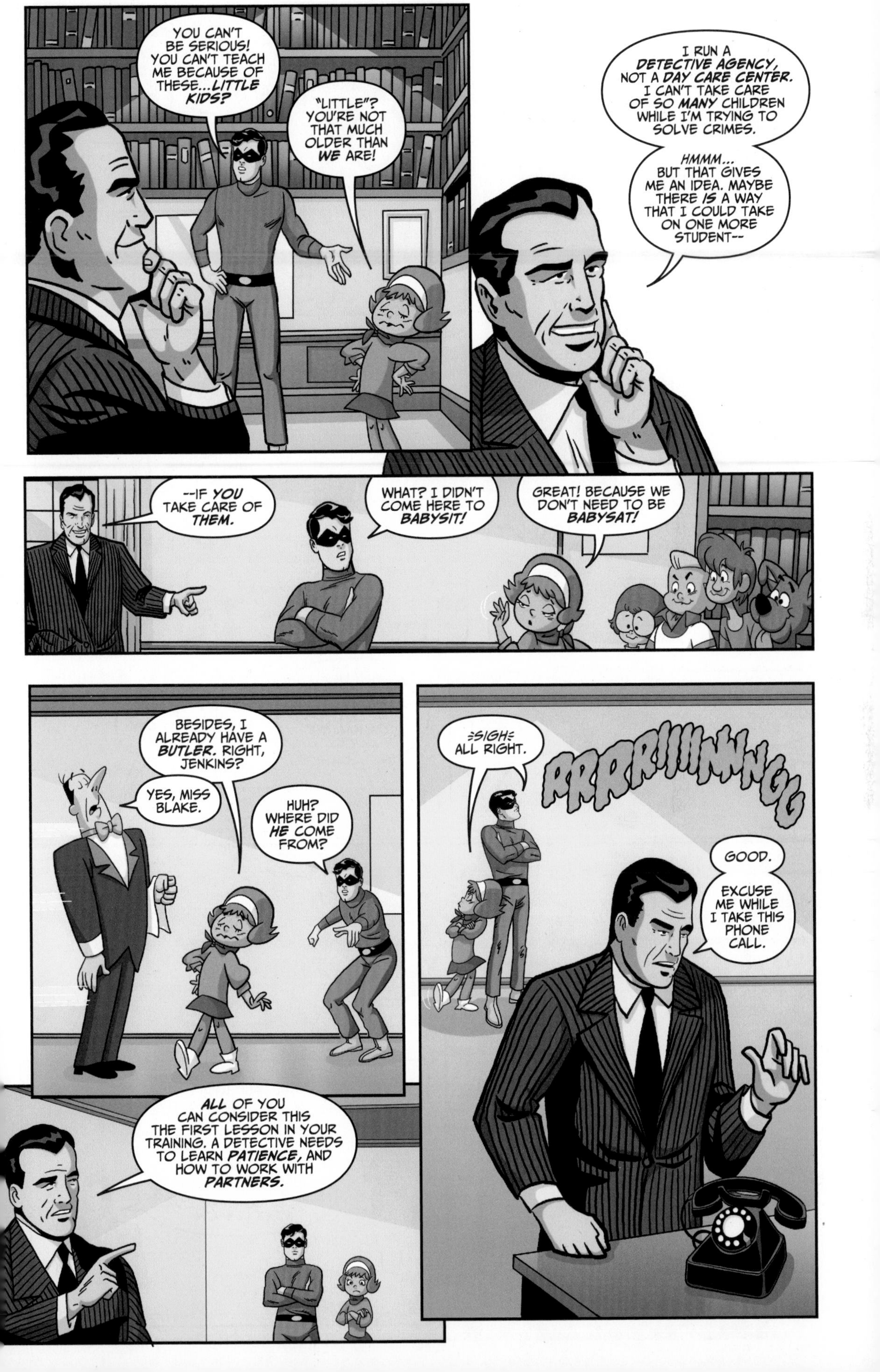
YOU CAN'T BE SERIOUS! YOU CAN'T TEACH ME BECAUSE OF THESE...LITTLE KIDS?
"LITTLE"? YOU'RE NOT THAT MUCH OLDER THAN WE ARE!
I RUN A DETECTIVE AGENCY, NOT A DAY CARE CENTER. I CAN'T TAKE CARE OF SO MANY CHILDREN WHILE I'M TRYING TO SOLVE CRIMES.
HMMM... BUT THAT GIVES ME AN IDEA. MAYBE THERE IS A WAY THAT I COULD TAKE ON ONE MORE STUDENT--
--IF YOU TAKE CARE OF THEM.
WHAT? I DIDN'T COME HERE TO BABYSIT!
GREAT! BECAUSE WE DON'T NEED TO BE BABYSAT!
BESIDES, I ALREADY HAVE A BUTLER. RIGHT, JENKINS?
YES, MISS BLAKE.
HUH? WHERE DID HE COME FROM?
ALL OF YOU CAN CONSIDER THIS THE FIRST LESSON IN YOUR TRAINING. A DETECTIVE NEEDS TO LEARN PATIENCE, AND HOW TO WORK WITH PARTNERS.
SIGH ALL RIGHT.
PRRRIIIINNNGG
GOOD.
EXCUSE ME WHILE I TAKE THIS PHONE CALL.

SINCE WE'RE WORKING TOGETHER, THE ONLY THING LEFT IS TO FIND OUT WHO YOU *REALLY* ARE!

WATCH IT! I WEAR THIS MASK FOR A *REASON*, YOU KNOW!

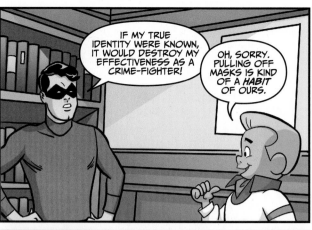

IF MY TRUE IDENTITY WERE KNOWN, IT WOULD DESTROY MY EFFECTIVENESS AS A CRIME-FIGHTER!

OH, SORRY. PULLING OFF MASKS IS KIND OF A *HABIT* OF OURS.

BUT I SUPPOSE YOU HAVE TO CALL ME *SOMETHING*. HOW ABOUT, *UM...*

...ROBIN.

OKAY, ROB. I'M *VELMA!*

PERSONALLY, SCOOBY AND I *LIKE* THE MASK, ROB. YOU LOOK LIKE A *SUPERHERO!*

I DO?

RUH-HUH!

"MASKED CRUSADER FOR JUSTICE," EH?

INTRIGUING...

YUP! LIKE OUR FAVORITE MASKED CRUSADER FOR JUSTICE-- *COMMANDER COOL!*

RAND *RELLOW RUTT!*

COMMANDER COOL & MELLOW MUTT #1

AH, YES. MY NIECE *WENDY* IS OBSESSED WITH COMIC BOOK SUPERHEROES, TOO. BUT THERE'S NO TIME FOR SUCH THINGS NOW!

THAT PHONE CALL WAS ABOUT A *ROBBERY* IN PROGRESS. WE'LL CONTINUE OUR *NEXT* LESSON--

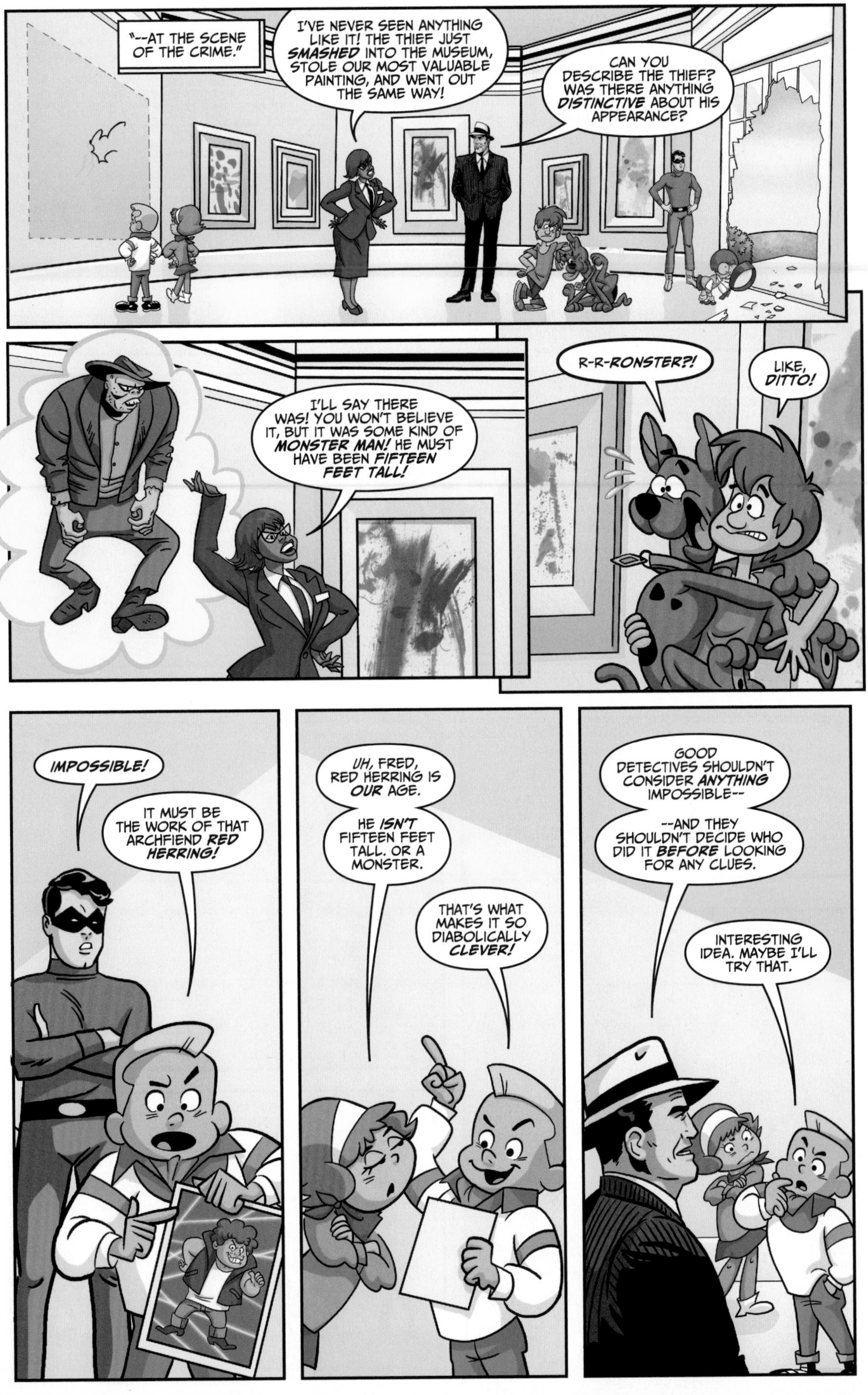
"--AT THE SCENE OF THE CRIME."
I'VE NEVER SEEN ANYTHING LIKE IT! THE THIEF JUST SMASHED INTO THE MUSEUM, STOLE OUR MOST VALUABLE PAINTING, AND WENT OUT THE SAME WAY!
CAN YOU DESCRIBE THE THIEF? WAS THERE ANYTHING DISTINCTIVE ABOUT HIS APPEARANCE?
I'LL SAY THERE WAS! YOU WON'T BELIEVE IT, BUT IT WAS SOME KIND OF MONSTER MAN! HE MUST HAVE BEEN FIFTEEN FEET TALL!
R-R-RONSTER?!
LIKE, DITTO!
IMPOSSIBLE!
IT MUST BE THE WORK OF THAT ARCHFIEND RED HERRING!
UH, FRED, RED HERRING IS OUR AGE.
HE ISN'T FIFTEEN FEET TALL. OR A MONSTER.
THAT'S WHAT MAKES IT SO DIABOLICALLY CLEVER!
GOOD DETECTIVES SHOULDN'T CONSIDER ANYTHING IMPOSSIBLE--
--AND THEY SHOULDN'T DECIDE WHO DID IT BEFORE LOOKING FOR ANY CLUES.
INTERESTING IDEA. MAYBE I'LL TRY THAT.

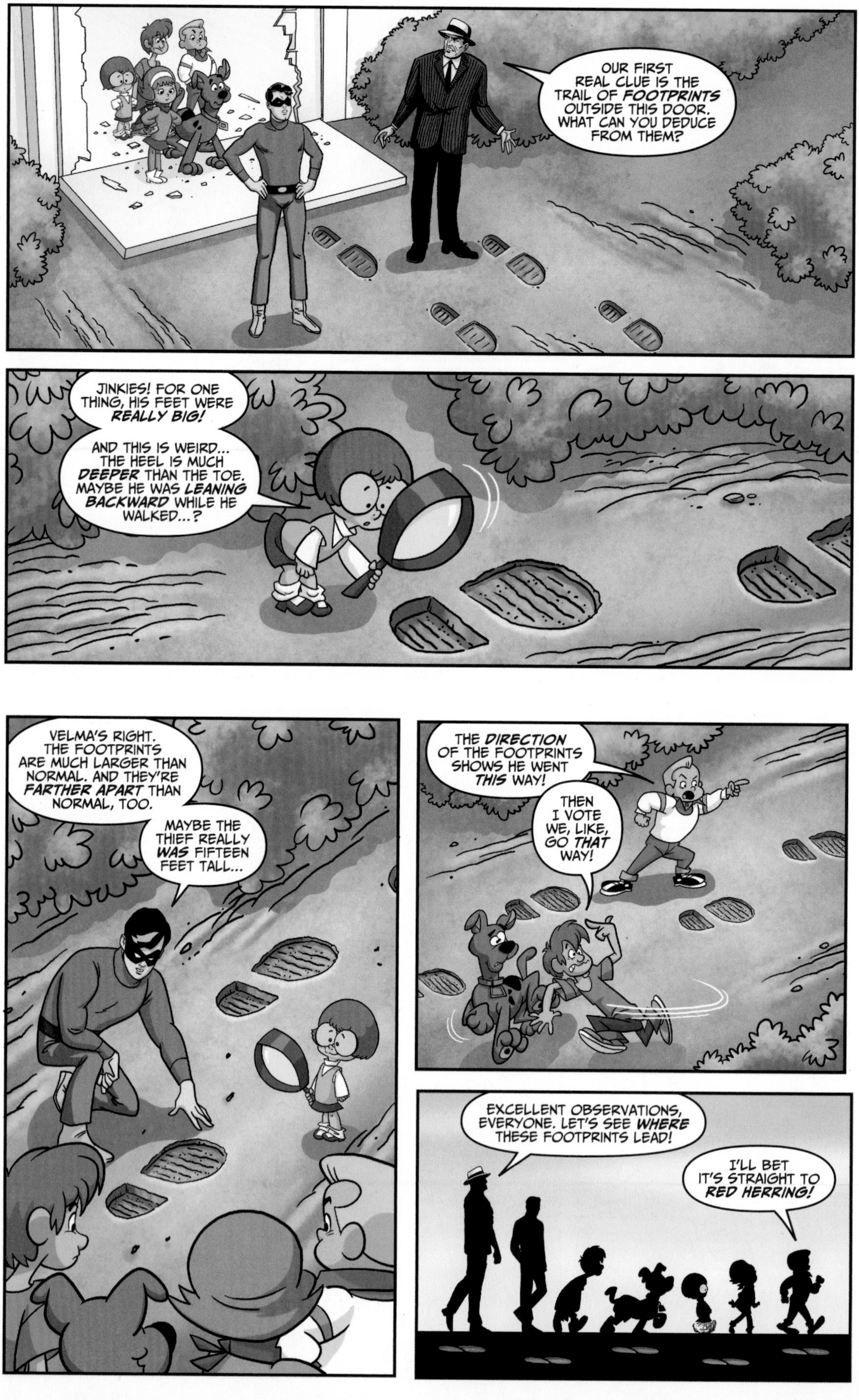
OUR FIRST REAL CLUE IS THE TRAIL OF FOOTPRINTS OUTSIDE THIS DOOR. WHAT CAN YOU DEDUCE FROM THEM?
JINKIES! FOR ONE THING, HIS FEET WERE REALLY BIG!
AND THIS IS WEIRD... THE HEEL IS MUCH DEEPER THAN THE TOE. MAYBE HE WAS LEANING BACKWARD WHILE HE WALKED...?
VELMA'S RIGHT. THE FOOTPRINTS ARE MUCH LARGER THAN NORMAL. AND THEY'RE FARTHER APART THAN NORMAL, TOO.
MAYBE THE THIEF REALLY WAS FIFTEEN FEET TALL...
THE DIRECTION OF THE FOOTPRINTS SHOWS HE WENT THIS WAY!
THEN I VOTE WE, LIKE, GO THAT WAY!
EXCELLENT OBSERVATIONS, EVERYONE. LET'S SEE WHERE THESE FOOTPRINTS LEAD!
I'LL BET IT'S STRAIGHT TO RED HERRING!

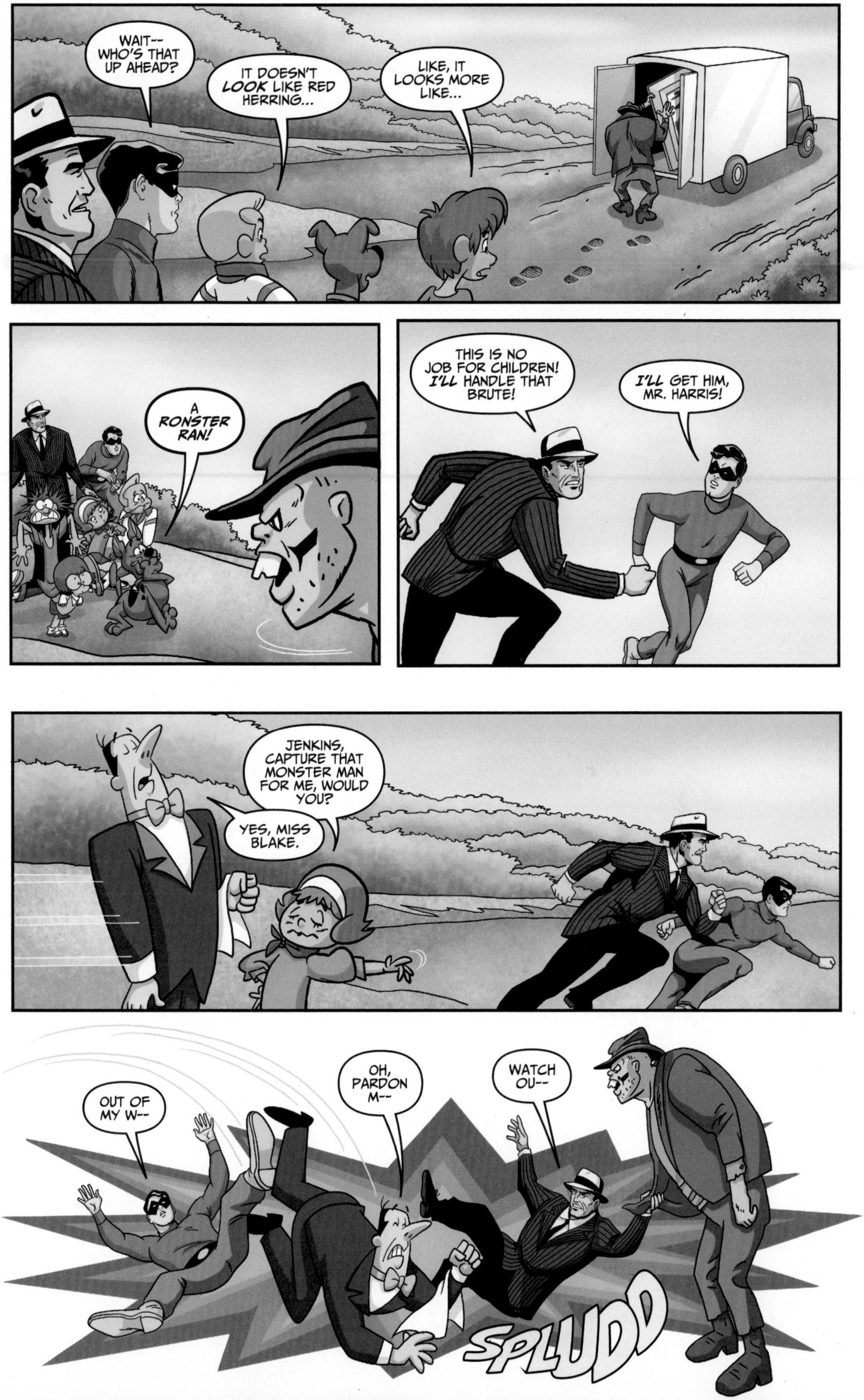
WAIT-- WHO'S THAT UP AHEAD?
IT DOESN'T LOOK LIKE RED HERRING...
LIKE, IT LOOKS MORE LIKE...
A RONSTER RAN!
THIS IS NO JOB FOR CHILDREN! I'LL HANDLE THAT BRUTE!
I'LL GET HIM, MR. HARRIS!
JENKINS, CAPTURE THAT MONSTER MAN FOR ME, WOULD YOU?
YES, MISS BLAKE.
OUT OF MY W--
OH, PARDON M--
WATCH OU--
SPLUDD

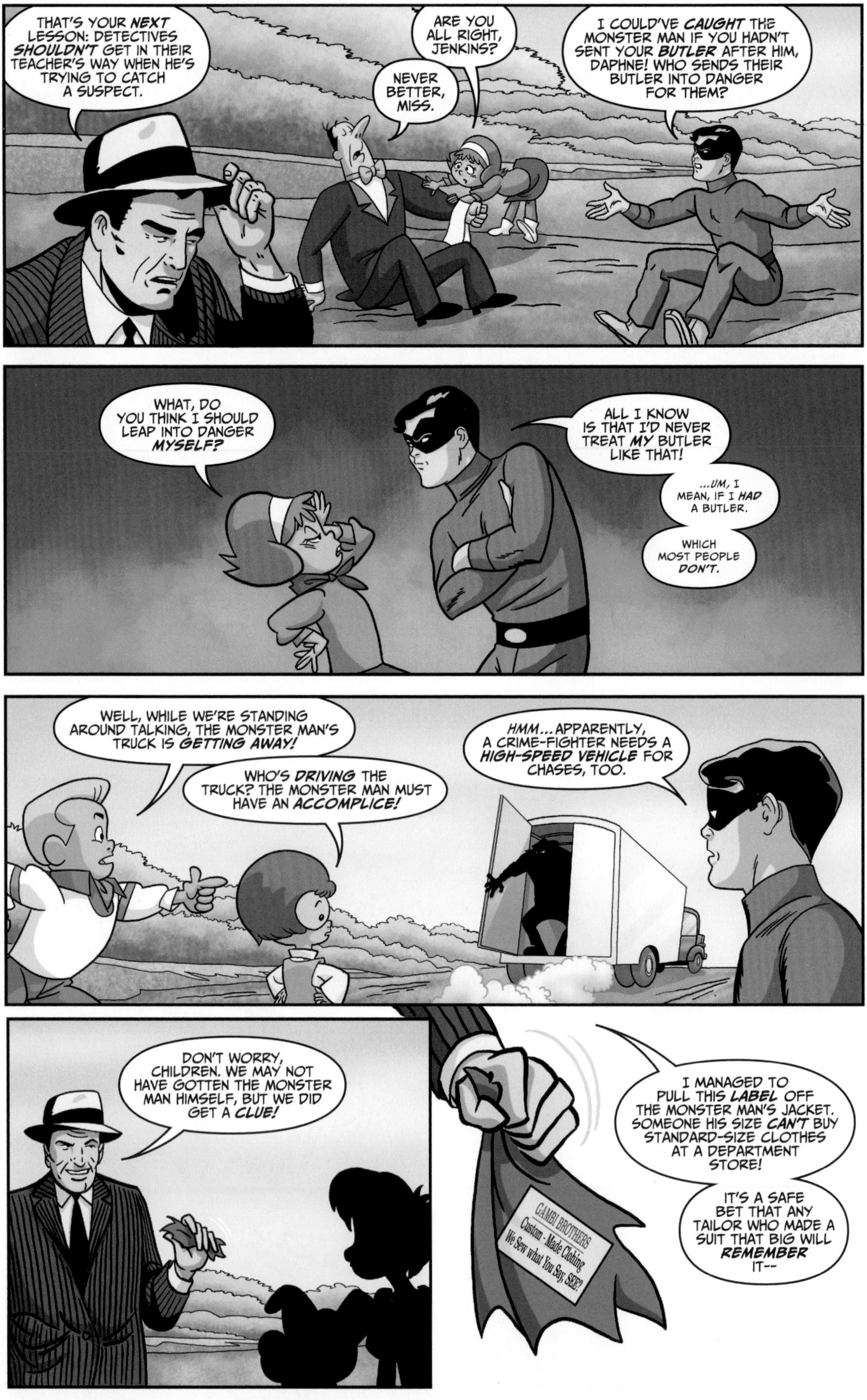

THAT'S YOUR NEXT LESSON: DETECTIVES SHOULDN'T GET IN THEIR TEACHER'S WAY WHEN HE'S TRYING TO CATCH A SUSPECT.
ARE YOU ALL RIGHT, JENKINS?
NEVER BETTER, MISS.
I COULD'VE CAUGHT THE MONSTER MAN IF YOU HADN'T SENT YOUR BUTLER AFTER HIM, DAPHNE! WHO SENDS THEIR BUTLER INTO DANGER FOR THEM?
WHAT, DO YOU THINK I SHOULD LEAP INTO DANGER MYSELF?
ALL I KNOW IS THAT I'D NEVER TREAT MY BUTLER LIKE THAT!
...UM, I MEAN, IF I HAD A BUTLER.
WHICH MOST PEOPLE DON'T.
WELL, WHILE WE'RE STANDING AROUND TALKING, THE MONSTER MAN'S TRUCK IS GETTING AWAY!
WHO'S DRIVING THE TRUCK? THE MONSTER MAN MUST HAVE AN ACCOMPLICE!
HMM... APPARENTLY, A CRIME-FIGHTER NEEDS A HIGH-SPEED VEHICLE FOR CHASES, TOO.
DON'T WORRY, CHILDREN. WE MAY NOT HAVE GOTTEN THE MONSTER MAN HIMSELF, BUT WE DID GET A CLUE!
I MANAGED TO PULL THIS LABEL OFF THE MONSTER MAN'S JACKET. SOMEONE HIS SIZE CAN'T BUY STANDARD-SIZE CLOTHES AT A DEPARTMENT STORE!
IT'S A SAFE BET THAT ANY TAILOR WHO MADE A SUIT THAT BIG WILL REMEMBER IT--
GAMBI BROTHERS
Custom - Made Clothing
We Sew what You Say, SEE?

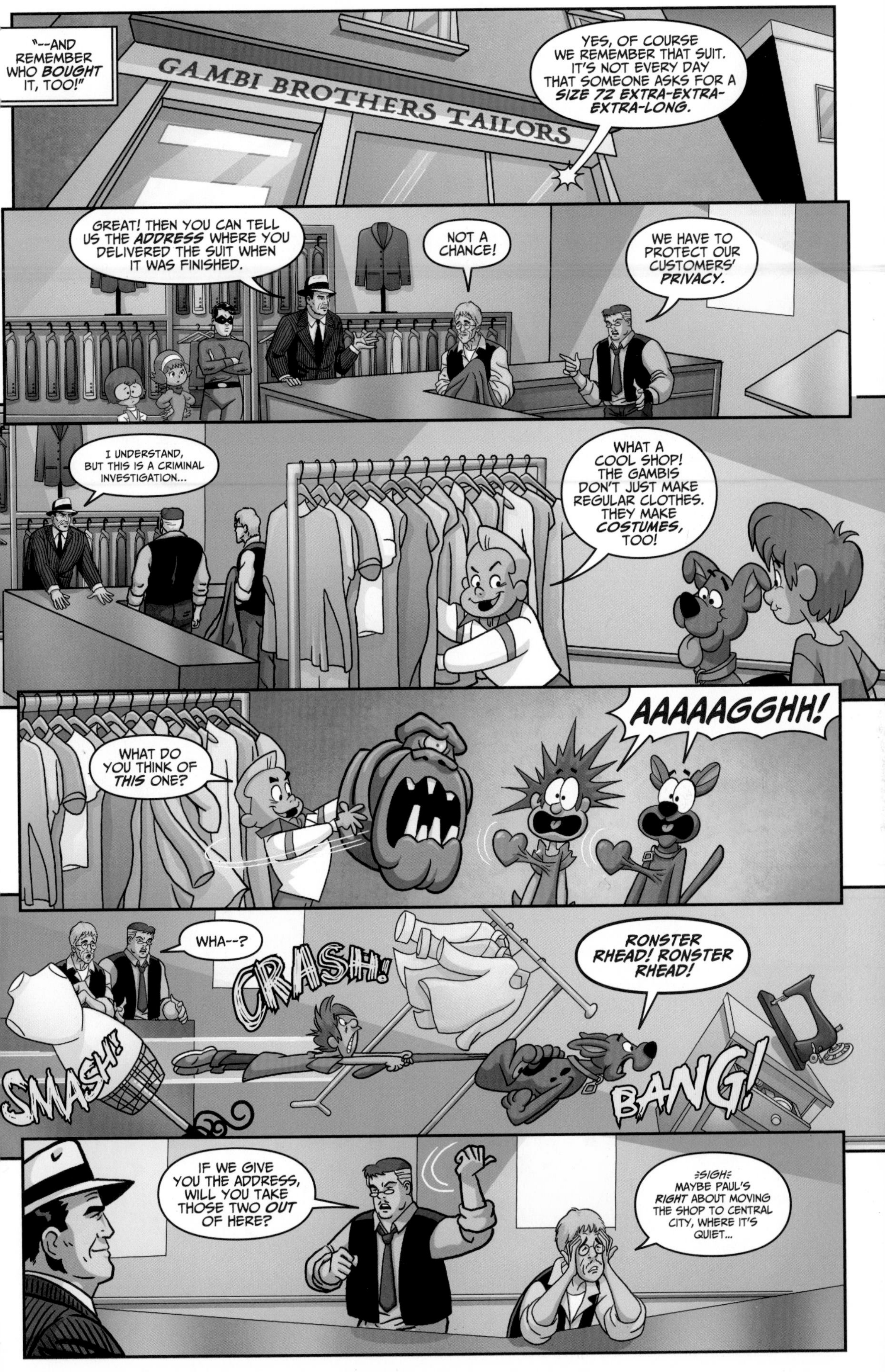
"--AND REMEMBER WHO *BOUGHT* IT, TOO!"
GAMBI BROTHERS TAILORS
YES, OF COURSE WE REMEMBER THAT SUIT. IT'S NOT EVERY DAY THAT SOMEONE ASKS FOR A *SIZE 72 EXTRA-EXTRA-EXTRA-LONG.*
GREAT! THEN YOU CAN TELL US THE *ADDRESS* WHERE YOU DELIVERED THE SUIT WHEN IT WAS FINISHED.
NOT A CHANCE!
WE HAVE TO PROTECT OUR CUSTOMERS' *PRIVACY.*
I UNDERSTAND, BUT THIS IS A CRIMINAL INVESTIGATION...
WHAT A COOL SHOP! THE GAMBIS DON'T JUST MAKE REGULAR CLOTHES. THEY MAKE *COSTUMES,* TOO!
WHAT DO YOU THINK OF *THIS* ONE?
AAAAAGGHH!
WHA--?
CRASH!
RONSTER RHEAD! RONSTER RHEAD!
SMASH!
BANG!
IF WE GIVE YOU THE ADDRESS, WILL YOU TAKE THOSE TWO *OUT* OF HERE?
SIGH MAYBE PAUL'S *RIGHT* ABOUT MOVING THE SHOP TO CENTRAL CITY, WHERE IT'S QUIET...

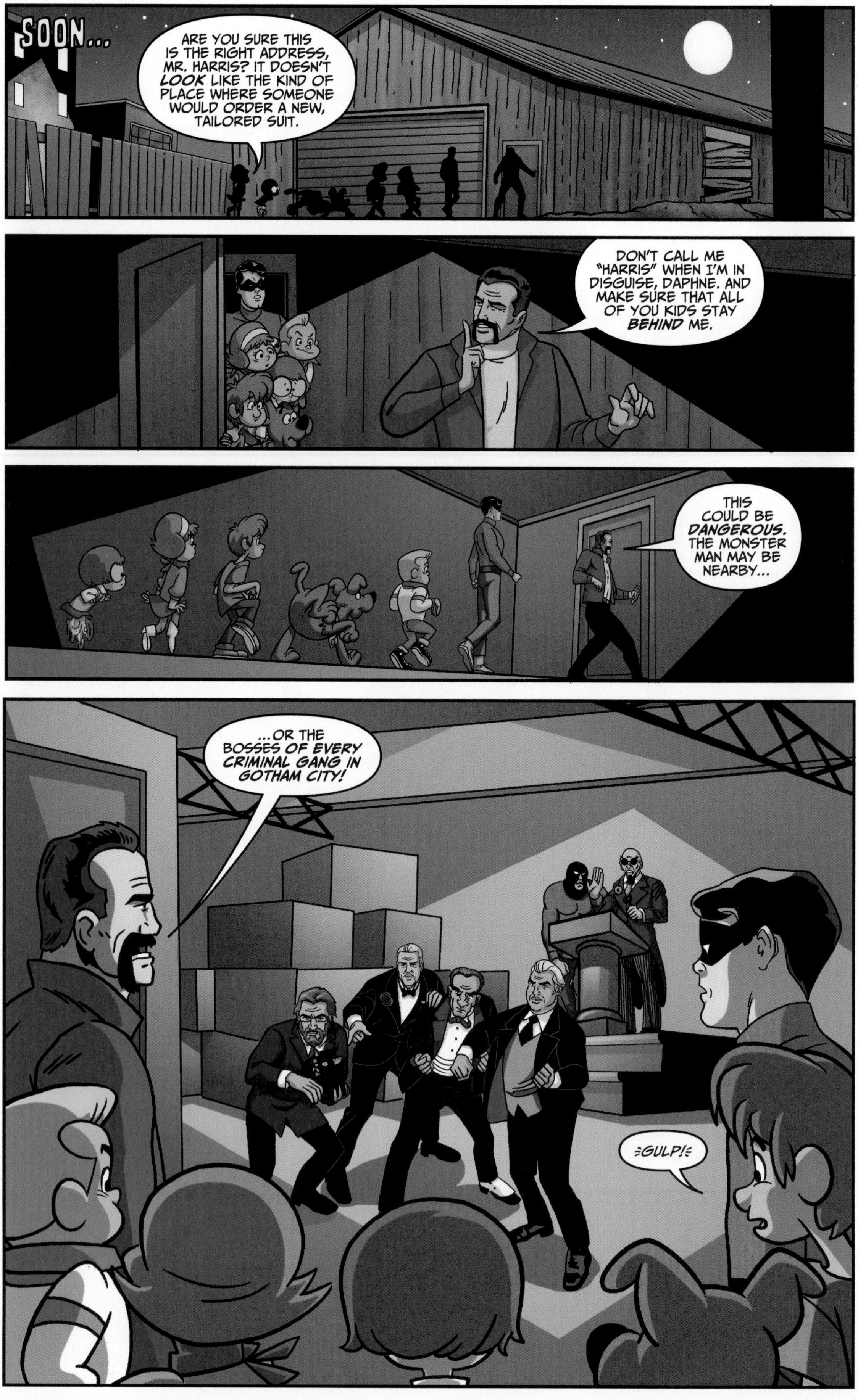
SOON...
ARE YOU SURE THIS IS THE RIGHT ADDRESS, MR. HARRIS? IT DOESN'T LOOK LIKE THE KIND OF PLACE WHERE SOMEONE WOULD ORDER A NEW, TAILORED SUIT.
DON'T CALL ME "HARRIS" WHEN I'M IN DISGUISE, DAPHNE. AND MAKE SURE THAT ALL OF YOU KIDS STAY BEHIND ME.
THIS COULD BE DANGEROUS. THE MONSTER MAN MAY BE NEARBY...
...OR THE BOSSES OF EVERY CRIMINAL GANG IN GOTHAM CITY!
GULP!

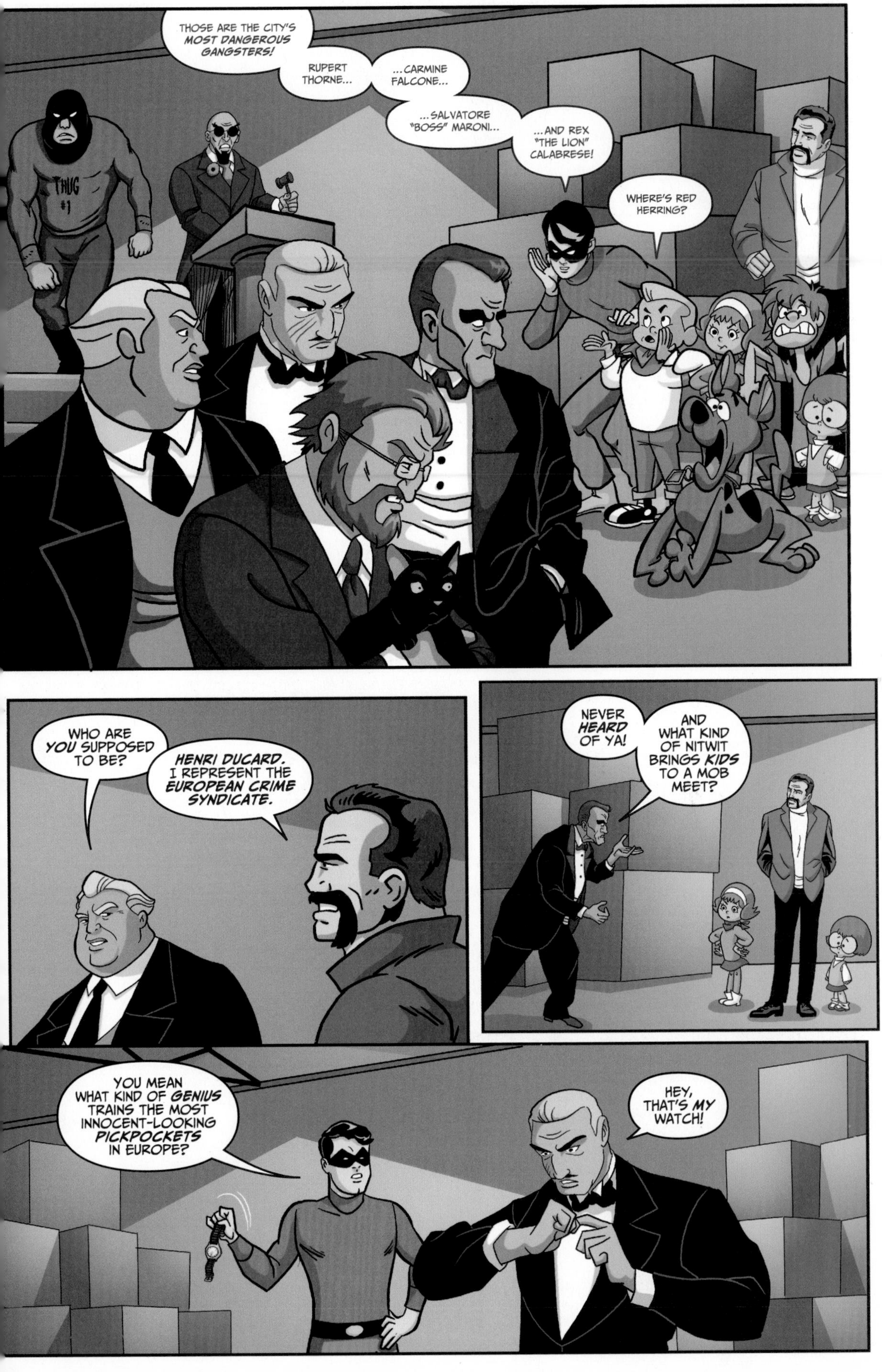
THOSE ARE THE CITY'S MOST DANGEROUS GANGSTERS!
RUPERT THORNE...
...CARMINE FALCONE...
...SALVATORE "BOSS" MARONI...
...AND REX "THE LION" CALABRESE!
WHERE'S RED HERRING?
THUG #1
WHO ARE YOU SUPPOSED TO BE?
HENRI DUCARD. I REPRESENT THE EUROPEAN CRIME SYNDICATE.
NEVER HEARD OF YA!
AND WHAT KIND OF NITWIT BRINGS KIDS TO A MOB MEET?
YOU MEAN WHAT KIND OF GENIUS TRAINS THE MOST INNOCENT-LOOKING PICKPOCKETS IN EUROPE?
HEY, THAT'S MY WATCH!

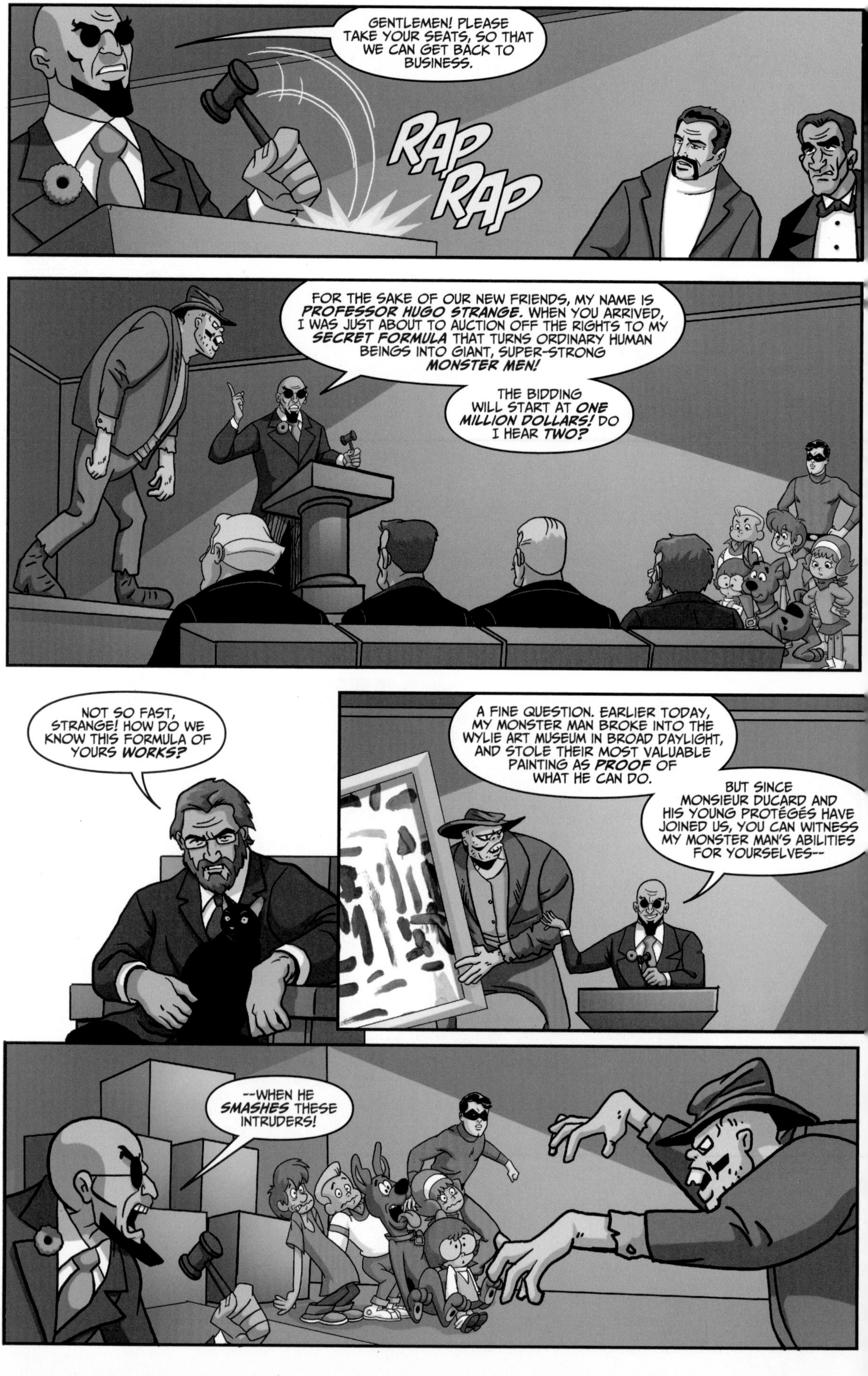
GENTLEMEN! PLEASE TAKE YOUR SEATS, SO THAT WE CAN GET BACK TO BUSINESS.
RAP RAP
FOR THE SAKE OF OUR NEW FRIENDS, MY NAME IS PROFESSOR HUGO STRANGE. WHEN YOU ARRIVED, I WAS JUST ABOUT TO AUCTION OFF THE RIGHTS TO MY SECRET FORMULA THAT TURNS ORDINARY HUMAN BEINGS INTO GIANT, SUPER-STRONG MONSTER MEN!
THE BIDDING WILL START AT ONE MILLION DOLLARS! DO I HEAR TWO?
NOT SO FAST, STRANGE! HOW DO WE KNOW THIS FORMULA OF YOURS WORKS?
A FINE QUESTION. EARLIER TODAY, MY MONSTER MAN BROKE INTO THE WYLIE ART MUSEUM IN BROAD DAYLIGHT, AND STOLE THEIR MOST VALUABLE PAINTING AS PROOF OF WHAT HE CAN DO.
BUT SINCE MONSIEUR DUCARD AND HIS YOUNG PROTÉGÉS HAVE JOINED US, YOU CAN WITNESS MY MONSTER MAN'S ABILITIES FOR YOURSELVES--
--WHEN HE SMASHES THESE INTRUDERS!

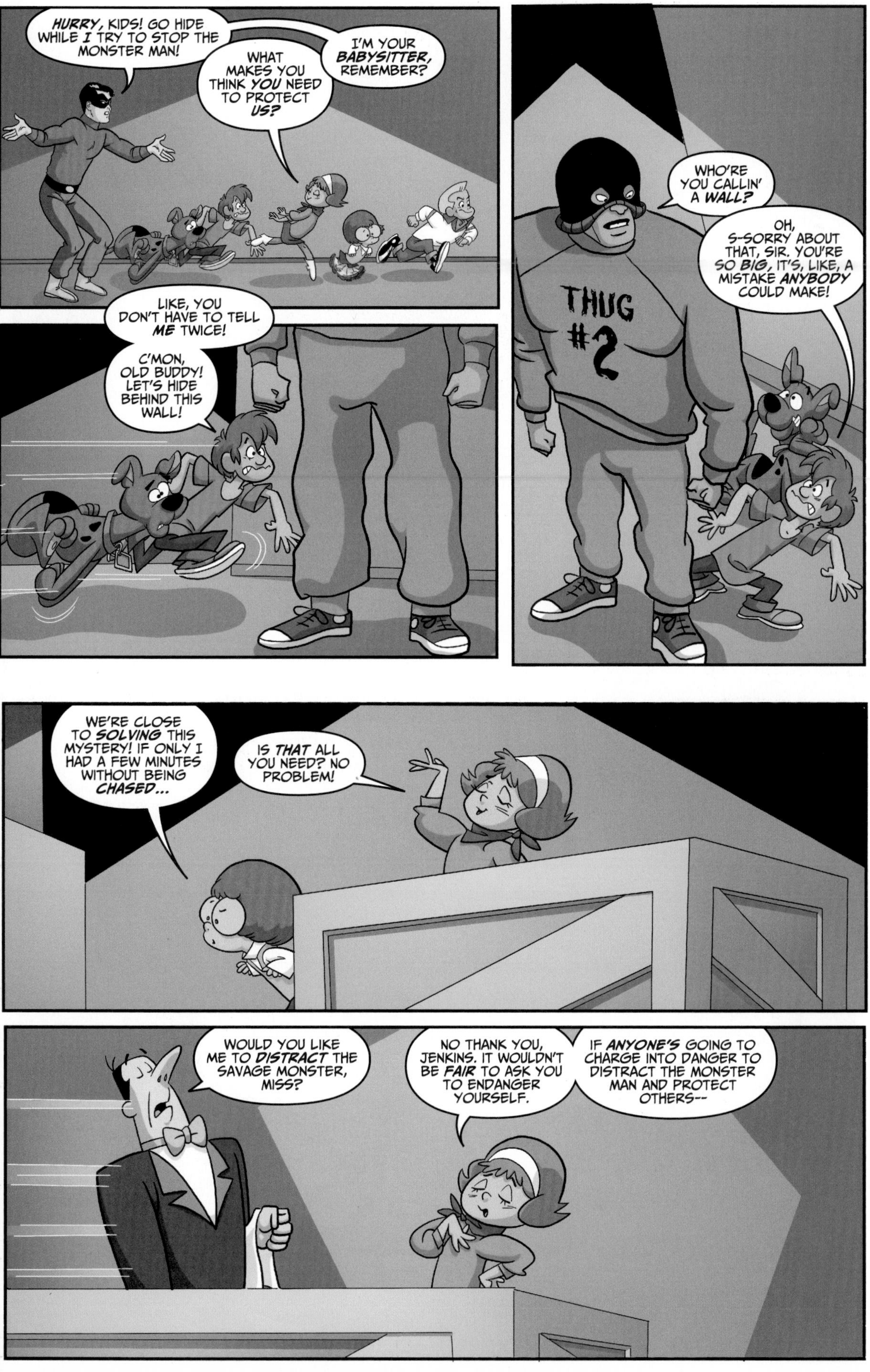
HURRY, KIDS! GO HIDE WHILE I TRY TO STOP THE MONSTER MAN!
WHAT MAKES YOU THINK YOU NEED TO PROTECT US?
I'M YOUR BABYSITTER, REMEMBER?
LIKE, YOU DON'T HAVE TO TELL ME TWICE!
C'MON, OLD BUDDY! LET'S HIDE BEHIND THIS WALL!
WHO'RE YOU CALLIN' A WALL?
OH, S-SORRY ABOUT THAT, SIR. YOU'RE SO BIG, IT'S, LIKE, A MISTAKE ANYBODY COULD MAKE!
THUG #2
WE'RE CLOSE TO SOLVING THIS MYSTERY! IF ONLY I HAD A FEW MINUTES WITHOUT BEING CHASED...
IS THAT ALL YOU NEED? NO PROBLEM!
WOULD YOU LIKE ME TO DISTRACT THE SAVAGE MONSTER, MISS?
NO THANK YOU, JENKINS. IT WOULDN'T BE FAIR TO ASK YOU TO ENDANGER YOURSELF.
IF ANYONE'S GOING TO CHARGE INTO DANGER TO DISTRACT THE MONSTER MAN AND PROTECT OTHERS--

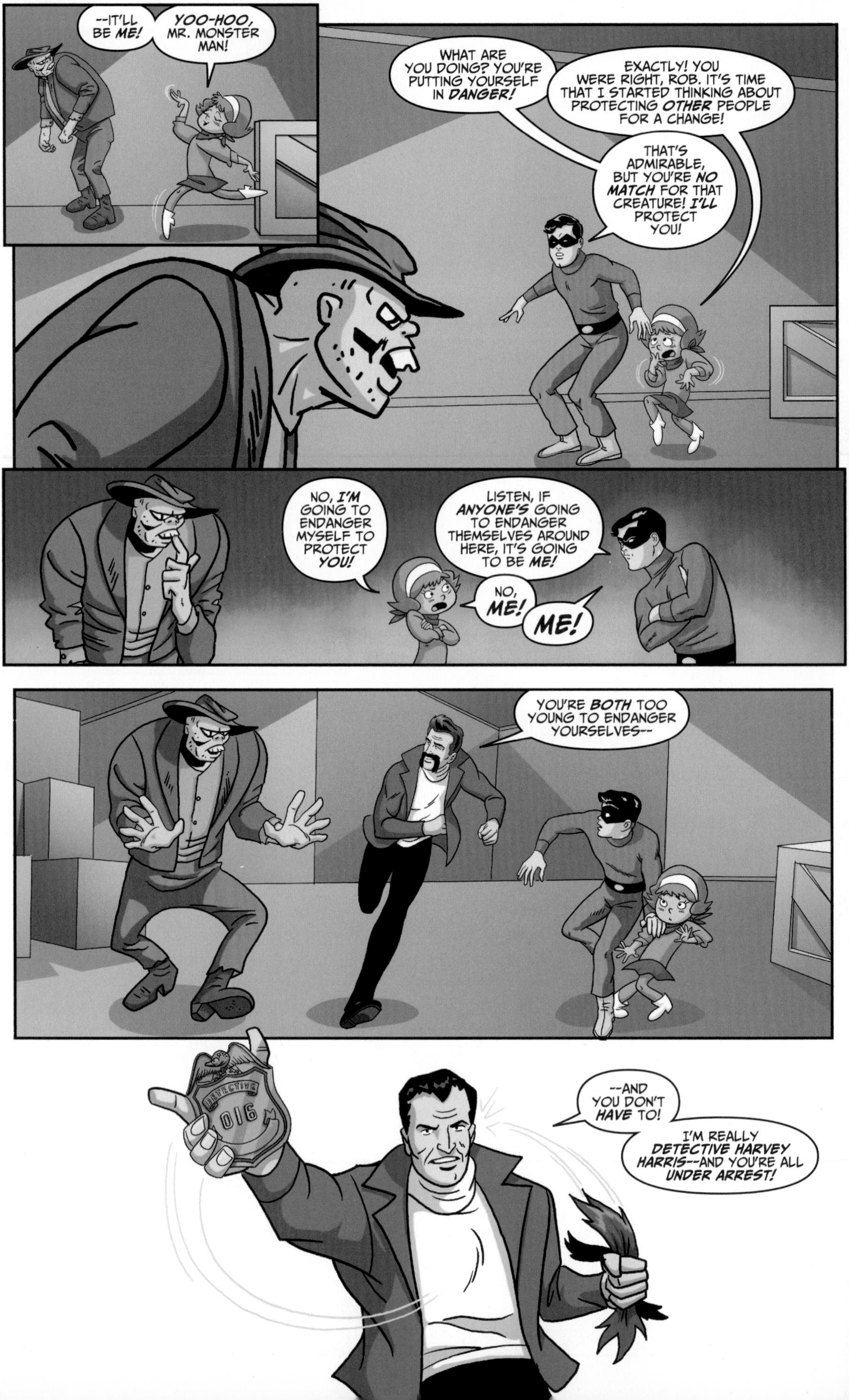
--IT'LL BE ME!
YOO-HOO, MR. MONSTER MAN!
WHAT ARE YOU DOING? YOU'RE PUTTING YOURSELF IN DANGER!
EXACTLY! YOU WERE RIGHT, ROB. IT'S TIME THAT I STARTED THINKING ABOUT PROTECTING OTHER PEOPLE FOR A CHANGE!
THAT'S ADMIRABLE, BUT YOU'RE NO MATCH FOR THAT CREATURE! I'LL PROTECT YOU!
NO, I'M GOING TO ENDANGER MYSELF TO PROTECT YOU!
LISTEN, IF ANYONE'S GOING TO ENDANGER THEMSELVES AROUND HERE, IT'S GOING TO BE ME!
NO, ME!
ME!
YOU'RE BOTH TOO YOUNG TO ENDANGER YOURSELVES--
DETECTIVE
016
--AND YOU DON'T HAVE TO!
I'M REALLY DETECTIVE HARVEY HARRIS--AND YOU'RE ALL UNDER ARREST!

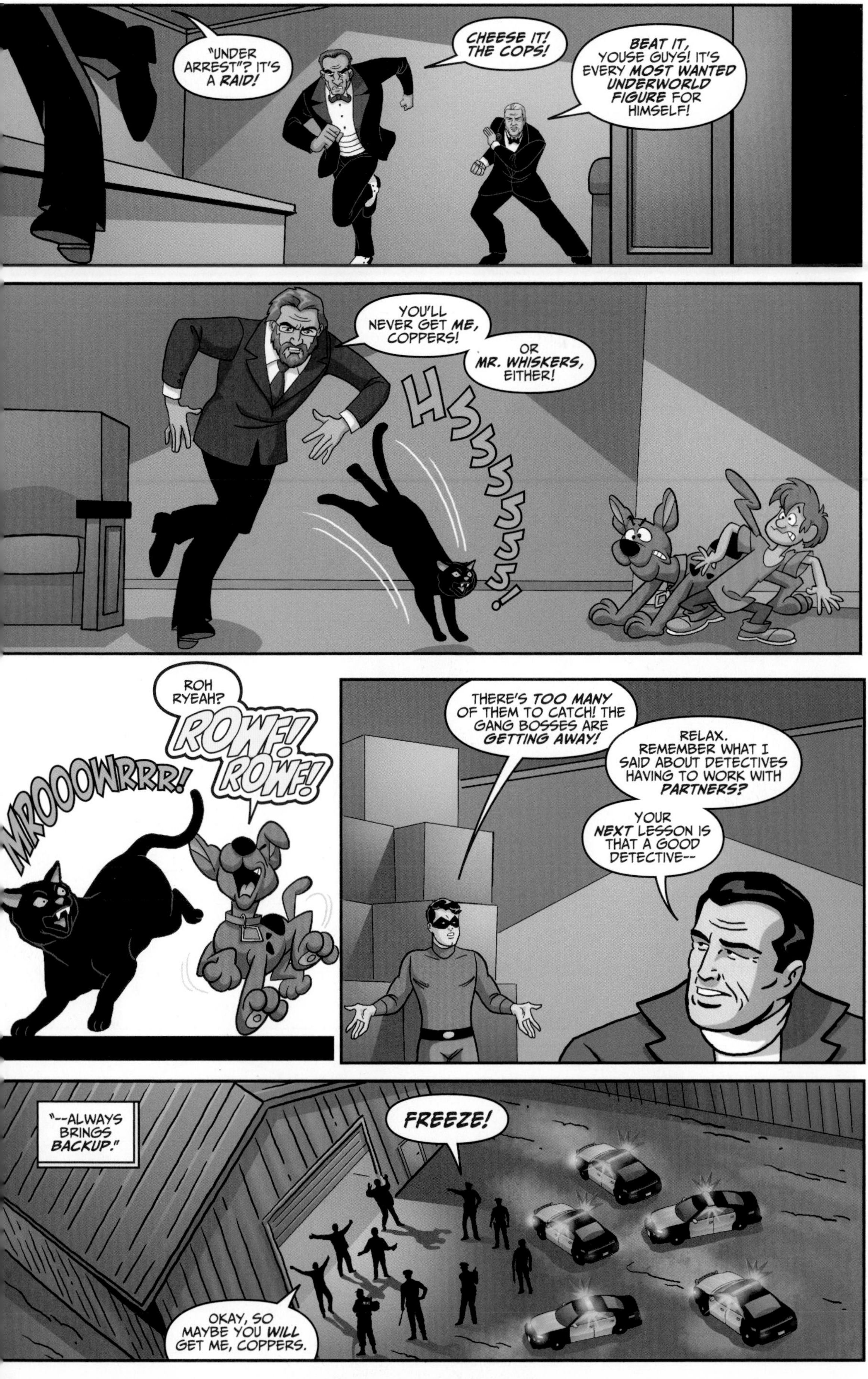
"UNDER ARREST"? IT'S A RAID!
CHEESE IT! THE COPS!
BEAT IT, YOUSE GUYS! IT'S EVERY MOST WANTED UNDERWORLD FIGURE FOR HIMSELF!
YOU'LL NEVER GET ME, COPPERS!
OR MR. WHISKERS, EITHER!
HSSSSSS!
ROH RYEAH?
ROWF! ROWF!
MROOOWRRR!
THERE'S TOO MANY OF THEM TO CATCH! THE GANG BOSSES ARE GETTING AWAY!
RELAX. REMEMBER WHAT I SAID ABOUT DETECTIVES HAVING TO WORK WITH PARTNERS?
YOUR NEXT LESSON IS THAT A GOOD DETECTIVE--
"--ALWAYS BRINGS BACKUP."
FREEZE!
OKAY, SO MAYBE YOU WILL GET ME, COPPERS.

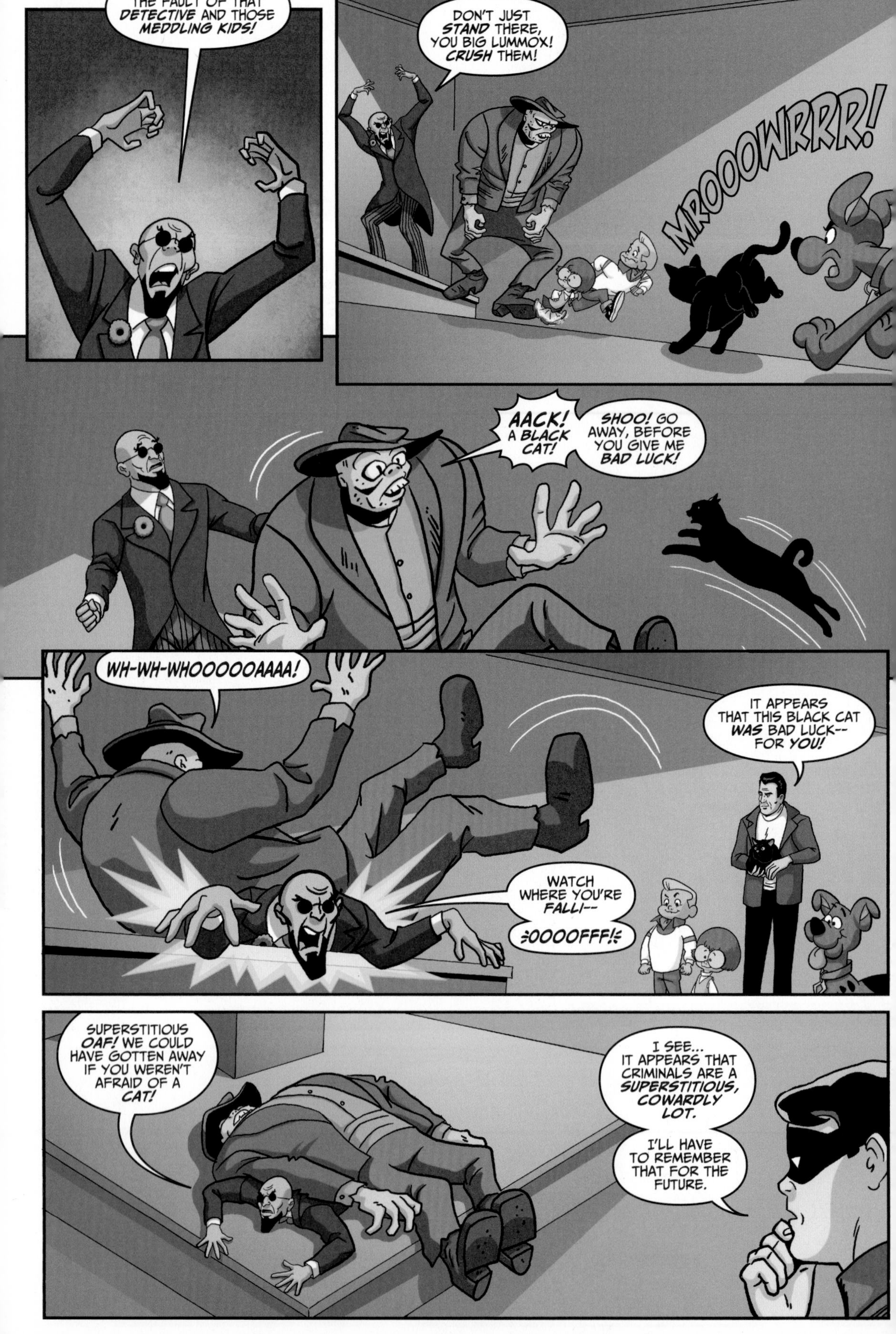
THIS IS ALL THE FAULT OF THAT *DETECTIVE* AND THOSE *MEDDLING KIDS!*
DON'T JUST *STAND* THERE, YOU BIG LUMMOX! *CRUSH* THEM!
MROOOWRRR!
AACK! A *BLACK CAT!*
SHOO! GO AWAY, BEFORE YOU GIVE ME *BAD LUCK!*
WH-WH-WHOOOOOAAAA!
IT APPEARS THAT THIS BLACK CAT *WAS* BAD LUCK-- FOR *YOU!*
WATCH WHERE YOU'RE *FALLI--*
OOOOFFF!
SUPERSTITIOUS *OAF!* WE COULD HAVE GOTTEN AWAY IF YOU WEREN'T AFRAID OF A *CAT!*
I SEE... IT APPEARS THAT CRIMINALS ARE A *SUPERSTITIOUS, COWARDLY LOT.*
I'LL HAVE TO REMEMBER THAT FOR THE FUTURE.

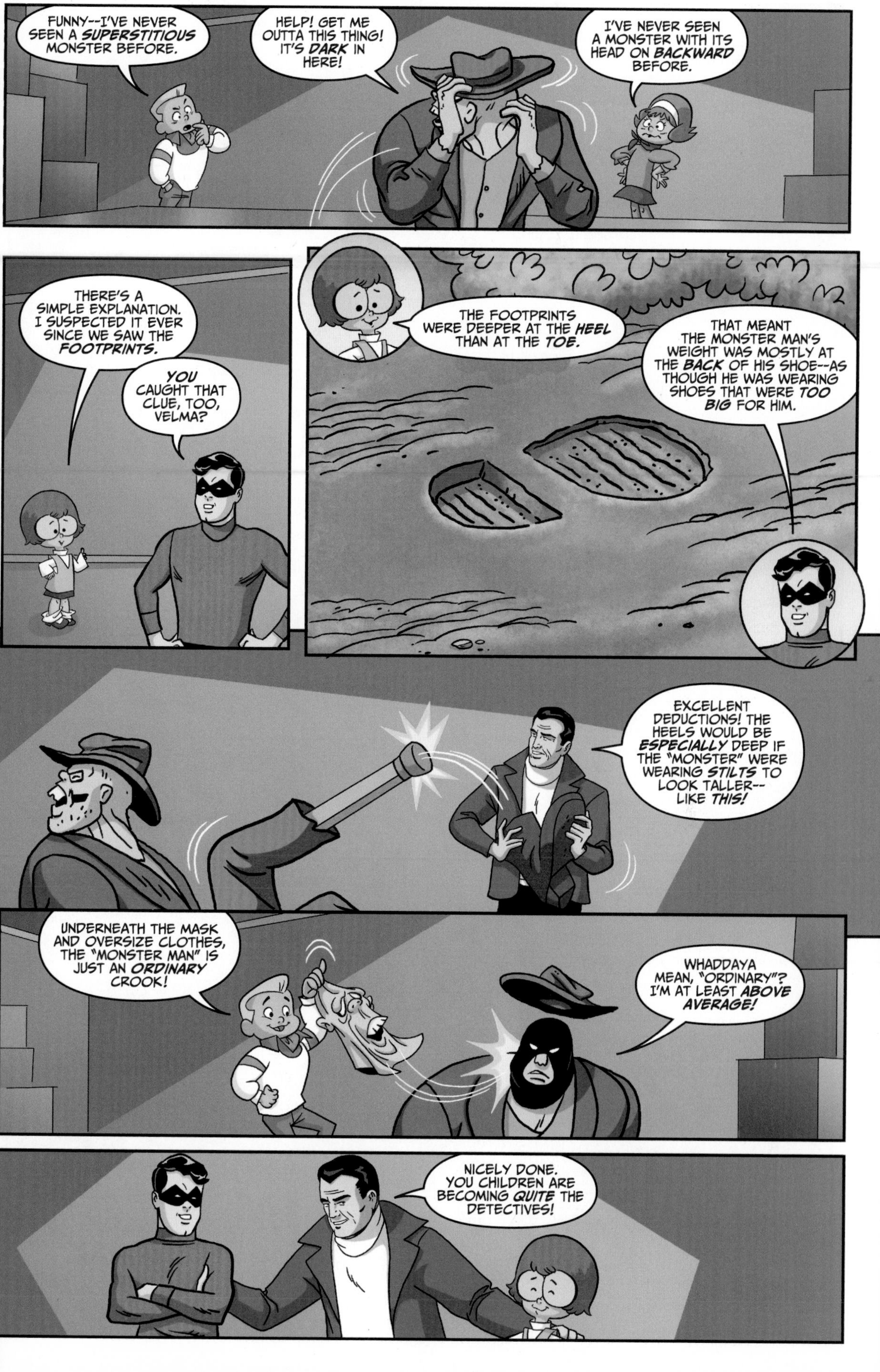

FUNNY--I'VE NEVER SEEN A SUPERSTITIOUS MONSTER BEFORE.
HELP! GET ME OUTTA THIS THING! IT'S DARK IN HERE!
I'VE NEVER SEEN A MONSTER WITH ITS HEAD ON BACKWARD BEFORE.
THERE'S A SIMPLE EXPLANATION. I SUSPECTED IT EVER SINCE WE SAW THE FOOTPRINTS.
YOU CAUGHT THAT CLUE, TOO, VELMA?
THE FOOTPRINTS WERE DEEPER AT THE HEEL THAN AT THE TOE.
THAT MEANT THE MONSTER MAN'S WEIGHT WAS MOSTLY AT THE BACK OF HIS SHOE--AS THOUGH HE WAS WEARING SHOES THAT WERE TOO BIG FOR HIM.
EXCELLENT DEDUCTIONS! THE HEELS WOULD BE ESPECIALLY DEEP IF THE "MONSTER" WERE WEARING STILTS TO LOOK TALLER-- LIKE THIS!
UNDERNEATH THE MASK AND OVERSIZE CLOTHES, THE "MONSTER MAN" IS JUST AN ORDINARY CROOK!
WHADDAYA MEAN, "ORDINARY"? I'M AT LEAST ABOVE AVERAGE!
NICELY DONE. YOU CHILDREN ARE BECOMING QUITE THE DETECTIVES!

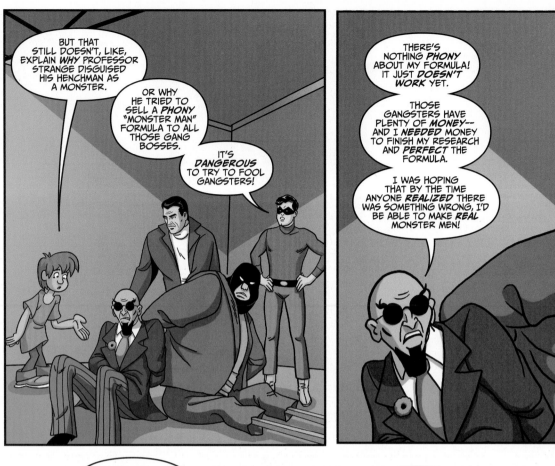

BUT THAT STILL DOESN'T, LIKE, EXPLAIN *WHY* PROFESSOR STRANGE DISGUISED HIS HENCHMAN AS A MONSTER.

OR WHY HE TRIED TO SELL A *PHONY* "MONSTER MAN" FORMULA TO ALL THOSE GANG BOSSES.

IT'S *DANGEROUS* TO TRY TO FOOL GANGSTERS!

THERE'S NOTHING *PHONY* ABOUT MY FORMULA! IT JUST *DOESN'T WORK* YET.

THOSE GANGSTERS HAVE PLENTY OF *MONEY*-- AND I *NEEDED* MONEY TO FINISH MY RESEARCH AND *PERFECT* THE FORMULA.

I WAS HOPING THAT BY THE TIME ANYONE *REALIZED* THERE WAS SOMETHING WRONG, I'D BE ABLE TO MAKE *REAL* MONSTER MEN!

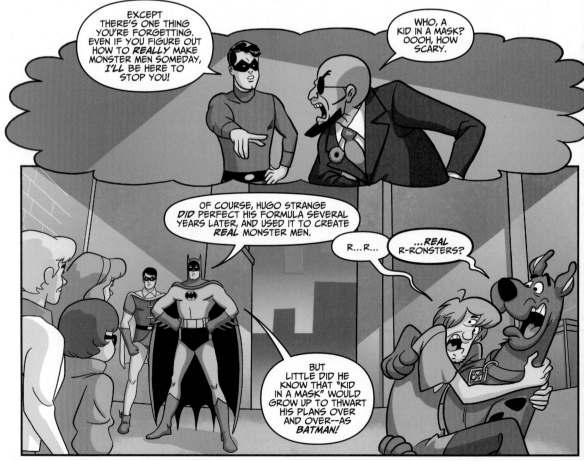

EXCEPT THERE'S ONE THING YOU'RE FORGETTING. EVEN IF YOU FIGURE OUT HOW TO *REALLY* MAKE MONSTER MEN SOMEDAY, *I'LL* BE HERE TO STOP YOU!

WHO, A KID IN A MASK? OOOH, HOW SCARY.

OF COURSE, HUGO STRANGE *DID* PERFECT HIS FORMULA SEVERAL YEARS LATER, AND USED IT TO CREATE *REAL* MONSTER MEN.

R...R...

...*REAL* R-RONSTERS?

BUT LITTLE DID HE KNOW THAT "KID IN A MASK" WOULD GROW UP TO THWART HIS PLANS OVER AND OVER--AS *BATMAN!*

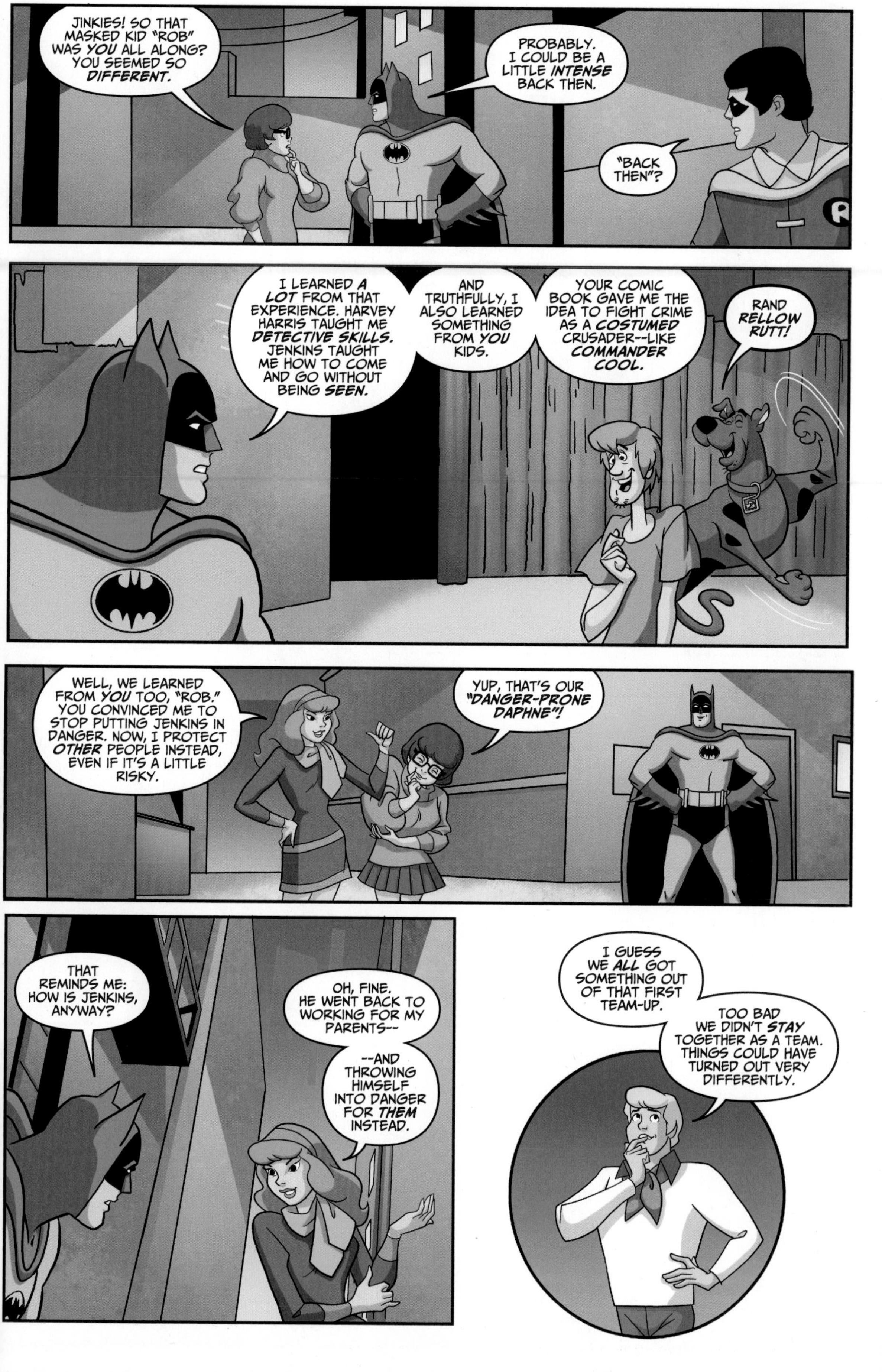
JINKIES! SO THAT MASKED KID "ROB" WAS YOU ALL ALONG? YOU SEEMED SO DIFFERENT.
PROBABLY. I COULD BE A LITTLE INTENSE BACK THEN.
"BACK THEN"?
I LEARNED A LOT FROM THAT EXPERIENCE. HARVEY HARRIS TAUGHT ME DETECTIVE SKILLS. JENKINS TAUGHT ME HOW TO COME AND GO WITHOUT BEING SEEN.
AND TRUTHFULLY, I ALSO LEARNED SOMETHING FROM YOU KIDS.
YOUR COMIC BOOK GAVE ME THE IDEA TO FIGHT CRIME AS A COSTUMED CRUSADER--LIKE COMMANDER COOL.
RAND RELLOW RUTT!
WELL, WE LEARNED FROM YOU TOO, "ROB." YOU CONVINCED ME TO STOP PUTTING JENKINS IN DANGER. NOW, I PROTECT OTHER PEOPLE INSTEAD, EVEN IF IT'S A LITTLE RISKY.
YUP, THAT'S OUR "DANGER-PRONE DAPHNE"!
THAT REMINDS ME: HOW IS JENKINS, ANYWAY?
OH, FINE. HE WENT BACK TO WORKING FOR MY PARENTS--
--AND THROWING HIMSELF INTO DANGER FOR THEM INSTEAD.
I GUESS WE ALL GOT SOMETHING OUT OF THAT FIRST TEAM-UP.
TOO BAD WE DIDN'T STAY TOGETHER AS A TEAM. THINGS COULD HAVE TURNED OUT VERY DIFFERENTLY.

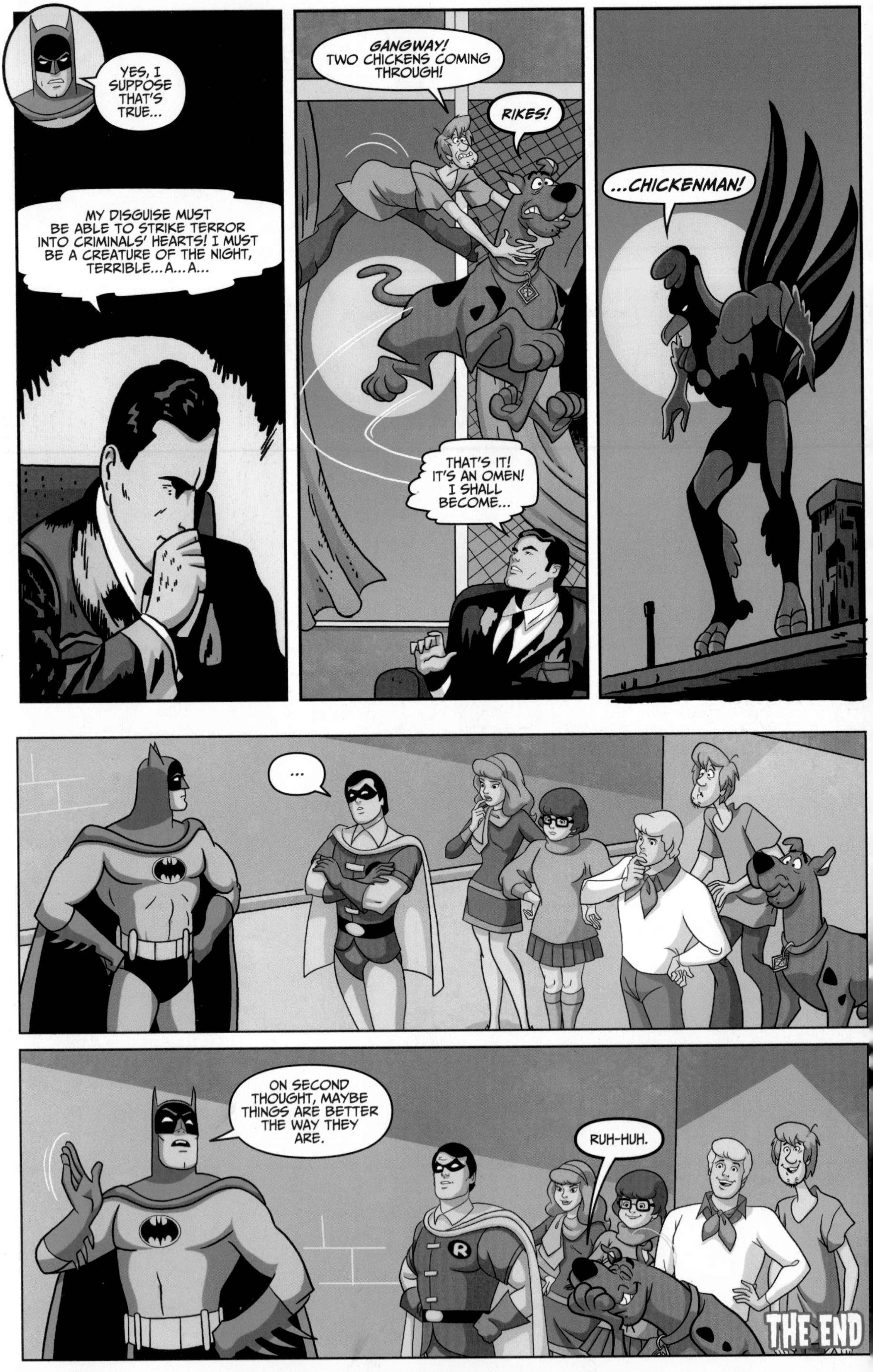
YES, I SUPPOSE THAT'S TRUE...
MY DISGUISE MUST BE ABLE TO STRIKE TERROR INTO CRIMINALS' HEARTS! I MUST BE A CREATURE OF THE NIGHT, TERRIBLE...A...A...
GANGWAY! TWO CHICKENS COMING THROUGH!
RIKES!
THAT'S IT! IT'S AN OMEN! I SHALL BECOME...
...CHICKENMAN!
...
ON SECOND THOUGHT, MAYBE THINGS ARE BETTER THE WAY THEY ARE.
RUH-HUH.
THE END